Agatha Arch is Afraid of Everything

A Novel

KRISTIN BAIR

alcove
press

This is a work of fiction. All of the names, characters, organizations, places and events portrayed in this novel are either products of the author's imagination or are used fictitiously. Any resemblance to real or actual events, locales, or persons, living or dead, is entirely coincidental.

Published in the United States by Alcove Press, an imprint of The Quick Brown Fox & Company LLC.

Alcove Press and its logo are trademarks of The Quick Brown Fox & Company LLC.

Library of Congress Catalog-in-Publication data available upon request.

ISBN (hardcover): 978-1-64385-500-4
ISBN (ebook): 978-1-64385-501-1

Cover design by Celeste Knudsen

Printed in the United States.

www.alcovepress.com

Alcove Press
34 West 27th St., 10th Floor
New York, NY 10001

First Edition: November 2020

10 9 8 7 6 5 4 3 2 1

Agatha Arch is Afraid of Everything

Also available by Kristin Bair

(writing as Kristin Bair O'Keeffe)
The Art of Floating
Thirsty

For all who face down their fothermucking fears with gusto and verve. You've got this.

Chapter One

It is quite possible Agatha Arch will be alone forever. Or maybe not. It's much too early to consider either eventuality. Today is her very first "my-husband-screwed-the-dog-walker-in-the-shed-and-left-me" day. Phrased that way, it sounds almost like a celebration. But it absolutely is not. Agatha smells like skunk. Her cheek is creased from lying on the porch all night waiting for Dax to return with their boys. Her big toe throbs. The house is quiet. Silent. Except for that bloody woodpecker pecking another hole in the clapboards near the roofline. *Tap tap tippity-tap.* Agatha's hands are full of splinters. No wonder. To say her heart hurts is an understatement. Or maybe an overstatement. Can she feel her heart? Is it even there? Did Dax pack it up and take it with him? *Hello, hello, heart? Are you in there?*

Agatha has so many questions. How long will it take for the skunk stench to wear off? Will taking a bath in tomato juice extinguish the odor or is that an old wives' tale? Who the hell were these old wives? And why did they have so many tales? Will her toenail turn black and fall off? If so, is that a sign of fortune or a warning of impending doom? Will her cheek be creased forever? Will she wear the crease like a scarlet letter? What is the best way to kill a woodpecker (not that she would)? What are her boys thinking? How are they feeling? When will they return?

Slumped against the porch swing, upright at last, she remembers the previous evening's posts in the Wallingford Facebook moms group, about her and the shed and the hatchet and the dog walker and Dax. Oh, god. The hatchet. The Moms know everything. High Priestess Jane Poston knows everything. Kumbaya Queen Melody Whelan knows everything. Agatha drops her head into her hands. Gingerly. The splinters hurt.

From her perch, she sees the shed. Or, rather, what's left of it.

* * *

Tap tap tippity-tap.

* * *

An hour later, a little more coherent, but probably not coherent enough, Agatha shuffles to her car and drives to Starbucks. "All hail the drive-through window," she mutters into the speaker. She is not presentable according to Wallingford standards. She is not presentable by anyone's standards. The crease. The stink. The hair. The splinters. The sobby eyes. That outfit. No shoes. If HP Poston catches a glimpse, she's toast.

"Excuse me? May I help you?" says the disembodied voice of the coffee-making person.

"A humongous latte with as many shots of espresso as you can stuff into it," Agatha says.

Met with silence, Agatha repeats, "A humongous latte with as many shots of espresso as you can stuff into it." She purposely sidesteps the lingua franca and imagines the Starbucks barista staring blankly at the wall, trying to translate *humongous* into *venti*. "Hey," she says, after yet another minute, "coffee-making person, can you or can you not make a big-ass latte with lots of espresso?"

"I can."

"Then please do so."

Agatha pulls around the corner. As she waits, she pulls splinters from her palms and piles them on the console between the driver and passenger seats.

When the window slides open, she grabs the latte and waves her phone in front of the swiper thing. She keeps her eyes on the gigantic cup so she doesn't have to see the look of horror on the coffee-making person's face when he sees and smells her. That wide-eyed grimace may have been the thing to push her over the edge, past the point of no return. The match in the powder barrel. The straw that breaks the camel's back. The exhausted, flabbergasted, emotionally wrecked camel's back.

Next stop, the pharmacy.

"All hail," she starts to mutter again as she pulls up to the drive-through window but stops. Enough hailing.

The young man at the window passes the cans of tomato juice to her with one hand. With the other, he pinches his nostrils closed. "When I saw the order, I couldn't figure out why someone would need so many cans of tomato juice," he says. "I thought, 'Tomato soup for a party of fifty, maybe?' Now I get it."

Agatha doesn't respond. She's getting used to the eye-watering stench.

"You know, we sell a wash for skunk scent," he says, blinking. "People say it works better than tomato juice. And it doesn't sting your eyes."

Agatha smirks. She's thinking about all the old wives and their tales, and she imagines their husbands likely screwed the milkmaids in the barn. Like Dax and the dog walker in the shed. She imagines they didn't have the same wherewithal as she to use the hatchet. Buying fifty cans of tomato juice feels like a virtual, time-traveling fist bump to those powerless old wives, as well as a nod to their wisdom. "Don't screw the milkmaid," she says to the young man, "or the dog walker." Then she drives away, leaving him in a cloud of skunk stink and confusion. Cans rattle on the passenger seat; a few tumble to the floor.

* * *

Back home, Agatha walks to the shed, big-ass latte in hand. The woodpecker starts again. *Tap tap tippity-tap. Tap tap tippity-tap.* Agatha eyes it and believes it eyes her back. She picks up the boys' basketball and hurls it at the determined bird. The ball hits the house but doesn't come close to its target. *Tap tap tippity-tap.*

* * *

On the day before, the steamiest Saturday of a very steamy September, for the good-god-gazillionth time, the boys had gotten the soccer ball stuck under the back porch where resident skunk Susan Sontag hangs her hat. Agatha chased them inside for lunch with an "if you're going to kick it in that direction, it's going to get stuck and I'm not retrieving it one more time," but after every single bite of grilled cheese sandwich, it was, "Mom, the ball," and "Mom, please," and "Mom, we can't leave it under there. It will smell like Susan," and "C'mon, Mom, for Big Papi's sake, go get the ball."

Thirty minutes later, she surrendered. They were dogged, their finest skill. "Okay, okay, but I'm using the rake," and she stepped into her flip-flops. "Finish your sandwiches," she said as the screen door slapped behind her.

She trotted across the driveway, noted the fuzzy pooch tied to the tree across the street yapping and yapping and yapping, spread her arms to touch each of the two towering oaks as she passed between them ["luck, Mom, luck!" the boys insist every time], righted a tipped soccer net, and skipped over the side lawn to the shed. Their yard is one of those endless New England lots that could double as a practice field for the Red Sox. The kind folks drool over in magazines. A white gazebo, a tree house, lilacs and rhododendrons as far as you can see. And, oh, the hydrangeas. So many quintessential hydrangeas.

Agatha pulled open the door and let out a sigh as the chilly air hit her. It was so damn hot out. The scurry of micely beasts with their tails and squeaks made her quake with fear, but she summoned her inner Bear Grylls and thrust her face into the cool interior.

"Fear sharpens us. Fear sharpens us. Fear sharpens us," she chanted. Bear says it all the time. He is her idol, her hero, her golden calf.

Then, between the yaps of the damned dog tied across the street, she heard a shuffling and the clattering of tools.

Chipmunk?

Squirrel?

Raccoon?

She sucked in a breath. "Fear sharpens us."

But, next, a gasp. A human gasp. A girly gasp.

And a grunt. A human grunt. A manly grunt.

Things in Agatha's brain got all jumbly as it started to make sense of what was unfolding, well before her pounding heart could even go there.

When her eyes adjusted to the dark, she saw the silhouette of her husband's erect penis poking out past the edge of the workbench. There was no mistaking that cock. The hideous, delightful knob at its end. She knows it as well as she knows the can opener in her kitchen drawer. She's had both since college.

She stepped over the threshold, stubbed her big toe on the snow-blower, and whispered, "Dax?" When she spotted the silky aquamarine muumuu-maxi dress puddled on the floor in a bit of sunlight—the same she'd seen earlier that morning on the dog walker who'd swaggered up their street with four corgis on leash, earbuds and glossy lips and hips in tow—her heart took a step in the direction of her brain.

WTF?

The next minute got all wobbly. Dax bent, grabbed the dress, and held it behind him. His hirsute back was bare. Then a hand reached from behind the ride-on mower and nipped the dress from him.

WTF?

Dax's glisteny knob wagged, then sagged. He found his britches and jammed a leg into them. "Agatha, go outside!" he said, toppling a stack of terra cotta pots. "I'll be out in a minute."

She was Agatha. She knew this. He was talking to her. But her head clanged and she felt a mad stinging all over her body as if she'd stepped on a nest of yellow jackets.

She remembers nothing after this moment and can only trust what the police officer tells her later. She got her hands on the hatchet. Naked people ran for their lives. A single shriek pierced the afternoon. She destroyed the shed. No one died.

Chapter Two

When Agatha snapped out of whatever state she'd snapped into when her heart finally caught up with her brain, the boys had left with Dax and the dog walker had been escorted to safety, generously draped with a tarp, a green tarp, the same green tarp under which, each spring, Dax protected his much-anticipated mulch delivery from rain. Black mulch, not red, absolutely not red, despite Kerry Sheridan's annual campaign for matching red mulch in the neighborhood. Even the dog walker's yappy charge, the very one she'd tied to the tree across the street before screwing Agatha's husband in their shed, had been tucked into the back of a squad car and delivered to its owner. An officer was waiting with Agatha until she was "calm."

"Are my boys okay?" she asked as soon as her voice returned. "Did they see everything?"

The officer shook his head. "They're fine. From what I heard, they'd been watching SpongeBob and didn't know a thing until an officer knocked on the door."

Agatha didn't think she'd ever have reason to thank the universe for SpongeBob, but life is funny like that.

She and the officer sat on the back porch staring at the jagged remains of the shed while she ranted. "You know that line about Janie in *Their Eyes Were Watching God . . . ,*" she said. "The one about her buttocks . . ."

"Whose eyes were doing what?" the officer said.

Agatha pulled an inch-long splinter from her thumb and side-eyed this young-not-young man. If his assignment was to help the crazed lady chill out, things were not starting off well. "What do you mean, *whose eyes were doing what*?"

The officer winced.

"*Their Eyes Were Watching God*. By Zora Neale Hurston. One of the best novels ever written by one of the best goddamn writers ever born."

He shook his head. "Nope, never read it."

"How in the world can you be a police officer without having read Zora Neale Hurston's magnum opus?" Agatha said, but really, she was asking, "How in the world can you be a human without having read Zora Neale Hurston's magnum opus?"

"I don't read many books," he said.

Agatha rolled her eyes as her soul rose up and towered over them. She doesn't trust people who don't read books—despises them really—but other than Kerry Sheridan, who was pretending to study her sun-scorched lawn but who was really trying to see if Agatha was going to go ninja on anything else, the officer was the only one around. "Well," she said, "Janie—Janie Mae Crawford—is the main character in this novel you really should read, and, in it, there's a line about her that goes, 'The men noticed her firm buttocks like she had grapefruits in her hip pockets . . .'"

The officer nodded in slow motion.

"That's how I'd describe this woman who just screwed my husband in our shed. Her buttocks, her ass, her behind, her derriere, is just like Janie's. Fothermucking grapefruits in her fothermucking hip pockets. Gorgeous work of art. You should have seen it." She was forgetting that he did see it, naked even, running wildly as Agatha chopped and chopped and chopped the shed into smithereens.

Holy crap, what a day.

Agatha stood and turned so her own buttocks were just a foot or so from the officer's face. "No grapefruits here," she said, smacking her bottom with both hands. "Just a couple of mushy, thirty-five-year-old, kid-chasing cantaloupes. Miss I-Screwed-Your-Husband-In-The-Shed walks dogs all day, firming those cheeks, while I slog after our children—*our children*—and end up with a couple of overripe cantaloupes stuffed into black leggings."

The officer slid back on the step, putting another foot or so between them. "Ma'am, how are you feeling now? Better? Calmer? More like yourself?"

This man was so young, so dumb. He had no idea Agatha may never feel like herself again.

"Yes, I'm fine. Go on back to the station and close your report on the woman who destroyed her shed. I'm all done chopping things up with a hatchet."

"You're sure?"

"I'm sure." And she was. Mostly.

The officer stood, clearly relieved. "Your husband and his friend will not be pressing charges. But, please, no more destruction."

If she had a single ounce of energy left in her limbs and this man wasn't a cop, Agatha would have decked him, laid him out right there on the sidewalk. He actually believed that she was the destroyer here and the shed the object of destruction. He saw the splintered wood but not the shards of her family, her marriage, and her heart piled up all around. Fuck the shed.

As the officer climbed into his car, her phone buzzed. An alert from her Facebook Moms group. Update! Update! Look! She shouldn't have looked. She would have bet the dog walker's silkiest muumuu-maxi it was about her. News traveled fast within the Moms group. Lightning fast. Cheetah fast. Peregrine falcon fast. Fothermucking supersonic fast. She pulled her phone from her pocket.

"Don't look," she told herself. "Do not look."

But she looked. Of course she looked. She always looked. All the Moms look. It's what they do.

Happy?

They look.

Lonely?

They look.

Sad?

Look.

Hungry?

Look.

Jealous?

Look.

Vengeful?

Look.

Bored?

Look.

Look, look, look, look, look, look, look.

Agatha stared at the new post. It was a photo of her shed. Now just a pile of broken sticks with tools and ride-on vehicles poking up here and there. A swatch of aquamarine fabric glinted in the corner. "Uh oh," the post said. She looked at the poster's name. Kerry Sheridan, aka her neighbor with the red mulch and shit-brown lawn. She looked up and spied Kerry cowering behind the hydrangea bushes their boys always used as a fort. Kerry's two and Agatha's two. The four musketeers. Comments flooded in.

Rachel Runk:	"Uh oh is right! Who's shed is/was that?"
Kerry Sheridan:	"Agatha Arch's."
phyliss-with-one-l-and-two-esses:	"agatha arch's?"
Agatha Arch:	"PHYLLIS, STOP WHISPERING IN ALL LOWERCASE LETTERS. YES, IT WAS MY SHED."

The splinter embedded in the tip of her thumb made typing a slow, agonizing task, but Agatha had to respond. She couldn't let such nonsense slide.

phyliss-with-one-l-and-two-esses:	"agatha, that's phyliss with one *l* and two esses. you know that."
Agatha Arch:	"It's also Phyliss with a capital P."
Rachel Runk:	"Forget that. Who destroyed the shed?"
Kerry Sheridan:	"Agatha Arch."

Kerry's smug satisfaction at being able to share this gold nugget of information dripped from Agatha's phone as nearly seventy-five Moms responded exactly alike in what Agatha calls the "stink bug syndrome." It went like this:

Priya Devi:	"Agatha Arch?"
Meena Johnson:	"Agatha Arch?"
Quynh Nguyen:	"Agatha Arch?"
Bridget Weller:	"Agatha Arch?"
Candice Anderson:	"AGATHA ARCH?"
Emily Patterson:	"Our Agatha Arch?"
Kimberly Stanton:	"Agatha Arch?"
Grainne O'Neill:	"Agatha Arch?"
Mary Devlin:	"Agatha Arch?"
Holly McCarthy:	"Agatha Arch?"
David Watkins:	"Agatha Arch?"
Susan Snow:	"Agatha Arch?"
Ava Newton:	"Agatha Arch?"
Olivia Charles:	"Agatha Arch?"
Mila Janssen:	"Agatha Arch?"
Tiana Samuels:	"AGATHA ARCH? *THE* AGATHA ARCH?"

Brigid Egan: "Agatha ARCH?"
Lin Zheng: "Agatha Arch?"
Isabelle Fish: "Agatha Arch?"
Erin Abel: "Agatha Arch?"
Abby Smith: "Agatha Arch?"

This would have gone on for many more minutes had Kerry not butted in and said, "Yes, ladies, Agatha Arch. The one and only Agatha Arch."

Agatha Arch: "I'm right here, Kerry. I can answer for myself."
Rachel Runk: "Why did she destroy her own shed?"
Agatha Arch: "I said I'm right here!"
Rachel Runk: "OK, Agatha, why did YOU destroy your own shed?"

Agatha paused, flagging slightly under the pressure of the 2,690 member Moms (and odd dads and guardians) waiting for her answer. Two thousand six hundred ninety Moms staring at their phones in line at Target, between sips of iced lattes at Starbucks, on treadmills at the gym, on conference calls in their offices, driving to work, blending kale smoothies, watching their little ones eat sand at the park. This was the kind of moment the Moms lived for. Better even than the big moment at a gender reveal party.

Agatha Arch: "My husband screwed the dog walker in that shed today. I destroyed it."
Rachel Runk: "With what? An ax?"
Agatha Arch: "Close. A hatchet."
High Priestess Jane Poston: "Holy shit."
Kumbaya Queen Melody Whelan: "Oh, sweetie."

Agatha clicked out. She and the High Priestess didn't occupy the same space very well. Ever. And pity from the Kumbaya Queen? That was the last thing she needed.

* * *

When Kerry Sheridan popped out from behind the hydrangeas for a follow-up photo, Agatha shot her the bird. Just above the tip of her middle finger, the daytime moon hung in the sky. It was the boys' favorite celestial phenomenon. Always there but not always visible. "Like you, Mom," Jason often tells her, "when we're at school or baseball."

Agatha lay belly down on the porch and rested her cheek on the boards, convinced that if she stayed in this insanely uncomfortable position until her bones ached, Dax and the boys would pull up in the minivan, she would wake from this nightmare, and life as she knew and loved it would resume. The brain is capable of such trickery.

But then the sun dropped behind Kerry Sheridan's historic Federal, and Agatha got a text. "Mom, it's us. Dad says we're staying at this hotel 2night. U OK? We love u. Weird & scary."

Agatha's heart sank with the sun. This day was not just a bad nightmare. Her husband had screwed the dog walker in their shed. She really had destroyed the shed with a hatchet. The Moms already knew, so, really, the whole world knew. Her sons were not coming home that night.

"All OK, J&D," she typed without lifting her head from the planks, thumbs stinging. "Don't be scared. Have fun in the hotel with your dad. A little vacation. I'll see you soon. Remember, daytime moon."

A text came back. "OK. Can you bring our swimsuits? Dad forgot them."

Even in the midst of such calamity, Agatha chuckled. Leave it to kids. Them first, no matter what.

Minutes later, Susan Sontag scuttled out from under the porch for her nightly rendezvous with Jerry Garcia, her shaggy beau from Kerry Sheridan's yard. When the motion light clicked on, Susan turned, spotted Agatha in the shadows, and jumped with surprise. Then she lifted her tail and sprayed, proving that even the crappiest of crappy days can get crappier.

Agatha groaned but didn't move. She had zero left. Zero energy. Zero pride. Zero huzzah. Zero urge to fight. Zero everything. Zero anything. As the cloud of skunk stink burrowed into her hair and clothes, headlights rounded the bend and paused near the bottom of her driveway. Her heart jolted. "Dax! Dax!" Maybe! Maybe?

But no. Not Dax. Lights too low to the ground, too golden, too bright.

The car crawled past the house. The first in a long line of looky-loos.

If Agatha were not Agatha—if she were Michelle or maybe Tanya or Katherine . . . geesh, even if she were a different Agatha—then a cavalry of friends might have arrived at that very moment. They would have galloped in on stallions, surrounded her, drawn swords to protect her, and shot poisoned arrows at Dax. They would have lifted her to the sky, pulled splinters from her hands, and tended her wounds.

But Agatha is Agatha. She is not good at friends. She has no cavalry in good times or bad.

If I did, she thought, they would not be called a cavalry. Too militant. Too male.

Just before drifting off to sleep, a mosquito bit her forearm. The final insult. The last screw-you of the day. When the itch began, Agatha didn't even attempt to scratch it. She just lay there. Belly down on the porch. Perfectly imperfectly still. And she stayed this way until morning. A teary, stinky, itchy, aching, creased, cantaloupe-assed mess of mad and sad.

* * *

Agatha Arch is Afraid of Everything

And now, a new day. Big-ass latte in hand, Agatha circles the remains of the shed and considers her favorite collective nouns:

dazzle (zebras)
quiver (cobras)
tower (giraffes)
prickle (porcupines)
crash (rhinoceroses)
mob (kangaroos)
shrewdness (apes)
maelstrom (salamanders)
murmuration (starlings)
rafter (turkeys)
wing (plovers)
knot (frogs)
descent (woodpeckers)

Each is clever, but her favorite is the first. A dazzle of zebras.

But friends? A collective noun for friends? If she had them . . .
Maybe a flicker.
A flash.
A quiver.
A clementine.
A zephyr.

So many possibilities. She can dream.

Chapter Three

By midafternoon, hordes of cars are inching past Agatha's house. Crawling as if they are stuck in looky-loo speed. Escalades, Humvees, Highlanders, and Mini Coopers line up behind three Teslas, an RV, and Wallingford's passionate gaggle of Subarus. A few shiny Mercedes join the parade, then the Range Rovers, the BMWs, and all the rest. Even Wallingford's favorite cupcake van does a lap. Everyone wants a glimpse of the shed. Or what's left of it.

Sitting on the porch, Agatha likens the procession to the crush of people who charge past the *Mona Lisa* every day. On their honeymoon in Paris, Dax had insisted they do the same. Agatha had not been impressed. "Who needs to stand in line for three hours to see another wry woman not speaking her mind?" she'd said.

But the shed. The shed in the late afternoon light. The golden light. The light in which all the best movie scenes are filmed. Now that *is* something to see. Hard evidence that women have the strength and the voice and—damn right—the skill and willingness to handle a hatchet.

As they pass, Moms lean out of their windows and snap photos with their phones. They wave to one another, call out, and *beep beep beep*. Jane Poston—who else?—introduces a new thread on the Moms page: The Shed on Sutton Circle. What better way to get back at

Agatha for one of the many insults she's hurled at Jane and her cohorts throughout the years? For her annual carol, "The 12 Days of the Wallingford Moms"?

What goes around comes around.

* * *

As the Moms stream past, Agatha soaks her swollen toe in a shallow basin and thinks about water, then swimming, then drowning, because this is the kind of human she can be, the kind who leaps from the mundane to the maudlin in seconds, the kind we all can be in our worst moments. She glances at the potted tomato plant at her side. "It's like that quarry I swam in during my first weekend in college," she tells it. She is also the kind of person who converses with plants when no other options exist. Sometimes even when they do. She remembers leaping into the greenish limestone water feeling brave and daring because all the other freshmen were lingering on the rocks, staring fearfully into the quarry. When she'd been accepted into college a few months before, she'd decided to let go of the fears that had nibbled at her through high school. "Go brave" was her new motto, and shouting that very thing while cannonballing into the quarry with an impressive splash symbolized the new Agatha.

She paddled around in her red-and-white-striped bikini flaunting her courage and breasts and calling out "Hey, come on in!" to potential friends. "Don't be chicken!" She felt intrepid and vulnerable. It was a new and welcome feeling.

It wasn't until she swam smack into the rotting carcass of the cow that she realized why her potential friends were not joining her and what they'd been staring at so fearfully. She back-paddled as fast as she could, but the rotting cow followed in her wake. Its eyes were gone. Its tongue nearly so. The hide on its hindquarters was flaking off like filigree.

As the squeals and laughter of her classmates echoed off the quarry walls, one boy offered a hand and helped her scramble to the rocks.

"I'm Dax," he said.

"Agatha," she whispered, trying not to look at the bits of cowhide stuck to her swimsuit.

"That was brave," he said.

"That was stupid," she said. "Never again."

* * *

A woman wearing a daisy-covered dress hops from her Lexus, jogs fifty yards into Agatha's yard, and takes a selfie with the remains of the shed. When the photo shows up on the Moms thread, Agatha admits it's a good one. The white daisies and gleaming teeth complement the splintered wood. She thinks again about the quarry and likens the Moms group to that poisoned pool and herself to the rotting cow. In that moment, she's quite sure the group had been just fine before she showed up. A harmonious, supportive clan of generous women.

"I am the rotting cow," she says to the tomato plant.

"You're not," it assures her.

Her phone buzzes with posts to the shed thread. "They disagree," she says.

Three fat tomatoes hang from the vines; two remain stubbornly green, the third offers a hopeful hint of yellow.

* * *

After dark, a dotted line of headlights moves up Sutton Circle. Agatha raises her binoculars. It's the Dads. The men. The humans with penises and power who, unlike the women, don't want to be seen eyeballing the shed. They don't want Agatha or their wives or their lovers or any other woman to glimpse their fear, thinly veiled as curiosity. They don't want any woman to know that the splintered shed represents the thing that scares them most: women rising up. Women grabbing a hatchet and hollering *uh uh, no more, ain't doing it*. If all their women rise up and do what Agatha did, how many sheds will look like this? How many lives?

As they cruise past, Agatha hears the sound of testicles shrinking. "*Shlooop*," she says to the tomato plant. "That's it right there. The sound of shrinking balls."

What if women start doing this with other things? What if the hatchet becomes the go-to response?

Unequal pay?

Grab the hatchet.

Glass ceiling?

Grab the hatchet.

Cat-called?

Grab the hatchet.

Sexually assaulted?

Grab the hatchet.

Cheated on?

Grab the hatchet.

"Get your shed-shattering hatchet here!" Agatha says to the tomato plant. "Hatchets on sale, two for ten bucks."

Women aren't supposed to think this way . . . act this way. Violence is not the answer after all. Children should not see their mother obliterating a shed while their half-naked father and his more-naked lover flee its confines.

This last statement is true. Children should not see this. And the fact that her boys might have caught even a glimpse will haunt Agatha until she decides it won't. But then there's Dax, right at this moment sitting with his pretty little cake and eating it too. She knows that at some point he'll look back and see all that he broke and pray he won't witness a ripple effect in his sons. But she also knows that some things travel that way, father to son. Some things you can't control.

* * *

That night, Agatha takes her first-ever tomato juice bath and reads an article about a mysterious outbreak of anthrax near the top of the world. The very tip-top of the world. In the morning, she can't remember the exact location. *Mongolia? Russia?* Just the fact that somewhere near the Arctic Circle thousands of reindeer and dozens of people have become deathly ill. A single child has died.

"What caused this?" her shrink asks the next morning when Agatha shares the story.

"Global warming," Agatha says. "Climate change." Her voice is high and trill-y. Like a buzz saw. "A recent heat wave thawed a reindeer carcass that had been infected with anthrax decades ago. Right at this very moment, scientists are running around vaccinating reindeer and trying to prevent other humans from keeling over, all while spores of unleashed anthrax are whizzing about trying to find new victims."

"The Arctic Circle is very far from here," Shrinky-Dink says. She knows Agatha well.

"We all breathe the same air eventually," Agatha says. "You do know pollution from China is causing health problems in California, right? China!" She ignores Shrinky-Dink's raised eyebrows. "Anyway, the article warned that global warming will continue to thaw corpses infected with all kinds of fatal viruses and bacteria: bubonic plague, smallpox, variants of the flu, and lots more we know nothing about."

"Agatha, please stop reading these types of articles," Shrinky-Dink says. "While they may be true, there is something to be said for perspective."

"Meaning?"

"Meaning an outbreak of anthrax at the top of the world is not going to directly affect you."

"You don't know this."

"I'm pretty sure."

"That's not good enough."

"So you're going to spend time fretting about this possibility because . . . ?"

"Because if I can anticipate it, I can avoid it."

"That philosophy doesn't often work."

"Sometimes it does."

"It didn't work with Dax."

"Meaning?"

"Meaning you got suspicious about Dax having an affair a few weeks ago, but you couldn't avoid the fallout."

"I wasn't suspicious."

"What were you?"

"Aware."

"Aware that he might be having an affair."

"Aware that something was shifting."

"Same thing."

"Stop it. We're talking about anthrax."

"We're talking about Dax."

Agatha purses her lips. This is a classic Shrinky-Dink switcheroo. "You're talking about Dax."

"Who is the woman?"

"A dog walker who's been walking past our house for years. Dax and I used to joke about her. Together. He says they met in the spring at the park."

"You don't have a dog."

"No."

"Dax hates dogs."

"So he said."

"He refused to get a dog when you and the boys begged."

"Indeed he did."

Shrinky-Dink pauses, and Agatha imagines it is one of those moments when a therapist has to stop herself from veering off the path of neutrality, like Switzerland when faced with a fondue crisis. A moment when she wants to say "What the fuck?" Maybe the greatest challenge of the job. Definitely the reason Agatha could never do it.

"So," Shrinky-Dink finally says. "A dog walker?"

"Yes."

"I assume she has dogs of her own."

"A Chihuahua."

"It's a fling?"

"No."

"No?"

"They're in love."

"Really?"

"So he says."

"What's next?"

"Dax has moved in with her and her Chihuahua."

"Already?"

"Already. He told me in a text."

"And the boys?"

"He said they're moving in, too."

"Into the dog walker's house?"

"Yes, he says they'll be living there with him and her, part-time, when they're not with me."

Shrinky-Dink shakes her head. "It's been barely forty-eight hours."

Agatha nods.

"Are you going to fight?"

"Fight?" Agatha can't imagine fighting any harder than she had with the hatchet.

"For full custody."

Shrinky-Dink's words echo in her brain. Full custody. "I don't know," she says, trying to imagine the boys never spending another night with their father. "How could I?"

"I'm sorry, Agatha."

Agatha wonders if Shrinky-Dink's measured response would be any different if they were out for drinks, if they were pals, not therapist and client, if Shrinky-Dink was an honored member of Agatha's imagined zephyr of friends. Maybe she'd sling back a whiskey sour and spit, "What a bloody jerk!" Or wrap her arms around Agatha and hold on tight. Perhaps she'd even answer the questions pummeling Agatha's heart: How does a man who hates dogs fall in love with a dog walker? How does a man fall in love with anyone but his wife? Does Dax now love dogs, too? Does he love the chirpy, snippy Chihuahua the dog walker sometimes carries in a pouch? What about their boys? Have Dustin and Jason fallen for the dog walker? Will they? How long will it take for Agatha to untangle the knot in her middle? When will she breathe again?

Not brave enough to ask her real questions, Agatha says, "Do I still smell like skunk?"

Shrinky-Dink nods. "And tomato juice. Have you gotten all of the splinters out of your hands?"

"Most. There are still two deep ones in my right. I can't dig them out with my left."

"May I help?" Shrinky-Dink opens the drawer of the coffee table between them and pulls out a sewing kit. She seems prepared for anything.

Agatha sticks out her right hand. When Shrinky-Dink takes it and holds it in her own, tears start to seep out of her eyes. She isn't sure she's crying because the needle digs so deep or because this is the first skin-to-skin contact she's had since discovering Dax and the dog walker in the shed. She makes little gulpy noises as tears soak the collar of her shirt.

"You could have called me on Saturday," Shrinky-Dink says. "I'm here in a crisis."

"I couldn't. I should have."

Shrinky-Dink makes the clucky sound she makes whenever Agatha admits to something she could have done differently. She doesn't cluck often. Her eyes go to the clock. "Time's up."

"Thank goodness." Agatha pulls her hand back into her lap.

"When is Dax dropping the boys?"

"Tomorrow evening after soccer practice."

"You could have demanded he bring them home immediately. You know that, right?"

"I know, but I didn't want them to see me like this."

Shrinky-Dink nods. "Take it easy between now and then. Remember, you're working on living in the moment."

Agatha nods, notes that her current moment is a crock of shit, goes home, researches symptoms of anthrax, and decides that yes, yes, she may, in fact, already be suffering from this horrid disease. Twenty-five years before, in the pre-internet era, she would have had to work way too hard to come by such information. Go to the library. Search in the card catalog. Jot the Dewey Decimal numbers on a piece of paper. Find the right section of the library. Find the right stack. Find the right book. Find the right page. But with Google at her fingertips, she is able to learn all too quickly that sore throat, fatigue, muscle aches, headache, and shortness of breath—all maladies she's been suffering since the shed incident—can quite logically be attributed to anthrax. She saves the information in the Hard Truths file on her phone. Despite Shrinky-Dink's doubt, the winds from that place near the very tip-top of the world must have blown directly to Wallingford. This is it, she thinks.

* * *

Agatha draws a bath, pours the remaining cans of tomato juice into the tub, and steps in. Why die stinking like a skunk? Sloshing around in what feels like slimy, day-old soup—sinking low enough to soak her hair and submerge her ears—she dares to shift her brain from the child who died of anthrax to her own children. Her healthy, hilarious, wear-you-out boys who are right at this moment exploring the new bedroom their father is putting together at the dog walker's house. That's what Dax's text said. "My love's name is Willow. The boys and I are at her house. I'll be living here. They'll have a room. I'm fixing it up now. I'll drop them to you at 6:30 on Tuesday after soccer practice. I'll pick up a few things, and we can figure out a child-sharing schedule."

My love's name is Willow.

What kind of corny crap is that?

In her best Lauren Bacall voice, Agatha repeats Dax's pronouncement. *My love's name is Willow.*

And the boys will be living part-time at this Willow's house?

Her boys? *Their* boys?

Though it's obvious Dax had put a good amount of thought into this plan over the past few weeks or months, Agatha doubts the plan had included getting caught screwing in the shed and having to escape the hatchet. That wasn't his style. Still, brand new to this unexpected twist, she is understandably bewildered, understandably heartbroken, and understandably pissed. She sits up in the tub and checks her body for blisters and dark scabs, further telltale signs of anthrax. She has a good many but isn't sure if they are left over from the shed incident or are symptomatic of her newly self-diagnosed disease.

A child-sharing plan. What does that even mean? How do you share children? Between houses? Parents? Lives? Hearts?

She could lawyer up and battle for full custody, as Shrinky-Dink suggested. It probably wouldn't be hard to win given the circumstances. But even in her current state, submerged in a pool of tomato juice, Agatha can't imagine doing that to the boys.

She turns on the shower, stands and rinses. In her head, she pens a farewell letter to the life she'd known and loved. What would it all look like now?

* * *

Agatha zips Dax a text. "Hope you and GDOG are happy."

He's fast. "GDOG?"

She's equally fast. "Your hussy. Your muumuu-maxi mama. You know, the Grande Dame of Grapefruits. GDOG."

Dax knows the reference. Of that, Agatha is sure. They'd read *Their Eyes Were Watching God* out loud to one another for a college

English class, back-and-forthing about Tea Cake and Janie and hurricanes and love, under trees and blooming bushes, in dorm stairwells and coffee houses, dog-earing pages, breaking spines, jotting notes in margins. Their first kiss was a post-TEWWG kiss in the college gazebo at midnight. Agatha has been standing on chairs and reciting best-loved passages to him ever since.

Dax: Her name is Willow.
Agatha: Grande Dame of Grapefruits

Chapter Four

Agatha stands at the bottom of the back stairs and looks up at the door to her office. *Lift your foot, you big crybaby. Lift your foot.*

She drops and curls on the floor. *Don't call yourself names*, she hears Shrinky-Dink whisper from somewhere far away. *Be kind to you. Try again.*

She stands.

Good god, if only she could will herself into action. *One step at a time. Go on.* She needs to climb these stairs, sit down at her desk, and get to work. Isn't writing the thing that always saves her? The thing that always keeps her from falling apart? When her father keeled over at the train station and died before she could get to the hospital, she wrote. When her mother suffered heartbreak-disguised-as-pneumonia a year later and died, she wrote. When Dax's sister married that feckless nincompoop from Texas, she wrote. When she miscarried, she wrote. When her fourth book flopped, she wrote. But this. This. This is something else. This is different. This is the hyena clamping her throat to weaken her. This is quicksand swallowing her limb by limb. This is the roller-coaster flying off its track. "Grief, when it comes, is nothing like we expect it to be," she whispers. All hail Joan Didion.

But upstairs, through that door, that beautiful crimson door, is the desk that Dax built. The solid, sturdy desk as big as a farmer's table with dozens of drawers and cubbies stuffed full of notes and letters and cards from the boys, along with balls of string and not-so-sticky-anymore fire truck stickers and pens and hair ties and all kinds of marvelous, mysterious whatnots. There's even an inch-high chamber carved into the wood on the right-hand side. A wee door, invisible to most eyes, that opens and closes on the tiniest of hinges. "It's for magical things," Dax had told her. For all these years, since her first big book deal, she'd stored a miniature photo of him and the boys in the secret cubby. Magical things.

She grips her right thigh with both hands and tries to drag her leg up onto the next step. She pulls; the leg pushes. She pushes; the leg pulls. It's like trying to wrestle a cranky toddler into a grocery cart. Giving in, surrendering to this impossibility, Agatha turns and trudges through the kitchen into the living room and up the front staircase to their bedroom. In the beginning of this house with Dax, she'd found it strange and unnerving to have two staircases, a front and a back. Who needs such convenience? Such luxury? Such a reminder of times past with maids and butlers? But after ten years, she loves the two equally. The boys love them for hide and seek, but she finds comfort in the fact that if a murderer ever comes for her up the front steps in the night, she can escape down the back.

Upstairs, she wraps herself in Dax's pit-stinky robe and curls in their king-size bed. For the next few hours, she binge-watches the most marvelous Bear Grylls leaping and crawling through brush and streams, clawing his way up a mountain and slip-sliding down a steep, shale-covered slope. He shimmies over a rocky crevasse, twenty feet in the air, one leg flung over a cord stretched taut from one side to the other. "It's all about the knots," he tells the camera.

"Bloody hell," Agatha says. She can barely tie her shoes.

Her nights with Bear always start this way, with Agatha unpacking her cornucopia of fears.

The first big one? Beans.

Years before, when she was just a teenager, she'd watched that horror movie about the serial killer guy who eats people with fava beans. Fava beans. It was hard enough to make sense of a movie about a man who eats people—actually *eats* them, with a fork and knife, and maybe some béchamel sauce—but to pair the main course with a particular type of bean? That was too much. As a writer, even at the tender age of seventeen, Agatha appreciated the specificity, but as a human . . . well. Never mind that she'd never eaten a fava bean, didn't know what one looked like, and had to look up the spelling of *fava* when she wrote about it in her journal. The experience had sent her into spasms of fear, and the only thing that helped her cope was complete abstinence. Not since that devastating cinematic experience has she eaten a single bean. Not any kind of bean. Not a green bean or a baked bean. Not a lima, wax, or snap bean. Not a kidney bean, despite her passion for chili. Not a black, garbanzo, or pinto bean. And, hell no, not a fava bean.

"Beans were my gateway fear," she'd told Shrinky-Dink at their first appointment. The fear that had opened the floodgates for all others: strangers, sand, mice, ghosts, alien invasion, fireworks, the dark, bridges, tunnels, not fitting in, the fact that raisins are dried grapes and prunes are dried plums, drowning. The list goes on.

"Fear is like that," Shrinky-Dink had said. "A slippery slope."

"Slippery slopes scare the shit out of me," Agatha had replied.

Dax once asked Agatha why she'd generalized, why she'd stopped eating all beans rather than just fava beans. She didn't have a good answer. It had felt like the right thing to do. The only thing to do. It sounds ridiculous described this way, but in Agatha's head, it makes complete sense. A person's head is a funny place. The heart is even funnier.

* * *

But an hour in, when Bear manages to spark a lifesaving fire as torrential rain pummels his hand-hewn leaf tent, Agatha stands on the bed and cheers. "I can do it, Bear!" she yells. "I can make it through this storm. I can climb this mountain."

And for this moment, she believes. Bear—the king of "I can do anything"—makes her believe. He makes everyone believe. It's his superpower. He is so focused and determined, so "no shit is taking *me* down out here," that for a few brief hours, Agatha Arch believes that she too can find her way out of a maze of vines and sinewy trees, keep her footing while crossing a river on a fallen log, and suck the innards from a poisonous creature whose sting can rot you from the inside out in less time than it takes you to say, "Holy shit, what is this thing?"

Courage is contagious after all.

She even believes she can write the psychological thriller about a murder in a Facebook moms group that she's promised to her agent. It had seemed like a great idea months before when she'd pitched it. Brilliant, really. Any woman shackled to such a group knows a murder within its confines is an absolute eventuality. Some of these moms are batshit crazy; take away their pumpkin spice latte on a day when their little one throws an epic tantrum in Whole Foods and *snap*. It's coming, no doubt about it.

After that, for a few all-too-brief weeks, dollar signs had *cha-chinged* back and forth in emails between Agatha and her agent, bestseller lists were alluded to, and images of Agatha in a sexy persimmony gown accepting an Oscar for best film adaptation of a book gave her palpitations. Thrillers are hot right now. Big sellers in the publishing world. Facebook moms groups drip with zeitgeist. So a murder in a Facebook moms group? Well, that is one hell of a plot.

When Agatha shared the news about her pitch at therapy, Shrinky-Dink had said, "Why in the world would you, of all people, offer to write a scary book? You are afraid of, well, according to you, everything."

"I know. The list of things I'm not afraid of is shorter than the list of things I am afraid of."

Shrinky-Dink nodded.

"The truth is," Agatha said, "all things of which good thrillers are made scare the living shit out of me. I remember the first time I read *Dracula*. I was in fifth grade, and to this day, I'm haunted by black flies."

"Black flies?"

Agatha rolled her eyes. She has no idea what to do with people who haven't read *Dracula*. "Yes, they're a sure sign a vampire is nearby. If I spot a fly in the house, within seconds I'm drowning in sweat just thinking about the vampire who is about to swoop down from the ceiling and sink his fangs into my jugular. Jason and Dustin think this is hilarious. They love to catch a fly outside and let it loose inside just to watch me leap and scream 'Vampire! Vampire!'"

"So why did you tell your agent you're going to write a thriller?" Shrinky-Dink said.

"I don't know. One minute Dustin was reading the Transitive Property of Equality to me from his math book and the next I was equating the whole thing to humans."

Shrinky-Dink cocked her head and waited.

"You remember, if A equals B and B equals C, then A equals C."

Shrinky-Dink nodded again. "Yes, that part I know. But how does this relate to humans and your next book?"

Agatha sighed. "People love thrillers, right?"

"Some."

"Many. Believe me, they're hot right now. Hot, hot, hot."

"And?"

"People don't really love me all that much."

"Not true. Your family loves you dearly."

"People besides Dax and the boys."

"Many other people love you."

"Still not true. I'm not easy to love."

"That aside, how does all this relate to the Transitive Property of Equality?"

"People love thrillers," Agatha said. "If I write a thriller, people will love me, too."

"That's quite a jump," Shrinky-Dink said.

"I call it the Transitive Property of Love."

Shrinky-Dink sat quietly with that for five very expensive minutes, then said, "I'm happy to hear that you're interested in forming stronger relationships with people, but there are better ways than committing to write a book that may send you over the edge."

"No, this is it," Agatha had said. "I can do it."

* * *

When she finally quits Bear at 3 AM, Agatha limps outside. Still wrapped in Dax's stinky robe, she turns her back on the remains of the shed and stares up at Orion, the mighty hunter, gleaming in the night sky. How can she, the biggest chickenshit in the world, write a thriller? Good god, she shivers just *thinking* about that horrid serial killer guy and his favorite fava bean meal.

When Orion winks at her, a Bear Grylls tweet flashes in her head: "Walk toward the dangerous and the difficult."

Damn. The universe is conspiring.

* * *

Tap tap tippity-tap.

* * *

The next morning, Agatha creates an Instagram account: "Infidelity: A Still Life." Her first post features a before-and-after mash-up of the shed. She writes, "Before I found my husband in the shed screwing a dog walker | After I found my husband in the shed screwing a dog walker. #infidelity #hatchet"

The use of the pronoun *my* before the word *husband* makes a faraway place in her middle ache and throb.

By noon, she has 739 followers and twice as many likes.

Chapter Five

At 4 PM Tuesday, Agatha flattens herself against the front window and waits there for Dax to arrive with the boys. How strange to be willing to stand against a window for well over two hours when there are so many things to be done: dinner to be cooked, dishes to be washed, sheets to be put on the boys' beds, calls to be returned, the last bit of skunk stink to be scrubbed away, and, of course, the writing, always the writing. A few days ago she would have guffawed at the thought of supergluing herself to the pane; now she won't leave the feeling of the cool glass or the view of the driveway for anything. Perhaps they will arrive early. When she says this to herself—perhaps they will arrive early—she feels as if she's been dropped into a Virginia Woolf novel, *To the Lighthouse* or *Mrs. Dalloway*. This is a Woolfian line, perhaps they will arrive early, something only a true Woolf woman would say. It is the introduction to a complicated set of social complexities that will lead to a more complicated set of psychological complexities that, hopefully, will lead to a simple but satisfying resolution.

Agatha looks through the pane at the porch and acknowledges that while the glider out there would be considerably more comfortable with its puffy pillows and cushioned armrests, from that vantage point she would look directly at the remains of the shed. The broken sticks, splintered roof, scattered tools, busted doorframe, rake handles and shovel heads, swatches of muumuu-maxi, pieces of her heart. She'd done a number on that shed and everything in it, that's for sure. A glance or walk-around now and again is fine, but two-and-a-half hours of gazing? That she cannot bear. Besides, there is comfort in discomfort.

Behind her on the living room wall, the Saturn-sized Roman numeraled clock ticks away the minutes.

4:10
tick
4:11
tock
4:12
tick
4:13
tock

Her swollen, splintered hands throb, and her big toe, poking over the edge of her flip-flop, resembles an overripe avocado.

4:57
tick
4:58
tock

The anthrax, she is sure, is snaking through her system, readying her for the final blow.

4:59
tick

5:00
tock

She rocks slightly with the rhythm of the passing minutes and fingers the crease on her cheek. Who designed such an audacious clock? Why has she never noticed this?

tick
tock
tick
tock

In a thousand years, when archaeologists dig up the ancient Wallingford society, they'll discover a similar humongous clock in nearly every home. *What of this?* they will inquire, turning the timepieces over and over in their hands. With little more to go on, they will assume Wallingfordites had had an extraordinary relationship with time instead of the unfortunate truth. Zero sense of design.

5:05
tick
5:06
tock

At 5:15 Agatha pulls away from the window, yanks the bloody clock from the wall, wrestles the *ticking-tocking* beast to the basement door, opens it, and shoves the monstrosity down the steps. She slams the door and listens to the clock *bumpety-bump* its way to the landing halfway down.

5:17
tick

5:18
tock
5:19
tick

Good god. She can hear the clock through the closed door. She thinks about "The Tell-Tale Heart," and, once again, rips herself away from the window.

tick
tock
tick
tock
ticktock
ticktock
ticktockticktockticktock

She opens the basement door, hobbles down the stairs, grabs the clock, and shuffles down the next set of stairs. "Fear sharpens us," she whispers, squinting to avoid the ghosts, then carries the ticktocking beast to the far end of the cavernous basement. Eyes closed, she stuffs it behind the old coal furnace they'd never had removed. "This is where we'll hide when the apocalypse comes," Dax always joked. "They'll never find us here."

Back upstairs at the window, it is finally quiet.

6:01
6:02
6:03

When Dax pulls into the driveway at 6:30, Agatha bounds out like a wounded deer, limping and gallumping to the car. Her heart beats in her throat, knees, and toes, and when the boys tumble out, she smothers them with kisses and buries her face in their hair. Ah, her beautiful, sweaty boys.

"Mom, you stink like Susan Sontag!" Dustin says. "I can't breathe."

"If you couldn't breathe, you wouldn't be able to speak." She squeezes harder. "I missed you."

"We missed you, too," Jason says. "And you only stink a little bit." He's younger and still expressing love without reservation. That will change, but not for a few years.

Agatha turns her back on Dax—she can't look—and herds the boys into the house. Dax follows. "Agatha," he says. His voice sounds strange and unfamiliar. "I need to get a few things."

She waits until she hears the boys upstairs in their rooms, then she turns. Her throat constricts. "This is the first time you've seen me since you screwed that woman in our shed and all you've got to say is 'I need to get a few things'? Not 'I'm sorry'? Not 'Are you all right?'? Not 'I'm so sorry Susan Sontag sprayed you'? Not 'Did you hurt yourself while chopping up our shed with a *hatchet*?'? Not even a mention of how the boys have responded? How they're doing?"

Dax tugs at the hem of his purple pullover, a shirt she's never seen before.

"You look like a plum in that thing," she says. "Is GDOG your new fashion consultant, too?"

"Her name is Willow."

Agatha looks directly at him for the first time. It is like looking directly into the sun. Black spots mar her vision. She squints. "Yes, you told me. In your text."

"Her name is not GDOG," he says, skating past the fact that he told his wife the name of his lover via text. "Her name is Willow."

"Willow what?" Agatha says. She studies the long, scabbed scratch on his cheek.

Dax pauses.

"Willow what, Dax?" A flash of him diving from her grip in the shed pops into her mind. The hatchet grazing his cheek. She'd made that scratch.

Her husband winces, looks at the floor, and says quietly, "Bean. Willow Bean."

Agatha freezes in front of the knife box on the kitchen counter. "Willow *what?*"

"Bean," Dax says a little more confidently, though he's still wincing.

"*Bean?* As in wax bean, green bean, baked bean, fava bean?"

"Yes."

"As in lima bean, snap bean, pinto bean, navy bean?"

"Yes."

"*Bean* as in the thing that scares me most in the whole world?"

"Yes."

Agatha stares at the knife box and considers the cleaver. "Bean," she says.

"Bean."

"You're joking?"

"I'm not joking."

Agatha takes a deep breath. "Well, that's just great," she says. "Get what you need and get out."

As Dax walks away, vulnerable with his back to her, she has to reason herself out of driving the cleaver through his skull. Her rage is that big, that powerful. She has no idea how she and her husband—her *husband*—have moved from discussing their Red Sox season tickets to discussing the fact that his lover's last name is Bean. Bean. Of all things, Bean. She has no idea how to reckon with a universe so cruel. So ironic. So merciless. If it weren't for the boys, she might actually do it. Heave that cleaver from the box, take three baby steps, and crack that motherfucker through his skull. Then leave him to rot behind the abandoned coal furnace in the basement. I'll give you an apocalypse, she thinks.

But.

But.

The boys.

She cannot kill her boys' father. No matter how far Dax goes with this infidelity escapade, she cannot kill him. Patting her hand against her thigh to keep it from reaching for the cleaver, she notes that for the first time ever she is not afraid of what might be done to her in the world, but what she might do to the world.

"So go thy ways," she quotes *Moby Dick*, "and I will mine."

Chapter Six

Agatha hoists the recycling bins onto the wagon in the garage, then starts down the driveway with the mountain of tomato juice cans rattling and clanging behind her like cowbells. Halfway down, Kerry Sheridan pops out from behind the hydrangeas.

"Jesus Christ, Kerry! Do you have to do that?" Agatha yells, her heart pounding in her chest.

"Susan got you good, didn't she?" Kerry says. She finds it hilarious that Agatha has names for the neighborhood skunks.

"There's a first time for everything."

Kerry sniffs the air and makes a face. "The juice didn't work too well, did it?"

"Feel free to move away," Agatha says. "Far away." She hits the dip in the driveway a little too hard with the wagon, and three cans tumble out. One veers into the yard. The other two pick up speed and roll all the way down the driveway and across the street.

"Not to poke the hornet's nest," Kerry says, following closely, "but when are you going to get this mess cleaned up?" She gestures toward the remains of the shed with a dramatic sweep of her arm. Everything with Kerry involves a dramatic sweep.

"Bringing up the most horrible thing to ever happen to me is your definition of not poking a hornet's nest?" Agatha says. She pauses, turns, and looks. Although Dax had cut the grass the morning before the incident, shorn it down to brownish nubs, it is already entering what Kerry calls "the shaggy phase."

"Well, we do have to think about the neighborhood," Kerry says.

"Screw the neighborhood." Agatha continues on. She stops at the mailbox, unloads the bins, and arranges them in a row. Then she hobbles after the runaway cans.

"Come on, Agatha. You cannot leave this mess in your yard."

Agatha picks up a can, tucks it under her arm, and goes after the second. A bit of tomato juice dribbles onto her shirt as she picks it up. "Watch me."

Kerry yammers on about expectations and "where we live," but Agatha pulls her phone from her pocket and gets distracted by an email from her agent. "How's the thriller going?" it reads.

Crap.

Crap, crappity, crap.

She hasn't yet told her agent that she hasn't started writing the agreed-upon thriller. How do you tell your amazingly brave, adventurous agent that you're a chickenshit? That you can't even think about a scary story, let alone write one? That you can't read scary books or watch scary movies? That you're afraid of the dark? And strangers? And beans?

This is an agent who, according to publishing lore, once waded through a lake with six alligators just ten feet away on the shore, faced down ghosts for the sake of a client's best seller about a haunted house, and climbed Everest without an oxygen tank.

The last may be a slight exaggeration, but still, Everest, with or without an oxygen tank.

How can Agatha admit to being a chickenshit?

She can't.

Instead, she lies. Lies like a purple shag rug in the 1960s.

"Thriller is going great!" she writes back. "Deep in it now." She props the two cans next to the bins, grabs the empty wagon, and heads back up the driveway. Her big toe is stinging.

"Agatha Arch, stop right there!" Kerry hollers. "What are you going to do about this mess? Don't walk away from your neighborhood responsibilities."

Agatha doesn't turn.

"Agatha! Agatha! I'll call Dax."

Agatha laughs. "I seriously doubt that will have an impact," she says. The farther she gets from the rhododendrons, the fainter Kerry's voice becomes. Thank goodness.

* * *

"When monogamous relationships come to mind," Agatha reads, "we typically think of geese, swans, or humans. Rarely do we think of prairie voles."

This may be the truest thing Agatha has ever read.

"If a member of either sex approaches the happy couple," she reads, "they will chase him or her away."

She takes a screen shot and saves it in her Hard Truths file.

It is Friday afternoon. Everything hurts. Hands, heart, big toe, all parts in between. She groans and thinks about the dog walker sashaying past their home, her Janie-grapefruit hips chugga-chugging this way and chugga-chugging that way. If she and Dax were voles, they would have chased that dog walker away, hollering "Begone! Begone!" in their squeaky vole-y voices. Then they would have hunkered down in their burrow and had beautiful vole-y sex. But Agatha and Dax are not voles. They are humans—flawed, flailing humans—and instead of chasing away the dog walker, Dax heard the beat of her beautiful Janie-grapefruit hips, fell into a trance, followed her to the park, and tumbled into a fling, an affair, and now, according to his latest text, an everlasting love.

My love's name is Willow.

Agatha clicks away from the nature blog to her favorite photograph of what used to be her family—her, Dax, Dustin, and Jason. Taken last spring at the home opener—just five months before—the boys are decked from head to toe in Red Sox gear. The Green Monster looms in the background. Dustin is leaning his head on Agatha's knee. Jason is on Dax's back.

Before the dog walker fed strychnine to Agatha's life, they'd been a Red Sox family. The four of them at Fenway on weekends, watching every game on TV until the very last up to bat, lucky Sox shirts holey with wear and love, and batting average bingo at breakfast in the morning. The boys are obsessed. Dustin has a Sox hat he's outgrown but loves so much he now wears it clipped to his belt loop with a carabiner. It was a tradition in their house, when they still had an "our house," when they still had an "our," that whenever the boys wanted to use the expression "for god's sake," they always said "for Big Papi's sake." Mom's rule. In the same vein, whenever Agatha wanted to say "motherfucking," as in "motherfucking unbelievable" or "motherfucking amazing," which was often because "motherfucking" was, and is, her favorite word, she had to say "fothermucking." Boys' rule.

Agatha wipes tears from her eyes and clicks over to the Moms Facebook page to peruse the usual litany . . . one Mom is desperate for a Bed Bath and Beyond coupon, another needs prayers for a sick cousin, Gem Lily's senile black lab has wandered away *again* (please don't chase!), another is collecting gently used toys for a local charity, three Moms need recommendations for orthodontists, seven more are seeking pediatrician recs, nine say they are "following" the pediatrician posts because even after years of being on Facebook they still don't realize they can simply "turn on notifications for this post" without announcing their intention to every single member of the group, and so on. Good god, the inanity. But then the High Priestess posts about a beggar, and, just like that, the everyday litany has fangs.

> Jane Poston: "Hey, ladies, anyone else see the young woman at Apple54 holding a can and a sign about being unemployed and going through tough times? Is she legit? She's looking a little rough."

Of course, the High Priestess does what the best of the best Facebook Moms do. She posts a photo. It's a terribly blurry photo taken through the window of her T-Rex Escalade, so it's hard to get a read on the woman. Yes, she's thin and unkempt with shaggy dyed-black ends on her dishwater hair. Familiar-looking in that down-and-out kind of way. But legitimately in need? Who can know for sure?

Three Moms report giving change to the woman. Each says she asked the obvious questions: *Who are you? What's your name? Where are you from? Where are you living? How long will you stay?* Two say the answers were vague. *I'm me. Don't worry about my name. From over that way. Around. Don't know.* The third says the young woman's voice was so raspy she couldn't understand a word she said.

As Agatha reckons with this new development, fear wraps its octopussian tentacles around her neck and gives a familiar squeeze. While the three Moms may have asked the obvious questions, none asked the most important: *What kind of trouble will you bring to our town?*

If Dax had been present, still bound in their marriage, he would have done what he'd always done—picked up on the scent of Agatha's fear, grabbed her hand, held it to his heart, and said, "No worries, Aggie-girl. I've got you." And she would have relaxed. A little bit. Enough. Just enough. For all those years, since freshman year of college, since the day she swam with the rotting cow, Dax had been her buffer, her shield, her warrior, the protective barrier between Agatha and the world. Is it fair to ask someone to hold you aloft in moments you cannot do it yourself? Is it fair to put such weight upon another? Was the responsibility too much? Is that what drove Dax into the britches of the dog walker?

Agatha clears her throat. Here's the thing. New people don't come to Wallingford this way. They come via international job placements. From the Netherlands. From Germany. From Israel and India and China. They come for the excellent schools, the high standardized test scores, and the unheard-of percentage of high school graduates who continue on to college. They come for the mostly white community with mostly conservative values. They come for the "we honor diversity" pretense. They come for the mammoth New England homes. The lawns and the fences between them. They come for the organic grocer, the trendy chalkboard shop, the local brewery, and the oyster/steak combo with a jalapeño martini at Westfall's. But beggars? Beggars don't come to Wallingford. This is unprecedented.

Agatha smacks her fingers on the keyboard and types as if her very life depends on it. It probably does.

Agatha Arch: "It doesn't matter if this woman's need is legit or not. No interlopers in Wallingford. She doesn't belong here."

But before she can chant "Interloper, Interloper, Interloper," the Moms choir is lobbing *kumbaya* grenades at her head. "Duck!" Agatha yells. "Dive, dive!" but it is useless. Within seconds, she is buried under an avalanche of manufactured love for this needy stranger who is most assuredly a dangerous ne'er-do-well of one sort or another.

Aren't these women on Twitter? Don't they read newspapers? Aren't they tuned in to NPR as they drive their littles to soccer practice? There are all kinds of real-life examples of overdoses, break-ins, burglaries, kidnappings, identity thefts, and murders in the world. The list is endless. But yet the Moms . . . and this:

Sally Snow: “Really, Agatha? Really? We don’t have room for empathy and kindness in Wallingford?”

Blonde Brenda What’s-Her-Name: “Ouch.”

phyliss-with-one-l-and-two-esses: “agatha.”

Agatha Arch: “Phyllis.”

Kerry Sheridan: “Agatha, perhaps you should put your energy to cleaning up the shed mess.”

Rachel Runk: “Or perhaps it’s time to write another book. Aren’t you on a deadline?”

The Moms know Agatha is an author. A good many of them read—and supposedly love—her books, and, on her mouthiest days, she is pretty sure her well-known-ness as the town’s most prominent literary figure is the only thing that keeps Moms group administrator Marty Snow from kicking her out for good.

Meredith Wilson: “Oh, Agatha, don’t be such a fraidy-cat. I’m sure this woman is harmless.”

Agatha Arch: “Fraidy-cat, Meredith? Is that all you’ve got? If you’re going to call me names, do it with gusto. Call me an invertebrate, a mollycoddled milksop, a lily liver. For God’s sake, call me a chickenshit. Show some creativity.”

Kelly Prescott: “Oh, Agatha, go eat a bean.”

Kelly Prescott—a flag-flying member of Poston's posse—is the master of hitting where it hurts. Various incidents throughout the years have revealed Agatha's soft underbelly and the fears that follow her this way and that: mice, spiders, the dark, ghosts, drowning, strangers, lightning, driving over bridges, alien invasion, and, of course, beans.

How dare Meredith and Kelly call her out on this. Fear is real. Fear is mighty. Fear is not to be fucked with.

But then . . .

Melody Whelan: "Agatha Arch, let's offer a gentle hand to this lost soul."

At this, Agatha's head pops off and shoots around her kitchen like an unleashed helium balloon. While all the Moms irk her from time to time, Melody Whelan catapults her into a frenzied state like no other. If it were up to the Kumbaya Queen, the citizens of Wallingford would throw open the gates, roll out the red carpet, and spoon-feed every lost soul in crisis. It takes everything Agatha has not to race to Melody's house, storm the front door, and stuff a potato in her yawning gob.

Agatha Arch: "Bah!"

She doesn't bother to read the rest of the responses. These women won't recognize danger until it leaps at them from behind a silver Mercedes.

She clicks out of Facebook, hops into her Mini Cooper (Coop, for short), flicks her Bear Grylls bobblehead, and heads to the intersection of Apple Street and Route 54. She needs to see this young woman for herself. She needs to make sense of this new development. Since the boys will be getting off the bus at Dax's new home a mile or so away, she is free to do as she likes. A strange and awful truth she may never get used to.

She parks in the grocery store lot and steps out with her binoculars. She lifts them to her eyes and scans the area. Traffic is light and this young woman—this Interloper—is nowhere to be seen, proving she has some smarts. No cars = no money. The swatch of grass in the center of the five-way intersection is empty other than a soda can, so Agatha adds "litterer" and "imbiber of unhealthy drinks" to the list of crimes she is compiling.

Then she opens the Moms group on her phone, writes, "At Apple54. Interloper nowhere to be seen. Anyone else spot her?" then hops in her car and putters to Hillway Elementary School to catch a glimpse of her boys as they board the bus.

She blasts her horn as she inches past the Moms idling in their Escalades and Teslas on the side road where they are not supposed to wait. Once in the proper parent pickup line, she turns off the car. No idling; it's a rule. Then she opens the Moms group.

Agatha Arch: "Car line tennis-whites ladies at Hillway, put down your skim lattes, get off your damn phones, and get in the parent pickup line with the rest of us riffraff. You and your snitty-snotty brats are not special rays of sunshine who get to avoid the chaos."

Minutes later, when Jason and Dustin exit the side door of the school and get in line for bus 9B, Agatha's heart goes kapowy. *Look at them.* She waves to Principal Bandolino, pulls out of line, and follows the bus all the way to what will be the boys' new stop a few days a week. Dax is waiting by the fire hydrant, smiling and waving, making sure they know to get off the bus right here on the first agreed-upon Friday at the dog walker's house. How thoughtful of him to hook up with a floozy on the same bus route so the boys' routine doesn't have to change all that much and how kind of Agatha to say yes when he'd asked for his first Friday dad day. It wouldn't be this way every week; they'd agreed to play it by ear until they figured out a schedule. But even this, one day at the new stop, hurt like hell.

Tears drip from Agatha's eyes as she watches them disembark, backpacks dragging on the ground behind them, Dustin's baseball cap clipped to his belt loop.

Jason needs a haircut.

Dustin needs longer pants.

She needs them.

She will follow these two to the ends of the earth.

Hands too sweaty to drive, she parks behind a pickup and plucks Bear from the dashboard. "Why, Bear? Why?" she says, cradling him against her cheek. "I'm so afraid I'm going to lose them forever."

"It's okay," Bear whispers in her ear. "Fear sharpens us."

"Shut up," she says, then sticks his foot in her mouth and bites down. Hard.

Chapter Seven

"I wanted to kill him," Agatha says. "Actually *kill* him. And I could have. I could have driven that cleaver right through his massive balding head." Her teeth hurt from gritting them together.

"What stopped you?" Shrinky-Dink sounds as impassive as ever. Her stylus squeaks against the screen of her iPad.

Agatha grunts. "The boys. I can't kill their father."

"Mm. That's good news."

"I suppose, but the urge is still there." A fireball in her belly.

"I'm not surprised."

"No?"

"No. It's quite a natural feeling."

"I'm afraid I might actually do it."

"Kill him?"

"Yes."

"You won't."

"You sound so sure."

"I am. If you could have, you would have, and I'd be visiting you in prison today."

"You think so?"

"Yes, I do. In the past few days, you've had a hatchet in your hand and a cleaver within reach. If you were able to kill Dax, you would have. You're a woman who gets things done."

Agatha rolls her eyes. "I wish I were a vole instead," she says. "Listen to this." She opens her phone, scrolls to Hard Truths, and reads the statement about voles.

Shrinky-Dink sighs. "Yes, I can see why you'd like to be a vole."

Agatha slides down in her chair.

"Is this in your Hard Truths folder?"

Agatha nods.

"I'm going to give you another hard truth. You are a human. You are not a vole. Dax is not a vole. Dax did not turn away from temptation. Dax cheated. You are alone."

Well.

"For fuck's sake," Agatha says, "I pay you. Money. Big money. Can't you be kind? Or at least give me a hard truth in a soft way?"

"You pay me to help you. You pay me to tell the truth. Even if it hurts."

"Fine," Agatha says. "Fine." She pretends to delete the screen shot and waves her phone at Shrinky-Dink. "There. It's gone. Happy?"

"Delete it for real."

Agatha smirks.

"Go on. For real this time."

Agatha does. "Happy now?"

"Satisfied. It's different than happy."

Agatha sighs. "Would you really visit me in prison? If I ended up there?"

"Of course."

"What if I couldn't pay you from prison?"

"We'd work it out."

Agatha wonders if anyone else would visit her in prison. Someone would have to bring the boys. Right? She imagines herself in an orange jumper, gray overtaking the brown in her hair, murmuring to the boys through the glass on a phone, with Dax and GDOG standing a few feet away.

Fothermucking Dax. If only she could. “So?” she says.

“So what?”

“So how should I handle this urge to kill my husband?”

“What’s that thing Bear Grylls always says? The one about fear?”

“Fear sharpens us?”

“Yes. Fear sharpens us.” It sounds much mightier coming out of Shrinky-Dink’s mouth. Like a sword.

“What about it?”

“Jot it down on a piece of paper. Hang it on your front door so you read it every time you leave the house.”

Agatha stares at Shrinky-Dink’s cherry red lips. They are startling against her pale skin. It’s a new color for her. Not a good one. “I’m talking about an urge to kill my estranged husband and you’re advising me to hang an inspirational quote on my door?”

“Yes.”

“Seriously? That’s what you’ve got for me today?”

“That’s what I’ve got for you today.”

“Okay, Oprah.”

Shrinky-Dink smiles.

“And that’s it?”

“For now. Time’s up.”

* * *

That evening, Agatha writes FEAR SHARPENS US on a blue sticky note. She pins it to the front door of her house. She pins another on the wall of the back staircase leading up to her office. It can’t hurt.

* * *

Kerry Sheridan—chief complainer of all complainers—grouses to Dax about the unsightly shed debris. "She says it's just awful, Agatha," Dax says when he calls. "An atrocity." He puts on his best Kerry-Sheridan-is-complaining-again voice, as if things, funny things, private jokes between him and his estranged wife, can still exist in the world, the too-bright world in which he's had sex with another woman in their shed, moved out of their home, and moved into the another woman's home. "She says wood and tools and bits of this and that are littering the lawn. 'What will visitors think?' she says. 'And when will the storm of shed tourists end?'"

Agatha bites her tongue until it bleeds. Shed tourists. Who ever thought such a thing would exist?

"But seriously, Aggie-girl," Dax says, his tone shifting into his own. "You need to get it cleaned up."

As he talks, Agatha's head swells to the size of a watermelon and starts to split. She looks around wildly, hoping, praying that a member of her imagined zephyr of friends has magically appeared and is at this very minute pouring her the biggest glass of tequila ever poured in the history of tequila pouring.

Aggie-girl?

Aggie-girl?

This man pulls the most horrific act a man can pull and now has the brass balls to use the nickname he'd given her all those years before on the day of the rotting cow? Her head explodes.

Aggie-girl?

As if nothing has changed between them?

Dax continues, oblivious to the explosion of Agatha's head. "As Kerry says, it is a bit of an atrocity."

Agatha gathers bits of her head and pushes them back into place before speaking. "Dax, first of all, do not ever call me Aggie-girl again. You have lost every right to that name, to that expression of affection. Do you hear me?"

Dax grunts quietly. "Yes, sorry about that, Agatha. It just came out. Habit."

"Second, you and Kerry Sheridan need to look up the definition of *atrocity*. The Rohingya genocide is an atrocity, Dax. The clampdown on free speech in Russia is an atrocity, Dax. The refugee crisis around the world is a fothermucking atrocity, Dax. But the shed debris? The shed debris in this yard? That shit is an annoyance. A first-world problem. A *who gives a royal fuck*."

She hangs up.

* * *

Despite Kerry's complaints, Agatha will not clean up the mess. Nor will she allow it to be cleaned up by the crew that arrives at Dax's behest.

"I'm happy with it just like this," she tells them. Happy is the wrong word but the right one is stuck somewhere between her heart and her mouth. "Do not touch it."

Two of the men look bewildered, eyes darting between the eyesore and the gleaming white Colonial behind it. The third leans against the We Haul It All truck with his arms folded across his chest.

One of the two bewildered men takes a step toward the debris. They have orders from Dax. Also a sizable check.

Agatha takes a step toward him. "Do not touch it," she warns, wondering if "All" includes sorrow, heartbreak, misery, anger, and fear. How much would it cost to haul that away? One hundred dollars? Two hundred dollars? A chest of gold doubloons? A miracle?

The leaning man grunts at his coworker and shakes his head. The other man backs away. Agatha offers the leaning man the blueberry muffin she'd planned to give to her shrink.

"*Gracias*," he says, taking it. "*Lo siento*." He says it with such feeling, such understanding, at least she imagines he does, that Agatha almost cracks in two. *Crack, crack, crack*, right down the middle. How in the world is a human supposed to stay whole for an entire lifetime? How is she supposed to survive all the emotions life dishes out?

Agatha sits down cross-legged in front of the remains of the shed, places a hand on each side of her ribcage, and squeezes, trying to hold everything in. "Gentlemen, if you touch this, if you dare to touch one stick of wood, one nail, one screw, one measly splinter, I swear to god I will erupt! I am a volcano right now! I am a volcano on the verge. On the verge of spewing lava and ash and rock from here to Antarctica." She pauses and Googles erupting volcanoes on her phone. Ah, the glory of technology. "At this very moment, I am Mount Sinabung in northern Sumatra," she says. "Do not fuck with Mount Sinabung." As the men stare at her, three looky-loos in an Audi yell, "Whoop! Whoop!" out their car window. Agatha closes her eyes and sticks out her tongue. Seconds later, a photo of this moment is posted in the Moms group. The We Haul It All truck is in the background. Kerry Sheridan's fuzzy red head is peeking out from behind the rhododendrons.

The number of cars in the procession burgeons as the post gathers likes and laughs, and Agatha thinks about all of the things Kerry has complained to Dax about over the years: the eight-foot-tall blow-up Santa (gaudy), Fleetwood Mac playing too loud ("the squawking of Stevie Nicks"), too many bikes in the driveway (road hazard), too many s'more parties (unhealthy), not enough potted mums around the mailbox in the fall (never enough in New England). Just as she remembers the time Kerry complained that Dax whistled too early in the morning, the cupcake van turns the corner and parks in front of Kerry's house. The cupcake-tess tweets "Parked from 11–12 today at the remains of the shed on Sutton Circle."

WTF?

Agatha tweets back, "Bring me a double chocolate."

The cupcake-tess tweets back a smiley face and a cupcake emoji.

It's something.

But then a Mom shares that OMG, Gem Lily's black lab is still missing—*still*—and Agatha hears the Moms machine screech into action like the old hand-cranked meat grinder in her grandmother's kitchen. Like most, she suspects the ancient beast has wandered off to die alone, with some dignity, but unlike most, she believes he should be allowed to do so. The poor wretch has to be at least a thousand years old, maybe more. Except for a small tuft of gray fur on his belly, he's bald as a baby, and his eyes are cloudy and moist. A single thread of drool hangs perpetually from his toothless mouth, and his legs are bent backward at the knee as if he is trying to move in reverse toward his days as a spry pup. A lovely thought, but futile, of course, since there's only one way into and out of this world. Despite his challenges, this hideous creature is loyal, and he's been holding on for Gem Lily, his ancient equal in the human world, for years.

The distraction from the shed feels good as the procession begins to peel away, but then HP Poston announces that the town-wide search for Balderdash will begin at the library and will be led by his devoted walker, Willow Bean.

Willow Bean.

Willow Bean.

The name echoes in Agatha's brain and she tips backward into the remains of the shed. Her legs poke up into the air with the handles of the rake, push broom, and hoe. A shard of terra cotta pot jabs into her hip. The back of her head clanks against a shovelhead. She moans. Willow Bean, of course, Willow Bean, the dog walker, *the* dog walker.

From that vantage point, Agatha watches the We Haul It All truck drive away slowly, offering up a single sorrowful beep as it rounds the bend.

* * *

Tap tap tippity-tap.

* * *

"This is why her name felt so familiar," Agatha tells Shrinky-Dink. "Because every single dog-loving Mom in Wallingford knows and adores Willow Bean. They extol her virtues almost as often as they ask for prayers and gently used toys and coupons for Bed Bath and Beyond. 'She's honest,' they sing. 'She's loyal and committed. She will love your dog more than life itself. She's a dog in human form. She's *dog* spelled backward. G-O-D.'"

"They say all that?"

"Yep."

"And not one Mom mentioned this the day of the shed incident?"

"Nope."

"No one said, 'Which dog walker?'"

"Not to me, but now I know there had to have been ten thousand DMs shooting around Wallingford." The Moms love direct messages.

"When Dax told you her name, you didn't remember seeing it in posts on the Moms feed?"

"No. No. Now I do, of course. Every time a Mom gets a new pup and puts out a call for reliable, loving dog walkers, the rest of the Moms holler, 'Willow Bean! Willow Bean! Willow Bean!' But then? That day? It didn't even ring a bell. How could I forget something like that?"

"You blocked it. The brain protects us when necessary."

"The head is a funny thing," Agatha says in a whispery voice.

Shrinky-Dink leans forward. "Excuse me?"

"Something my mom always used to say. The head is a funny thing; the heart even funnier."

"Smart mom."

"Dead mom."

"You miss her."

Agatha nods.

"Have they found the dog?"

"Balderdash?"

Shrinky-Dink nods.

"Not yet. Gem Lily must be so lonely."

"You must be so lonely."

Agatha doesn't answer.

* * *

When she gets home, Agatha finds a double chocolate cupcake in a box on her stoop. No card, no note, just the cupcake she'd longed for. It's something.

Chapter Eight

Agatha stares at Jane Poston's photo of the Interloper, so fuzzy, but so telling, like many of the Moms' "Look at this!" posts. God-awful photographers, the Moms are, with no artistic sensibility and no interest in quality, just quick snaps with a corner of a wall included or a husband's elbow or the shadow of a barista's arm. The photos are about the things at which they demand you look and nothing else, no spirit, no song, no rhythm, no secrets. Agatha minimizes Facebook, then pulls the first such post she'd ever seen from her WTF folder, her genesis "Look at this!" post, the one that stole her Moms group virginity.

"Moms!" Sandra Block had posted with her photo ten years before. "Pus is oozing from my son's butt! Look at this!"

"Nooooooooooooo!" Agatha had wailed at the time, Dustin suckling at her breast. She remembers it as clearly as she does Dustin's birth. "I will not look at this."

But look she did. At that post and many more. Unfamiliar with the whos, whats, and hows of a Facebook Moms group, she'd been flabbergasted by the pictures of wounds, stories of private woe, descriptions of melodrama, and general over-the-top inanity the Moms shared so willingly, so passionately. "Quit reading. Don't look," Dax had said.

He was always full of advice about restraint, though in retrospect he has shown none himself. But not looking was impossible. Facebook moms groups are addictive. Once you're in, you can't get out. "They're the glory and suck-duckery of modern-day parenting," Agatha had told him again and again. "A moms group is a high school clique on steroids. Or Scientology."

Back then, when Sandra Block had pleaded "What should I do?" Agatha had done the unthinkable. She'd told the truth. "For Big Papi's sake," she wrote, "stop writing FB posts and get the kid to a damn doctor."

Rookie mistake.

After scolding her like a naughty toddler, the Moms began offering up their own solutions to Sandra's emergency, clearly preferring their ignoramus home-brewed solutions to life-threatening dilemmas:

Tiana Samuels:	"Have you tried an herbal enema?"
Tina West:	"How about an essential oil rubbed on the buttocks? I sell a wonderful blend of tea tree, lavender, and myrrh that might just do the trick."
Stella Bender:	"Bananas."
Lila Due:	"Fewer bananas."

So far that was the only truth Agatha could cull from this herd of wackadoodles. They were bananas. All of them.

Mackenzie Tucker:	"Time heals all wounds."
Sandra Gilliam:	"My cousin's son seeped a similar pus. He died of a rare rectal cancer a few months after first seepage (prayers welcome). I'm sure it's not the same thing."
Melody Whelan:	"Sending love and light."

Agatha had longed to ask what love and light were going to do for a pus-seeping butt, but instead she'd quietly created a "The 12 Days of the Wallingford Moms" folder on her desktop and slipped this gem into it.

* * *

She closes the folder and looks back at Jane Poston's post about the Interloper. If there was some other distraction—a vote about next year's school calendar, untethered teens climbing all over public property, the loss of another beloved business in the downtown's overpriced rental market—the Moms might shimmy right on past the Interloper and the Interloper might move on to another town, another state, a new place to hide, a new place to take money from unsuspecting people. But other than the search for Balderdash and the shed on Sutton Circle, there is nothing. The Moms latch on.

Rachel Runk:	"Hi Moms! I drove through Apple54 this morning and the young woman is still there. What's it been, a week? Have we figured out if her need is legit? I'd like to give her a little money, but only if she is truly in trouble. The last thing I need to do is provide funds for a heroin addiction. Much better things to do with my money than that."
Agatha Arch:	👏👏👏👏👏👏👏👏👏👏
Lara Lynch:	"Rachel, I saw her today, too. She is skinny, as are most opioid addicts I know."
Agatha Arch:	"Oh, come on, Lara, exactly how many opioid addicts do you know?"
Melody Whelan:	"Let's not make assumptions, ladies. People also become skinny because they do not have enough to eat."

Agatha Arch:	"Hungry or not, this young woman has permeated our borders and introduced life-threatening danger."
Ava Newton:	"Life-threatening danger? As far as we know, this young woman hasn't done a darn thing except stand at an intersection and ask for money. It may be frustrating and even annoying, but it certainly isn't putting anyone's life at risk."
Agatha Arch:	"Wrong, wrong, wrong. With this woman comes danger."
Ava Newton:	"You have no proof of such a thing, Agatha."
Agatha Arch:	"Some things you just know."
Ava Newton:	"And some things you make up because you're scared to death of the world. Signing off."
Agatha Arch:	"Good riddance. Hope the Interloper gets you first!"
Rachel Runk:	"Ladies, if I can direct us back to the young woman. Any info on her need?"
Jane Poston:	"I actually stopped and gave her some change today. She seemed okay. Maybe a little hungry, as Melody suggested."
Agatha Arch:	"You sure did, didn't you, Jane?"

Agatha posts a photo of Jane handing money to the woman through the window of her Escalade. Unlike Jane's photo, this one is crisp and clear, courtesy of Agatha's Nikon DSLR.

Jane Poston:	"Seriously, Agatha? You're stalking the young woman? Taking pictures?"
Agatha Arch:	"Just trying to keep our community safe."

Mary Devlin: "Sidebar here, but, Jane, your new Escalade is sweet."
Jane Poston: "Thanks." 😉
Melody Whelan: "Jane, you agree she may be hungry?"

Right then, the unmistakable beat of "Kumbaya" shakes the Moms page. The thump of Melody's empathetic heart rolls through like the call of a timpani drum.

Jane Poston: "Melody, she just seemed a little faint or weak."
Melody Whelan: "That's not a good sign. No one should go hungry, no matter the circumstances. I'll check on her tomorrow."

The Moms have heard this thump before, and they all know what it means. Melody Whelan will be leading the charge, parting the Red Sea for this woman. Agatha stares at the screen and remembers her mother's favorite bit of advice whenever a controversy arose: "If you can't beat them, join them." Can she beat the 2,690 member Moms (and odd dads and guardians) once Melody Whelan picks up the reins of empathy?

Probably not.

Can she join them?

Definitely not.

What else is there?

* * *

"Sing it to me," Shrinky-Dink said when Agatha first told her about her "The 12 Days of the Wallingford Moms," the parody she'd written of everyone's favorite "The 12 Days of Christmas."

"Right here?"

"Yes."

"Right now?"

"Yes."

"I can't. I'm a terrible singer."

Shrinky-Dink leaned back and smiled. "I'll close my eyes. Pretend I'm not here."

"I guess I asked for this," Agatha said. She cleared her throat and began. "On the first day of Christmas, the Moms gave to me, a cure for pus-seeping butts. On the second day of Christmas, the Moms . . ."

Shrinky-Dink opened her eyes and checked the clock. "How about just the final verse? Start with the twelfth day. That will give me everything I need."

"I thought you weren't here?"

Shrinky-Dink closed her eyes again. "I'm not."

Agatha nodded and began again:

On the twelfth day of Christmas, the Moms gave to me
twelve mani/pedis,
eleven summer nannies,
ten essential oils,
nine squashed turkeys,
eight eyebrow threaders,
seven Disney cruises,
six recs for date night,
five pulled pork recipes,
four car line cheaters,
three cans of Edgecomb Grey,
two rash creams,
and a cure for pus-seeping butts.

Shrinky-Dink laughed out loud and made a note on her iPad. It was the first time Agatha had heard that laugh, and it felt a little bit like friendship. Therapy was sneaky that way.

"Edgecomb Grey?" Shrinky-Dink said.

"The paint color that best complements Benjamin Moore's Revere Pewter," Agatha said. "It's one of the three most frequently asked questions on the Moms page."

"Really?"

"Oh, yes. And it's asked passionately, as if lives will be forever altered if the right color gets on the right wall, as if this choice will stop world wars, end the opioid epidemic, curb female genital mutilation, and get girls to school in developing nations."

Shrinky-Dink chuckled. "Edgecomb Grey, huh?"

"Nantucket Fog is a close second."

"Good to know."

Agatha sighed. "Well?"

"Well," Shrinky-Dink said, "I can see why the Moms got mad. The carol sounds a bit judgmental."

"No, it doesn't. It's funny."

"It is, but it also hits close to home."

"It's supposed to. It's a parody."

"I'm curious. What are the other two most frequently asked questions?"

Agatha laughed. "The first, what is your favorite pulled pork recipe?"

Shrinky-Dink smiled so big Agatha knew she, too, loved a good pulled pork sandwich. Who didn't? "And the second?"

"Is this a fox or a coyote? That one is always accompanied by a photo."

"The Moms can't tell the difference between a fox and a coyote?"

"Nope."

Shrinky-Dink sighed and shook her head. Agatha did the same, knowing that while the Moms weren't a dumb lot with half of them being full-time career Moms who Tasmanian-deviled the shit out of the world in order to stay afloat, they did play into Facebook's algorithms, willingly engaging in the group energy they counted on.

"I've got a theory," Agatha said.

"I'm not surprised," Shrinky-Dink said. Agatha is good at theories. It's part of what makes her a good writer. Big picture stuff.

"I call it Mouse to Cheese."

Shrinky-Dink waited.

"Biggie Z," Agatha's nickname for Mark Zuckerberg, "is the esteemed leader of a group of aliens from another galaxy intent on studying human behavior. Facebook groups are his human terrariums. Moist nourishing environments in which his victims can thrive or fail."

"And?" Shrinky-Dink said.

"We have to wait and see."

Chapter Nine

Each day, Agatha adds a little something to Infidelity: A Still Life. A splintered rafter. A bent nail. An overturned bucket. A shard of terra cotta pot. A doorknob. An errant gardening glove. An aerial shot from one of the oak trees. A swatch of the dog walker's aquamarine muumuu-maxi snagged on a pickax. Even a close-up of a single tear rolling down the seemingly permanent crease on her own cheek, although that one feels a little maudlin. Rhythm matters on Instagram. As do song, artistry, spirit, and secrets. She learns to use filters and pays attention to angles. Vignettes are her secret sauce. In her posts, she's quippy and clever, wry and witty. She becomes a master of hashtags.

On day three, she has 1,475 followers.

Within the first week, 9,328. Her phone pings with each new follow. It's addictive. Pavlovian. The more pings she hears, the more photos she posts.

Her followers, she notes, are mostly women, many, like her, who've been cheated on, wronged, sliced to the quick by husbands, wives, lovers, boyfriends, girlfriends. These aren't women looking for love, understanding, empathy, and support. They're pissed-off women looking for a posse.

Many Moms from her FB group follow her IG, too. Jane Poston. (ping) Melody Whelan. (ping) Rachel Runk. (ping) And so on.

When she hits 10,000 followers, Agatha orders a pair of spy pants. They're glorious.

If you can't beat them, join them.

If you can't join them?

Spy on them.

"Spy on them?" Agatha doesn't lay out her plan for Shrinky-Dink, doesn't show up at her appointment and say, "Hey, I'm going to start spying on my estranged husband and his hussy," mostly because Shrinky-Dink would do everything in her power, with typical shrinkerly restraint, to stop her. She would apply logic where Agatha wants none. Is there anything worse than being in a highly emotional state and someone, anyone, a dermatologist, a grocery clerk, a lawn specialist, but especially a shrink, turning themselves inside out to apply logic to an illogical situation?

But even though Agatha doesn't reveal her secret plan, in her head she hears what Shrinky-Dink would say if she knew. She hears the tsks, the admonitions, the warnings, the caution, the "Agatha, this isn't going to end well."

* * *

Agatha's new pants aren't marketed as *spy pants*, of course. That would be strange. But they are equipped with dozens of pockets that will allow Agatha to tote all the items she needs. Some, like the "long-knife pocket" that stretches from the middle of Agatha's thigh to the top of her calf, are unusually large. Others are quite small. In preparation for the work ahead, she packs them with necessities.

A good-sized camera lens goes into the drawstring pocket. From the loop at the waist, she hangs her binoculars. She tucks a can of spray paint in the calf pocket of the left leg. Fluorescent pink. Her high-tech voice recorder fits nicely in the hip pocket, along with a mini-speaker and microphone. The pencil and paper are for old-fashioned note taking. She's not sure she'll ever need invisible ink, but she packs the pen anyway. She stashes a small bag of the boys' favorite candy in the calf pocket of the right leg so that if they happen to catch her in a suspicious activity, she can sweeten them up. Anything for Sour Patch Kids. In various other pockets, she stashes a headlamp, gum, rubber bands, a nail file, a mini-roll of duct tape, waterproof matches, a whistle, firecrackers, a ball of twine, and a few other bits and pieces. She Googles what Bear takes on his adventures, then adds a survival blanket, a sewing kit, and snare wire to her stash. You never know.

While the kitchen cleaver would fit just fine into the long-knife pocket, she opts for a Leatherman Super Tool 300 EOD with a fold-down blade not more than an inch long. Better to avoid temptation, no matter what Shrinky-Dink believes.

* * *

The first nor'easter of the season hits that Tuesday, and for twenty-four hours rain pelts houses and slams into windows, pools and puddles in low-lying areas. Agatha watches Kerry Sheridan chase her garbage cans down the road, tumbleweeding past Mrs. Crichton's house and moving on to the intersection with Brumpy Loop, the road on which Agatha had wanted to live. Forget the fact that when she and Dax had househunted, there'd been no houses for sale on it, and that, yes, the Sutton Circle house was a charmer that she eventually fell for. Even so, the writer in her wanted Brumpy Loop. She'd imagined a castle with a turret and the ability to say to people, "Address? My address? Oh, eleven Brumpy Loop." What a wonderful name.

Hours into the storm, the bombshell news anchor with ripe breasts barely contained by a blue seersucker jacket reports that highways have slowed to a crawl, and when she passes the baton to the weather team, glee drips from their faces like fat from a roasting pig. In New England, there's nothing like a good nor'easter. For newbies, the blonde one explains in a driving, breathy voice that mimics the one she likely uses during sex: "Nor'easters are brilliant storms along the East Coast of the

United States. With them come extremely heavy rain or snow, flooding, coastal erosion, and hurricane-force winds." Her face is pinked up, and Agatha expects bubbles to shoot from her ass as she announces, "Get ready, people, this is just the beginning."

By Tuesday evening, the "thank goodness this isn't snow" post on the Moms page has garnered 439 likes, 67 amens, and something in the realm of 1,309 snowman emojis.

"It is true," Agatha says to the tomato plant. "If this were snow, we'd be screwed."

The shed debris gets soaked for the first time. The snowblower, ride-on mower, push mower, drills, saws, rakes, shovels, hoes, picks, and even the hatchet from hell all get drenched. Rain saturates the earth, and hundreds of nails, screws, and bolts sink into the mud. The mammoth, monogrammed tool chest Agatha gave Dax on their fifth anniversary tips over and its wheels spin in the gale-force wind. When Dax drops off the boys, he whines about the state of things. "Do you have any idea how much that snowblower cost?" he says. "The ride-on mower? It's bad enough you destroyed the shed, but letting all these tools get ruined, too?"

Agatha gulps. In little more than two weeks' time, the reason she destroyed the shed has escaped Dax's memory, along with the fact that sales of her middle-grade series paid for most of these toys. She thinks about the police officer who sat with her just after the incident, the one who had never read *Their Eyes Were Watching God*, who'd never been stunned by the power of Janie Mae Crawford or her magnificent grapefruit hips, the one who'd believed Agatha was the destroyer and the shed the object of destruction, the one who'd seen the splintered wood but not the shards of her family, her marriage, and her heart piled up all around.

Agatha does not respond to Dax's rant. Instead she snaps a photo of the shed debris in the rain and posts it to Infidelity: A Still Life. The wet red fender of the ride-on mower gleams brightly in the headlights of Dax's car.

Dax pulls open the kitchen door. "I need to get a few more things."

Agatha looks up at him from the porch swing. "From now on," she says, "if you want to 'get a few more things,' you'll need to make an appointment. You have thirty minutes. After that, I call the police." She hopes he doesn't test this pronouncement. She's quite sure the police will care as much as the woodpecker.

Tap tap tippity-tap.

Listening to his footsteps heading up the front stairs to what used to be *their* bedroom, she notes that tiny bites have been taken from the underside of the still-green tomato. "Someone nibbled your low-hanging fruit," she says.

Chipmunk?

Squirrel?

Groundhog?

Susan Sontag?

Agatha nods. Damn skunk.

Tap tap tippity-tap. Even in the torrential rain. *Tap tap tippity-tap.*

Agatha pulls her blanket close and listens to the boys greet their dad. Their cries are gleeful and loud. Louder than the rain. Louder than the woodpecker.

She looks beyond the remains of the shed to the street. The hill that climbs in front of their house is steeper than most in Wallingford. It's one of the big reasons Dax fell for the house ten years before. That and the massive glacial boulders that dot the yard. "When you walk up Sutton Circle and see our house halfway up, you know you're heading somewhere and you have to do a little work to get here. It's a symbol for marriage and us," he'd said when they'd decided to buy. She'd been holding newborn Dustin in her arms and they were all in love. Deeply in love. Forget Agatha's fears. They could survive anything.

Anything, it turns out, except the dog walker.

Agatha can't remember when Willow Bean started using Sutton Circle as her daily route, but she knows that for at least a year, maybe two, GDOG had been the subject of her and Dax's daily shtick. "There she is again," one of them said nearly every morning. "Woof! Woof!" Then they'd call out the breed of pup she was walking.

"Dalmation!"

"Pug!"

"Mastiff!"

It became a game of who could name the breed first. Sometimes Agatha won. Sometimes Dax. Occasionally the boys took the prize, but they worked as a team and cheated using Google. All of them failed whenever GDOG walked the Shih Tzu. Dax always yelled, "Pomeranian!" The boys tried out various possibilities, including Afghan, Yorkshire terrier, and poodle. And that little furball always made Agatha think about a kumquat-eating Havanese that had lived next door to her growing up. In fact, that had been her name, or maybe her nickname, Kumquat.

In all those days/weeks/months, the dog walker never slowed, spoke, or waved. She never showed any sign of even noticing the Arch family, let alone Dax. She just walked up the hill and down the hill, earbuds in place, doing her job, firming up those hips.

Agatha hates this history. This story that will become romantic lore for Dax and Willow Bean.

Chihuahua up the hill.

Labradoodle down the hill.

Bernese up the hill.

Scraggly mutt down the hill.

Ridgeback up.

Beagle down.

Surly shepherd up.

Surly shepherd down. (That one needed a lot of exercise.)

Pitbull up.

Chocolate Lab down.

Dachshund up.

Shaggy something down.

Muddy mutt up.

Australian shepherd down.

Boxer up.

Maltese down.

She wonders how in the world she was able to name so many dog breeds over the days/weeks/months but miss the slow seduction of her husband. The rhythm of those grapefruit hips drawing him in.

Dax up.

Dax down.

Dax up.

Dax down.

Dax up.

* * *

Even on the morning of the shed incident, Dax had looked up when the dog walker passed and said, "Corgi," winning the game once again. Then he'd bent his head to the sports section of the paper.

* * *

The rain stops by noon on Wednesday and bullet-force winds clear the clouds from the sky. By midnight the moon is so hot and shimmery that when Agatha spots Kerry Sheridan making her way through their yards, Kerry is shining like a star that has fallen to Earth. Who would have thought Captain Complainer could look so beautiful? Mary Cassatt could have painted her. García Márquez could have written about her. But when Agatha realizes that the beautifully illuminated Kerry Sheridan is crossing their yards toward the remains of the shed carrying a bag the size of her own body, she cries out, hobbles down from the porch, bends into the wind, and sets off after Kerry. No one is clearing that debris. Not the We Haul It All gents, not Dax, not Agatha, and certainly not Kerry Sheridan.

"Kerry!" she hollers. "Kerry Sheridan, stop right there!" She's loud, but her voice is toted away by the gale. Nearly horizontal, Agatha pulls her mega-flashlight from her spy pants and zaps Kerry with its beam. Kerry freezes, swings a look back at Agatha, and pushes on.

Agatha pulls a bullhorn from her pants and lifts it to her mouth. She pauses and glances at the boys' bedroom windows. Dark. No sign of movement. Thank goodness they're heavy sleepers. "Kerry Sheridan!" she shouts. Her voice cuts through the roar of wind.

Kerry stops and turns to face Agatha. She cups her hand to her ear, shrugs, and feigns innocence.

Agatha trods closer. "Kerry, what are you doing?" she yells into the bullhorn.

"What do you think I'm doing? I am cleaning up this mess."

"No, no, you're not. This is my yard, Kerry. Your yard ends over there." She gestures with the bullhorn.

"This is not a yard, Agatha, unless you're calling it a scrapyard. It's an eyesore. A hideous eyesore. A hideous eyesore that I have to look at from my living room. *Your* hideous eyesore."

"The key word in that sentence is *your*, Kerry. No matter what you call this area," Agatha waves her arms, "it is *mine. Mine, mine, mine!* You can't touch it without my permission and you do not have my permission."

Kerry yells something back but the wind sweeps it away. She leans down, picks up a bucket, waves it at Agatha, then stuffs it into the bag. Next she grabs a gardening glove. A screwdriver.

"Put those things down, Kerry! Put it all back!" Agatha pushes deeper into the grass and hobbles toward the debris. When she gets close, she climbs onto an overturned wheelbarrow and leaps onto Kerry's back. She wraps her arms around her neck.

Kerry tips sideways and falls to the ground. "Agatha! Agatha Arch? What are you doing? Get off me!" she yells.

"Not until you put all that stuff back."

The two roll this way and that in the tangled grass until they slam into Dax's gigantic toolbox.

"Ow!" Kerry struggles to her knees, rubs her head, drops the bag, and surrenders. She crawls toward home, disappearing into the protective ring of forsythia bushes.

Agatha stays on her back and watches clouds whip across the moon. "A soufflé of clouds," she whispers.

The wind is brutal. In any other year, she would have raced inside and written about this altercation. In any other year, this altercation wouldn't have taken place.

"Write hard and clear about what hurts," Hemingway once said. Easy for him to say. He was a man. A man among men. A hairy, chase-the-bulls, scratch-the-balls kind of man. But still. Agatha stands and dumps the bits and pieces of shed debris out of Kerry's bag back into the hideous mess.

* * *

An hour later, she sits on the bottom step of the stairs leading up to her office. Bear sits on the second stair, bolstering her brave. She Googles "voodoo dolls" on her phone, and while this particular search turns up nothing productive, she discovers that Etsy offers a few options for "reflection dolls," dolls created in the "likenesses of your loved (or not so loved) ones." Close enough. Agatha can make it work.

"Attach a clear photo of each desired model when ordering," the instructions read. Dax would be easy enough, she had so many photos of him, too many photos of him, Dax standing, Dax sitting, Dax bending, Dax climbing, Dax smiling, Dax frowning, Dax laughing, Dax pretending to be a bear, and so on, but a photo of GDOG? That would take some work.

The red door taunts her from above, so close but yet so far. Bear nods appreciatively from his perch.

"Look at us," she says to him. "Two steps up. Progress."

Chapter Ten

Every story has a beginning. A genesis. An Adam and Eve. An apple. A sneaky serpent. Therefore it must have been so for Dax and Willow Bean. Right? A glance. A whisper. A breath. A dropped leash. A slipped collar. A dog treat.

But maybe there is something even before that. Maybe every story begins before the beginning.

With a shadow, a twitch, a fractured something.

"Maybe," Agatha thinks, "this is where I should begin with the Interloper."

She moans.

A moan of lamentations.

She writes that down.

Then she opens *The Book of Saint Albans*, first edition, 1486. It is a treatise on "hawking, hunting, and heraldry," written, supposedly, by a nun and sportswoman. Agatha appreciates the *supposedly* and the mystery of authorship that has taunted scholars for centuries. The Olde English is a tangle of squiggles and whorls, but she unravels the collective nouns that call to her: *a slewthe of beerys* [a sleuth of bears]; *a sege of herons* [a siege of herons]; *a synguler of boores* [a singular of boors]; *a multiplieng of husbondis* [a multiplying of husbands].

This one stops her. The last thing she wants is a multiplying of husbands. One husband is/was more than enough.

A noonpacyens of wyves [an impatience of wives]. This one makes her laugh.

She likes this mysterious, ballsy author-nun and adds her to her imagined zephyr of friends.

* * *

Agatha's agent blitzes her on Twitter. "Hey Beautiful," she writes, using thirteen of her allotted 140 characters to woo. "You still out there? Looking forward to new ms."

Crap.

Crap.

Shit.

Crap.

Shit. Shit. Shit.

"Been kidnapped," Agatha types furiously. "Send $$$."

This will hold her agent for a bit. She loves funny stuff.

* * *

"In a past life," Agatha tells Shrinky-Dink, "I'm pretty sure I was one of those beggars used as bait in the Roman Colosseum."

"Really?" Shrinky-Dink never shows much interest in Agatha's past life banter. Not the "I once was a worm" story she often shares when big fears pop up or the "I was one of Joan of Arc's minions" tale she told a million times before Bear replaced Joan as her guiding light.

"Yep. When the lion shot up through the trap door in the floor from one of those underground tunnels, I lasted all of ten seconds before it caught, smothered, and shredded me to bloody bits while the Emperor and his Senators cheered and jeered."

"You remember this?"

"Vaguely."

"And this experience in what, AD 100, solidified your fate almost two thousand years later?"

Agatha growls like a lion and nods.

"You're afraid of beans today because you were devoured by a lion in the Roman Colosseum in a past life?"

"It's possible."

"Agatha, technically anything is possible, but not likely. Do you see the difference? Any other thoughts on why you fear so many things?"

"I was born this way."

"Too easy. What else do you have?"

"When I was three years old, I got my head stuck between the bars in a fence at a mall. This was before they all started using that safety glass. Have I told you about this?"

"No, and this is a real story, not a past life story?"

"Real as you and I sitting right here, right now. I was trying to see the Build-a-Bear store on the first floor and I stuck my head through the fence. When I went to pull back and follow my parents, I couldn't. I was stuck. A guard had to pull the bars open a bit in order to release my head."

"That must have been scary."

Agatha smiled. Finally, a bit of respect. "It was. For years I dreamed my parents left me there, head stuck out over the open space, looking down longingly at the Build-a-Bear store. Every once in a while, a mysterious hand would reach in from behind and stick a cheese doodle into my mouth."

Shrinky-Dink nods and leans a little closer. She likes dreams.

"And when I was six," Agatha says, "my dad insisted I learn to swim. 'I'm done with this nonsense,' he said, referring to my insistence on staying in the shallow end, then tossed me into the deep end of the pool and walked away. I couldn't even doggie paddle. The lifeguard saved me."

"At six you couldn't doggie paddle?"

"No, I was afraid of the water."

"Even before your dad tossed you in and left you?"

"Yes."

"Why do you think that is?"

Agatha raises her eyebrows. "Aaaaand, we're back to the lion in the Colosseum."

Shrinky-Dink ignores her. "What else?"

"Well, you already know about the flies and Dracula."

Shrinky-Dink nods. "Keep digging."

Agatha turns and swings her legs onto the sofa, then lies down with her head on a pillow. Even though she can't see Shrinky-Dink now, she knows she's giving a private cheer. Agatha never lies down. Much too vulnerable a position.

"When I was seven, my parents moved us to a new town and a new school. It was torture. I hid in a bathroom on the second floor for the first three weeks."

"Did anyone look for you?"

"No one remembered I was supposed to be there. My new teacher assumed they'd moved me to another class."

"Who finally figured it out?"

"A janitor found me and called down to the office."

"What else?"

Agatha is on a roll. "When I was eight, my mom's best friend died. She was one of the best people in my little world and she just out-of-the-blue died. No one had ever died in my life before."

"What was her name?"

"Susie. She was funny and didn't distinguish between adults and kids. She just talked to us all in the same way. I liked that."

"What happened?"

"One morning before school, my mom was sobbing in her favorite chair. Crying and crying like I'd never seen her cry. I asked her what was wrong, but she wouldn't tell me. She just waved me off to the bus stop."

"By yourself?"

"Yes. I worried all day. At dinner that night, my dad put a piece of meat loaf on my plate and said, 'Susie died this morning.' That was it. 'Susie died this morning.' No explanation. No hugs. No books about death and what it means. No discussion of heaven and hell. Just a slab of meat loaf I was expected to finish. You know, the whole *clean your plate* thing. A few days later we went to the funeral home and my mom made me look at dead Susie in her coffin. I didn't have a clue what 'dead' was."

"Stop there."

"Stop there?" Agatha hears the tick of the clock that indicates the end of her hour.

"Yes, there's a lot to unpack in this memory, but time's up. We'll start with this at your next appointment."

Agatha swings her legs to the floor. She sits up and fingers the crease on her cheek. "You know," she says, "therapy isn't much different than writing."

"How so?" says Shrinky-Dink. Agatha can tell by the tone of her voice that she's moving on mentally and emotionally, likely already thinking about the woes and wherefores of the woman waiting in the vestibule, the one who follows Agatha in the lineup every week, the one who always wears gray.

"We both like to leave the day's work on a cliffhanger."

* * *

Agatha limp-hobbles through the bruised shadows toward GDOG's House of Sin. She shouldn't be limp-hobbling through the bruised shadows toward GDOG's House of Sin. She should be at home resting her foot and her hands, nursing her anthrax. She should be at home moisturizing the crease on her face so that one day it will go away. She should be at home writing the thriller she has promised her agent. But here she is, doing everything she shouldn't be doing, but not being able to help it. She has to see Dax and what he's up to.

Plus, she needs a good, clear photo of GDOG for the reflection doll order.

Ten minutes before, she'd set off thinking stealth and Bear and creeping-into-GDOG's-yard-unnoticed but the tools in her spy pants are clunking against one another as she limp-hobbles along. *Bump. Clang. Bang. Diggity-Dang.* She's a one-woman band on a mission.

Bump. Clang. Bang. Diggity-Dang-Dang-Dang.

Her boots slush through dry leaves like brushes on a snare, and eighth-grade band flashes in her head. She on her clarinet trying to *toot-tootle-toot* through the *1812 Overture* just moments after her secret saxophone crush whispered to the whole band that he'd had sex—actual sex—with his drummer crush the night before. What did that even mean in eighth grade? And sex with that giant-mawed drummer-girl with glisteny gums? Ew. Could Agatha's heart hurt any worse? She remembers watching the freshly skewered girl bang away on the bass with newfound power and the band director trying to cover the battle cry of lust with audacious arm arcs and hollered 1-2-3-4s.

Poor Tchaikovsky.

When she reaches the House of Sin, Agatha smirks. It is one of a handful of Victorians in town. Purplish, asymmetrical, narrow, and crazy tall. Much more ornate than the steadfast Colonials and Capes that surround it. A turret crowns the roof. Stained-glass windows glow like paintings. It is an obvious house. A sexy house. A *hey-hey-hey-look-at-me* house. The perfect house for a husband-stealing, grapefruit-buttocked dog walker. An ordinary human might miss the symbolism of this story, but Agatha is a writer. Symbolism is her second language. Her husband has moved from a massive white Colonial to a towering purple Victorian. He's replaced his Red Sox jersey with a lavender pull-over, and his frightened wife with a fearless lover. This means something. Everything means something.

Agatha lifts her binoculars to her eyes. There are no curtains on the first-floor windows so she quickly spots her husband and Willow Bean.

They are sitting on the couch, tossing back their heads and laughing. The two look incredibly comfortable, as if they've been laughing and leaning against one another for years. The goddamn Chihuahua is curled between them, its head resting on Dax's knee. How is this possible? This snapshot. Not even three weeks since the shed incident. What could they be laughing at? A show on the television? A private joke? Her?

Agatha snaps the long lens onto her camera and takes a few close-ups. The weight of the camera feels good in her hands.

A passerby pauses, follows the direction of the camera, frowns, and moves away. Another says, "Good evening?" in a questioning tone, asking "What are you up to?" without asking "What are you up to?" A dog on a leash nuzzles her ankle, and its human says, "Can I help you with something?"

"Nope," Agatha says, snapping another photo, "unless you're willing to sic your pup on that woman in there."

The dog lifts its leg and pees on the telephone pole. He and the man move on.

When the lovers start kissing on the couch, Agatha drops the camera. The strap around her neck saves it from crashing to the sidewalk but its weight snaps her head. "Ow!" she hollers, loudly enough that Dax and Willow Bean break apart, turn to the window, but seeing nothing—or perhaps seeing and not caring—return to each other's mouths. Hunger means something, too.

Agatha pulls the can of pink spray paint from its pocket. Somewhere in that head of hers she hears Shrinky-Dink groaning and saying "Don't do it," but she uncaps the can and points it at the closest tree trunk in Willow Bean's yard. Spasms of pain from the camera snap begin to undulate down her neck. She can't move without grunting but she raises her arm higher anyway. Fuck pain. She writes an H, the first letter in HUSSY, but then thinks of Jason and Dustin and how much she loves them and how much she never wants anything—even this terrible mess—to hurt them.

Instead of USSY, she adds EART.

HEART.

HEART instead of HUSSY.

That's what she writes on GDOG's tree.

HEART.

If the boys find out she did it and ask why she wrote HEART, she can fib and say it's so they always remember how much she loves them, even when apart. Like the daytime moon.

But when Dax asks, she can tell the truth. She can tell that fothermucking SOB it's meant to serve as a reminder of what he broke, shattered, snapped, blew up, destroyed.

Her heart.

Agatha limp-hobbles back to her car, not even trying for stealth this time. What's the point? *Bump-bump-bump. Clang-clang-clang. Bang. Bang. Diggity-dang.*

Above, the stars are bright and shiny. The kind of shiny that makes her want to believe in something. Anything. Reincarnation. God. Buddha. Mother Nature. Druids. Past lives. Fairies. And wanting to believe, she thinks about Heaven's Gate, the UFO religious cult that participated in a mass suicide back in the 1990s. Thirty-nine members believed they would get to the "Next Level" via an extraterrestrial spacecraft right after a comet named Hale–Bopp did its comet-y thing, and thirty-nine members committed suicide to do so. Suicide. The permanent choice. Thirty-nine. Thirty-nine permanent choices. Agatha scans the sky for a savior ship. If only.

She climbs into her car and picks up bobblehead Bear from the dashboard. "I did believe in something," she says to him. "I believed in love. I believed in Dax. In me and Dax. Look where that got me." She tries to drop her head dramatically to the steering wheel but pain ripples down her spine and she cries out. She won't be able to turn her head for a week.

Moments later, her phone pings. The Moms. Of course, the Moms. It seems the best gel manicurist in town has moved to Utah. She's getting married. This is a catastrophe. A travesty. A cry for next-best goes up. Sharon at Glamour Nails is very good. Tildi at Passion is highly rated. Vanilla at Sweet Spa gets many likes. But whatever you do, do not use Samantha at Nail Love. DM for details.

And so it goes.

Until you spend time in a Facebook moms group, it's impossible to fully fathom the range of topics these Moms can discuss, argue about, champion, and/or beat to a bloody pulp.

Jaywalkers?

Yup.

The cars that nearly mow down jaywalkers?

Yup.

Moms who defend the cars that nearly mow down jaywalkers?

Yup.

Jaywalkers who challenge the cars who challenge the jaywalkers for jaywalking?

Yup.

Moms who defend the jaywalkers who challenge the cars who challenge the jaywalkers for jaywalking?

Yup.

Slow-cooker recipes?

Especially in winter.

ADHD therapists?

Taking names.

Best keratin stylist in town?

Mm hm.

Cheapest keratin stylist in town?

Every week.
Worst keratin stylist in town?
A must.
Best cookie baker in town?
Yup.
Least painful place to get a bikini wax?
Yup.
Refreshing yoga studios?
Yup.
Kick-ass cycling studios?
Yup.
Best Disney hotels?
Bring 'em on.
Best resorts in Punta Cana?
Oh yeah.
Warmest slippers?
Yup.
Marriage therapists?
Indeed.
Divorce lawyers?
Of course.
And on and on it goes.

* * *

Back home, she uploads the photos and picks one of GDOG she's sure will make an excellent reflection doll likeness. GDOG is looking straight at the camera. Her eyes are wide, as if Dax is telling her a delicious secret. Her mouth is slightly open.

As she fills in the Etsy form, Agatha notes how strange it is that she's come to a point in life in which she is ordering voodoo dolls, officially reflection dolls, in the likenesses of her husband and his lover.

Will the dolls even work? If she sticks a pin in Dax's arse, will he flinch? If she dangles GDOG over the edge of the balcony, will adrenalin rush her veins? Does any of it matter?

Agatha goes to the order page at Etsy, attaches the photos of Dax and GDOG, and pays the fee, along with expedited delivery charges. Then she opens her Hard Truths file and scrolls to the vole post that she never really deleted in Shrinky-Dink's office. She closes her eyes and for the millionth time imagines herself and Dax as the little rodent-y creatures shunning the sexy vole sashaying past their home. "Begone!" she whispers. "Begone."

Chapter Eleven

"You haven't died of anthrax," Shrinky-Dink says at Agatha's next appointment.

"Not yet," Agatha says, moving only her eyeballs as she speaks. Her neck hurts that much. "They say the official incubation period for pulmonary anthrax is one to seven days, but I suspect that's a conservative estimate."

Shrinky-Dink nods. "Let's hope for the best." She's so matter of fact it stings. "What's wrong with your neck?"

Agatha turns at the waist like a marionette and tells her about the spy pants and taking photos and the kissing and the snap of the camera strap and the spray paint. She does not mention the voodoo dolls.

"Spying is not what I meant by 'try out a new hobby,'" Shrinky-Dink says.

"I figured," Agatha says.

"Nor is graffiti."

"I figured that too."

"You do smell better though. Note even a hint of skunk now."

"Thank you."

"And your hands are healing nicely."

Agatha holds out her hands, palms up, and studies them. "Yes."

"Rather pink though."

"The paint. It's messy when you're moving fast."

"Mm hm. How's the toe?"

"Getting there." Agatha slides her foot out of the flip-flop and waggles her big toe. Less like an overripe avocado, more like a dill pickle.

"So now just the neck?"

"And the anthrax."

"Right."

Agatha is quiet.

"And the heart," says Shrinky-Dink.

Agatha nods ever so slightly. "And the heart."

* * *

Later that evening, Agatha shovels shrimp lo mein into her mouth with a pair of the boys' Red Sox chopsticks, notes the cultural misstep of that combo, as well as how quickly dinner on boys-with-Dax nights has become an informal, almost slovenly affair, and, when the carton is empty, pulls the fortune from her cookie: "Conquer your fears. Otherwise, your fears will conquer you."

"Bloody hell." She crumples the fortune and tosses it over the railing into a forsythia bush. Dustin would yell at her for littering but he isn't here and Agatha can't see how littering is really littering if it's on your own property. She tucks away the guilt, nibbles the stale cookie, and opens the Moms group on her phone.

Agatha Arch: "Moms, I need an exterior house painter. Best recs. Go!"

Agatha doesn't *need* a house painter. The house was painted two years ago and will be good for four or five more, depending on the number of nor'easters that hit. But if sticking Dax in the wallet means one less silky muumuu-maxi for GDOG, bring on the brushes.

While she waits for the Moms to pounce—they adore "Go!" posts almost as much as "Look at this!" posts—Agatha combs the feed looking for contenders for her annual "The 12 Days of the Wallingford Moms":

Lauren Stage: "Best place to buy a mattress? Go!"

Boring.

Sandy Stone: "Favorite orthodontist? Go!"

Equally boring.

Lauren Stage: "Electric toothbrush for sensitive gums? Go!"

Seriously?

Dolly Eggers: "Favorite venue that can handle 50 to 60 guests for my baby's first birthday party? Go!"

Aha! Agatha saves the first birthday gala post as "Dolly's Diamond" and wonders if any of the many Moms who host these supersized parties for their one-year-olds realize the absurdity of such events.

Lauren Stage: "Best vibrator? (TMI?) Go!"

Score. After saving Lauren's vibrator post for the carol, Agatha also saves Elizabeth Kingly's most recent inquiry. Undeniably one of the year's best.

Elizabeth Kingly: "OK, ladies, a bit of an embarrassing question, but you all know best and I know you are

	discreet. What is your favorite method of birth control? We've been using condoms, but they're ruining a bit of our fun. Go!"
Tessa Rivers:	"IUD!"
Sandy Stone:	"Nuvaring."
Dolly Eggers:	"The pill."
Wanda Watson:	"Having four kids under the age of 5. I don't have enough energy to wave goodbye to my husband let alone spread my legs for him."
Rachel Runk:	"Pull-out method!"
Tessa Rivers:	"You've got to be kidding, Rachel?!"
Elizabeth Kingly:	"Rachel, DM me!"

Agatha is not sure if Elizabeth wants a direct message from Rachel for a how-to on the pull-out method or if she just wants to tell her she is batshit crazy, but either way, her Go! post will get high honors in this year's carol.

Minutes later, the recs for a house painter start to pour in. Big Al of Big Al's Painting Crew is cheap but always leaves a few drips. Duncan Weber is great for spot jobs. Cyrus Little is awesome but *oh my god* so pricy. Isai Corona—also known as the Tush—is affordable, efficient, skilled, and responsible. He is also hot, seven Moms report. Very, very hot, three Moms add. Agatha texts him immediately.

* * *

Agatha's agent comes for her on Instagram. "Where, oh, where, is Agatha Arch?" she posts, tagging Agatha, with a photo of a world map with a smiley face plastered on it.

Agatha tags her back in a Where's Waldo? post.

* * *

The first late September chill hits just days after the nor'easter, and the leftovers of summer begin to decompose in the dirt. All those lilac petals and forsythia blooms, discarded fortunes and marigold dust mixing up with the carcasses of bees and beetles, deer dung and turkey feathers, even those sad little tufts of rabbit fur left over by the ravenous fox.

Agatha sniffs at the early autumn rot and shifts the ice pack on her neck. The nail of her big toe has fallen off and there's no sign of a new one growing back. The skin is smooth and shiny; still bruised and tender but far less painful.

Tap tap tippity-tap. The woodpecker continues its work. Agatha lifts her binoculars. Seven holes and counting. Bastard.

She so wants to spend the day lounging in misery. Eyeballing the remains of the shed. Crying about *that* day . . . *this* life. Wallow-wobbling in woe-is-me. She glances at the tomato plant. The hopeful tomato is now ever so slightly tinged with red. Prick.

She throws on her spy pants, hops in her car, and heads to Apple54. On the way, she's sure she feels sad enough to join the Interloper in her life on the road, to squat in a carbon dioxide–soaked patch of grass and hold out a can for small change. For one brief moment, it seems like a fantastically uncomplicated existence.

But the moment she spots the Interloper in the distance that fantasy explodes. Hang out with this coo-coo-cachoo in the newly brisk air for hours on end? No, thank you. She takes a deep breath and pulls off the road to consider her options:

1. Turn around and head home without further action.
2. Pull into the grocery parking lot, take photos, and study the Interloper from afar.
3. Pull up next to the Interloper, roll down the window, say hello, and give her some cash.

Option #3 gives her palpitations, but it's the only way forward. Agatha cranks up her go-to brave song—the theme from *Rocky*—and envisions herself in a dumpy pair of gray sweats and a headband running up those famous Philly steps.

Thump-thump-thumpy-thump-thumpy-thump-thumpy-thump.
Thump-thump-thumpy-thump-thumpy-thump-thumpy-thump.

She plucks Bear from the dashboard, gives him a loud smooch, and apologizes for biting his foot. He bobble-nods his forgiveness.

She pulls a dollar from her wallet and sets it on the passenger seat. She needs to be ready. No fumbling when she comes face to face with the Interloper. She must appear strong and not-to-be-fucked-with. First impressions are everything. She practices.

"Hello, Interloper," she grunts.

Too tough.

"Hi there, Interloper person."

Too familiar.

"Howdy, Interloper."

Too western.

"Hi."

Too meek.

"Hello, Ms. Interloper."

Too formal.

Screw it. She revs Coop's engine, turns on her blinker, and pulls into traffic.

As she closes the distance between them, her heart bangs harder and louder than the *Rocky* beats. "Fear sharpens us," she whispers. "Fear sharpens us." When there are just two cars between her and the ne'er-do-well, the light turns red. The Interloper takes money from the car in the lead, plods past the next car whose window stays tightly sealed, and moves in Agatha's direction. Agatha turns down the music.

She wants to wait and roll down the window, but how? How? This is too much. She is too scared. What was she thinking? When the young woman is right there, right outside her window, Agatha freezes with terror. The greasy hair, the chafed cheeks, the dim eyes. What horror is this monster about to unleash on Wallingford? Images of death and destruction whip through Agatha's mind: a plague of locusts, an all-consuming fire, a nuclear bomb, a swarm of killer bees, catastrophic flooding, a bomb, poisoned water sources, rabid dogs, the reintroduction of dinosaurs. The irrational possibilities are endless.

Just as she is about to pass out, the light turns green and Agatha drives right past the Interloper, the dollar still gripped in her hand. She is so distraught she forgets to go straight and accidentally turns onto the highway heading north. "The highway! The highway! The highway!" her brain screams.

Agatha never turns onto the highway heading north. She is terrified of that highway. She is terrified of any highway. All highways. Those heading north. Those heading south. Heading west? Nope. East? No way. The speed. The blur. The trucks. As an eighteen-wheeler roars past, she swerves toward the barrier and thankfully away just before slamming into it, then she slows to a dangerous crawl, and creeps off the highway a mile down the road at the next exit. A bevy of cars tries to beep her to death.

By the time she pulls into her driveway and puts the car in park, she is soaked with sweat. "The Interloper almost killed me," she thinks. "I could have died just now."

She pulls Bear from his spot on the dashboard and presses him to her cheek. "Bear," she groans, "what kind of nonsense are you selling me? Fear sharpens us? Fear sharpens us?" She shakes her head and lifts him to eye level so he can see how wrecked she is. "Fear does not sharpen us," she says. "Fear weakens us. Plain and simple. Fear reduces us to the smallest reduction of the smallest reduction of the smallest reduction of ourselves." She plucks a speck of dust from the cup holder and holds it up for him to see. "You see this, Bear Grylls? You see this speck? This wee speck is now bigger than me."

She picks up the tissue box from the passenger seat and stuffs Bear headfirst through the slot. Only his brown-booted feet poke out. One boot forever marked by her teeth.

* * *

The next morning Agatha wakes to the beeping of her phone. It's Balderdash. He was spotted crossing the road near town center last night. Unfortunately, Priya Devi reports, by the time she got stopped and out of her car, he was gone. On another day, in another week, in another year, this might have gone differently, but, Priya says, she's hobbled by a surgical boot and a knee walker. Bunion surgery. The Moms sigh, grumble, offer condolences for the bunions, then cheer. Sure, Balderdash is still missing, but there's hope. What was it badass Emily Dickinson wrote? "Hope is the thing with feathers." In this case, it's a hideous pup with drool and a single patch of fur, but still, hope. Balderdash is alive.

Agatha clicks through to the picture of Dustin and Jason lined up at the ice cream truck, right behind the Sheridan boys. It's a good shot, taken just a few weeks ago, a shot that captures their essence, their verve, their humanness. Sure, they're sweaty and goofing and Jason is pointing at the picture of the ridiculously gross-tasting SpongeBob popsicle, his favorite, but Agatha can also see their hearts, their joy. She remembers the moment she snapped it, then the moment she texted it to Dax. He'd sent back two red hearts, one for each boy.

She presses her hand to her chest and assesses the status of her own heart.

Still beating?

Yes.

Still aching?

Oh yes.

Still in there?

Just barely.

How long has it been since the shed incident? Two hours? Two weeks? Two years? Two decades? Two lifetimes?

* * *

The boys shove through the basement door. Each is holding one side of the enormous clock that Agatha had hidden behind the old coal furnace.

"Mom? What's this doing downstairs?"

Agatha sighs. "What are you doing down behind the old furnace?"

"Playing hide and seek."

"Well, don't." She glances at the large wall behind them. It's weirdly empty.

They glance, too.

"Why did you take it down? You love this clock."

Tick tock.

"I do not. It's too loud. Listen to it."

"Since when?" Dustin says.

"Since I decided it was too loud."

Tick tock.

"Dad gave you this clock," Jason says. "Remember? He said it was because you guys always have the time of your life together."

"Dad isn't here anymore."

The three of them look at the clock, and the boys turn back to the basement door as if they'd figured out a great mystery. "Oh," Dustin says. "I get it. Come on, Jason." He opens the door and they wrestle the beast back down the stairs.

* * *

In an eensy-weensy garden in her brain, Agatha Arch is not afraid of anything. In this garden, she *is* Bear Grylls. Brave, ballsy, strong-jawed, covered with dirt, and not giving a shit. In this garden, she cartwheels through life with gusto and laughs off the FB Moms who invite her to play Candy Crush instead of taking them to task. In this garden, Agatha Arch jaywalks and speeds and sleeps at night without the lights on. She drives on the highway for miles and miles in any direction with the windows down. For Big Papi's sake, she doesn't even wash grapes before eating them. When she walks down the street, people, even HP Poston, gawk, point, and growl, "Fearless, that one. Look at her go."

But Agatha lives in the world, the real world, so when a 2 AM infomercial ignites an obsession about what to do if she ever plunges her car into a lake, pond, ocean, or, god forbid, humongous puddle left on the side of the road by a nor'easter, she does what anyone would do. She buys three of those special hammers that will slice her seat belt and shatter her car windows.

"I'm prepping for any and all disasters," she tells Shrinky-Dink at her next appointment. Remembering how quickly Shrinky-Dink pulled the sewing kit from the drawer to help remove her splinters, she's sure she'll be impressed. "Do you have one of these in your car?" As if they'd agreed to a game of show-and-tell, she pulls one of the hammers from the pocket of her spy pants and holds it up.

"No," Shrinky-Dink says. "I don't."

"No?"

"No."

"Why not?"

"The likelihood of ever needing one is too infinitesimal for me to worry about."

Agatha glares at Shrinky-Dink's bravado, shoots disdain and envy at her with her eyeballs. "Well, this one is the best of the best."

"What makes it the best of the best?"

"It has dual steel hammerheads that can shatter side *and* rear windows with a quick bang-bang." She whips the hammer back and forth to demonstrate.

"I see."

"And if you shut off the light, I will show you that this pin right here," she points to a pin in the center of the hammer, "actually glows in the dark. I'll be able to find this thing even if I plunge to the bottom of the ocean." Agatha reaches for the light switch.

Shrinky-Dink shakes her head.

Agatha shrugs and drops her hand. "Take my word for it. It glows."

"Does it fix broken hearts?"

"Excuse me?" Agatha will not meet Shrinky-Dink's eyes.

"Broken hearts. Does this particular model fix them?"

"The literature doesn't mention it."

"Does it mention how to actually deal with fear as opposed to spending money on objects you'll never be able to operate at the bottom of the ocean?"

"It assuages fear."

"Really?"

Agatha grunts and cradles the hammer in her lap. She and Shrinky-Dink sit in silence for the remaining three minutes of the session.

When Agatha gets to her car, she pulls the product pamphlet from the glove box. "Once your seat belt is cut and your car window is shattered," she reads out loud, "you can slip out the window, and, like a mermaid, swim to safety." The pamphlet actually says "like a mermaid." Three words that manage to transform the terrifying experience of plunging to the depths into something magical. And these three words are the real and true reason she bought this particular hammer.

"Like a mermaid."

She didn't buy it for the dual steel hammerheads or the glow-in-the-dark pin. Not really. She bought it because by using it, she has been promised that she might momentarily be as carefree and intrepid as a mermaid. For someone who fears the world, this seems like a lovely option.

Chapter Twelve

Agatha jams her right foot on the first step. "Go up!" she commands. "Go up!" There's no one to hear her. She smacks her own arm. "Now!" She makes it to the second step.

The boys are at school. Dax is fluffing about somewhere with his new hussy, probably wearing a shirt with ducklings on it.

She reads the note on the blue sticky. FEAR SHARPENS US. She chants the line over and over. "Fear sharpens us. Fear sharpens us. Fear sharpens us." If she repeats it a million times, will it work? Will she be sharper? Fearless?

Repetition hasn't worked with the boys.

Pick up your underwear.

Clean your room.

Comb your hair.

Flush the toilet.

Close the door behind you.

Don't pee on the floor.

Say thank you.

Drink more milk.

Get the mail.

If you pee on the floor, wipe it up.

Eat your grapes.

Don't hit your brother on the head with your shoe.

Do your homework.

Read a book.

Don't hit your brother with the bat.

If you pee on the floor and wipe it up, throw the tissue in the trash.

Over and over she delivers these lines, these bits of wisdom, these lessons of life, yet the boys do none of these things, despite her efforts, despite the repetition.

She studies the red door eleven steps up. She'd painted it herself. Welcome, a red door says. You are safe here. Bye-bye, evil spirits.

Who is she kidding? She knows she'll never be sharp. Fearless. She'll never again make it up those stairs to that red door, to the desk that Dax built. It will gather dust for decades, centuries, millennia, then disintegrate. Perhaps, if luck is a real thing, its bones will be discovered by the same archaeological team that discovers the mammoth clock behind the old coal furnace in the basement.

Yet she tries.

"Fear sharpens us." She says it in a British accent.

Then a Russian accent.

Then Texan. Yee ha!

She tries it as an Irish lass.

Aussie.

Boston.

Godfather gangster.

Indian.

Scottish.

Frenchie.

She raises her left foot to the third step, but lowers it again. She can't. She lifts Bear from his perch on the step until they're at eye level. “I’m unworthy,” she whispers. Then she tucks him back into her pocket. He shouldn’t have to witness such cowardice.

* * *

The boys are home when the UPS guy delivers the Etsy package, and while they chuckle at his nerdy way-too-high brown socks, Agatha hides the package on a shelf in the kitchen and goes the whole day nervous and excited about opening it. When they finally tumble into bed, fresh and soap-smelling from the commanded bath and still guffawing about who knows what, it’s 9 PM, and Agatha cherishes a thank-god-they’re-asleep-but-what-marvelous-boys moment, retrieves the package, then, with hands shaking, peels back the plain brown paper, unties a black silk bow, then rips through the hot-pink tissue paper with black handheld mirrors stamped all over it. Inside the box, the reflection dolls look astonishingly like Agatha’s estranged husband and his lover. Dax’s hair, or lack of hair, is precise, as are the shape of his head, his ears, and the unusual way in which his nostrils ripple. His belly is a bit smaller than in person, but that depends on the week. His mouth is curled in the “I care, I really do” expression that she’d believed in all those years. It hurts to look at him. The GDOG doll is as beautiful as the real thing, blond hair pulled into a messy bun, a sweet nub of nose, and the longest eyelashes ever seen on a human being. The buttocks don’t quite compare, but, to be fair, the glorious grapefruits weren’t featured in the photo.

The attached card reads, “a reflection of those you love (or those you don’t).” There is no mention of jabbing a pin into your doll’s derriere, wrenching its arm, stepping on its shoulder, pulling individual hairs from its head, dropping it into a vat of boiling oil, or sticking grains of rice up its nostrils, but Agatha takes the reference to “those you don’t” as a subliminal nod to the possibilities.

She moves outside to the porch, a doll in each hand, and watches the moon, then counts the woodpecker's roundish holes. Eight.

There, in the dark, the woodpecker is diligently starting a ninth.

Tap tap tippity-tap.

Do all woodpeckers peck at night?

"Fothermucking bird." She sits, puts Dax and GDOG on her lap, then checks the Moms group on her phone.

Melody Whelan: "Moms, I'm pulling together care bags for the young woman at Apple54. Let me know if you'd like to contribute."

The Moms are on it. With summer over (thank god!), kids back in school, and time their own again, the Moms are up for a good charity case. Responses fly fast and furious, but only after a Wallingford dad airs his frustration.

David Watkins: "Melody, you know very well there are fathers in this group, too. Wonderful, nurturing fathers. The exclusive address to 'Moms' is offensive."

Oh, for Big Papi's sake. Equity and inclusion. This is David's life quest. Everyone has one. Everyone is born with one. Some forget theirs by the time they can walk; others by the time they start school; others by the first time they have sex. Some never know theirs; some, like David, never forget.

Agatha Arch: "Go play on your own Ferris wheel, Davy Crockett."

Melody Whelan: "Apologies, David. I was distracted by the young woman at Apple54. I typed too quickly."

David Watkins: "Thanks, Melody. And, Agatha, this is my Ferris wheel. I'm pointing out—for the millionth time—this is a communal space for mothers and fathers."

Agatha Arch: 

David Watkins: 

Agatha respects David's prowess, as well as his willingness to go head to head with her, master of emoji war. She revs her thumbs and scrolls through her well-built collection.

Agatha Arch: 

Take that.

The long pause before David's response indicates he is searching an emoji database bigger than he is used to. He is stretching, growing for this exchange, and, once again, Agatha is impressed. Others would have folded and resorted to words. Or bowed out. Not David. He is a worthy opponent.

David Watkins: 

Symbolism. Agatha nods approvingly. He's good. So good that for a brief moment she thinks that maybe she should welcome him into the Moms group. Not all men, mind you. But David. That might be okay. "Maybe I should rally for a name change," she thinks. "'The Parents' would be a shit name. No music at all. But 'The Guardians'? Yes, yes, 'The Guardians' is kind of fun. Rather rock-bandish, if you will."

She is running out of time. The longer she engages in an emoji war, the closer the Interloper gets to destroying the world. Agatha does what she has to do.

Agatha Arch:

This is it. David doesn't fight back. He's clearly a man who knows when he's lost. He goes quiet. And then:

David Watkins: 

The end. Agatha wins. And not once during this exchange does it cross her mind that she is a grown woman fighting a grown man with a series of wee cartoon pictures. Not once does she think, "Wow, this is classic preschool behavior." She is so into the fight, she can't even see the inanity.

Besides, she wins.

High Priestess Poston: "Melody, if I can draw us back to the subject at hand, what kinds of items do you want in the bags?"

Melody Whelan: "Self-care items. Nonperishable food (light-weight, as I'm not sure how far she has to carry the bag). Maybe a shirt or a pair of pants."

Wanda Watson: "Self-care items?"

Watson is not the brightest bulb on the string of chili pepper patio lights.

Melody Whelan: "Soap. Shampoo. A washcloth. Deodorant. Small items that help you take care of yourself."

Agatha Arch:

High Priestess: "Should we drop the items at your house, Melody?"

Melody Whelan: "Yes, Jane, please. If I'm not home, you can leave a bag at the door or, if small, in the mailbox. I live at 164 North Circle Street."

With this, Agatha's head pops off again. Only the Kumbaya Queen is trusting enough and/or stupid enough to offer her address to every Barbara, Stella, and Mary (and, yes, David) in the Moms group. Who in their right mind gives out their address publicly these days? It's like inviting the devil into your bed. Why not just holler "Come get me!" to robbers and rapists and druggies? Or the Interloper?

Tap tap tippity-tap.

Agatha sets Dax and GDOG on the table, plucks one of the two still-green tomatoes from the plant at her side, winds up, and hurls it at the woodpecker. It hits the house just inches from her target, ruptures, and, although she won't see it until morning, leaves a green splotch on the white clapboard. The woodpecker flees. "Clay Buchholz has nothing on me," she says. The plant is left with two tomatoes. One still green; the other—now beautifully reddish on one side—holds tight to hope.

* * *

Frustration aside, Agatha knows she's been handed the opportunity to end all opportunities. A chance to slip a message to the Interloper without Melody or any of her Kumbaya cronies sabotaging her efforts. She bows out of the discussion, composes a short note in her head, and prints it on small cards.

Time to move on, Interloper.
Time to move on.

She pulls a few candy bars from last year's Halloween leftovers, peels the wrapper from the first without tearing it, then slides one of her notes between the wrapper and the candy bar. She glues it shut again.

She does this with the second. And the third.

Before going to bed, she puts Dax back into the Etsy box, tucks him in with some tissue paper, and sets him on the kitchen counter. She puts GDOG into the bottom of a wine box in the garage.

That'll teach them.

* * *

The next morning, Agatha puts the candy bars in a red-and-white grocery bag, drops the boys at school, and drives to 164 North Circle Street. As described by Melody, the house is a white Colonial with green shutters, as New Englandy as you can get. The lawn is perfectly manicured; hostas encircle each tree. Bags of all shapes, sizes, and color are piled up on the porch. Evidence the Interloper is the Moms' feel-good project of the month. Agatha hops out of her car and runs to the door. Before dropping her bag, she peeks into a few others. A comb, soap, toothpaste, a few toothbrushes, some hideous shirts, gift cards for the grocery, and more. She lingers just a moment too long because right after she drops her bag of tampered-with chocolate bars on the pile, Melody opens the door, pearls and toothy grin firmly in place.

Agatha freezes.

"Agatha Arch!" Melody exclaims, as if she's been expecting her for days. Such joy in her voice. Such welcome. Such relief.

Agatha doesn't buy it for a second.

"Agatha Arch, how are you? I'm so happy you decided to bring a little something for the young woman."

Agatha feels the tiniest bit of shame. "It's not much," she says. "Just a few candy bars. Not the healthiest choice, but sometimes you need chocolate more than broccoli."

WTF? This has got to be the stupidest thing she's ever said.

Even so, Melody smiles and nods. "You are so right, Agatha. That is very thoughtful."

"I have to go, Melody," Agatha says. It is true. She hasn't driven past the House of Sin in hours. Her dual spy missions are starting to compete for her time.

"How are you?" Melody asks, hinting at the shed incident. How does one reference another's cheating husband? The total destruction of a shed? The wielding of a hatchet? "Would you like to come in for a cup of tea?"

A cup of tea? Clearly Melody has to be talking to someone else. Agatha glances over her shoulder. She is the only one there. "Excuse me?" she says.

"Tea," Melody says. "I wish you could come in for tea."

It takes a moment, even a few, for Agatha to register the words *come in* and *tea*, connect them, and realize that Melody, the Kumbaya Queen, is issuing an invitation to her. When is the last time someone invited her to tea? To anything? "I don't drink tea," she says when the putting-it-all-together process is complete.

"Really?"

"Well, sometimes I do." She has two cups every morning. "But not today."

"Not today?"

"Not today."

"Why not today?"

"Because today is . . . don't worry about why not today. It's not your business."

"How about coffee then? Or wine?"

Good god, this woman is relentless with the invitations. Agatha swings another look over her shoulder, quite positive Melody is speaking to someone else. "Me?"

"Yes, you."

"Why?"

"Why not?" Melody says.

The kinder Melody is, the guiltier Agatha feels. All she can think about is the note she'd slipped into the chocolate bars.

Time to move on, Interloper.
Time to move on.

With Melody smiling and extending invitations for tea and coffee and wine, it hits Agatha just how mean her note is. It's fine for her to make such a choice, but if the boys find out, they'll never again listen to a lecture about kindness and generosity. They'll scoff when she pulls out that *do unto others* mumbo jumbo and may even begin to make unkind choices themselves. For Big Papi's sake, what had she been thinking?

Agatha stares into the sea of bags and tries to locate hers. "Um, Melody, I have to go, and I have to take the chocolate with me. Clearly this young woman needs broccoli more than sweets."

"Agatha," Melody says, "you did a nice thing by bringing chocolate bars for this young woman. I realize that was hard for you. Skip tea if you must, but I am not going to let you take away the treat."

More than anything in that moment, Agatha wants her note to reach the Interloper. She wants her and the possibility of a plague gone, gone, gone. But her boys. Her sweet boys. She can't risk their morality, their trust, their beautiful shiny hearts, for anything. Good lord, why does no one ever tell soon-to-be moms how limiting motherhood will be to their ability to ruthlessly take down an enemy?

Agatha shakes her head.

Melody shakes hers back.

Agatha is surprised that this pearl-wearing woman is proving to be as formidable in person as David was in the online emoji war. Who knew she had it in her? Still, Agatha has to get that bag. She crouches into a gorilla-like stance and starts to circle the pile. Her bag is white with red lettering, as are at least half in the pile.

"Agatha, leave the chocolate," Melody purrs.

"I can't do it, Melody. I realize now that chocolate isn't the answer. I'll come back with broccoli. Fresh, green broccoli, full of nutrients and goodness."

Oh, the absurdity.

Melody looks at Agatha as if she's lost her mind, but she crouches, too. Her eyes dart between Agatha and the pile of bags, arms outstretched. "Don't do it, Agatha Arch," she whispers. "Allow yourself this wonderfully generous act. It will feel good. I promise."

They circle like a couple of wrestlers, and Melody's face contorts into a puddle of lovey goo.

"I have to take the chocolate bars, Melody. It's old chocolate from two Halloweens ago."

"It will be fine. Chocolate ages well."

"Not American chocolate. I'm sure it's dry and flaky by now. Besides, the Interloper needs nutrients, not empty calories. Broccoli will be a much better choice."

"Nonsense," Melody says, and she starts to hum "Kumbaya." The air burbles, and waves of rainbow-y love waft toward Agatha. A tsunami of kumbaya is headed straight for her. Her knees wobble, but she holds on. She must resist.

"Let the goodness out, Agatha Arch," Melody says.

"I'll come back with broccoli," Agatha says. "That's much gooder than chocolate."

Gooder? *Gooder?*

Did Agatha, brilliant scribe of the written word, just say *gooder*?

"No!" Melody says. "Leave the chocolate."

Right then a gaggle of Moms appears on the street calling "Balderdash! Balderdash!" The search party. They're moving slowly, stretched in a line across the road, heads shifting from left to right, the end pieces crouching to look under pine trees and rhododendrons. "Balderdash!"

Taking advantage of the distraction, Agatha leaps gazelle-like across the pile of bags. She grabs the smallest, lightest one and bolts for her car. Melody's voice closes the distance between them. "Agatha! Agatha Arch! No!"

But Agatha has a head start, and before Melody can reach her, she jumps into her car, whips it into gear, and peels away, kind of. Behind her, in the rearview mirror, she sees Melody standing in the middle of the street, hands raised to the sky. In front of her, the line of Moms sweeps the street looking for Gem Lily's pooch. Each wears a pale blue

T-shirt with a photo of Balderdash on the back. It's almost more than she can bear.

A few blocks down North Circle Street, Agatha pulls over, rips open the candy bars, and eats them faster than you can say, "Interloper, Interloper, Interloper." Then she tosses the mean-girl notes out the window and waits until a brisk wind whisks them away.

Bear's feet are poking out of the tissue box where she'd stuffed him the day before. "Oh, be quiet," Agatha says to him and pushes him deeper into the box with the tip of her finger.

* * *

Agatha's agent messages her on FB. Who does this? Agatha never reads FB messages. No one reads FB messages.

But because it's her agent, she reads. "Agatha? Agatha? Trying to track you down. Holler when you come up for air."

Chapter Thirteen

Agatha drives the boys to Taco Bell. They love Taco Bell. They love tacos. She orders their usual, then adds, "One enchilada with refried beans."

The boys look at each other, then lean as close to the front seat as their seat belts allow.

"Mom, are you okay? You just ordered something with refried beans in it," Dustin says.

"Hush," she says.

"Mom, you don't eat refried beans," he says. "You're afraid of refried beans."

Agatha considers the foolishness of this statement coming from her ten-year-old's mouth. A ten-year-old shouldn't have to say "you're afraid of refried beans" to his mother, to anyone.

"Mom?" Jason says.

She pulls to the pickup window, pays, and takes the food from the clerk. She parks in the lot, then pulls her enchilada from the bag. The wrapping crackles. She hands the rest to the boys.

"Mom?" Dustin says. His voice carries the trepidation of someone trying to talk a loved one off a ledge.

"It's just beans, right, boys?" Agatha says.

"Yeah," the boys say. They unclip their seat belts and stick their heads into the front seat.

Agatha unwraps the enchilada. The beans are leaking a bit. She grimaces at the dirt-colored mush. With a deep breath, she pulls bobblehead Bear from the tissue box and stands him up on the dashboard once again. He's never banished for long. She gives his head a firm tap, and he nods encouragingly. "Fear sharpens us," he whispers.

She picks up the enchilada, closes her eyes, hovers it just inches from her lips. She knows Jason, Dustin, and Bear are cheering her on, but the only thing she hears is that serial killer guy in that movie sucking his teeth and talking about fava beans. "Give me the bag!" she hollers. "Give me the bag!" She grabs it from Jason, shoves the enchilada into it, and tosses it into the backseat. "You two eat it. You love enchiladas."

Jason puts his hand on his mom's shoulder. "Mom, that was so awesome. You almost did it."

"Yay, Mom!" Dustin yells.

Agatha wipes sweat from her forehead. She's nauseated and dizzy. But, yeah, she almost did it.

"What do you always tell us, Mom?" Jason says.

"Try again," Agatha whispers.

"Try again," the boys say in unison.

"How about next week?" she says, pretty sure she won't be able to try again for at least a decade.

"We'll be here."

* * *

When Agatha wakes all alone to the first stink bug post of the season, just a month or so after the shed incident, she knows for sure Dax is never coming home. It is a strange way to have your fate confirmed—the appearance of a prehistoric-looking bug that reeks when squashed—but there it is. Each September since moving to Wallingford, the two of them had waited impatiently for the first panicked "OMG! Look at this! What is it?" post on the Moms page when the insect appeared on a windowsill or lampshade. Each September they'd read that initial post aloud to one another, then giggle and guffaw.

As is often the case, this year's post is written by a New England newbie. Nothing is different, except that Dax isn't there to share it. Agatha is alone when she reads it out loud. She doesn't giggle or guffaw.

Susan Snow: "Yikes, found this in my house today! What is it?"

She attaches the photo, and the Moms begin . . .

"Stink bug."
"Stink bug."
"Stink bug."
"Stink bug! Do not squish! They smell like grass!"
"Stink bug."
"Stink bug."
"Looks like a stink bug to me."
"Definitely a stink bug."
"Stink bug."
"Stink bug."
"Stink bug. Flush the fucker!"
"Stink bug."
"Definitely a stink bug."
"Stink bug."
"Stink bug."
"Stink bug."
"Stink bug. Don't squish it. The scent will attract more stink bugs."

"Stink bug."
"Stink bug."
"Stink bug."
"Stink bug. Pick it up gently. Place it outside far from your house."
"Stink bug."
"Stink bug."
"Stink bug."
"Stink bug."
"Stink bug. Don't smoosh it!"
"Stink bug."
"Stink bug."
"Stink bug."
"Stink bug."
"Stink bug."
"Stink bug."
"Stink bug. Whatever you do, DO NOT SQUISH!"
"Stink bug."
"Stink bug."
"Stink bug."
"Stink bug."
"Stink bug."
"Stink bug."
"Stink bug. Squish it! I love the smell." (There's always one.)
"Stink bug."
"Stink bug."
"Stink bug."
"Stink bug."
. . .

* * *

"How about walking up to her and saying, 'Hi. How are you?'" Shrinky-Dink says.

Agatha is incredulous. "Are you out of your mind? Ask the Interloper how she's doing?"

"Agatha, you just shake hands with her. If it's hot, you say, 'Good gracious, you must be sweltering out here. I brought you a cool beverage with ice. It will refresh you.'"

"I would never say *good gracious*."

"It's my turn of phrase. Put your own spin on it."

"I would never say *cool beverage*."

"What would you say?"

"Cold drink."

"Use that."

Agatha nods.

"If it's cold outside, you say, 'Good gracious, you must be freezing. Here's a hot coffee. It will warm you up.' Then you invite the young woman to sit, encourage her to tell her story, give her a candy bar or an apple, buy her lunch, show good listening skills, and perhaps even offer sympathy."

"This is what a nice, somewhat normal person would do," says Agatha.

"Yes."

"I am not a nice, somewhat normal person."

"Yes, you are."

"No, I'm not."

"You are. You're just in a crisis."

"I'm not. Even before Dax ruined my life, I could not have done what you're suggesting. I've always been not nice. Not normal." She means this about herself, though she's never said it out loud before. Saying such a thing out loud about yourself is almost the same as throwing yourself in front of a moving car because you have to live with the consequence forever. In this case, she'd have to live with knowing that she'd known she wasn't nice or normal but hadn't made any kind of conscious decision to do anything about it. She thought about her imagined zephyr of friends. If only she were a little nicer or a little more normal, it might be hers for the taking.

"First," says Shrinky-Dink, "Dax did not ruin your life. He's thrown a wrench into it, for sure, but it is *your* life. And it has been your life all along. Second, you could do what I'm suggesting but you are choosing not to."

"Wrong on both counts." Agatha puts both hands on her chest. Just talking about communing with the Interloper is sending her heart into some kind of syncopated rhythm. "This beggar," she says, "could sneak into my home in the middle of the night, kill me, and eat me with fava beans."

Shrinky-Dink clucks and raises her eyebrows. "So could the grocery store clerk or your accountant or your agent. Anyone could kill you and eat you with fava beans if they really wanted to."

Agatha stares at her. "This is not helping me."

"But it's the truth."

"It's not. Those people don't have a motive."

"And this young woman at Apple54 does?"

Agatha looks up at the ceiling. "Maybe."

* * *

Agatha leaves Shrinky-Dink's office, drives across town, parks in the grocery store parking lot, and blows her horn at the Interloper. She's nowhere near ready for "I brought you a cold beverage with ice." She's at the I-want-to-put-you-on-notice stage of things and nothing can deter her.

She grabs her camera from the passenger seat and takes a few dozen photos. She turns up her music. Disruption is everything.

All is going just fine until Melody Whelan appears at the driver's side window and startles the bejeebies out of her. At first Agatha thinks she is an apparition, Melody's round pinkish head bobbing just inches from her face. But when Melody's voice cuts through the Beastie Boys, she realizes she is not an apparition.

Agatha turns down the music.

"Agatha Arch, just what are you doing?" says Melody.

Agatha makes a few weird *blarghy* sounds that one tends to make when one is caught doing a not very nice thing.

"Agatha Arch, are you still stalking this girl?"

"*Blgjhryssssytpsa*."

"Agatha Arch, you have to stop making this girl's life tougher than it already is. Stop this at once."

Agatha takes a deep breath and revs her engine. "I will not, Melody Whelan. We've got to drive this girl out of town. She's trouble."

"She's not. She's just a girl *in* trouble. Now go home."

Agatha watches Melody walk up to the Interloper and sit down in the grass with her, just like the nice, somewhat normal human being Shrinky-Dink had referenced. She watches Melody hand a drink to the Interloper that Agatha knows damn well is warm and comforting.

"Dammit," she says.

She lifts her camera and begins to shoot. For a few fleeting seconds, she is one hundred percent sure the prosecution is going to need these photos as evidence when the girl steals, maims, or even kills. The team will be forever thankful that Agatha risked her own life to take the photos. She'll be lauded as a hero. The *Wallingford Townsman* will do a cover story on her. And, yes, Dax will fall to his chubby, hairy knees and thank her for protecting their children. Then, brimming with gratitude, he'll leave GDOG tangled in her sexiest muumuu-maxi and return to their marriage bed. All this shoots through her brain as she click-click-clicks even though she knows damn well, or at least is starting to know damn well, that such projection is simply a way to protect the scared little thing inside her.

Chapter Fourteen

When the boys find the hammers in the car, they worry themselves silly that Agatha is getting scared of even more things in the world and rat her out to Dax. Kids shouldn't have to worry about their parents; worrying is a parent's job, but does it ever work out that way? Being a parent is still being a human and being a human is still making mistakes, and making mistakes means anyone gets to worry.

At the news, Dax is exasperated but serene. From what Agatha has seen, his relationship with Willow Bean is built on catchphrases like "wing it," "go with the flow," and "be in the moment." It is the antithesis of his relationship with her.

During their next face-to-face, he lectures her. "Agatha, could you even get to that hammer if you crashed the car and sank into a body of water?"

Agatha.

Agatha.

She tries to remember the last time he called her by her formal name, but can't. And even though she was the one who'd told him no more Aggie-girl, not hearing his nickname for her hurt worse than all the splinters or toe stubs or neck snaps in the world.

"Blah, blah, blah," she says, but in her head she knows he is right. If submerged in a car, would she really have the wherewithal to open the little box, feel for the hammer, cut the seat belt, shatter the window, slip free, and swim, like a mermaid, to safety? And if the boys were with her, would she be able to cut their seat belts, too?

"Even if you do manage to open the little box," Dax says, "won't the hammer float away in the water?"

"The hammer is attached to the side of the little box with Velcro. It does not float away." She feels good about this.

The literature that accompanies the tools insists that adrenalin will help you save yourself and your loved ones. It demonstrates such delightful success in a cartoon, a mom bursting through the surface of a pond with her trusty hammer in one hand and a smiling, soaking-wet tot in the other.

Plus, there's the whole "like a mermaid" thing.

But it's bullshit. Total bullshit. Shrinky-Dink knows it, Dax knows it, and Agatha knows it. Her adrenalin would do nothing more than make her curl into a ball and sob, causing her to suck in gallons of putrid water and hasten the drowning process.

In an attempt to counteract this eventuality, Agatha practices. Every day for three days, she drives to a shallow stream not far from the boys' school where she can manage her fear of water, pretend she's crashed her car and sunk to the bottom, and go through the lifesaving steps laid out in the literature (while parked safely *beside* the stream). The first day, she couldn't have saved a soul. But on the third day, she goes through the steps wearing one of Dustin's old Halloween masks. The scary kind. Freddy or Jason. The holes don't line up with her eyes. She can't see a thing. That's the point.

"Go!" she yells, pretending the car is sinking. She whips open the box next to her, puts her hand on the hammer, pulls, and in her excited state, swings the hammer and hits the driver's side window. Then the windshield.

In the second between the hitting and the shattering, the second in which she realizes she's gone a step too far, she says, "Holy shit," but it's too late. The glass explodes. As promised in all the videos, the glass stays mostly in a single sheet. Safety and all. Agatha lifts the mask from her eyes and looks at Bear. "Well, it works."

* * *

Two hour later, the tow truck drops her at her house. As it pulls away with Coop firmly on its flatbed, Kerry Sheridan looks up from the yellow mums she is potting at the end of her driveway.

"Agatha?" she calls. "Agatha, are you all right?"

Agatha groans, wishes she had an invisibility cloak she could throw over the car and herself. The look on Kerry's face reflects the state the windows are in, shattered.

"Agatha, did you get into an accident?"

"No, no," Agatha says. "I'm fine. Just a mishap."

"A mishap? A mishap? What kind of mishap shatters a car window? And a windshield?"

"Don't worry about it, Kerry. I'm fine. Go back to your mums."

Two thoughts linger in Agatha's mind as she makes her way into the house. First, the old adage "Practice makes perfect" may be true after all. Despite the broken windows, she really kicked ass with those hammers. Second, is it really autumn in New England if you haven't planted your mums?

* * *

Agatha's agent sends another email. Good god, doesn't this woman have other clients? Doesn't she have a family to tend to? Doesn't she have a mountain to climb, a river to swim? Doesn't she have a wing of dragons to slay?

As soon as the email pops up on Agatha's phone, she panics. Sweaty pits, racing heart, urge to run.

"When can you send me pages? I can't wait to read this!"

An exclamation point. A true blue exclamation point. Her agent never ever uses exclamation points. She hates exclamation points. What new madness is this?

After pacing for a good hour, Agatha writes back: "Not yet! Just discovered a second murder suspect!"

This will hold her for at least a day.

* * *

The music from Kerry Sheridan's annual "lanterns on the lawn" party is light and twinkly. Perfect for a midsummer evening, but tone deaf for an unseasonably cold autumnal affair. For the ninth year in a row, Agatha declined the invitation, or actually ignored the invitation Kerry slipped under her door, never responding, never offering a yay or nay, but also for the ninth time, from the porch, she half enjoys watching the bare-shouldered revelers shiver and huddle in clumps like macaque monkeys to keep warm. Who hosts an outdoor evening party in New England on the cusp of October? Who trusts Mother Nature enough not to ruin such a shindig with a cold snap? Who sends an invite for such a trusting event but doesn't add "Bring a wrap"? What numskull attends without bringing a wrap? A silk shawl. A light cardigan. A Canada Goose jacket with a hood.

When the moon appears from behind a cloud, a tight gaggle of ten shimmies to the street, then into Agatha's yard. Usually Kerry's grilled lobster tails, the highlight, keep partygoers close, but this year the remains of Agatha's shed lure them away. In the ambient light of the lanterns, the shards of wood look downright ghostly. Paired with the swishy silk skirts and colorful tuxes, it's a worthy shot. Agatha snaps a photo and posts it to Infidelity: A Still Life.

As the likes accumulate, she scrolls through her IG feed. The usual nonsense. Selfie of a foiled-up woman who "can't yet yield to the grays." [Fist bump, sister!] A freshly minted mom sporting perfectly applied ruby red lipstick, her newborn splayed on her bare chest. [#rubyred #momlife] Rainbows over Montana, Texas, and Illinois. [Can you spell S-T-E-R-E-O-T-Y-P-E?] A luscious lemon meringue pie. [#homemade] The careful curation nauseates Agatha. Where's the pain? Where's the struggle? Where's the honesty?

Murmurs of the dog walker, her disgruntled husband, and a hatchet reach Agatha's ears. She can't make out faces in the growing crowd near the remains of the shed, but she'd know the squawk of the High Priestess anywhere. Poston is out there, for sure. Agatha swipes to the sprinkler app on her phone, then to the "front yard east zone." As her finger hovers over the "on" button, she considers the wonders of technology.

When the water bursts forth, the revelers shriek and leap into the crisp arc of the sprinklers. Backlit by the lanterns and the moon, HP Poston arches her back and screams, "Agatha Arch! I'll get you!" Her lavender gown looks lovely in the light and spray. Agatha adds the shot to her feed, then edits a photo of Melody handing a can of soda to the Interloper. She lightens the shadows, intensifies the contrast, deepens the saturation, adds a filter, and uploads it to the Moms group.

Agatha Arch: "Stop communing with the Interloper, Melody Whelan. She's a danger to you, our families, and our community."

Agatha knows she should be upstairs working on the thriller, not watching a party she refused to attend and writing mean Facebook messages about a kind woman who likes to sing "Kumbaya," but . . .

The Moms come at Agatha like a ravenous cackle of hyenas—jaws snapping, drool frothing. These are the same women who cower in their homes for hours when they witness a fox eating a rabbit in their yard, a perfectly natural part of life. But throw some real danger at them—a potential murderer and thief—and they act like you're the crazy one.

Inez Walker:	"Agatha, get a life. Quit sneaking around with your camera."
Cindy Swatten:	"OMG, this is an invasion of privacy, isn't it? Any lawyers on here?"

On and on they go . . .

Agatha heads upstairs and curls in bed, turns on Bear's latest episode, and responds to the Moms' nonsense while listening to the revelers decimate "Sweet Caroline."

An hour later, somewhere near midnight, as Kerry Sheridan's guests are drunk-slamming the doors of their Ubers, the most unexpected response of all comes through.

"Agatha, how about lunch at my house next week? DM me."

Melody Whelan.

Agatha sits up, grabs the clicker, and pauses Bear in mid-leap over an icy gulch.

Lunch with Melody Whelan? At her house? *Her house?*

Agatha looks around her bedroom, half expecting a film crew to jump out from behind the curtain and yell, "Agatha Arch, you're on *Candid Camera*!" What is this unexpected move by the Kumbaya Queen? Some strategic effort to get Agatha into her grip? An attempt to brainwash her? Kidnap her?

She has no idea, but she stays up half the night trying to figure it out.

Tap tap tippity-tap.

Chapter Fifteen

Agatha pulls herself up on the lowest branch of the pine, delighted to be hands-free. The minute she snapped that GoPro on her head, she knew it was her most brilliant spy investment of the year. Better than her camera. Better than the neon-pink spray paint. Better even, and she can't believe she's saying this, than her spy pants.

Somewhere in the back of her head she imagines Shrinky-Dink saying, "Agatha Arch, get down! You cannot climb a tree across the street from your estranged husband's new house. You cannot spy on him." But she ignores the imagined voice and pulls herself up branch by branch, choosing the fattest, the sturdiest, just like when she was a kid. It's funny how things come back; it's also funny how her fear of heights takes a back seat to her urge to spy on Dax, to see her sons, to know what their new life in this new house with this new grapefruit-arsed woman is like. Sure, her hands and neck still hurt like hell, and that toe isn't a hundred percent, but what's a little pain in the face of an important mission?

When she's parallel with the second floor of GDOG's house, she turns and straddles a branch. Her crotch hurts way more than when she was ten but she can survive it. "What would Bear do?" she asks herself, then pulls binoculars from her pants and lifts them to her eyes.

As she suspected, Willow Bean is messy. *HOME Magazine* would call it shabby chic, but messy is messy. It is audaciously bright, too. Pink throw pillows. Orange curtains. Turquoise everything.

She guides the binoculars to the second floor. In a front bedroom she sees GDOG sitting cross-legged on a meditation pillow with a single lit candle on a bedside table.

"Meditator," she says and adds it to GDOG's list of sins.

Then she watches Dax—her Dax—walk into the room, drop another pillow onto the floor, and sit down next to GDOG. He puts his hands on his knees and closes his eyes. "Oh, for Big Papi's sake. Him too?"

When she finds the boys' room with the binoculars, a sob rolls up through her middle and bursts out of her mouth. It's a marvelous room at the top of the house. Every kid's dream. The bunk beds are tethered to a treehouse-like structure with rope. There are walkways and cubbyholes. It's like something out of *Swiss Family Robinson*. Dustin is swinging on a swing; Jason is lying on a hammock.

As tears begin to gather in her eyes, she hears, "Hey, lady!"

She ignores the voice, hoping it goes away.

"Hey, lady, what are you doing up there?"

She glances down. A kid maybe seven or eight is looking up at her. He's got his foot on the lowest branch. "Oh, nothing," she calls, "just practicing my climbing skills."

"Grownups don't climb trees."

"This grownup does."

"What's on your head?"

Agatha feels the GoPro. "A crown."

"Uh uh. That's a camera. My cousin wears one when he skateboards."

"No, it's not. It's a crown."

"What are you doing up there with a camera?" The kid pulls himself up to the second branch.

"Nothing. Now go on your way."

"I'm coming up, too."

"No, no, don't do that."

"Why not? This is my favorite tree. I always climb it."

"Well, I'm having some quiet grownup time. Come back later."

"But I want to climb up."

"No!" Agatha twists a pine cone from a branch and tosses it at the boy. It hits his arm.

"Ow!"

"What?" She feigns innocence. It was a super-light papery cone. It couldn't have hurt.

"You threw a pine cone at me."

"I did not."

"You did, and it hurt."

"I didn't. It must have shaken loose from a limb."

The boy starts to climb down. He's crying. "That hurt. I'm telling my mom."

"Come back later," Agatha says. "Sorry about the pine cone."

She looks back at the House of Sin through the binoculars. Dax and GDOG have moved into the bedroom with the boys. The four of them look like a family. A cool family. A cool, meditating family. A cocl, meditating, treehouse-living family.

Moments later she hears the boy's voice again. "That's her, Mom. Up there."

Agatha looks down. She sees the boy and his mother looking up at her through the branches. "Lady? Lady? Excuse me," the mother says. "Did you throw a pine cone at my son?"

Agatha aims the binoculars at the House of Sin again. How in the world is she supposed to get a sense of Dax's new life with all these interruptions? "Oh, for Big Papi's sake," she says. "I'm trying to have some quiet time here. I asked your very sweet son to come back later."

"Lady, you do know you're up a tree, right?"

"Of course I know I'm up a tree. Now go away. Please."

"I am not going away. This is all very suspicious. I'm calling the police. You can't get away with climbing trees, looking into houses with binoculars, wearing GoPros, and hurling pine cones at innocent children."

"I didn't hurl anything. I accidentally dislodged a pine cone and it fell in your son's direction."

Five minutes later a police car pulls up. Lights, no siren, thank goodness.

Agatha climbs down, but rips a hole in the knee of her spy pants while doing so.

Although it seems impossible, the officer is the same one who sat with Agatha on her porch after the shed incident. He looks as young and dumb as ever.

"You again," he says.

"I could say the same thing to you."

"Officer, this is the woman who threw a pine cone at my son. She's been hanging out in this tree with that GoPro on her head. It's unusual and suspicious."

Agatha glances at the boy. "It's a crown." She leans down and touches her knee through the hole in her pants. Damn.

The officer sighs. "Ms. Arch," he says. She's shocked he remembers her name. She doesn't remember him ever using her name. "Exactly what were you doing in the tree?"

Agatha stashes her binoculars in the pocket of her spy pants and pulls the GoPro from her head. "Nothing. Reliving my kidhood. Having some quiet time."

"Ma'am, who lives in that house?" He gestures to the House of Sin with his sunglasses.

Agatha rolls her eyes. "My husband and his . . ." She can't finish the sentence.

The officer nods. "His friend?"

Bile gathers in the back of Agatha's throat and the prickles on her knee remind her she hasn't shaved since the morning of the shed incident. Why shave when your husband is feeling the knees of another woman? "Yes," Agatha says, "his friend."

"That's what I thought."

The boy's mom catches on. She clicks her phone, obviously scrolling through the Moms group on Facebook. "Oh, I know you!" she says. "You're . . ."

The officer steps between them. "No need to determine who's who," he says. "Let's just call this a day. Nothing unlawful is happening here, nothing unlawful is going to happen."

The woman snaps a photo of Agatha, then says, "Are you not going to cite this woman for harassing my son?"

"No, your son is fine." He turns to Agatha. "Ma'am, please stay out of this tree and be more careful about dislodging pine cones in the future."

Agatha nods. "I promise."

The woman stomps off, dragging her son behind her. "I'll see you on the Moms," she spits back.

Agatha sighs. "I'm sure you will."

"I'm serious about staying out of this tree," the officer says when the woman is out of earshot.

"I know. I'll steer clear of it." Agatha turns to walk away.

"By the way," he calls, "I've been reading that book you talked about."

Agatha turns to face him. "Seriously? *Their Eyes Were Watching God*?" She is incredulous. No one ever does what she tells them to do.

"The very one."

"And?"

"I'm only a third of the way into it, but it's a pretty good book."

"Told you," she says. "Learn anything yet?"

"I'll let you know when I'm done."

The officer gets back into his car.

"Hey," Agatha says before he closes the door. "How about Janie?"

He laughs. "I see the comparison."

* * *

Her agent's next email arrives with hot flames licking its heels. "Agatha, so much silence. You haven't become the victim of your own murder mystery, have you?"

Agatha sends back a GIF of a girl being bludgeoned to death on a mountaintop, blood spurting everywhere.

* * *

"Don't give in to your fears. If you do, you won't be able to talk to your heart." Paul Coelho, *The Alchemist*

Agatha stares at the quote on the back of the passenger seat. She sniffs back tears, then catches the Uber driver looking at her in the rearview mirror.

"You okay?" he says.

She nods. Lying to an Uber driver is easy.

She stares at the quote. When was the last time she was able to talk to her heart? She looks down. Her neck is still a little stiff, so really she can only see her boobs. Close enough.

"Hello, heart," she whispers.

What does one say to one's heart?

"Heart, are you in there?"

No response.

"Hello, heart? Heart?"

Nothing.

The Uber driver turns. "Excuse me? Did you say something?"

Agatha shakes her head. "I have to get out of your car."

"What? Now?"

"Yes. Please stop."

"Right now?"

"Yes!" Agatha puts her hand on the door handle.

"But we're only halfway to your destination."

"Please stop the car." Agatha pulls the handle.

The driver swerves out of traffic and pulls to the side of the road.

Agatha taps her Uber app. "I've paid. And I'll give you a solid recommendation."

"Ma'am, it's not that. Are you sure you're okay? It's a busy road. It's starting to get dark."

Agatha steps out of the car. "I'm fine." She closes the door and leans against the stop sign. Thank god for stop signs.

It's dusk. Agatha needs to get to the service station before it closes to pick up her car, but the quote keeps rattling around in her brain like a dime in a clothes dryer: "Don't give in to your fears. If you do, you won't be able to talk to your heart."

Handfuls of cars pass. Some stop at the stop sign. Some roll right through. It's this kind of cavalier nonsense that makes the world so hard to trust. The authorities say you must stop here. They put up a big red sign so you know. But not everyone listens. Not everyone adheres to the rules.

Five out of ten cars eschew the stop sign. A man eats people with fava beans. A husband has sex with a dog walker in a shed. The Interloper hunkers down at Apple54. Just how far can the world go?

Agatha hears a beep, then a familiar voice. "Agatha? Agatha Arch? What are you doing out here? It's almost dark."

Agatha leans down and peers into the car. Of course. It's the Kumbaya Queen. Who else would the universe send? "Melody?"

"Yes, it's me."

"Oh, hi."

"Are you okay out here? Where are you going?"

Agatha looks around. Is she okay?

"I was on my way to get my car, at the station, in an Uber. I had to get out. It's been too long since I talked to my heart. I got out."

There's so much of that in life. The getting in and getting out.

Agatha's words make no sense to an outsider looking in, but Melody doesn't address any of that. She just says, "Get in, Agatha. I'll take you to the station."

Once again, getting in.

Agatha looks around. It's at least another mile to the station. It's close to pure dark now, and her fears are kicking in. "Okay," she says.

At the station, she thanks Melody.

"What was wrong with your car?" Melody asks.

"Broken windows."

"Rock?"

"Hammer."

Melody squinches up her face. "Huh?"

Agatha thinks about how much her recent life is about tools that start with H. Hatchet. Hammer. She tries to think of others. Hacksaw. Hackle. "Just an accident," she says and climbs out of the car. "Thank you for the lift."

"Any time. And Agatha?"

Agatha leans down and looks at Melody.

"Have you decided about lunch?"

Agatha slams the door and runs into the station.

* * *

Over the next few days, she frets and broods over Melody's unexpected invitation to lunch because, really, when was the last time someone asked her to anywhere, wrote down the words "how about doing this with me," other than, of course, Kerry Sheridan and the invitation to her ridiculous autumn-in-New-England garden party? And while Agatha feels a trill of joy somewhere down so deep she almost doesn't recognize it, it's smothered by a dense, lardy sack of fear, so gasping for air and not knowing how to respond, she does what any broken-hearted, somewhat maniacal person does when mysteriously invited to a meal in the enemy's lair: She buys a new pair of spy pants and adds 164 North Circle Street to her spy route. The pants, identical to the first, which she tore climbing the tree and accidentally/on purpose lobbing the pine cone at the boy, are a little bit baggier in the arse and legs because eating since the shed incident seems harder than usual and a few pounds or more have slipped away. Not so much that she needs a smaller size, not yet, but definitely enough to require a belt. And because she anticipates a few more rips and tears on her mission, she orders not one, but ten replacement pairs, five her current size and five one size smaller.

Though she strives for Bear's level of stealth—shifting into neutral and drifting to her parking spot outside Melody's Colonial, turning off her headlights three houses before, pretending to hit the button for her secret invisibility cloak, and so on—she knows she's failed on the third night when Melody appears at Coop's window with her iPhone flashlight shining brightly, then leans close and whispers, "Agatha? Agatha Arch? Is that you?"

"Crap," Agatha says.

"Agatha, what are you doing out here?"

"Is this your house, Melody?"

"Yes, it is. You know that."

"Oh, I'm sorry to have disturbed you. I was having trouble with my brakes as I was going home. I had to pull over."

"You just happened to pull over on *my* cul de sac? In front of *my* house? That seems rather unlikely. My house isn't anywhere near your house."

"No, no. I was heading home on Wayton." Agatha points back at the main feeder road. "And my brakes felt funny so I pulled off here." She looks around wild-eyed, feigning bewilderment.

Melody sighs.

"I don't think I've ever been on this street except to drop off that bag for the Interloper," Agatha says.

"That's odd," Melody says. "I'm pretty sure I saw your car here last night. And the night before that."

"Melody, are you spying on me?" Agatha asks, voice rich with shock.

Oh, the irony, the performance.

"No," Melody says. "I wasn't spying. I was simply looking to see who was shining a giant beam of light in my living room window."

Agatha shoves the spotlight from the passenger seat to the floor. It's the size of a toolbox. The only indispensable spy tool that doesn't fit neatly in her pants. "Someone has been shining a beam of light into your house? Are you sure? Who would do such a thing?"

This masquerade might have worked in Agatha's favor had she been driving an Escalade. Melody would have been too short to peer into the vehicle to see the evidence. Even standing on tippy-toe she wouldn't have been able to see a thing. But Mini Coopers are low to the ground, so low even GDOG's Chihuahua could have peered in.

"What's that?" Melody says, shining her light on Agatha's spotter.

"Nothing."

"Really, Agatha? Nothing?"

Agatha tosses a sweatshirt over the spotter. She and Dax had bought it years before when they'd driven around New Mexico looking for mountain lions. That's the kind of young lovers they'd been. Reckless and brave. When they'd finally found a lion feeding on an elk, it looked up at them all bloody and wild-eyed, and they were thrilled. Well, Dax was thrilled. Agatha was terrified but putting on an "I'm thrilled" front. Young love and all. Now that Dax is shacked up with Miss Please-Don't-Kill-That-Mosquito-Even-Though-Its-Bite-Will-Give-You-Dengue-Fever, he has no use for such a light. "I'll leave this for you," he'd told her. And thank goodness he had.

Agatha starts her car, drifts forward a few inches, and taps her brakes. "Oh, look at that," she says. "The brakes feel much better now. They must have gotten too hot."

"Too hot?" Melody says.

Agatha nods. "It's a thing with Mini Coopers. It will be fine."

Melody moves her light from the spotter to Agatha's face. "Are you sure, Agatha?" she says. "I wouldn't want you to drive an unsafe vehicle. I could drive you home. Or you could spend the night here."

Agatha's eyes pop wide. Spend the night at Melody's house? Good lord, no. She shoves her foot onto the brake and taps again. The car jitters and jolts. "Oh, no, all seems just fine now. False alarm. Thanks for checking on me but I need to get home to my . . ." She almost says *boys*, but the word catches in her throat. Her boys aren't at home. It's a "boys with Dax" night. She doesn't need to get home to them. She doesn't need to get home to anyone. Aside from Susan Sontag lying in wait under the porch and the woodpecker continuing his assault on Agatha's sanity, there is no one there. Unable to say another word without sobbing, Agatha hits the gas. Melody's flashlight shines like a beacon in the rearview mirror.

* * *

During the next few days, Melody mentions the Interloper in every post she writes on Facebook and insists on calling her Lucy. Not "the Interloper." Not "the beggar." Not even "the young woman at Apple54." Just Lucy. "That's her name," she explains. "Let's all use her name."

Somewhere in the middle of the barrage of Lucy posts, just after Agatha mocks her for this blind support of the Interloper, Melody reissues her invitation, right there on FB, publicly, for all the Moms to see: "Agatha, please come to my house for lunch sometime soon. You know how to find it." Then she adds a winking emoji, calling attention to their private joke.

Lunch with Melody Whelan at the Colonial Kumbaya house?

Um, no, thank you very much.

* * *

"You did what?" Shrinky-Dink says. "Why in the world would you climb a tree, spy on your estranged husband with binoculars, and film him with a GoPro?"

"Stop making it sound so dramatic."

"It is dramatic, Agatha. And it's serious."

"Stop. It's not a big deal."

"It is a big deal. You need to donate that GoPro to a local school immediately."

"No way," Agatha says. "I have to see my boys."

"You have your boys four out of seven days every week."

"I have Dustin and Jason. I don't have Dax. I don't have all three of them together. They have been my boys for years, and I believed they'd be my boys forever. How is a woman expected to go from three to two without even a say in the matter? Without even being asked?"

Shrinky-Dink visibly softens. "I see," she says. "This isn't about custody, is it?"

Agatha sighs. "Not at all. It's about the fact that my life has changed without me even being involved in the decision to change it."

"You do have a say in deciding how things move from here," Shrinky-Dink says.

"But I had no say in how we got here. And that fact will never change."

Chapter Sixteen

Agatha lies in bed trying to assure herself that the scritchy-scratchy noise over by the stuffed chair is not a wee rodent scrounging for nuggets of food and plotting her demise but just a branch on one of the oaks grazing the window in the breeze. If that's true, she reasons, perhaps the oak trees need a trim. They're massive things that drop more leaves in the fall than is humanly possible to collect into bags, therefore a major pain in the ass that requires a hired team, but not until you stand in their cool shadows on a hot day in midsummer do you realize their power and worth. There are many such trees in Wallingford. Old, thick-trunked behemoths that tower over yards, arch across roads, and frequently crash to the ground during nor'easters and similar storms, crushing roofs, dragging down power lines, and leaving sections of Wallingford in the dark for days on end. It's the charm and tragedy of old wood. As Agatha makes a note in her phone to call TreeLife about a checkup, good old Ava Newton posts a photo of the rangy quadruped that has been loitering in her yard for the past thirty minutes and asks: "Ladies, is this a fox or a coyote?"

Agatha bolts into an upright position. Good lord, here we go again. No matter how many times these Moms have studied pictures of these two very distinct animals, no matter how many times they've hashed out the characteristics of each, they are still incapable of distinguishing one from the other.

Rachel Runk:	"Ava, that could be a wolf. They've been working their way east again."
Ava Newton:	"A wolf?"

With that, panic permeates the page.

Priya Devi:	"Definitely a coyote. They're killers. Keep little Chloe and your pets inside until help arrives."
Lara Lynch:	"Fisher cat, for sure. If it sounds like a screaming woman being murdered, that's it."

Agatha posts a photo of Janet Leigh doing her famous shower scream in *Psycho*.

Grainne O'Neill:	"Wolf."
Rachel Runk:	"Right, Grainne? Definitely a wolf."
Holly McCarthy:	"Neighbor's dog? Too small to be coyote or fox."
Lin Zheng:	"Groundhog."

There's always one.

Olivia Charles:	"Damn coyotes."
Emily Patterson:	"Is it growling?"
Isabelle Fish:	"Is it howling? Foxes howl."

Agatha posts a link to an article about why coyotes howl.

Quynh Nguyen:	"Fox."
Anne Pape:	"Coyote."

Agatha posts a photo of a lemon. "Ladies, is this a lemon or a lime?"

Jane Poston:	"Oh, Agatha."
Rae Stein:	"I vote fox."
Cherry Stenson:	"Is it rabid? Is it frothing at the mouth?"
Jane Poston:	"OMG, Ava, have you seen *Cujo*?"
Erin Abel:	"Ava, call animal control right now. Officer Ed will be there pronto."

Agatha leans back into her pillow and lifts her thumbs off her phone. Who in New England doesn't know what a fox looks like? Haven't these women ever read *Peter Rabbit*?

Reddish. Brownish. Furry. Knee high. With a classic bushy tail.

But then Agatha thinks about GDOG, whom she'd mistaken as an innocent dog walker. Even with all the sashaying past with pups, she hadn't pegged her for a husband-stealing hussy. Yet here they were.

She's quiet for a moment, hesitant to jump back into the controversy knowing damn well there's no messing with the Moms once Officer Ed enters the conversation. Their absurdity is funny until it's not. She'd learned this the hard way years before when one of the Moms posted that she'd spotted a turkey strutting around a busy intersection. Like a lot of New England towns, Wallingford is one of those rural/not rural places in which it's common to see coyotes, foxes, deer, skunks, groundhogs, raccoons, fisher cats, and, yes, turkeys. How this woman hadn't known that many *Meleagris gallopavo* roam the land is beyond comprehension. Unless she'd just moved to town from Laos (hadn't) or was blind (wasn't), it would seem impossible for her not to know this fact. But she hadn't, and when she spotted the dislocated tom cocking about near the hardware store, she'd called Officer Ed in a panic and was stunned to learn that he wouldn't do anything about it. What exactly she'd wanted him to do was unclear—usually you just watch and admire them, or mock them, or shoo them with a beep of the horn if they're in the road—but the Moms jumped in enthusiastically, most showing support by explaining the wildlife of Wallingford and assuring her the turkey was not a dangerous outlier. It was all going along well, with women telling stories about how they, too, had seen the turkey, where they'd seen it, estimating how long it had been around, and hypothesizing about why it was on its own. One woman even had an emotional epiphany when she opened up about being attacked by a turkey as a kid. Another shared that a group of turkeys was called a rafter. Moms' camaraderie at its best.

But then, in a very preachy, pokey tone, Jane Poston slung the question that had been quietly percolating in every Mom's mind: "What exactly do you want Officer Ed to do with the turkey?" Saying without saying that the Mom wanted him to remove it. Or worse yet, kill it.

But wait.

Kill it?

Kill an animal?

Kill an *animal*?

Oh, no.

Oh, no, no, no, no, no, no, no, no, no.

There will be no killing of any animal in this politically correct town. Not even that rabid coyote lumbering about with blood and slobber frothing at its jawline and a two-year-old's leg hanging out of its mouth.

So with Poston's question on the table, the gloves came off, with so-and-so accusing so-and-so of not understanding anything about turkeys. Then so-and-so accusing so-and-so of thinking she was the kind of person who didn't understand turkeys. And within an hour, it had deteriorated into a pathetic slinging of elementary school nonsense.

Abby Smith: "I do so understand turkeys!"
Tiana Samuels: "You do not!"
Abby Smith: "I understand turkeys way better than you!"
Tiana Samuels: "Do not!"
Abby Smith: "Do, too!"
Tiana Samuels: "Nuh uh!"
Abby Smith: "Uh huh!"

Three hours after the final "Uh huh," the poor, dislocated tom was accidentally squashed by a passing car.

Aaaaaaahhhhhh!

The Mom who witnessed the slaughter posted a photo of the great beast lying dead in the triangle of grass. Stick-legs akimbo; feathers galore.

* * *

Tap tap tippity-tap.

* * *

Just four weeks have passed since the shed incident, or maybe four weeks and a few days. Has it been longer? Five weeks? Six? Agatha is losing track, and the grass now tickles her calf. She turns in a circle with her arms outstretched, like a sundial, although faster, much faster, because who could ever turn as slowly as a sundial?

In the moonlight, she watches Susan Sontag wade through the grass, Jerry Garcia a few steps behind, a loyal disciple, his sexy shock of white fur blowing back in the breeze. It's no wonder Susan hangs out with him.

In the corner of the yard, near the street, Agatha sees a shadow move, a tall, leggy shadow that could be a fox or coyote, but a familiar limp, the backwardish bends in the shadow creature's knees, the drag in its gait, all make Agatha lean forward and squint. "Balderdash?" she whispers. The creature sidles into the shadows of the forsythia. The leaves shake, then still.

"Balderdash? Is that you?"

She inches toward the bush, pauses briefly to reflect on the fact that it is she, the spurned, the rejected, the tossed-away, who is likely spotting the dog that her husband's lover walks and boards and loves, her husband's hussy, minx, coquette. Agatha Arch, the woman in the world trying hardest to avoid anything canine, anything related to dogs, leashes, fur, soapy tin tubs, biscuits, peanut butter in toys, soft beds, barks, mournful howls, because right now, in this moment, any reference, even the slightest, to dog-related details makes her hair stand on end. But there he is, she's sure now. Balderdash. Not more than thirty yards away. Her husband's lover's keep.

"Balderdash," she calls.

Susan Sontag stops a few yards from Agatha, almost but not quite to the forsythia, turns her behind to Agatha, raises her tail, and sprays. Agatha drops to her knees, the stench filling her face. Again.

* * *

"You again? I knew it."

Agatha smiles. "Me again."

"Sure you don't want the bottle of skunk wash this time?" The boy looks so earnest.

"Nope, I'm sticking with the tomato juice. All fifty cans."

The boy grins and hands another can through the window. "I'll let my manager know to order more. Just in case."

* * *

"Tell me three ways you are different from any other mom in that group," Shrinky-Dink says. She's dubious. As usual. Agatha wonders if she was born this way or if she was seasoned into it.

Agatha takes a deep breath. "Fine. Here goes. One, most Moms do not skulk around other people's homes. Two, most Moms do not skulk around other people's homes wearing spy pants packed with spy equipment. Three, if a Mom does skulk around other people's homes wearing spy pants packed with spy equipment, I'll bet my last dollar she chooses to carry the slim, sleek Leatherman Juice C2 as her tool of choice, not the Super Tool 300 EOD, like me." Agatha yanks open the Velcro on a pocket of her pants, whips out her Super Tool, and displays it on the palm of her hand.

Shrinky-Dink pulls back with that "I don't know what you're talking about" look on her face, which, in Agatha's opinion, she gets way too often. Scrunched-up lips. Squinty eyes. Head cocked like a dog that hears the faraway call of the wild.

"This baby right here," Agatha says, tapping the Super Tool, "is designed for Explosive Ordnance Disposal technicians. Get it? EOD. Super Tool 300 EOD. For folks who defuse explosive devices. This right here is one serious fothermucking tool." She strokes the handle. "As they say at Leatherman, 'An everyday carry tool, with some not-so-everyday features.'"

Shrinky-Dink laughs.

Agatha stares. "I do not know what is so funny."

"And I do not know why in the world *you* would need to carry a tool designed for people who defuse explosives."

"I'm prepared."

"For what?"

"Anything. Everything. One commenter on the Leatherman Super Tool 300 EOD website is a jungle survivalist. A jungle survivalist! He says that the punch and awl tools saved his life."

"Saved his life?"

"Saved his life."

"How?"

"He was dying of thirst in a jungle. There were coconuts everywhere but he couldn't get to the coconut milk until he dehusked the coconut with the awl and poked a hole through the shell with the punch. Saved his life."

Shrinky-Dink blinks. "He was in the jungle?"

"Yes."

"In Wallingford?"

"No, we don't have a . . ." Agatha eyes Shrinky-Dink. "Oh, be quiet."

"Listen, Agatha, if you need to carry the Super Tool 300 EOD, fine, but let's not pretend that you are in the kind of bind that guy was in."

"Not yet. But when I am, when the Interloper decides to make her move, I'll be prepared."

"You keep saying that. 'I'll be prepared.' Every new tool or gadget makes you feel more prepared for danger."

"Exactly."

"But then that feeling of safety and protection wears off and you're off in search of the next tool. The next fix."

"You're comparing me to a drug addict?"

"In a way, yes."

"Just because I'm making sure I'm prepared?"

"Yes, because no matter what you do, you can't be prepared. Not in the way you're trying to be. These things will not keep you safe. They will not shield you from potential harm. They will not protect you."

"They will."

"They won't. Life will still happen. If something dark and dangerous is coming, owning and carrying a particular tool is not going to stop it."

Agatha sighs, folds the tools into place, and tucks the Leatherman Super Tool 300 EOD back into its pocket.

"How are you feeling now?" Shrinky-Dink asks. Her voice is soft again.

Agatha stands and reaches into one of the deep pockets on her hip. Something jingles.

Shrinky-Dink sits up straight with her "Oh boy, what's next?" look on her face, a look she wears almost as often as her "I don't know what you're talking about" look. Eyebrows up. Eyes wide. Lips pursed to one side. Or her "I know exactly what you're talking about, but, oh my god, you're out of your tree." Eyes cast to the ceiling.

Agatha dives into another pocket and pulls out a ball of purple twine the size of a clementine. "You want to know how I'm feeling now?" she says. "How I'm feeling right now?"

Shrinky-Dink nods.

Agatha turns the ball of twine in her hand until she locates the end of the thread. She pinches it between thumb and pointer, then leans down and tucks it under the leg of the table. With the twine firmly rooted, she begins to unfurl the ball. On the floor, she makes large circles and figure 8s. She loops the twine around chair legs and Shrinky-Dink's ottoman. The office is small and requires her to make curlicue after curlicue. As she does, she remembers doing a similar thing in the woods, looping and twirling and whirling long-stemmed wildflowers into some kind of fanciful creation. She thinks, "Did this happen this morning?" But no, no, it was eons ago when she was a kid, when the looping and twirling and whirling was fun and freeing. It was warm then, too, she remembers. It is cold outside now. Another autumnal cold snap in New England. And this looping and twirling and whirling is different. Much different. Sad and confining.

Shrinky-Dink watches silently. She lifts her feet when Agatha needs to reach under them, and Agatha accepts this as encouragement. She doesn't stop until she is holding the tail end of the twine.

After six minutes, she spreads her arms and looks up. "Ta-da! My life."

"And how do you feel now?" Shrinky-Dink asks.

Agatha tucks the tail of the twine under Shrinky-Dink's shoe, then holds out her hands, palms up, and shakes them. "Unfurled."

Chapter Seventeen

Crap always happens when you try to do too many things at the same time, as in the case of Agatha tripping on the stairs when she reads the text that her agent sends, because her agent never texts, has never texted, could not have been presumed to ever make such a move, and it isn't just a "hey" text or a "how r u?" text. This text is a piece of art, a stuttering of questions marks, a single purple heart, and a pencil. A line of independently insignificant emojis that strung together mean something, mean everything, especially in the moment when Agatha looks up from the floor where she's smashed to after tripping on the stair and sees Bear, her bobblehead Bear, her beloved, has been beheaded by their fall. The alliteration of the accident doesn't escape her, despite the buzz and shock in her own noggin. She's still a writer through and through, and she lets the words run off her tongue: beloved bobblehead Bear beheaded. If only she'd tucked him into her spy pants before heading down the stairs. If only she hadn't been gripping him in her hand. "Life is full of if-onlys," she thinks. She stares at his body lying east of the chair leg in the kitchen, or maybe west, far off, that's for sure, and, although it takes a moment to spot it, discovers his head lying not far from hers, bobbleneck up.

That's what she gets for attempting, once more, to climb the back staircase to the red door that leads into the office that houses the desk that Dax built. That's what you get, she tells herself. But also the text, at least there's that. If only she had waited to read it. With her outstretched arm, she takes a screenshot, can't lose that text, then begins to assess her injuries. A sharp pain in one knee, a sure bruise on both elbows, but, stretching out this limb and that limb, bending her neck this way and that way, nothing broken, except Bear, beloved Bear.

With one hand, she reaches out and grasps his decapitated head. With the other, she types a reply: a long line of hearts, kissy faces, one margarita glass, three typewriters, one dagger. The last a promise of the thriller to come.

Her phone buzzes and she opens the Moms group to find, first, that the Moms are raging about Crystal MacLeish's audacious post about how using a mensural cup has brought unexpected joy and freedom to her menses life, and, second, that Balderdash has likely been spotted in a park not far from Gem Lily's house on Rodderdale Street. This time there's a photo of a shadow near a brick wall. A shadow so dark and abstract it could be Balderdash, maybe, or a duffel bag in a wagon or, perhaps, three chickens on the run from a fox. But no matter, the chase is on and Willow Bean reports that she's dragging a corgi and two mutts behind her on leash as she races to the spot. A hundred Moms, maybe more, are circling the park trying to block all exits from the shadow that may or may not be the missing pooch.

Agatha saves the mensural cup post in her "The 12 Days of the Wallingford Moms" folder, then shimmies on her belly across the kitchen floor, screeching *ouch, ooh, ugh, ouch* every time a bruised part bumps or bangs. She sets down her phone and picks up Bear's lower extremities. She thumbs the bite marks on his foot, rolls onto her back, lifts her arms, and tries to fit his body back onto his head. She shoves it, wiggles it, twists it, but, in the end, fails. The neck is irreparably, forevery broken. Rolling slightly onto one side, she reaches into a pocket of her spy pants, pulls out a roll of duct tape, rips a piece to fit, then wraps it properly around his neck until his head is firmly in place. He no longer bobbles, but at least he is whole.

* * *

"How's GDOG?" Agatha says when Dax stops by to suggest moving forward with a divorce, as if this is something Agatha would even allow through the door, let alone into her brain or heart. She goes on the defensive, and Dax acts as if this is something he didn't expect, couldn't fathom, and she wonders if this dog walker, this Willow Bean, this firm-butted bombshell, has somehow devoured his brain, his memories, his way-he-used-to-be-ness. She's never heard of such a phenomenon, a devouring of a man's way-he-used-to-be-ness, even in relationships that have gone awry, but maybe she hasn't paid close enough attention, for Dax is definitely not the way he used to be.

"GDOG, Agatha?" he says. "Seriously?"

"Seriously, Dax. Grande Dame of Grapefruits. GDOG, GDOG, GDOG."

"C'mon, Agatha. Please call her Willow," he says. "For the boys' sake."

"I do call her Willow when talking to the boys. For their sake. I am the only one of us doing anything for their sake. I call her whatever the hell I want when talking to you. For my sake."

"What am I supposed to say to that, Agatha?" he says. "My therapist tells me you need to let off steam and that I should allow it."

"Your therapist? When did you get a therapist?"

"Months ago," he says. "When my feelings for Willow started to grow."

"And this therapist supports your recent behavior? Your romp in the shed while the boys and I were in the house?"

"I admit he was concerned and upset that things with Willow came to light in this way."

"Came to light in this way? That's a merry way of describing the fact that you screwed this woman in our shed while the boys and I were eating lunch, while the boys were watching SpongeBob. SpongeBob, for fuck's sake."

"You know what I mean."

"And is this therapist at all concerned, or encouraging you to be concerned, about how the incident in the shed is affecting your wife and your children?"

"He is. And he's suggested the boys may need a little therapy themselves once things calm down a bit."

"Ya think?"

Dax blows out a loud breath.

"And you? What about you?" Agatha asks. "Are you at all concerned?"

Dax looks at his hands. "I am, of course I am, but I am equally concerned that you are being cruel, intentionally cruel. Even so, I am trying to take the high road."

Agatha closes her eyes. Clearly, irony is invisible to this new Dax, now that the way-he-used-to-be-ness has disappeared. This new Dax who cheated on his imperfect and complex, but still pretty damn amazing wife and dismantled his beautiful family has the gall to say *she* is being cruel, intentionally or otherwise. She wonders what he'll think about on his deathbed and kind of, but not really, but, yes, kind of, wishes that were something to which they'd know the answer sooner rather than later.

"Dax," she says, squeezing the loaf of raisin bread on the cutting board so hard raisins pop from each end. "From where you sit, you can't even see the high road."

Despite the morning sunshine, the house is still dark. "Jesus, Agatha, open the blinds," he says. He walks across the kitchen and pulls the cord.

When light fills the room, she sees he is wearing a hot-pink shirt with a patchwork pocket on the breast. "Nice shirt, Gandhi," she says. "Whatever you're here for, get on with it."

He sits across from her, rests his hairy, lumpy forearms on the table, and leans close. She can tell he is working hard to speak in a conciliatory tone but instead sounds so condescending she has to resist the urge to stuff the loaf of raisin bread up his right nostril.

"Listen, let me help you out," she says. "Unless you're here to profess your love for me, declare temporary insanity, and denounce your dalliance with that marriage-destroying monster, I've got nothing to say to you." Agatha is tired. The house is disturbingly quiet. And it is heartbreaking to have Dax at the table without also hearing the boys' pounding down the stairs to breakfast, banging off the walls and hollering about sticks and forts and the enemy they will conquer.

"Agatha, you know that's not why I'm here."

"Then get out."

"Agatha, listen."

She meets his eyes and gives him a withering look, one that makes it clear they are not going to be having the rational discussion about divorce proceedings he'd proposed via text the day before. "You get out," she says. "Get out of this house." Each word she speaks is quieter and more clipped than the one before it. "And do not come back here again unless you've got the boys and suitcases in the car."

She can tell that this is the first time Dax is afraid of her. She's seen him annoyed, pissed, flabbergasted, and frustrated, but until right this very moment she's never seen him afraid. There's a strange comfort in that, one she wouldn't have felt a few weeks before.

He stands, keeping the table between them, and backs his way to the door. She knows he wants to tell her that his lawyer will be in touch with hers, wants to toss out that classic line they'd heard in so many movies, but for once he keeps his mouth shut. When the door clicks behind him, Agatha winds up and hurls her coffee mug at the refrigerator. When the pieces settle, she is shocked at how completely the thing has shattered—a gazillion brilliant shards glitter in the blast of sunlight shooting through the now-open blinds. "That's your heart, Agatha Arch," she says. "Your fothermucking heart."

She stomp-storms to the junk drawer, yanks the Dax reflection doll from the tangled jumble of seashells, plastic sunglasses, kite string, rubber bands, pens, and whatnot, then puts him on the cutting board and glares at him. So many options, but still, the boys. She moves the bread knife to the sink, out of reach, the best place for it, then picks up the loaf of raisin bread and plops it on top of him. "Ha," she says, "see how that feels." But as she holds it down, she wonders, briefly, what happens when someone is no longer able to be the way they used to be. Maybe Dax could no longer be the Dax she knew and loved. Maybe this because of GDOG or maybe this not because of GDOG. Maybe this because of something deep inside that other people can't see. Even so, she presses harder until Dax is completely enveloped in the raisin bread. He hates raisin bread.

She is barely breathing when there is another knock. She wipes sweat from her forehead, steps over the shards, and opens the door. A man in painter's whites smiles and says, "Agatha Arch? I'm Isai Corona. The house painter." His eyes flicker from Agatha's face to the shattered mug and back. "Oh, I'm sorry," he says. "Accident?"

"Not really," Agatha says.

Just as the Moms promised, Isai Corona is handsome. Very handsome. Lots of thick, curly hair. Not a hint of jelly-belly. Muscular forearms. And when he turns to walk down the steps, Agatha sees that their comments about his tush are spot on.

"I've got a problem with peeling," Agatha says, leading him outside to the corner of the house, "and I want the house painted as soon as possible."

Isai Corona is thorough. He looks at the peeling bit, then circles the house. "Just a touch up then," he says. "The bulk of the house looks good."

Agatha wags her head back and forth. "No, no, no. I would like you to paint the whole house."

"The whole house?" he says. "But your whole house doesn't need to be painted. You don't need to waste your money. The whole house is a big, expensive job. Fifteen thousand dollars."

"Money is not an issue," she says. "Please paint the house. Can you start next week?"

Isai Corona eyes Agatha in the same way one might eye a hungry velociraptor squawking on a nearby rooftop. "I'll have to juggle a few things, and I'll need a check right away for the first third," he says. "Then a check for the second third after we've sanded, and another for the final third when the job is done."

"I'll give you a check for the whole thing right now."

Isai raises his eyebrows, but nods. She can see him reciting in his head, "The customer is always right. The customer is always right." He seems like that kind of upstanding guy. "See you in a week or so," he says. Before getting into his truck, he pats both oak trees by the driveway. "These are impressive," he says.

Agatha nods, then texts Dax. "Getting the house painted. Pulled $15,000 from savings this morning. Happy weekend to you and GDOG."

While Isai had come highly recommended by many of the Moms, a handful had criticized his work, saying he didn't sand thoroughly enough and took long coffee breaks, but Agatha knew how to read between the lines. She knew they were really saying they didn't like the fact that his skin was not white. It is dark. Dark dark. Much darker than some Wallingford women are comfortable with. He's from the Dominican Republic and has a strong accent some say makes it tough to understand his words. But that's just made-up crap from a gaggle of women who prefer their houses painted by white men. If you listen to his words the same way you listen to the words of a white painter, you hear him just fine.

Race is a tricky thing in Wallingford. Indians, the non-native kind, are A-okay to most Moms. Many have good-paying jobs, money to spend, and nice homes. Asians, the whole lump of them despite country of origin, are on the "accepted as long as they stick to the library, orchestras, and Chinese restaurants" list. But a painter with dark skin and an accent from the DR? That is too much for some of the Moms. For them, the DR is good for one thing and one thing only: high-end resorts in Punta Cana.

Agatha doesn't care one way or another about Isai Corona's skin color. Or his tush. She just needs a quick and easy way to gouge her estranged husband.

Revenge is sweet.

And bitter.

* * *

"What do you think?" Agatha asks the TreeLife guy.

The man scratches his beard and circles the oaks. He's one of the many bearded millennials in the world today, so bearded that Agatha wonders if he knows anything about trees at all or if he has just been hired to play the part of Paul Bunyan.

"There are no visible signs of disease." He pats the trunks of each oak. "Should be fine with just a trim. I'll come back with the truck and my crew next week."

Agatha nods. An hour later she drives to the grocery store, parks, and climbs onto Coop's hood. Her eyes flicker between the sky and the Interloper. It's a clear, crisp night, and the stars are as bright as they can be next to a well-lit parking lot. When the Interloper looks up, Agatha thinks about that thing Oscar Wilde once said—"Two men look out a window. One sees mud, the other sees the stars." The same must hold true for two women, but, Agatha wonders, which am I?

Chapter Eighteen

Dax:	Agatha, I just saw the payment to the painter. It's outrageous. We have to talk about this.
Agatha:	Tra la la
Dax:	Agatha, you can't continue to spend money this way.
Agatha:	Just return the turquoise silk muumuu-maxi you bought for GDOG to replace the one lost during the shed incident. That should cover the painter's fee.
Dax:	What I buy for Willow is my business. It has nothing to do with painting the house. Nothing to do with you.
Agatha:	Tra la la

Agatha thinks about Hubert Selby's Tra La La in *Last Exit to Brooklyn*. She lives a brutal life but offers up some gems in the quiet spaces. "Getting laid is getting laid," says Tra La La.

Maybe, Agatha thinks, but making love is making love. She misses that.

* * *

That night she reads an article about a man in New Hampshire who released his coterie of wild animals into the woods behind his house just before taking his own life. A lion. A grizzly bear. One strange anteater. A leopard. Seven giraffes. Three gorillas. Two tigers. Three hippopotami. Three flamingoes. One kangaroo. All cages were empty when the authorities arrived. Nothing left but piles of dried-up dung.

It is illegal to own such animals in this small town, but the man had gotten away with it for years. That's New Hampshire for you. Live free or die.

Days after the man's death, the police assure the public they've tracked, caught, and killed each of the animals. "The lion got as far as the Maine coastline," a sergeant says. "We intercepted and extinguished him there."

But who can know for sure if the police are telling the truth? Perhaps the trackers lost the lion's scent at the Massachusetts border and gave up. Perhaps one of the two tigers slipped into the Piscataqua River and swam south. The White Mountains are dense with stone, and Mount Washington is known for its inhospitable climate, but once you get a whiff, freedom is powerful stuff.

Agatha imagines the lion sleeping next to the remains of the shed. Good god. As if life hasn't been hard enough. Now this to worry about.

She wonders if perhaps the man had had more animals than outsiders had known. Has anyone considered that? A man with the balls to build a private zoo might not have been a reliable record keeper. Maybe there was a fourth gorilla. Or a lioness. A snow leopard. Maybe a grizzly cub snuck away unnoticed while the officers were shooting at its mother. Maybe that cub is slowly making its way to Wallingford, gorging on turtles and berries. Growing enormous along the way. Sharpening its claws on aspen trees.

There are so many maybes in the world. How does anyone live with them all?

Agatha saves the article in her Hard Truths file and turns off the light.

* * *

When she brings all this up in her session, Shrinky-Dink plunks it right next to the fear that caused Agatha to buy three window-smashing hammers for Coop. "One of these animals devouring me in Wallingford is as likely as me plunging my car into a body of water and not being able to escape," Shrinky-Dink says. "I can't waste time worrying about it."

Agatha is always surprised when Shrinky-Dink so honestly shares her own feelings about something. That seems out of the realm of a therapist's responsibilities.

"Shouldn't you keep judgmental opinions to yourself?" she says. "Isn't that part of your job?" She shakes her head and thinks about the Interloper. Shrinky-Dink doesn't worry about that danger either.

"If we set aside the possibility of a lion lying in wait at the remains of your shed," Shrinky-Dink says, "what is it that really upsets you about this situation?"

Agatha sighs. Saying it out loud will be excruciating. Holding it in even more so. "How lonely the man must have been to gather this gaggle of wild animals. To want to care for and be cared for. How alone the man must have felt to take his own life. How even his desperate gathering of living things failed to satiate him."

Shrinky-Dink nods, but doesn't speak. The two sit with that between them, silently thrashing the hell out of it.

A streak of tigers, Agatha thinks.

A sloth of bears.

A candle of anteaters.

A whoop of gorillas.

A leap of leopards.

A pride of lions.

A tower of giraffes.

A stand of flamingos.

A bloat of hippopotami.

A mob of kangaroos.

One lonely man.

Me.

* * *

Tap tap tippity-tap.

* * *

Run. Run fast. When it happens, when you've done the deed, run like the wind. Just like Ding, Dong, Ditch.

Agatha crouches behind a tree, not the oak tree in her yard, not the tree in GDOG's yard on which she'd painted HEART, but the pine tree just beyond GDOG's property, the tree in which she'd been caught spying, first by the boy, second by the boy and his mad mad mother, and third by the police officer who'd babysat her after the shed incident.

When Dax's car pulls into the driveway, she waits for GDOG to step from the passenger seat. When she hears the door click shut, she envisions herself leaping out of her crouch from behind the tree, grabbing GDOG's ponytail, and holding tight. She sees herself whipping scissors from the waist loop on her spy pants and snipping off all GDOG's hair with one great snip. All of it.

Snniiiiiippp!

If she does this, if she follows through, GDOG will scream, and Agatha knows for sure, one hundred percent, it will be the shrillest sound Agatha has ever heard, shriller even than the scream of the fisher cat that hunts in her neighborhood after midnight, the one Kerry Sheridan complains about year after year.

Agatha presses her hand to the scissors on the waist loop of her spy pants. So damn much she wants that ponytail—that sleek blond plait—but moving from painting HEART on a tree trunk to cutting off GDOG's hair is moving from annoyance to assault. She knows it, and as much as she longs to do it, all she can think is *the boys, the boys, the boys.*

Instead, she creeps back to Coop, drives home, and, in the kitchen, shears the hair off the GDOG reflection doll until there's nothing left but stubble. It's something. She runs her thumb over the bristly remains, then pulls her estranged husband from the drawer. "Look at her now," she says, holding up GDOG and letting Dax get a glimpse of her stubbly, wubbly head.

Agatha sits like this for a long time, GDOG in one hand, Dax in the other, wondering where she'd be right now, in this moment, if she'd followed through and leapt from behind that tree and chopped off all that hair. This would be a very different moment, this one here. Maybe she'd be in GDOG's yard being questioned by the officer. Maybe she'd already have been taken in to the police department, hands cuffed behind her back. Maybe she'd be staring out from behind bars.

Needing air, fresh air, she tucks the dolls back into their respective drawers and steps onto the porch. As she leans over to chat with the tomato plant, a police cruiser makes its way up the street, pausing in front of her house, as if knowing her intention, which is impossible, because she'd shared her hair-chopping plan with no one. Not Shrinky-Dink. Not even Bear.

When the cruiser is in line with the driveway, the window rolls down and Agatha sees the young officer, whose name she still can't remember, looking at her. He smiles, waves, and holds up his copy of *Their Eyes Were Watching God*. She gives him a thumbs-up, gives herself a thumbs-up, then turns to go back into the house.

* * *

"You what?" Shrinky-Dink says.

"I almost cut off a bit of GDOG's hair." Agatha says it the same way she might say, "I cut the tags off my new dress."

"With what? Please do not tell me a hatchet."

"Scissors. Just scissors."

"But you didn't do it?"

"I didn't do it. I just kept thinking about the boys." She doesn't mention the reflection doll.

"Thank goodness. That could have landed you in jail."

"I know."

"What were you feeling?"

Agatha rolls her eyes.

"What pushed you to consider going so far?"

"I was scared."

"Scared?"

"And mad."

"Mad as in angry? Or mad as in crazy?"

"You tell me."

Shrinky-Dink leans back in her chair and makes a weird gulpy-wheezy noise in the back of her throat. Agatha has never heard a sound like this from Shrinky-Dink. It's unexpected and unnerving. "Are you okay?" Agatha says.

Shrinky-Dink clears her throat. "I am." Then she says, "You know, you're not afraid like other people."

Agatha cocks her head. "What?"

"You're afraid of things, but you're not afraid like other people."

"What do you mean?"

"Many people—most people—who suffer from fears and phobias hide and cower and retreat. They turn inward when they're afraid."

"Yeah, so?"

"You do the opposite. You strike out."

Agatha is quiet.

"When another person—let's say a woman named Gloria—is afraid of the dark, she sits in a corner with all the lights on. You? You turn off the lights, grab a sword, and stab anything that comes close."

Agatha nods. Sounds about right.

"When Gloria is afraid of strangers, she goes in her house, locks the door, and stays there until pried out by her family. When you are afraid of strangers—the Interloper, for example—you drive to where she is, take photos, yell at her through a bullhorn, blast the Beastie Boys, and put her on notice."

Agatha half smiles, chuffed. This line of reasoning kind of feels like a compliment. Also kind of not.

"When Gloria is cheated on, she retreats. When you're cheated on, you grab the nearest weapon—hatchet, spray paint, scissors—and go after the cheaters."

"And you're saying that most people are like Gloria?"

"Absolutely."

"How boring."

"Maybe, but they leave less carnage in their wake."

Agatha thinks about the carnage in her wake. The shed. The tree. Almost GDOG's hair. "And?"

"And I think getting mad allows you to avoid your true feelings."

A chime dings quietly from Shrinky-Dink's vicinity.

"What is that?"

"My new way of indicating that we're at the end of a session. The clock felt too abrupt."

Agatha smirks.

"For next time, spend a few minutes thinking about your relationship with fear and anger."

When Agatha opens the door, the woman in gray is sitting, as always, in the small vestibule just outside Shrinky-Dink's office. She's staring out the window. "Gloria?" Agatha whispers as she passes.

The woman doesn't look up.

Chapter Nineteen

Agatha steps off the pavement of the grocery store parking lot, shoves through a tangle of branches, and disappears into the copse of trees, thinking with every step about how Shrinky-Dink says she is different from other chickenshit people, how she, unlike other chickenshit people, unlike this imagined Gloria, unlike all Glorias, runs at the thing she's most afraid of instead of cowering from it, runs at the thing with her Leatherman Super Tool 300 EOD glinting in the sun, blade drawn, mouth ripped wide with warrior cry. If it is true, and she's not one hundred percent sure it is, what do you do with such a revelation?

It's warm again, hot really, tank top hot, hiking sandal hot. Welcome to early October in New England. Hot, cold. Summer, winter. Hot, cold. Steaming, freezing. It's a crapshoot.

Agatha is well prepared for this journey. Looking like some kind of adventure zealot determined to find the secret cave, the hidden grail, she's sporting her brand-new "Fear Sharpens Us" tank, dark blue with white letters, her spy pants are well stocked, and her GoPro is firmly strapped to her head. Back home, she left a note on the kitchen table: "Braving the Krug to spy on the Interloper. If I don't return, call Bear Grylls. He's the only one who can save me."

She grins at the idea of Bear's helicopter hovering over the Krug, heat sensors pinpointing her location, and Bear, oh brave brave Bear, swinging down on a rope to save her from whatever escaped beast that New Hampshire cuckoodoodle released into the world, her world. Lion, gorilla, grizzly.

While most land in Wallingford has been overdeveloped so that as many people as possible can unpack their lives in their very own five-plus-bedroom McMansion, the Krug—a 5,000-square-acre splotch—was designated "protected forever" when the owner gifted it to the town decades before. Agatha has never spent time here; few have. It is wild and woolly, full of dark hidey-holes and ghostly glacial boulders. In some places, strange, fingerlike fronds hang from trees and scrape at your head as you pass beneath them. The hills are too steep for decent walking trails, and there are no playgrounds, skate parks, or splash pads. It isn't a place where a mom takes her kids, unless she's at her wits' end and is kind-of-but-not-really hoping a bear will lunge from one of the hidden caves and devour her little miscreants. Agatha once made this joke on the Moms page and got her noggin gnawed off by the hoard of politically correct mothers who don't believe in even joking about wanting to feed their children to bears. "What if it actually happens?" one Mom argued. To that Agatha had posted a picture of poor Basil being assaulted by bears in *The Gashlycrumb Tinies*. Edward Gorey knew the drill.

Trudging deeper and deeper into the forest, her steps as close to silent as a human can get on dry, crunchy leaves, Agatha realizes that the Krug would make an excellent setting for the murder in her proposed thriller. It is, after all, the most densely wooded area of Wallingford, the kind of forest in which a Mom-on-Mom crime could occur, the kind of forest in which a Mom could disappear without a trace.

Poof.

Right here at this junction, on this hill, in these woods, a story starts to take shape.

The only people who love the Krug are mountain bikers, and their narrow, rutted trails cross creeks, follow the most challenging swells, jump off crazy-high precipices, and take you up and over every boulder in the woods. The Interloper skirts most of the challenging choices, opting again and again for a work-around, but Agatha channels her inner Bear and follows the path almost religiously, even shimmying under a fallen tree on her belly instead of walking around it.

Just as they are making their way into the densest part of the Krug, Agatha turns on the live feed for the GoPro and streams it onto the Moms page. “Moms,” she shout-whispers when she is sure the Interloper is out of earshot, momentarily turning the camera’s eye on herself, “it’s Agatha Arch. I’m out here in the Krug following the Interloper, trying to figure out what the hell she’s up to.” Then she turns the camera’s eye to the Interloper, a hundred or so paces ahead.

A few minutes later, thirty-one Moms have commented on her feed. None is positive:

Esther Ma:	“Seriously, Agatha? Seriously?”
Sandra Snow:	“Don’t you have anything better to do?”
Linh Hong:	“I hope you get eaten by a bear.”
Rachel Runk:	“Agatha Arch, this is nuts. Leave that poor girl alone.”
Jane Poston:	“If anyone doubted that you’re completely out of your tree, that doubt is now completely gone.”
Coco Kitty:	“Marty Snow! Marty Snow! Block this feed immediately and throw Agatha Arch out of the group. Now!”
Kelly Prescott:	“Ooh, be careful, Agatha, if that girl’s a killer, she could be luring you to her trap right this very minute. You could be walking into a setup.”

That last one gets Agatha. It's not that she hasn't considered the possibility of a trap, but having Kelly Prescott point it out makes it all the more possible.

She pulls the Leatherman Super Tool 300 EOD from her pocket and stares at its jumble of tools.

She tugs one.

Ruler.

She tugs another.

Bottle opener.

Another.

Phillips screwdriver.

Another.

Electrical crimper. What the hell is that?

Another, and another, and another.

Needle-nose pliers, stranded-wire cutters, C4 punch.

Where the hell is the knife? If the Interloper turns on her, Agatha is going to need the knife.

Trying to focus on the positive, Agatha bows to Bear's spirit in the woods. Both the Grylls variety and the furry variety that used to roam these very lands. She's quieter than a grasshopper on a leaf. Quieter than an ant on a blade of grass.

As they climb higher, she closes in on the Interloper, narrowing the distance between them to twenty-five paces. "Are you watching?" she whispers to the Moms. "I'm getting closer."

Minutes later, maybe a half mile into the woods, maybe ten miles into the woods, the Interloper stops next to a humongous tree with a trunk broader than a pickup truck. She reaches into a hole so big it could have housed three Hobbits and a Honda Pilot and pulls out a black bag. It is the kind of bag that murderers drag out from under beds in late-night cop shows, black and canvas, long enough to hold a body, or a weapon.

Convinced the Interloper is about to pull a gun, shoot a thousand bullets into her, and leave her dead in the woods where she won't be found for at least six years when a wealthy developer finally bribes his way to developing this land, Agatha hurls herself to the ground with a terrific thud. So much for silence.

Although she can no longer see the Interloper, she hears her whip around and imagines she is staring down the hill at the place where Agatha now lay.

"Who's there?" the Interloper calls. Agatha hasn't heard her voice before, but it is very, very murder-y, just like she imagined.

Agatha flattens herself in the dirt. "Be Bear," she whispers. "Be Bear."

"Hey?" the Interloper calls.

While Agatha is pretty sure the Interloper can't see her in the bed of prickly bushes she's crashed into, the panicked rustle of branches and leaves and panting lets Agatha know she's on high alert.

As Agatha waits for her to trust the silence and continue with her task, a creepy-crawly something wriggles into her pant leg and nibbles on her ankle. She has no idea if it is a snake or an ant or a chupacabra, but does it matter? It's a thing nibbling on her ankle.

Nibble, nibble.

Nibble, nibble.

By the time the thing reaches her knee, she knows it isn't a snake. No slithery wrap of a tail. No horrible hiss. No rattle. She's also pretty sure it isn't a chupacabra.

But what?

What?

A black widow spider? A tick? Some other human-eating bug making its way toward her jugular?

Good god, here she is doing everything she can to protect the citizens of Wallingford. Here she is performing a civic duty. Here she is making sure this intruder is not out in the woods building bombs, stashing weapons, making meth, or hiding stolen children. Here she is, doing Good. Good with a capital G.

And this monster tries to eat her.

She lies there, wincing, trying to squelch her fear—"fear sharpens us, fear sharpens us, fear sharpens us"—but when the thing reaches the top of her thigh and continues north toward her cootchie, there is only one option. She wraps her hands around her head to protect the GoPro, pushes off with her elbows and feet, and starts rolling down the hill. As she picks up speed, rocks and roots rip open her skin and a long, pointy branch tears a gaping hole in her spy pants. When she slams to a halt against a boulder, she raises her head and sees the Interloper standing at the top of the hill next to her tree, craning her neck.

Agatha jumps up, reaches through the gaping hole in her britches, and pulls the humongous human-eating bug off her upper leg. Who knows what the hell it is, but while Agatha screams, the Interloper makes her escape, stomping over the hill like an angry boar and disappearing behind a curtain of dark fronds.

She is gone.

With her thigh wagging about, Agatha makes her way up the hill once again to the Interloper's tree. The canvas bag is lying on the ground and Agatha ever so carefully unzips it, praying she isn't about to set off a bomb and be blown to bits. Inside, she finds a bottle of water, a pen and notebook, and some food. No body. No bones. No weapons.

There must be another hiding place, but Agatha is too spent to look for it. She switches off the GoPro, turns, and heads for home. Half an hour later, when she plunges out of the woods, shaken, dirty, bloody, panting, and stinky, she sees Melody Whelan leaning against the bumper of her car, knitting. Melody looks up and shakes her head. "How could you, Agatha Arch?" she says, gesturing to Agatha's gear and filth.

"How could I not?"

* * *

That night, she downloads the GoPro video feed of the Interloper to her computer, then uploads it to the cloud. Unable to resist, she shares a couple of screenshots on the Moms page. Recriminations fly like cannonballs:

Melody Whelan: "Agatha Arch. Really? Doesn't this young woman have it hard enough?"

Erin Abel: "Where do you get all the money for this high-tech equipment? As far as I know, you haven't sold a new book lately."

Ouch.

Priya Devi: "Marty? Can you delete Agatha's post please? It is offensive and breaks the rule of posting offensive material to this page."

Agatha Arch: "What is offensive about this? No one is naked. No one is having sex. I'm not inciting violence. I'm not advocating for an overthrow of the Wallingford government. I've simply posted photos of an outsider who is doing suspicious things in our forest."

Grainne O'Neill: "You are infringing on this young woman's privacy. That is offensive. None of these photos show anything suspicious. All I see is a sad, lost girl. That should be private. You of all people should recognize this."

Bridget Weller: "Don't you have anything else to do in your life than follow people who do not want to be followed?"

Agatha Arch: "Nope. I've got all the time in the world right now, thanks to my husband. On some nights, no meals to cook or kids to care for. All the time in the world."

There is a pause in the posts here. In a different moment, Agatha might have picked up on the fact that at least a few of the Moms are feeling for her. She might have recognized the possibility of that zephyr of friends she secretly longs for. A genesis. But it is not a different moment, it is this moment, and Agatha charges like a gladiator at the enemy, sword drawn. Thirty minutes later, Marty Snow pulls her post.

* * *

"You followed the young woman into the Krug?"

"I did."

Shrinky-Dink stares so hard at Agatha that she knows she's supposed to be deducing something profound. "What?"

"You do see how fear motivates you, right?"

"Motivates me?"

"To act, not hide."

"This again?"

"Yes, this again. It's important."

"I followed the Interloper into the Krug. Big deal. Someone has to keep an eye on her."

"But you, Agatha Arch, are terrified of the woods, the dark, strangers, getting lost, too many trees over your head."

Agatha had forgotten about the too-many-trees-over-her-head fear. "So?"

"You went into the Krug anyway."

"So?"

"You are not the chickenshit you profess to be. You are a warrior. A fierce warrior."

Agatha pulls Bear from her purse and sets him on the table between them. "You hear that Bear? I'm a fierce warrior." She flicks his head but because of the accident and the duct tape neck brace, it doesn't bobble as it should, just wags back and forth the slightest bit.

Shrinky-Dink smiles. "Hi, Bear. Good to see you again."

Agatha preens. She loves when Shrinky-Dink plays along. It makes her seem more human. More like the rest of them.

"What happened to him?" Shrinky-Dink says. She reaches out and touches his neck.

"Accident."

Shrinky-Dink fingers the deep bite mark in his boot. "And this?"

"A moment of weakness."

The chime chimes.

"I've been meaning to ask, are you eating?"

"Eating?"

"Yes, eating. Meals, snacks, you know, eating. You look a little skinny."

"It's not easy to eat without the boys around. I don't have much of an appetite."

"Try."

"Okay."

"Are you writing?"

Agatha drops Bear back into her purse and snaps it shut. "Scribbling in my journal. Playing with a few things."

"Have you gone up to your office yet?"

"No."

"So no deep writing?"

"No deep writing."

"No thriller?"

"Not yet, though I do have the beginning of an idea."

* * *

Later that day Agatha stands on the third step of the back staircase and looks up. The red door actually stings her eyes. She thinks about her favorite Shirley Jackson quote: "As long as you write it away regularly, nothing can really hurt you." This had always worked for her. Get hurt.

Write your way through it. Death. Heartache. General malaise. Politics. First-world problems. Arguments with store clerks. Highway stress. Fears. Kid problems. Write and you shall be free. Write and the most unmanageable becomes manageable. She knows she should write about Dax and GDOG and the shed and the tree and the dolls and the hair. She knows she should climb those stairs and face the page. "Go up," she says, but good gracious, she just can't.

The desk.

The desk.

The desk.

* * *

Then a letter arrives. From her agent.

A handwritten letter.

It seems impossible in modern-day society that anyone, especially her agent, would take time to write and mail a letter. But there it is, a bright white envelope lying on the weedy black mulch under Agatha's mailbox, a bold handwritten address on the front.

What kind of madness is this? Is her agent retiring? Is she going to dump Agatha? Break up with her? Good god, there is no way she could take that rejection right now. One shattered relationship is enough.

Agatha carries the letter into the sunroom, then digs Dax's beloved mail opener from a drawer. She slices open the envelope and takes out the letter: bright white paper with loopy cursive words running up hill.

No sign of an assistant's help on this. And the voice? The voice is all agent, and it feels as if she is standing right there in the room, an intense but loving look on her face. Agatha remembers their first meeting in New York City after her agent had read and adored her first novel. She'd hugged her, then pulled her into a full face-to-face grip. "I want it," she'd said. "And every book after."

The letter reads:

Heellllloooo? Heellllloooo, Agatha?

You still there? Listen I know you're up against something big. Maybe in life? Maybe in the writing? Whatever it is, I'm here. Waiting for the next installment. Take your time. I'm looking forward.

* * *

Tap tap tippity-tap.

Chapter Twenty

Agatha fidgets under the heat lamp and listens to the gaggle of women gobble on about this, that, and the other thing:

"Have fun tonight."
"Are you excited about the wedding?"
"My fifth," hands on swollen belly. "Gender reveal party tonight."
"Pink at the Garden. We have amazing seats."
"Adele has a new album coming out?"
"I need my autumn colors."
"Yes, a mimosa, please. Skip the orange juice."
"A rainbow, please. I want to look like a unicorn on ecstasy."

So much gets shared at Salon Brava, private things, announcements, secrets, complaints, pleas, and decrees. While a handful of men dare to venture in—the brave, the desperate, the clueless—it's mostly women in tinfoil folds, plastic caps, eyebrow dye, lash serum, and various other states of disarray. Delighted to be out of the public's gaze while they primp and pluck and gussy up, the women get peeled, massaged, threaded, blinged, volumized, moisturized, and more, moaning happily, breathing, dropping the façade.

"Perhaps a facial?" Calliope asks, pointing at but not touching the crease on Agatha's cheek. "And a manicure, for sure." She grimaces while delicately fingering the tender scars that decorate Agatha's hands.

Much like Homer's muse, this Calliope is beautiful, though Agatha doubts she has the know-how to turn men into beasts. Too young, too sweet.

"My god, what happened to you?" Calliope says, and, when she does, fifteen sets of eyes snap in their direction, all the eyes that had been pretending not to see Agatha, not to register her presence.

"Nothing," Agatha says, tucking her hands under the cape. "No manicure. Just my hair today." Then, ignoring the jab of eyes and swelling tsunami of whispers, she taps into the Moms group on her phone and gets caught up in Stella Bender's request for recommendations on where to buy a desk lamp. Agatha's heart seizes. A desk lamp? Who needs recommendations for where to buy a desk lamp? Walk into almost any store and you'll find desk lamps for sale. Who would need help with this simple decision? It's like asking for recommendations about where to buy bananas. Or toilet paper.

Yet welcome to twenty-first-century America. Agatha pounces.

Agatha Arch: "Seriously, Stella? You need a recommendation for a place to buy a desk lamp? A desk lamp? Your inbox is not like every other inbox in this world? It is not inundated with emails from Pottery Barn, Crate & Barrel, and Wayfair.com? You have not passed the HomeGoods store one million times on your way to the YMCA? You never sneak away from your kid's soccer game to pop into Marshall's? You haven't heard of Macy's or Ethan Allen? How about IKEA? Have you heard of IKEA? IKEA has 45 million desk lamps to choose from. Forty-five million! It would be a perfect place to buy a desk lamp.

"How about Home Depot? Or Lowe's? Either of those ring a bell? Maybe you're familiar with Staples or Office Depot? They are both office-y stores that sell desk lamps by the dozens. In fact, dear Stella, every single one of these stores sells desk lamps! And because of this, there is absolutely no reason that you need the collective advice of nearly 3,000 Moms to make this decision.

"I encourage you, Stella, to set off on this mysterious adventure alone and see what happens. Be brave, sister! Go forth! This is your chance to see what wares you come up with ALL BY YOURSELF.

"And when you finally get to the point where you have to make a final decision between two equally useful and almost identical desk lamps, I warn you, DO NOT POST PHOTOS OF BOTH TO THIS PAGE AND ASK, 'WHICH ONE SHOULD I BUY?' Believe me, sister, both lamps will give light, both will sit on a desk, and, I assure you, dear Stella, your college-bound daughter will not give a shit.

"Good luck and happy shopping."

Agatha hits *post* as her heat lamp buzzes. Calliope lifts the lamp, then peels the cap from her head. Agatha stands, rustling in the plastic cape, and sees most of the women in the salon eyeballing her. Damn Moms.

"Stella just needed a boost, Agatha. Some camaraderie," the unicorn pips. She's in the purple stage of layering. It's quite profound, though Agatha doesn't say so. "You'll understand when your kids are getting ready to leave the nest for college. You didn't need to slay her."

"Someone did," Agatha says. "It's a lamp, Bernice. A desk lamp." She lies down on the reclining chair to have her hair washed.

"Nothing is just a lamp," Calliope says, upping the temperature of the water, knowing Agatha likes it hot, not warm, not extra warm, but hot. Remembering that and offering up spritely but powerful statements about life are the only reasons Agatha returns to Calliope's chair, because, honestly, she's a terrible hairdresser, a bloody awful one who always cuts the left side of Agatha's hair shorter than the right or colors the top darker than the bottom or scrapes her forehead with one of her dagger-like fingernails. Agatha has considered changing stylists or salons but the gems that bubble from this young woman's mouth keep her coming back.

Nothing is just a lamp, which, for no reason and all the reasons, makes Agatha think about Dax and GDOG and the shed and the dogs going up the hill and down the hill for months, years, before that day.

* * *

"Fear is a reaction. Courage is a decision." Winston Churchill

It's on a sign at the post office.

"Is the post office allowed to hang such offensive signs?" Agatha asks. She needs stamps, the flower kind, not the flags. She isn't into the nationalism of flag stamps, the ones that yell, "I am an American. Look at my flag." Plus, even though she will never admit this to Kerry Sheridan, she really likes flowers. Hydrangeas are her favorite, the pale blue blooms especially so, but almost any flower pleases her. "Isn't there a law about signs like that?"

The postal clerk in the black beret turns and looks at the sign. He mouths the words as he reads it. "What is offensive about that? Seems pretty straightforward to me."

"That statement makes it seem as if a human can just decide not to be afraid of something."

"So?"

"So it's not true. You can't just decide not to be afraid."

"Who says?"

"I say."

The man in line behind Agatha clears his throat. He's slumping under the weight of three large boxes.

The postal clerk shakes his head. "Why can't you just decide not to be afraid?"

"Fear is fear. It's not easy to kick it out of your life."

"Churchill didn't say anything about courage being easy. He just said it's a decision."

"That's bullshit."

"Listen, if you don't like the sign, don't look at it."

"There should be a law about signs in government offices."

The clerk's eyes move to the picture of Bear Grylls on Agatha's T-shirt. "Pretty sure he'd like the sign." He gestures at Bear with his thumb as he looks for flower stamps in the stack. "He's not afraid of anything."

Agatha shrugs. "Leave Bear out of this."

"I'm just saying it's probably not cool for you to flaunt a Bear Grylls shirt and then complain about a sign like that." He hands her a pack of flag stamps. "We're out of flower stamps. Sorry."

"Seriously?"

"Seriously."

Agatha doesn't believe him, but pays and turns to go. "I'm going to write to someone about that sign." She lifts her phone and snaps a picture.

"You do that," says the clerk, and he turns to the man behind her.

* * *

Just after posting a photo of the Winston Churchill quote on Infidelity: A Still Life, Agatha hears the TreeLife truck pull into the driveway.

The bearded guy knocks. "Good morning. We're here to trim the oak, as promised. Can you please move your car to the street? We don't want to damage anything."

Agatha picks up her keys and heads outside, only to find three more densely bearded men in the driveway. She can't tell one from the other. By the time her car is well out of the way, the cherry picker and the chipper have arrived. More bearded men emerge from the vehicles. She's sure she's in some kind of comedy skit about beards, but no one laughs when she says so. They're very serious about their facial hair.

Back in the house, her IG followers hug her in the best virtual way:

"Bullshit."

"Clearly Churchill was never cheated on."

"Burn the sign!"

"Bullshit!"

And so many 💕.

Chapter Twenty-One

"Agatha! Agatha Arch! Come out here this instant!"

Agatha peeks out the window though she doesn't have to. She'd know that squeaky squawk anywhere. It's Kerry Sheridan, and she's hopping mad.

Kerry knocks. "I'm not going away. Better open this door."

Agatha opens the door. "What is it, Kerry?"

"Thomas, my sweet Thomas, has poison ivy! Look at him!" She pulls her sweet Thomas into view and spins him around and around. "It's all over his hands and arms. His face." She cups his chin and lifts. "It's everywhere."

Agatha clears her throat. It is everywhere. Poor sweet Thomas looks like a sunburned puffer fish. "Oh, that's terrible," Agatha says. She means it. "And?"

"And it's your fault, Agatha. This, this, this . . ." Kerry waves her arms at the mess of weeds and grass that used to be the yard surrounding the shed. "This atrocity."

Back to that word.

"How is this my fault?" Agatha says.

"You know very well that this atrocity is full of poison ivy. Thomas lost his lucky baseball in there two days ago and went in after it, even though I told him not to. 'You are not allowed in that mess of weeds, Thomas,' I told him. But did he listen? Does he ever listen?" She looks from Thomas to Agatha and waits.

"No?" Agatha says.

"No, he did not. You know very well he did not listen. My boys listen no better than your boys. They do exactly what they want when they want. Thomas dug around in that mess until he found that ball. He came home itchy and red. Now he's on steroids. Steroids, Agatha! He's allergic to poison ivy."

Thomas moans. His face is an over-boiled beet. One eye is swollen shut; one arm is in a sling. "Oh, Thomas," Agatha says. "I'm sorry."

"It's okay, Mrs. Arch. It's not your fault."

Kerry bristles. "Not her fault? Thomas, this is most certainly Mrs. Arch's fault."

Thomas moans again. "Mom, can I go home now?" he says.

"Yes, go on. I'll be there in a minute." Kerry waves at Thomas. "See, Agatha? See?"

"I'm sorry Thomas is hurting, Kerry. Truly I am. But you can't know that it was poison ivy in my yard that did this."

"I can't? Really, I can't?"

"No, he could have gotten it anywhere."

"Where, Agatha? He's been at school and home and in your . . . your . . . wilderness."

"Maybe there's some in the field at school."

"There's not."

"You know this?"

"I know this. If there was, every boy in fifth grade would have poison ivy. They don't."

"You know this for a fact?"

"I know this for a fact. I called the school nurse."

Agatha looks at the remains of the shed. "I don't know what you want me to do, Kerry."

"I want you to clean it up, Agatha. It's simple. Please. Just clean it up." She turns and storms off down the steps.

* * *

Tap tap tippity-tap.

* * *

Rachel Runk :	"Ladies, I just saw Balderdash on the corner of West and Grayson streets! I'm in my car. Can't stop. Too much traffic. Someone get there. Who's close? Quick! Call Willow Bean!"
Melody Whelan:	"On my way! I'm just down the street."
Jane Poston:	"I'll call Willow."

Of course you will, Agatha thinks, then turns on her blinker to head for Grayson. Like Melody, she's close. Just three intersections away. Two right turns, one left. Physically, a hop, a skip, and a jump.

Emotionally, she might as well be on Neptune.

While heading to Grayson will mean helping Balderdash get home to sweet, old, hanging-on-for-dear-life Gem Lily, it will also mean meeting face to face with GDOG for the first time since the shed incident, a personal sacrifice for which Agatha doesn't feel the least bit prepared.

"Leap into a volcano spewing hot lava in order to save the world?" she says to Bear. "Or jump into a waiting helicopter to save myself?"

Save the world? Save myself?

"C'mon, Agatha," he says. "It's time to save the world." Oh, that accent.

"Bastard," she says. "I knew you'd say that." As she pulls into a spot on West, she swears she hears Shrinky-Dink cheering from the shrinks' section of life. "Oh, for Big Papi's sake, all of you!" She jumps out, bumps both swollen elbows, hollers in pain, then whips her head around, looking for the damn pooch in every direction at the same time.

Nothing. Nothing but a steaming pile of dog poop right smack dab in the middle of the sidewalk with GDOG and her gorgeous grapefruit hips leaning over it. Willow glances up. "Agatha," she says. "You came to help."

"I came to help Balderdash. And Gem Lily."

GDOG straightens. "I get that, but you're here, and I've been wanting to talk to you."

"Why?" Agatha looks at everything but GDOG. The sky, the blue Prius, the stop sign, the steaming pile of poop.

"I've been wanting to apologize for how things happened the day of the shed incident. We're both women, members of the sisterhood . . ."

Oh, for fuck's sake. The sisterhood? What sisterhood? The one in which the sisters steal one another's husbands? That sisterhood? Agatha wants nothing to do with it. "Willow, this isn't the time."

"No, no, it's not, is it? We have to move fast to find Balderdash, but please know that I'm sorry and I'd like to talk."

Thankfully, Melody appears beside them. She points at the pile, cheeks shining. "Is this Balderdash's?"

"It is," GDOG says. Her voice is breathy and excited. "I'd know his BM anywhere." She squats and holds her hand just inches above the pile. "It's still warm. He can't be far."

Agatha wonders how Dax, the man who refused to get a dog because he didn't want to pick up dog poop, the man who insisted he got nauseated just talking about dog poop and therefore could never ever have a dog, how he would feel if he saw his lover holding her hand just inches above a stray pile of the stinking stuff. She hums Huey Lewis's "The Power of Love," then says, "Really? Seriously, Willow? You can tell Balderdash's poop from any other dog's?"

"Absolutely."

"I find that hard to believe."

"No time for debate now," GDOG yells. "Divide and conquer!" She pushes off and heads down an alleyway between two houses. "Go!"

For the next ten minutes, Agatha, GDOG, and Melody run between houses and behind sheds. GDOG stops traffic with her hips and lies down on the street to look under cars. "He loves shady spots!" she hollers.

Agatha dives under a thicket of bushes, banging the shit out of her bruised knee. He's not there.

When they've covered every inch of the West/Grayson intersection, they meet again at the pile of poop.

"He's gone," GDOG says. She sniffles. Tears well in her eyes. She snaps a photo of the poop with her phone and uploads it to the Moms group. "This is Balderdash's," she writes. "If you happen upon another pile, let me know asap." Then she pulls a plastic bag from her pocket and scoops the poop. The consummate dog walker.

"Don't lose heart, Willow. Balderdash was here and he's still alive," Melody says. "We'll get him home."

GDOG nods. "Thanks for helping me, Melody." She looks at Agatha. "Thank you, too."

"I was close. That's all."

"Still."

Agatha's phone buzzes. Anti-canine-fecal-matter activist Winky Moran is upset about Balderdash's pile of steaming poop. "I sure hope you're cleaning up that mess before heading off on your merry way, Ms. Bean," she writes.

"Of course," GDOG writes.

This is not Winky's first such rant, nor will it be her last. She's a big believer in what she calls "home pooping" for dogs, a philosophy that insists dogs poop only on their home lawns in order to save civilization. Most, even Agatha, have learned to tune her out, but David Watkins has a special knack for egging her on.

David Watkins: "People, do not be alarmed, but just hours ago I watched a rabbit poop on my lawn! This hopping beast did not pick up its own poop, nor did it have a human attached to it. Advice before my lawn dies, my family perishes, and our entire street is wiped out?"

Sandra Locke: "Last night there were seven deer in my yard. Seven! ALL OF THEM POOPED! Save us!"

Candace Smith: "And what of the grasshopper in my garden this morning? Its imperceptible poop must be more lethal than any of us can comprehend."

This rather formal Brit wins the prize. Grasshopper poop.

Winky Moran: "You'll all be sorry."

"I need to call Gem Lily," GDOG says to Agatha and Melody. "She's going to be devastated. Again."

Agatha turns to walk to her car.

"Hey, Agatha," Melody calls. "Ready for that lunch yet?"

Agatha pretends not to hear.

Chapter Twenty-Two

Agatha shields her eyes from the blinding sunlight in the Krug, a reminder that all too soon fall will smash to its magnificent end and another horrid New England winter will begin. Leaf peepers around the world wax poetic about autumn in New England but anyone who lives in the thick of it knows that old-fashioned autumn is a thing of the past. A pre–global warming delight. In a good year, autumn—the beautiful bright-blue-skied brilliant-yellow-and-orange-leaved autumn that makes those peepers *ooh* and *aah*—now lasts no more than a couple of weeks. "It's so brief, it doesn't even deserve to be called *autumn* anymore," Agatha once told Dax. "It ought to be *aut*."

Dax had laughed and laughed. He used to do that all the time at things said, laugh and laugh.

Winter haunts Agatha. All those people skating around on frozen ponds and lakes, daring Mother Nature to melt a single spot under the bustle of berry bushes so they all plunge to their frigid deaths. But with Dax gone and the boys now a part-time gig, the thought of a dark freezing winter terrifies her even more. It's not the heavy hauling tasks that scare her. She's more than capable of moving patio furniture to the basement and she builds a much better fire than Dax ever could. She can salt walkways and call the plow guy. But how will her feet stay warm in bed without Dax to tuck them under? Who's going to drink Earl Grey with her after the boys are asleep? Who will investigate when she hears a mouse, an annual visitor in a house as old as theirs?

Keeping a safe distance between herself and the Interloper, Agatha pushes through a tangle of vines so entwined she imagines they are making love. An image of Dax and GDOG and the shed explodes in her brain. Good god, she thinks, I'm a walking stereotype, a jilted wife who can't get through a simple stalking exercise without envisioning her husband in vile acts of infidelity.

As always, she is well prepared for her mission. Her GoPro is in place. She put fresh batteries in her headlamp. Her spy pants are packed with all the familiar necessities, though this time the Dax and GDOG reflection dolls have joined her, Dax in the left cargo pocket, GDOG in the right.

Rounding a glacial boulder, she considers the animals loosed by the sad man in nearby New Hampshire. Is the hungry lion hunched on the other side? Will the gorilla swing down on a vine? Will that bear they promised had been eliminated storm out of a cave? Agatha runs a hand over the Leatherman Super Tool 300 EOD and takes another step.

When the Interloper reaches her tree, she grabs something from inside the trunk, then slumps to her bum. She closes her eyes and wraps her hand around what Agatha imagines is a photograph of two young girls. She imagines the Interloper has two daughters, one still alive back home and one dead. It's a story. A made-up story. A writer's story. For all Agatha knows, the Interloper is gripping the last Oreo in her self-care stash.

When the Interloper's head bobs to her chest, Agatha sneaks closer, making her way across roots and branches and leaves, pretending she is Bear Grylls sneaking up on a rabbit he's snared for dinner, his only hope against starvation.

Tiptoe, tiptoe, tiptoe.

All goes well until she gets close to the Interloper. Then, oh. Sometimes seeing just isn't what you imagine it's going to be, even for Agatha. She expects to feel powerful and dominant, superior to this young woman begging for money, but instead she feels like a felled tree. Up close she can see that the Interloper's hair is matted and gnarled. Up close she can smell her sour stink. She peeks into the tree and sees that Melody had indeed given her the self-care bags. She sees a flashlight, a jar of peanut butter, and many cans of beans with pull tops. There are bottles of water and a bunch of rotting bananas. Also two rolls of biodegradable toilet paper, candy wrappers, the coffee can with a handful of bills and coins, and a plastic bag of notes from Moms in the group. Agatha opens the bag.

"Stay strong," one note says.

"Here's a phone number for a shelter where you can sleep at night," says another.

When Agatha sees the filthy blanket, she knows the Interloper has no intention of using the phone number printed on the slip of paper. For some impossible-to-understand reason, this young woman would rather trudge through the most challenging terrain in Wallingford, climb this unbearably steep hill, pull this atrocious blanket from this tree trunk, and wrap it around her sad self. Agatha wonders what could drive someone to this place, all alone in the wilderness. Then she thinks of herself destroying the shed with the hatchet, spray-painting the tree in GDOG's yard, spying, and almost cutting off GDOG's hair. Do the Moms think the same thing of her? Do they DM one another about what could drive *her* to such behavior? Where will it end, for the Interloper and for Agatha?

Without taking any photos, without turning on the GoPro, Agatha turns and tiptoes back to her hiding place. She watches a squirrel pick up a leaf, super-fast fold it many times as if an ancient origami master, then race up a tree to pack it into its nest.

A scurry of squirrels.

Three black-capped chickadees scamper up and down an aspen trunk, performing acrobatic feats with their strong tiny legs. *Chicka-dee-dee-dee. Chicka-dee-dee-dee.*

A banditry of chickadees.

A garter snake rustles under a mound of fallen leaves and pokes its head up near a rock.

A nest of snakes.

The horror.

Agatha begins a sprint down the hill, chanting a tongue-twisting poem of sorts:

A prickle of porcupines
A cauldron of bats
An obstinacy of buffalo
A mischief of rats

A flamboyance of flamingos
A thunder of hippos

A smack
Yes, a smack,
of jellyfish

Ravens, a storytelling
Bullfinches, a bellowing
Larks, an exalting
Cormorants, a gulp

Lions, a pride
Bears, a maul
Kangaroos, a troop
Gorillas, a whoop

When she crashes through the last tangle of brush into the grocery store parking lot, she's caught up in the irony of collective nouns. A maul of bears. Bah!

No one is waiting to share her preoccupation. The Dax and GDOG dolls are shaken but silent. So what of a group of friends?

A devour
A rebuke
A censure
A stricture

But better,
A soul
A luminescence
An aurora
A syzygy

* * *

High Priestess Jane Poston and her dazzle of zebras cross Main Street with their heads high, their manes shiny and keratin-smooth, and their colorful stripes breathtakingly lovely. As good, law-abiding Moms, they stay in the crosswalk, swishing back and forth between the lines, and when they make it to the parking lot, they disperse as if they've found a good watering hole. A pot of water buffalo now.

Minutes later, safe in their cars, they sing the praises of Salon Brava, then their favorite lunch spot. Photos of the roasted salmon with autumn vegetables inundate the Moms page.

Priya Devi: "Major shout out to Dalton's today! New tablecloths are to die for!"

Agatha guffaws. The new tablecloths are hideous. Purplish things with putrid orange pumpkins. In response, she posts a photo of a man falling to his death when he sees a woman in a pumpkin costume.

The Moms bombard Agatha with frowny faces and continue their mission to lift Dalton's to new heights.

Blonde Brenda What's-Her-Name:	"The walnut/goat cheese salad has been seasonally updated with mandarin oranges and pine nuts. Heavenly."

Agatha posts a photo of oranges dancing in a conga line.

phyliss-with-one-l-and-two-esses:	"agatha arch, quit it. you're just jealous you weren't invited to the salon + lunch outing."

Agatha posts a photo of a troll sobbing under a bridge.

phyliss-with-one-l-and-two-esses: "i said quit it!"

Agatha posts a photo of Bam-Bam banging his giant bone into the earth.

To Jane Poston's photo of a bowl of three miniature scoops of sorbet, she adds a cartoon of a deer pooping in the woods.

And as a final comment, she posts a photo of the Dallas Cowboys Cheerleaders doing their thing. "Go Dalton's!" she writes. "The restaurant of choice for divorcees, old ladies, and Wallingford Moms!"

* * *

Later, sipping tea on the porch and waiting for Susan Sontag to appear, she considers Phyliss's comment about jealousy. Is she right? Is Agatha jealous of the camaraderie these women seem to find in one another and this group? Does she really want to be part of the swishing tail of the dazzle, dutifully following High Priestess Poston hither and thither? Does she really want to share photos of salmon and sorbet?

She searches for the collective noun for skunks.

Surfeit.

Yes. And no. And maybe. But rather than admit such complexity, she'd rather get sprayed by a skunk.

* * *

"When I was a girl, before my father tossed me in the deep end and before beloved Susie died, I dreamed of effervescence. I was strong and powerful and unbreakable." Agatha's voice trails off. She is lying down again.

"Life is hard," Shrinky-Dink says. "And wonderful."

An effervescence of friends.

This is a good one. Maybe the best.

Chapter Twenty-Three

The 3,000,000th "IS THIS YOUR CAT? post pops up in the Moms group just minutes after Agatha wakes from a dream about being stuck in a submerged vehicle with High Priestess Poston. Unable to access her dual steel-headed hammers and gasping for air, Agatha had turned to find the High Priestess relaxing next to her in Coop wearing some kind of fancy, blue-lit underwater breathing apparatus on her head like a giant bubble. Agatha was drowning. The High Priestess was not.

Agatha squints through soggy, drowning-next-to-HP eyes at the image of the cat on her phone. Like seventy-five percent of the lost cats in Wallingford, it is black with a bit of white at the neck.

"OMG," she types, "is this Tuxedo?!" Because they're all named Tuxedo and she's grumpy from the dream.

Phyliss isn't amused. "agatha, that is not funny. someone is missing this darling creature and you should not poke fun."

"And you should learn the rules of capitalization," Agatha writes, as if that will ever happen.

In any other conversation, their tiff might distract from the topic at hand, but nothing—absolutely *nothing*—blazes brighter in Wallingford than the passion of cat people.

Melinda Bates: “Oh, this sweetie-magoogle-toogle of a feline. Where do you belong, sweet thing?”

Agatha Arch: “The cat isn’t reading the posts, Melinda. No need to address it directly to her. Believe it or not, cats don’t read.”

Ava Newton: “Is kitty-kitty OK? Is she hungry? Thirsty? Ill? Lonely? Does she need a little rub behind the ears?”

Agatha Arch: “Ava, Ava, Ava. I’m pretty sure if Coco is posting this, she’s also taking care of the cat’s basic needs. She doesn’t have the nickname Coco Kitty for nothing. As far as I know, she hasn’t let one of the many lost cats she’s saved starve. Coco, weigh in here?”

Coco Kitty: “I am taking good care of her, Agatha. Thank you.”

Agatha Arch: “👍😺”

The wild tagging begins as Wallingford’s cat passionistas pull together to get this little kitty home, the great meow crescendoing via the FB waves.

Wanda Watson: “Mary Waters, is this Tuxedo?”

Esther Ma: “Barbara Bancroft, is this your missing kitty?”

Linh Hong: “Darlene Smith, this cat looks just like yours! Is Blackie safe in the house?”

A frenzy of “Blackie? Blackie? Is she safe?” posts follows.

Sheila Craft: “Coco, important question. Does this cat purr? My neighbor, Julie Pastor, has a cat that looks

	just like this but it doesn't purr. Some kind of vocal cord injury at birth. It's a silent cat."
Kerry Sheridan:	"Oh, poor, poor kitty. No voice. Julie Pastor, I didn't know."
Coco Kitty:	"Yes, lots of sugary purrs, especially after the saucer of warm milk."

And that is it. The saucer of warm milk stirs the cat passionistas into such an orgasmic state that Agatha has to sign off. She moves to the kitchen, makes a cup of tea, and tries to quell the *burble-gurgle, burble-gurgle, burble-gurgle* sounds left over from the nightmare. The sound of herself drowning and HP Poston laughing.

* * *

Agatha pulls up behind GDOG's silver Volvo Xwhatever in the after-school pickup line, and even before she taps the horn, Willow Bean's eyes shoot to the rearview mirror. She knows when Agatha is close, senses it. It's hard not to when Agatha oozes jealousy and hate like some people ooze sweat.

When their eyes lock, Agatha winks and gives her the royal wave.

It is Tuesday, and on Tuesdays the boys take swimming lessons after school at the Y. In their former life configuration, Agatha used to pick them up at school, buzz through Dunkin' for a coffee (her) and donuts (them), then take them to swim. In their present life, Tuesday is a Dad Day so the dog walker fills this role, though she skips the Dunkin' stop and provides organic apples for the boys instead.

The line creeps forward, kid after kid tumbling from the mouth of the school into a waiting car, heading for dentist and doctor appointments, piano lessons, soccer practice, Girl Scouts, and/or any of the zillions of activities available to overscheduled children these days. Finally, Agatha sees Dustin and Jason poke their heads out of the door. Principal Bandolino is between them, a hand set lightly on Jason's scruff, knowing he'll bolt to the playground given half a chance.

When the boys clear the door, they both turn their heads to see Agatha's car. They know she's there, as she is every Tuesday—daylight moon—and both grin as if they've just spotted a bowl of chocolate pudding with a thousand marshmallows stuck in it.

She waves at them, rolls down her window, and yells, "Hi, sweeties!" Technically she's not supposed to get out of her car in parent pickup line—school rule—but technically Willow Bean is not a parent, so neither is adhering strictly to the rules. She throws Coop into park, leaps out, and smothers the boys in a hug. Mucky hands squeeze her hard. "Mom, take us to swimming!" they yell.

Willow Bean's voice floats into their circle. "Hello, boys! Hop in! I'm taking you to swimming today."

"No way! We want Mom!" they yell.

Agatha feels Mrs. Bandolino's hand on her shoulder. "Agatha," she says. Her voice is calm and even, as always. Agatha loves that. She reminds her of her fifth-grade teacher who let her explore the world the way she needed to, whether that meant climbing a tree or lying in a pile of dirt or jumping in puddles to measure how high the splash rose.

Agatha pulls back. "Boys, go on with . . . ," she says. "With . . ." *Brazen hussy* is tickling the tip of her tongue, sitting right there, wanting to deliver its sting. But these are the boys. Her boys. She wants them to shine and show respect no matter what nonsense the world or their father introduces. She clamps her lips together and keeps that *brazen hussy* in. "Go with Willow," she says.

"But, Mom," they say, again in unison.

"Go. I'll see you on Thursday."

"But . . ."

Agatha opens the back door of the dog walker's car, eyes down. "Go. I love you two birds." She smooches the top of each of their heads as they climb in.

GDOG is working hard to meet Agatha's eyes. A thank-you, she presumes, for not making a scene. Or at least not much of a scene. Agatha avoids them. Mrs. Bandolino's hand stays on her shoulder. She wishes she could keep it there all day.

As the Volvo pulls away, both boys wave wildly at Agatha through the rear window. She is crying again. And the cars behind her are beeping. Children are lined up in the hallway. Dentist appointments are looming. The clock is ticking.

Agatha shakes free of Mrs. Bandolino and raises her arms at the line of cars. "Be quiet!" she yells at them. "All of you, be quiet!" She knows there are at least a dozen FB Moms in those cars, witnessing Agatha's weak moment. "Be quiet!" she yells again. Then she leaps into Coop and pulls away. She rolls slowly over the speed bumps, tears obliterating the signs warning about children crossing.

* * *

The grass and weeds in the yard around the shed tickle Agatha's calves. Dax is pissed.

"C'mon, Agatha, get this cleared," he insists, as if he gets to insist on anything.

"Did Kerry call you again?"

Dax doesn't answer.

"Did she? She's been hounding me about this every damn day."

"She sent me a photo of Thomas's poison ivy. He looks like he has the plague."

"Oh, for Big Papi's sake. He's fine. It's almost gone."

"It's not just poison ivy, Agatha. The buckthorn and knotweed are raging out here. Hire someone. Let me hire someone. Heck, get out there and do it yourself."

"Tell me, Dax," Agatha says, "what exactly is buckthorn?"

Dax sucks in a breath and pats his belly, a telltale sign he doesn't have a clue what he's talking about. Agatha has seen it a million times. It used to be endearing. Not anymore.

She smiles. "Thought so."

"I know what poison ivy looks like, Agatha, and there's enough of that out here to strangle an elephant. Our boys are going to get it, and then you'll be sorry."

"The boys don't go in there."

"Of course they don't! It's turning into a jungle."

"Bullshit."

"They used to play here all the time. They want to again. This was their baseball field with the Sheridan boys."

"We have enough land around this house to fit four baseball fields. They do not need this particular spot."

"It's their favorite. The boys have played here for years. The shed was always second base and you know it."

Agatha rolls her eyes. Damn Sheridans. "Those Sheridan boys can walk an extra fifty feet to play ball."

"That's not the point."

"You don't get to make a point, Dax. We'd still have a shed and a beautiful swatch of yard and the perfect second base for ball games if you hadn't done what you did. This is not your concern. This is not your home. Take care of the yard at the House of Sin if you're compelled to take care of something. The end."

* * *

Agatha posts a photo to Instagram of the note taped to her front door: FEAR SHARPENS US.

3,639 people like it.

She creates a hashtag: #fearsharpensus.

Instagrammers start using the hashtag to share their triumphs over fear.

Some seem small but loom large. One man walked around the block all by himself. Another went to the dentist for the first time in seventeen years. One got dressed and combed her hair.

Some shine. A woman in Tennessee sang on stage to 5,000 people, realizing her lifelong dream. The people clapped and cheered. Another published her first book of poetry.

Agatha doesn't share her triumphs. She's not sure she has any.

* * *

When the Tush finally arrives, a few days later than expected, he and his team, sporting painterly whites, pull ladders from the truck.

"We'll be scraping and sanding for the first few days," he tells Agatha when she steps out to greet him. "Sorry for the noise."

"Make as much noise as you can," she says. She misses noise, kid behavior, farting, peeing behind the shed, burping, big laughter, yelling things you can say just as well in a conversational tone, "I NEED BUTTER!" instead of "I need butter" and "WHERE IS MY BASEBALL GLOVE?" instead of "Where is my baseball glove?"

"Bring it on," Agatha tells the Tush. He looks at her funny. She doesn't explain.

Closing the door, she continues with the list of things she misses: sharing donuts with Dax and the boys, Friday family pizza night, falling into an exhausted lump on the couch with Dax after finally getting the boys to bed, listening to Jack Johnson as they wait for the boys to stop coming downstairs for water/snacks/hugs/a lost ball, and sex, yes, yes, that, the sex.

Dax calls just after she adds sex to the list. Bad timing. He's upset about her visit to the school before swimming class. "You've broken the agreed-upon rules of our co-parenting situation," he says.

"Baloney," she says. "I haven't agreed to any rules of co-parenting. I haven't even agreed to co-parent. I'm still back at, holy shit, my husband cheated on me and left me to rot."

"I didn't leave you to rot."

"Well, you left and I'm rotting. And while I'm sitting in our house rotting like a discarded piece of cauliflower under the table, you came up with a bunch of co-parenting rules and assumed I would adhere to them."

She heard Dax chuckle, hold back a chuckle, guffaw in the back of his throat the way he does, has always done. "Dax, are you laughing at me? At my rot?"

"No, Agatha, I'm not laughing at you. I wouldn't laugh at you, especially right now. I'm laughing at the discarded piece of cauliflower rotting under the table."

Agatha smiles a tiny bit, the teeniest, tiniest bit possible. He's always loved her descriptions, as exaggerated as they may be. But then she gulps down the smile because this man, this used-to-be-husband who has morphed into somebody-else's-lover, doesn't have the right to enjoy her creativity, her brilliance, her humor. "You don't get to laugh with me anymore, Dax. You gave up that right. And I'll tell you here and now, I'm going to see my boys as much as possible, even on days when they are technically yours. If you try and stop me with lawyers or rules or judges or anything, you'll be sorry."

It's a threat. And while Dax is brave about his love fest with GDOG, she's pretty sure he'll do anything to protect it.

"Agatha," he says, his voice much less I'll-take-you-to-court-ish and more I-wish-we-could-work-this-out-over-pancakes, "I am sorry. This isn't what I wanted to have happen, not how I wanted you to find out. I am . . ."

Agatha hangs up, gathers her boombox and Beastie Boys CD, and heads to the House of Sin. The boys are at school and Dax is at work. She parks under the umbrella of yellowing maple leaves. One window in the living room is open. A light breeze bustles the white sheers. She pops in the CD, cranks the volume, and props the boombox in the open car window. She leans her head back. She knows every bounce and run in this song.

At minute 1:38, the dog walker's turquoise-y self appears in the window. The woman thinks she's a piece of Southwestern jewelry. Agatha waves. Willow Bean doesn't wave back. Then Dax appears behind her and places a hand on her hip. What is he doing home from work? He was talking on the phone to her from GDOG's house? Agatha seethes and boosts the volume. He shakes his head, says something in Willow Bean's ear, and slides the window shut.

While Agatha waits out the song, she checks the Moms page. Raquel is once again fascinated by the mundane wildlife in her yard.

Isabelle Fish: "Four deer today. Nibbling the leaves on the bushes. Any known deterrents?"

Rae Stein: "I have some excellent repellent (aka poison) that can help with that problem." 😉

That no-kill policy in Wallingford goes out the window when the garden is affected.

Melody: "Oh, the deer are beautiful, aren't they?"

Oh, for fuck's sake. Agatha starts the car and heads off, offering up a double beep to Dax and the Grande Dame of Grapefruits as she goes.

Chapter Twenty-Four

Just when it seems Agatha can't get any more invasive, she buys a drone. An ultra-fancy drone equipped with a state-of-the-art camera, which, with the *right touch*, the literature promises, can hover close enough to a subject to record even the most intimate of moments.

"Whose intimate moments?" Shrinky-Dink asks when Agatha slips it out of her bag.

"Dax and the Grande Dame of Grapefruits."

"You're going to film them?"

"Yes."

"Your ex and his lover?"

"He's not my ex."

"Technicality."

So blunt.

"Yes, my estranged husband and his hussy."

"Where?"

"In the House of Sin."

"In Willow Bean's house? Now their house?"

"Yes."

"Doing what?"

"Whatever they do."

"You want to film them doing whatever they do?"

"No, but I want them to see me filming it."

"Agatha, I can't condone this."

"I'm not asking you to."

"Yes, you are. You brought the drone to your session. This implies you're looking for support or permission."

"I just wanted to show you my new toy."

"This is not Show and Tell, Agatha. It's therapy. You know I feel that way, so I assume that subconsciously you're uncomfortable with your drone acquisition and you wanted to be confronted about it."

Agatha grunts. Subconsciously hadn't she just been looking for a friend to say "that's so cool," but forgot that she didn't have a friend so accidentally turned to her therapist and is now feeling like more of a failure than ever? She could say this, should say this, it would save them months of unraveling the thread, but instead says, "Wasn't there a 'make your tone nonjudgmental so your client/patient doesn't know when you're unhappy with her' course offered when you were in school?"

"I'm not unhappy with you. I'm unhappy with your choice. And, no, there's not a class like that."

"Obviously."

Shrinky-Dink waits.

"Listen, it's a cool drone. The best on the market."

"You said the same thing about the hammers and the Leatherman."

"The Leatherman Super Tool 300 EOD." Agatha smiles.

Shrinky-Dink does not. "Yes," she says. "The one that saved a man with a coconut in a jungle."

"And you hate those tools, too."

Shrinky-Dink opens her mouth to speak, but Agatha jumps in first. "I know, I know. You don't hate the tools; you hate my decision to buy the tools."

"I don't *hate* anything."

* * *

Determined, Agatha takes to practicing in a nearby park with the gaggle of nerdy teens who congregate each day for drone practice. Most are working toward dive-bombing their friends' unsuspecting mothers or stealing answers to next week's test from their teachers, but tech-obsessed teens know their shit.

On her first day at the park, Agatha crashes the drone into the statue of Wallingford's esteemed founder so hard it busts into pieces. "Holy crap," she grunts, panicked that she's ruined the most expensive and most advanced drone on the market. But within five minutes, those marvelous magical teens have it back together and are skating it along tree branches and around corners of the park shed. It draws significant attention. "Wow," one kid says, turning it this way and that. "What did you pay for this thing? It looks like NASA built it."

Agatha doesn't tell him because she knows he won't be able to afford this particular category of drone for at least fifteen years. "I got a good sale," she says.

A girl named Blue becomes her primary tutor. All the kids jockey for the position but since Blue is the only one who compliments Agatha's spy pants, she gets the gig. Once their partnership is established, Blue swoops in each afternoon on a well-worn skateboard carrying two coffees. Agatha brings cookies.

"My mom hates my drone obsession," Blue tells Agatha. "She's a librarian and she thinks drones signal the end of society as we know it. 'Why go to a library when a drone can deliver books to your home?' she says at least once a day. 'Why go to the mall if a drone can drop socks at your door?' She goes on and on about the end of society as we know it. Just what is so damn great about society as we know it?"

It's a worthy question.

Blue then lists the atrocities the world has seen during her lifetime: school massacres, terrorist attacks, Malala getting shot in the face, racial profiling, the proliferation of Starbucks, *Zoolander 2*. She is a smart, well-informed librarian's kid, and she has her own ideas for making the world a better place. Agatha gets it, but she gets her mom, too. She can understand why she is working so hard to make sure Blue touches library shelves and walks through a mall to pick up socks in the hosiery department in Macy's.

Agatha likes hearing about Blue's mother and all the ways she makes her crazy, but it gets her thinking about the things that will someday drive Jason and Dustin mad. She imagines them playing baseball with their friends and saying "My mom is afraid of everything. Everything. She is even afraid of butterflies. Who can be afraid of butterflies?" Maybe they say this already.

Blue's big question sticks with her. What is so damn great about society as we know it? Not much, as far as Agatha can see. Even if a human manages to create a cozy nest of a life, Dax has proven it can be blown to smithereens in an instant.

Kapow! Kaplooey! Kaboom!

While Blue teaches Agatha about the ins and outs of controlling a drone, they make a list of the things they do think are great about society. Ginger ice cream. Coffee. Free Wi-Fi. Blue: skateboards. Agatha: her sons. It's a powerful but pretty short list, which makes Agatha realize that she and Blue aren't as far apart in their lives as one would think.

"What are you going to do with this thing anyway?" Blue asks one day.

"Impress my kids," Agatha says.

"Liar," Blue says. She's a keen kid an eye for honesty, but how can Agatha tell a fifteen-year-old girl that she plans to film her estranged husband and his lover?

Agatha smiles. "What about you? Why are you so big on these things?"

"I'm designing drone programs that will deliver food, water, technology, and education to people in remote areas," Blue says. She looks

Agatha right in the eye as she speaks. This girl has vision. And know-how. And drive. Yes, she is only fifteen, but she's doing the work.

By the time Blue is done with her, Agatha can maneuver her drone between branches of trees, around tight corners, and into the smallest of small spaces. She can hover it a mere inch from a window, so still the images it shoots back are as clear as if the camera were sitting on a tripod. She can even make that thing fly alongside a car in motion, filming the driver and the passenger. Blue dubs her Hummingbird.

Agatha likes this nickname. She's never had a nickname other than Aggie-girl, and that no longer counts.

With her new skill set, she is going to glean even more information about the lovers and see as much about her boys' life as she needs to.

This is powerful. And totally screwed up.

* * *

"If you can't come up with anything nice to say, parrot someone's words back to them," Shrinky-Dink advises.

"If you can't come up with anything nice to say, parrot someone's words back to them," Agatha says.

"Change the pronouns," Shrinky-Dink says.

"Change the pronouns," Agatha repeats.

Shrinky-Dink smirk-smiles.

Agatha smirk-smiles back at her. "If I can't come up with anything nice to say, parrot someone's words back to them."

Shrinky-Dink smile-smiles. "You got it."

"I got it."

* * *

Scrape, scrape, slide. Scrape, slide, scrape.

Tap tap tippity-tap.

Slide, scrape, scrape.

Slide.

Tap tap tippity-tap.

Between the Tush's team and the woodpecker, all the noise sneaking in the window sounds like a jazz tune.

Agatha hates jazz, always has, hates its dissonance, its wonky rhythms, its improvisation. She depends on structure and form and routine and doing what is expected.

Dax used to say she listened to it wrong, but that was a load of bullshit. She listened just fine.

She sips her coffee.

Scrape, scrape, slide. Scrape, scrape, slide.

Tap tap tippity-tap.

Gggrrr.

The doorbell rings. She tiptoes to the hallway, peers around the corner, and sees the top of Kerry Sheridan's hot-pink babushka through the window. Kerry calls it a workout kerchief whenever Agatha calls her out about it, but it's no different than the babushka Agatha's grandmother used to wear.

Dammit.

Agatha throws open the door. "Hello, Kerry."

"Hello, Agatha."

Shrinky-Dink's words echo in Agatha's head: If you can't come up with anything nice to say, parrot someone's words back to them. A timely challenge if ever there was one.

"I need to talk to you."

Change the pronouns. "You need to talk to me?"

"Yes."

"Yes."

Tap tap tippity-tap.

Tap tap tippity-tap.

Scrape, scrape, slide.

Scrape.

Slide, scrape, slide.

Agatha looks at Kerry.

"It's about that." Kerry points toward the yard-cum-meadow that surrounds the shed.

"It's about that?"

"Yes."

"Yes?"

"Your yard."

"My yard?"

"It's still a mess. A bigger mess."

"A mess?"

"Yes, Agatha, the giant, hideous, gnarly mess full of poison ivy. When are you going to clean it up?"

"The problem is that it's ugly?"

"And full of poison ivy! Thomas is finally over it and he wants to play ball in the yard again."

"Why don't the boys play ball on the other side of your house? You've got loads of yard."

"You know very well they play ball right here, on this side."

"Well, they should change yards. Change is good."

"Agatha, they're playing ball with your boys."

"Yes, I know. I'll tell my boys they have to play on the other side of your yard."

"Agatha, that's not the point. Not the only point. It's the mess. It's the poison ivy. It's the weeds. Rats are going to come, you know."

Agatha stops. Her heart seizes. Rats? Rats? She hadn't thought of rats. "Do you think so? Have you seen one?"

"No, but they'll come. That's what this kind of mess draws."

Agatha slams the door in Kerry's face and leans against the wall. Rats. She's got to get the yard cleaned up. "Well played, Kerry Sheridan, well played."

Chapter Twenty-Five

"Hey, Hummingbird, are all ladies your age afraid of so many things?" Blue asks. She's tightening a screw on the drone, the tiniest screw Agatha has ever seen and the one that proves getting older stinks. Agatha can't even see it let alone tighten it.

"I doubt it," Agatha says. "I'm a bit of a special case."

Blue nods. "Maybe you should ask them."

"Why?"

"I don't know. It might help to know you're not the only one in the world afraid of butterflies."

There are so many reasons to like this kid. Vocabulary is one. Honesty another. Huzzah is a third. Agatha suspects she's likely right about the Moms having their own fears, but asking is like admitting out loud that there is just so much to cower from in the world. So much that can break you.

That night, after obsessing about the boys, butterflies, the Interloper, the rogue grizzly cub, and, ugh, the rats that are right now marching to their new life in her yard-cum-meadow, Agatha sucks down a glass of wine and opens the Moms group on her phone.

Agatha Arch: "Unexpected question, Moms, but what are you afraid of in life?"

She expects guffaws, smirks, and whatnot. She's never actually used the Moms group as a soft place to fall; that was Dax's domain, he was her soft place. She waits, but instead of a raking over the coals, she gets a landslide of honesty.

Erin Abel:	"Oh, god, perfect question for tonight. I'm petrified of having my seventeen-year-old daughter drive by herself. I've been sitting here waiting for her to come home. I made her text me before leaving the mall. Now I wait, like I do every day, staring at the front door, waiting for it to open. It's ridiculous. I know she's a responsible kid and she has to grow up, but I'd like to keep her in the passenger seat until she's thirty."
Katherine Stot:	"I'm afraid of the dark. My husband died last year, and I never realized how afraid I was of the dark until then. Maybe I wasn't before. Maybe the dark was different. Maybe I was just fine in the dark. I'm not now."
Meghan Wilson:	"Germs. I'm so afraid of germs. I wear gloves all the time, which embarrasses the hell out of my kids. They beg me to take them off when I visit their schools for a parent/teacher conference or ice cream social, but I can't. They're getting old enough to know most mothers don't wear gloves 24 hours a day, and they're starting to hate me for it. Soon they'll hate me completely. I'm even typing with my gloves on."
Samantha Yang:	"Dogs."
Priya Devi:	"I'm afraid of mice, and I know there's one in my basement. I spotted his droppings a few days ago, and I haven't gone down since. It's a

	fucking mouse, for god's sake. I'm a million times bigger than him. But still, I'm terrified. I'm going to send my laundry to the dry cleaners so I don't have to go down there."
David Watkins:	"Not being accepted for who I am."
Carla Met:	"Failing. At my job, at parenting, at life. It keeps me from taking any kind of risk or trying something new. Drives my husband batty because I talk about it constantly. Sometimes I think he's going to take off and leave me behind because I'm so annoying."
Grainne O'Neill:	"Me, too. Fear of failure is my greatest weakness. I was passed up for a promotion because of it. A promotion I wanted and that I was quite qualified for. But the hiring director said they needed a risk-taker and I hadn't shown that characteristic in the three years I'd been at my job. It sucked. But I still haven't taken a risk."
Katie Kim:	"White water rafting."
Deirdre Heathers:	"Scary movies."

Agatha gives her a fist bump.

Blonde Brenda What's-Her-Name:	"My kids dying."
Tanya West:	"Sneezing in public cuz it makes me pee my pants and I don't want to wear Depends."
Anne Pape:	"Getting old."

Lots of funny-face emojis pop up after the getting old one. It seems everyone but Agatha is afraid of that. That's the one thing that doesn't worry her.

High Priestess Poston: "Just saw this thread and scrolled up to see who posted the original question. Honestly did a double-take, Agatha, when I saw your photo next to the post. Kudos."

Kudos for what?

She doesn't ask. For once she keeps her mouth shut. She just sips her pinot noir and reads through the crazy-ass fears the Moms are sharing.

Faith Flanagan: "Flying. My kids live all over the world. Hong Kong. Scotland. France. And I rarely see them because they're too busy to visit and I'm too chicken to fly. I'm retired. I have money. My kids love me and want to see me. But I can't get on a plane. How f'd up is that?"

Amanda Stout: "Leaving my house, at all. I haven't gone out the door in two years. Not once."

Melody Whelan: "I'm most afraid that the people who are most afraid will not achieve their true potential because they remain governed by their fears."

If anyone else had spit out this mumbo jumbo, Agatha would have called them on it, but knowing Melody the bit she does, she knows she is telling her truth. Melody Whelan's fear is all about others not achieving their true selves. Agatha doesn't know what mix of DNA and voodoo occurred at the moment this woman had been conceived, but this is who she is.

Agatha also knows that while she wasn't specifically mentioned, Melody is talking directly to her.

Agatha Arch: "Thanks for all the input, ladies."

She despises the word *ladies* but it feels right in this context. Convivial even.

High Priestess Poston: “Agatha, have you been abducted by aliens and forced to engage in a congenial and helpful conversation with the Moms? Type a poop emoji for yes.”

Agatha laughs. She is actually kind of glad someone says it out loud.

Agatha Arch: “Nope, no aliens, Jane. Thanks, all. Nice to know I’m not the only one afraid of shit in the world.”

She called her Jane. Not High Priestess. Not HP. Not *you giant pain in the ass.*

High Priestess Poston: “🙂”
Melody: “Never the only one, Agatha Arch, never the only one.”

* * *

Agatha dreams about Susie. She asks all the questions she wants to ask the world.

Is it possible to feel afraid and brave at the same time?
Happy and sad?
Hopeful and bleak?
Benevolent and malevolent?
Awake and dormant?
Horny and hideous?

* * *

In response to the last, she wakes lustful. She wants to roll over and into and onto some body that wraps itself around her. Legs and arms and tongues. Weeks have passed without a single touch. Weeks. Good god. Weeks. All this post-shed turmoil is hard but this may be the hardest part. Definitely the loneliest. Who can I kiss? she wonders.

Scrape, slide, slide.

Slide, scrape, slide.

The Tush?

Kiss the Tush?

No.

Slide, slide, scrape.

Maybe.

Agatha hauls herself out of bed and pulls her "Who Can I Bonk?" hat from a pre-marriage box in her closet. She smiles and puts it on.

"You have a 'Who Can I Bonk?' hat?" Shrinky-Dink asks when Agatha shares the story.

"Not a real one," Agatha says, rolling her eyes. "It's metaphorical."

Hat in place, she digs around in drawers and boxes until she finds a couple of silky dress-up things from her pre-kid life that were too snug when she'd tried them a few months ago for a night out with Dax but that fit just fine now that she's been on the my-husband-screwed-the-dog-walker-in-the-shed-and-left-me diet for a few weeks. They smell like mothballs, but they'll do.

She peeks out the window, spots the Tush on the ladder near the east corner of the house, and targets him as her very first my-husband-screwed-the-dog-walker-in-the-shed-and-left-me lover. He's perfect. Convenient, responsible, and, just as the Moms promised, he has a great tush.

In a few hours' time, she develops a strategy for the development of their tryst. It's simple really. She will sashay about the yard in alluring clothes, then saunter into the house and toss back a look of longing and lust. The Tush will come to the door and growl, "I'm thirsty." She will wag a bare shoulder at him and say, "I'm thirsty, too." He will narrow his eyes, raise his eyebrows, and smile ever so slightly. Then he will throw open the screen door, whip her into his paint-spattered arms, and take her right there and then on the kitchen table.

Perfect plan.

It lasts three days.

* * *

Day 1: Agatha pulls on the low-cut lavender bubbly thing with a pair of white jeans and some jingly-bell sandals. Then she delivers a cold, sweaty glass of iced tea to the Tush, holding her own sweaty glass against her now mothbally cleavage.

* * *

Nothing.

* * *

Day 2: Agatha dons the shortest dress in the world—a shirt, really—but forgets she is wearing her faded gramma gutchies until a gust of wind whips up the dress and reveals her truth to the world. And to the Tush.

* * *

Nothing.

* * *

Day 3: She steps into her roller skates ["Roller skates?" Shrinky-Dink is incredulous when she hears this.] and spins around the driveway in a yellow tank top with her boobs poking out like torpedoes. When, for whatever unfathomable reason, this final display of desire does not cause the Tush to swoon with desire, she tries a double spin, loses control, and slams face first into one of the oak trees. This, at least, makes the Tush leap down from the ladder, run to her side, and inquire about her well-being. After confirming that she is not critically injured from the impact, he eyes the swell of her cheek and says, “That’s going to bruise. You might want to ice it.” Then he makes his way back up the ladder, his adorable tush swishing and swagging in his painter whites. “Perhaps women your age should avoid roller skating,” he adds when he gets to the top. “My mother gave it up years ago.”

Chapter Twenty-Six

Though she's not sure why, Agatha accepts Melody's third invitation to lunch. Maybe she is curious or lonely. Maybe she's worn down. Maybe some greater cosmic energy intervenes and calls out in a deep, echo-y voice, "It is time to have lunch with the Kumbaya Queen." She's not into the God thing, but every once in a while, she does get the feeling there's something more than mere humans governing the beauteous fuck-up of a world.

When Melody answers, "Great! Does next Friday at noon work for you?" Agatha panics. *Does next Friday at noon work for you?* This response is so normal—so banal—she knows it has to have some hidden meaning.

But finally, she responds, keeping it just as simple. "Yes," she writes.

"You know the house," Melody writes back, letting Agatha know she has not forgotten the spying incident.

"Oh, I'm not sure I do," Agatha replies. "Address?"

She can hear Melody *tsking* through the internet.

"164 North Circle Street."

* * *

During the week leading up to the lunch, Agatha obsesses. Is this going to be some kind of intervention? Are five hundred Wallingford Moms going to be present, encouraging Agatha to be kinder and gentler? Will the Moms join hands in a circle around her, sway like pines in the wind, and sing "Kumbaya"? Will Marty Snow deliver notice of her final eviction from the Moms group, citing lunacy and erratic behavior? Will Melody have a therapist waiting in the wings to whisk her away to a rehab center immediately following the gathering, like they do on afternoon talk shows?

But the scariest question of all is, will Melody invite the Interloper? Will she use this lunch as an opportunity to introduce the two of them, to cajole Agatha into seeing the Interloper as a wounded soul instead of imminent danger? This is the possibility that gets Agatha's stomach churning, and that week she gets even less sleep than normal. She tosses and turns, tosses and turns, from the time she gets into bed to the time she gets out.

* * *

"For in the end, freedom is a personal and lonely battle; and one faces down fears of today so that those of tomorrow might be engaged." Alice Walker

Fears of today. Fears of today. Agatha slams the book closed and tries to pick one to face down.

Mice?

The dark?

Fireworks?

Tunnels?

Bridges?

Men with tiny patches of hair on their chins?

Alien invasion?

Ghosts?

Beans?

Drowning?

Not fitting in?

Public bathrooms?

Anesthetic?
Surgery?
Shadows?
Nope, nope, nope.
That stranger on the street?
Uh uh. Cross the street before you have to deal with that one.
Butterflies?
Can't they just stop flitting around and land on something?
Being alone?
Grrr.
The rats Kerry promises will be invading the yard?
Absolutely not.
The Interloper?
Hell no.

* * *

The second nor'easter of the season blows in overnight. It's a doozy, but by dawn still no snow, just rain and wind and more rain, and the Moms thanking goodness for that. Agatha is awake early, monitoring a cupcake kerfuffle in the group when an ad for brush-clearing goats pops up in her FB feed. Brush-clearing goats? She has never heard of such a thing, but vacillates between finding out if one of Wallingford's finest specialty bakers is going to make a new batch of Minion cupcakes for the Mom who is royally pissed that her cupcakes look more like penises than Minions OR finding out if the goat thing is real.

She stares at the yard-cum-meadow—wet, muddy, beautiful, and beastly, like her heart—posts a GIF of a Minion waltzing with a cartoony penis, and calls the goat company. "Is this a real thing?" she asks the woman who answers. "I can hire goats to clear a yard? An overgrown yard? An eyesore, as my neighbor calls it?"

"It's a real thing, ma'am. Better than poisonous chemicals. Better than a bulldozer. Better than a hundred lazy men. Eyesores are our specialty."

"The goats eat the weeds?"

"The goats eat the weeds."

The Moms are mad as hell about the cupcakes. "Damn the Penis-Maker-Baker," one Mom writes. The specialist baker, previously known as Barbara, will now be referred to as Penis-Maker-Baker until the end of time or the end of Facebook.

"The goats eat poison ivy?" Agatha asks the goat woman.

"They eat poison ivy."

"Do they smell?"

"Absolutely not. Goats are very clean creatures."

"How about their poop? Does it stink?"

"No, goat excrement is odorless, and it's terrific fertilizer. A true gift of nature."

Another Mom asks if anything was broken or thrown or hurled in the bakery during the altercation. Fists, cupcakes, spatulas?

There was hand-slapping, a tossing of the receipt, and lots of yelling, the poster assures.

"How quickly do goats clear an area?" Agatha says into the phone, trying to stay focused.

"It depends on the size, density of brush, weather, and so forth. Baseline, four goats can eat a quarter of an acre of shrubbery and weeds in a week."

"Wow."

"That's what our customers say."

The Moms are piling on. It's like that king of the hill game-not-game you play as a kid.

"Do goats destroy structures?"

"Structures?"

"Like a shed. Or what used to be a shed."

Agatha hears the wind pick up. It sounds like a train coming out of a tunnel.

"No, no, that's the beauty," the goat woman says. "These sweet peas eat the unwanted stuff and leave everything else intact."

"Amazing," Agatha says.

"Now they might climb on a structure. They are climbers and leapers. It's a goat thing."

Agatha nods. "Not a problem. The shed is in shambles already."

"Perfect," the goat woman says. "Anything other questions?"

The Moms are pulling orders from Penis-Maker-Baker, vowing to ruin her hard-won reputation. They've loved her desperately until this very moment, for her Thomas the Train cakes, the Having-a-Baby vagina cake, and her flowers, oh, her flowers, but that's how it goes in the Moms group, as Heidi Klum says on *Project Runway*, "One day you're in, the next day you're out."

"No," Agatha says. "It just sounds too good to be true."

"It's good. It's true."

"How soon can I book them?"

Agatha clicks back to the Moms group. It turns out that Penis-Maker-Baker has refused to bake another batch. Her Minion cupcakes are loved near and far. She knows it and she stands her ground. "She said, 'I will not do it! They are not penises. They are Minions,'" the poster reports.

The next crack of lightning is followed by a deafening boom, and one of the two mighty oaks is felled. It hits the house, shakes it, scoots the furniture a few inches this way, and rattles the windows a few inches that way. The boys come running, and Agatha's heart jumps all the way to the moon and she thinks about the "My Favorite Things" scene in *The Sound of Music* but can't bring herself to utter a note or dance with her curtains because there is no Dax to calm the waters, so she holds on to those boys in the room now darkened by the oak flush against the window and thinks about Janie and Tea Cake fleeing the hurricane and the cow swimming in the flood with the massive dog on its back.

That book. About so much more than a hurricane.

This tree. This downed tree. About so much more than a nor'easter.

In the days that follow, Penis-Maker-Baker receives two death threats as a result of the altercation, and as far as anyone knows, these are the first death threats ever to be issued as a result of a Moms group posting. It is frightening but thrilling.

It also affirms Agatha's prediction about an eventual murder in a Moms group.

It comes that close.

* * *

Agatha shimmies through a narrow space between the driveway and the trunk of the oak.

"Agatha? Agatha!" It's Kerry Sheridan. "Are you and the boys okay?"

"We are," Agatha says. She pushes a bunch of orange leaves out of the way and tries to step through the tangle, but a branch blocks her path. "Storms make you stronger," she says.

Kerry's eyes get wide. "What?"

"Storms make you stronger. Bear says that."

"He does?"

"Yup."

"I hope he's right."

Agatha pulls her Leatherman Super Tool 300 EOD from a pocket and opens the saw. She pulls the blade back and forth against the thick branch. "He's always right."

Kerry looks dubious.

"This tree hit the house hard." Agatha sighs. The northeast corner is smasheroo'd. It's pretty clear the Tush isn't going anywhere soon.

When a blister starts to form on her thumb, she stops sawing, gets outs her phone, and calls TreeLife. There has to be some kind of guarantee.

* * *

"Do not bark," Shrinky-Dink says. "Do not bark at Melody Whelan. Do not bark at Jane Poston. Do not bark at the Interloper. Do not bark at Dax or Willow Bean or Kerry Sheridan or . . ."

"I cannot bark at Kerry Sheridan?"

"You cannot bark at Kerry Sheridan."

"This is what I pay you for?" Agatha says.

Shrinky-Dink nods. "Money well spent."

* * *

The drone bumps into the downstairs window at the House of Sin and Agatha turns on the feed. No one is home, of that she is sure, this time, because after the boys' bus departed, she waited in the pine tree across the way until Dax kissed his lover at the door then climbed into his Honda and until GDOG left for work on foot, a bag of dog treats strapped to her hip.

She cowers behind the tree with HEART painted on its trunk. She didn't know until right this moment that Dax had tried to sand off the word, but up close she can see his efforts. Funny that it didn't work, but here it is, HEART, still clear and bold, as if written in hot-pink blood.

On the feed, she sees the dining room table with four plates of breakfast leftovers. Pancakes and yogurt, blueberries, pineapple, slices of orange. The boys' plates are nearly empty, and the fact that they are eating fruit salad for GDOG when they won't eat an apple for her unless she slathers it in Nutella sinks her heart.

She sends the drone to the window of the boys' room, studies the tangle of pajamas on the floor, Dustin's plaid flannel and Jason's SpongeBob tatters which he refuses to give up and insists on toting between his two homes like treasure. Tears start to drip so she calls the drone back and slumps to the ground just as a police car pulls up. It's him, as always, him, the same officer who sat with her on the porch and called her down from the tree and waved with *Their Eyes Were Watching God* at dusk, as if Wallingford has only one officer who goes out to do any work. That's what she wants to ask him: "Are you the only officer on our force? Aren't there others? Why you? Always you? Who else is keeping our citizens safe? Who else is watching the Interloper?"

"Ma'am?" he says. "Ms. Arch?"

Agatha stands. "You might as well call me Agatha."

"And you might as well call me Henry. We got a call you were here again."

"Henry?"

"That's my name."

"Okay, Henry, so who called you? The lady with the kid who got hit with the falling pine cone?"

"It doesn't matter. Just a call."

"I'm not doing anything wrong." She holds the drone behind her back.

"You do know spying with a drone could be considered trespassing, right?"

"Yes, of course, I wouldn't do that. I'm just watching. Making sure my boys have a safe and healthy life in this second, unexpected house."

Henry nods. "I understand that need," he says. Perhaps he is not as young and stupid as Agatha thought. "But I also need to make sure you stay safe and healthy."

Agatha feels like he's telling the truth. She turns to go, tucking the drone under her shirt.

"Ma'am," the officer calls. "Agatha?"

Agatha stops, pretty sure he's going to bust her for the drone. She considers taking off through the trees and into the back yards and remembers doing that very thing in high school when cops busted an underage kegger. That officer had grabbed her arms from behind and she'd peeled right out of the yellow cardigan she was wearing, leaving it in the officer's clutch. Then she'd run and hid under a bunch of bushes. The president of the class was hiding there, too. "Wanna make out?" he'd said while they waited for the police cars to go. He'd never spoken to her before, and she'd declined.

"Yes, Henry," she says.

"That book? *Their Eyes Were Watching God*?"

Agatha smiles. "Yes?"

"It's good. Thanks for the recommendation."

* * *

"Put your phone in here," Melody says when Agatha walks into the house, along with many other things that Agatha doesn't hear because she has to zigzag herself around in the foyer to avoid the weird, white basket Melody shoves at her.

"No, no, thank you," Agatha says, as she tucks her phone into the hip pocket of her spy pants where it will be safe from Melody's grip. There's no way she's going to enter the enemy's lair without access to communication with the outside world. She practiced her emergency call on the way to Melody's house and she's ready: "This is Agatha Arch. I'm being held against my will at 164 North Circle Street by Kumbaya Queen Melody Whelan. Please rescue me."

Once the weird, white basket disappears, Agatha says, "Thanks for inviting me, Melody."

"Thank you for accepting my invitation."

And after that there's a long, awkward pause that Melody tries to fill with a description of the stone turtle that serves as a doorstop and the dozen tiny stone turtle babies around it.

"Beautiful house," Agatha says, following Melody into the living room, not meaning beautiful at all, really wanting to say there are a lot of doilies and knickknacks and padded rocking chairs and weird-ass shit cluttering the house, but trying, really trying, to channel Shrinky-Dink's advice about kindness.

"You don't mean that," Melody says.

"You're right. I don't. But it does make me feel nostalgic for my grandmother's house. And you do stop short of plastic couch coverings, which is nice."

When Melody turns her back, Agatha peeks around a corner, sure that while the Moms weren't waiting in the foyer, they are going to jump out of the shadows soon enough.

Once in the dining room, Melody carries out two plates of salad and perfectly cooked tuna to the table. "Let's eat. Do you like tuna?"

"Love it."

And Agatha does love tuna, but it hits her that she should have brought a taste tester, the kind kings and queens employ to test their food for poison, the kind paid to take the fall. Despite the uneventful opening ceremonies, Agatha is still quite sure Melody's motives are devious and deceptive, except that from time to time she finds herself lured into comfort by Melody's warmth and seemingly genuine care. Is this some kind of intervention, she thinks, or the beginning of a zephyr?

Melody smiles and takes a small bite of tuna, then excuses herself to get the salt. While she is gone, Agatha switches their plates. Knowing that Melody took a bite and hadn't keeled over comforts Agatha only until she figures out that Melody may have done this purposely, that she'd taken the only non-poisoned bite of her tuna, then conveniently left the room, knowing Agatha would switch the plates during her absence.

Good god, life is complicated.

When Melody returns, Agatha doesn't mention the possibility of poisoning, but she does spend the rest of the meal pushing the tuna around on its greens.

"Not hungry?" Melody asks. Her tone is so banal Agatha knows she made the right decision about not eating.

"No, I had a big breakfast. A late breakfast. Really a late brunch. No offense."

Melody forks a piece of tuna into her mouth. "None taken. It is delicious though. I got the recipe from the Moms."

Agatha imagines the post: "Best tuna recipes in which you can successfully hide the flavor of poison? Go!"

No way, Melody Whelan. No way.

* * *

When the cheesecake hits the table, Melody finally broaches the subject of the Interloper. Agatha knew it was coming.

"Her name is Lucy Strums," Melody says through a mouthful.

"Please don't talk with your mouth full. I can't understand you," Agatha says. Melody's mouth isn't really full. Just kind of full. The kind of full people talk through all the time. A bit of cheesecake tucked in one cheek. But Agatha needs a minute to channel Shrinky-Dink's advice about barking.

"Don't bark," she chants silently. "Don't bark. Don't bark." She mashes a spot of possibly poisoned cheesecake into oblivion.

"Okay, you can talk now," she says to Melody in the most non-barky tone she can summon. She can tell she's achieved an unprecedented level of non-barkiness because Melody looks at her like she has three heads. Agatha considers smiling. Shrinky-Dink says that particular maneuver will catapult her to new heights as a human, but come on. Smile? She just can't do it. Not yet. The amount of self-control it takes to offer up that non-barky tone has just about done her in.

"Her name is Lucy," Melody repeats. "Lucy Strums."

Channeling Shrinky-Dink's advice a second time, Agatha simply parrots Melody's words back to her. "Her name is Lucy," she says. "Lucy Strums."

At the sound of her voice delivering the Interloper's name, Agatha swears she hears a bell ring somewhere in the distance at the same moment satisfaction merges with joy on Melody's face.

"Do you like cheesecake?"

"I do, but, again, I'm just not hungry."

"I should have served cupcakes. I know you like those. The chocolate especially."

"How do you . . ." Agatha starts to ask, but then it hits her. Melody had left the cupcake on her stoop.

"You left me the cupcake?"

"Of course I did. You needed one. You deserved one after all you've been through. Probably should have left you a dozen."

Agatha stares at her plate and fingers the crease still deep in her cheek.

It becomes obvious as Melody happily shuffles Agatha out the door with a Tupperware of cheesecake in hand that she has achieved her unspoken goal. Agatha said the Interloper's name out loud, therefore, in Melody's mind, she has acknowledged her as a person. A fellow human. A soul.

As Agatha bolts down the walk, Melody waves vigorously from the porch, pearls bouncing on her bosom, and calls, "See you next time," as if lunch together is going to be a regular occurrence. And then, as if *that* isn't enough, she adds, "Let's do a yoga class together next Tuesday."

"Sure," Agatha calls back without turning. "That sounds great."

Yoga class?

On Tuesday?

With Melody?

When Agatha finally gets to the end of the stone walkway and leaps into her car, she drops her head to the steering wheel and sobs with relief. She hadn't been kidnapped, brainwashed, poisoned, or made to talk to the Interloper. She hadn't been subjected to an intervention. She'd simply eaten lunch. Or rather, she'd simply sat with Melody Whelan while Melody had eaten lunch. And, although the experience wasn't so bad, she tosses the Tupperware of cheesecake into the first garbage can she sees. Just in case.

Chapter Twenty-Seven

Tap tap tippity-tap. A single life does not happen in isolation. Humans are connected to fish are connected to whales are connected to flashes of lightning are connected to trees and ants and roots of the tallest stalk of corn and sunflowers and raindrops and exploding stars. Humans are connected to one another. This human to that human. Big human to little human. Black human to brown human to white human. Newborn human to ancient human.

For better or worse, Agatha is connected to the Interloper. The Interloper is connected to Melody. Agatha is connected to Melody. As Carl Sagan said, "We are made of star-stuff," connecting the matter in our bodies to the previous generations of stars in which it was formed.

WTF is it all about?

Agatha is also connected to Willow Bean, despite the fact this is the woman falling more and more deeply in love with Agatha's husband. It's an unwelcome connection, but an unavoidable one. Even Jason and Dustin are beginning to like Willow. Not love. Not yet. But like? Yes, like. "It's hard not to," Jason says.

Tap tap tippity-tap. Agatha is also connected to the woodpecker.

* * *

The guy from TreeLife strokes his beard. He's shocked the oak came down. "I apologize for the misdiagnosis," he says.

"What didn't you see?" Agatha says.

"The tree was diseased on the inside, but it wasn't visible on the outside. No symptoms."

Agatha knows exactly what he means.

"Someday we'll be able to x-ray a tree and diagnose sooner, but that technology is still developing. We'll give you six months of tree work to compensate you for the loss."

"No need," she says. "I'm just glad no one was hurt." Really she wishes Dax had been standing under the tree at the very moment it fell, but she can't say that out loud.

* * *

Without the tree in front of the window, the northeast part of the house is fresh with light. In an unseasonable surprise, a charm of goldfinches gathers on the sill.

Agatha warms to this. A charm of friends.

* * *

"Agatha, just keep a lid on it," Shrinky-Dink advises. Her tone is more abrupt than usual.

* * *

When Stella Bender posts photos of her two identical desk lamp options, Agatha does the unthinkable. She grabs Bear, marches up the back stairs, passes the FEAR SHARPENS US note without even a glance, throws open the red door, snaps three photos of her desk lamp, slams the door, marches back down the stairs, slaps Bear onto the counter, and posts the photos to the Moms group.

Agatha Arch: "This, Stella Bender, is a desk lamp. A fine desk lamp. Any desk lamp will do. I warned you."

Fifteen minutes later, the truth hits her. She just walked into and out of her office, the first time since the shed incident, and she didn't melt, explode, spontaneously combust, or even cry. This is something.

* * *

The following day, Agatha gets a text from Melody. "Agatha? Agatha? Did you write this?" A photo of the piece of paper Agatha had tucked into one of the chocolate bars is attached. The message is still legible. "Time to move on, Interloper. Time to move on."

Agatha's heart races as she types. "Where did you get this?"

"Agatha, please answer. Did you write this?"

Crap.

If you're not impulsive, it's easy to be evasive in a text exchange. You simply choose not to answer right away. Later, once you've gathered your thoughts, you make up a lame excuse:

- Totally missed this!
- Big meeting at work. Couldn't talk. More soon.
- Kids hid phone. Just found it.
- Was driving. Never text while driving.
- Phone dead when you texted. Thx for waiting. What's up?
- Sorry so late! Feet in stirrups for annual pap smear when you texted.

But when you're impulsive, like Agatha, evasion rarely works. Since she immediately wrote back "Where did you get this?" Melody knows damn well she isn't in the middle of her annual pap smear. She also knows her phone isn't dead.

"Low on phone juice," Agatha texts back. "More after recharge."

Shit.

Shit, shit, shit.

How in the world had this note gotten into Melody's hands? She'd thrown the notes out the car window, watched them blow away, never to be seen again. But what's worse is why she is so upset that the note got into Melody's hands. So what? Who cares? Who cares if Kumbaya Queen Melody Whelan is upset? Who cares if she read the nasty note?

Agatha's hands and pits are sweating. She is upset, truly, honestly upset. What is happening? She paces the kitchen.

Her landline rings. Normally she wouldn't pick up because who answers a landline nowadays? But she does . . .

because . . .

because . . .

Oh, for fuck's sake, because it's Melody! And like it or not, she realizes she has started to care about Melody.

Agatha Arch cares about Melody Whelan.

Agatha doesn't say anything, just holds the receiver an inch from her head, grimaces, and thinks about this realization.

"Agatha Arch. Did you write this note? You cannot avoid answering this question."

"Melody? Is that you?"

"Of course it's me."

"Oh, hi! Sorry about my cell phone. You know how it is."

"Agatha, can you please tell me if you wrote this note?"

Agatha paces back and forth in front of the empty space on the wall where the clock used to be.

"Agatha?"

There's a long pause.

"Agatha Arch!"

"Oh, for Big Papi's sake, yes. I wrote it. I'd planned to get it to the Interloper via the candy bars. But after running into you on your porch that day and having you invite me in for tea, I felt guilty. That's why I grabbed my bag and ran away. It didn't have anything to do with wanting to give her broccoli. Then I ate the candy bars and threw the notes out the window of my car."

"You wrote a horribly mean note, decided not to give it to Lucy, then tossed it out the window without a thought to littering our world? Do I have it right?"

Good lord. Agatha hadn't even considered the littering issue.

Agatha leans her head against the pane of the living room window. She stares out at the remains of the shed.

"Agatha, do I have it right?"

Agatha nods, but doesn't speak.

"Agatha Arch, do I have it right?"

"Yes."

The line goes quiet.

"Melody? Melody?"

Then Melody Whelan, the Kumbaya Queen, hangs up.

Chapter Twenty-Eight

"Alexa, what is an interloper?" Jason asks when he overhears his mom bemoaning the Interloper to the tomato plant.

Alexa: "An interloper is a person who intrudes or becomes involved in something in which they are not wanted. An interloper is considered to be someone who doesn't belong."

At first Agatha feels a little pleased—smug even—that she chose a perfectly fitting moniker for the ne'er-do-well, but then she sees Jason staring at her. He's close to tears.

"Mom, who is this Interloper you're talking about?" he asks. "Why doesn't she belong?"

As a family, they've spent enormous amounts of time talking about the importance of including everyone, about how every person brings something unique to the table.

"She's someone who has come to town for a questionable reason."

"What questionable reason?"

"Well, she . . . she . . . she's begging for money in town."

"She doesn't have any money? Does she have food?"

"Jason, sometimes there are people who seem dangerous. This young woman seems a little dangerous," Agatha says. "We've talked about how we do have to be wary of some people."

"How do you know she's dangerous?" Jason asked. "Have you talked to her? Do you know her?"

Agatha wants to fib, but this is her kid. She can't fib to her kid. "No, I don't know her."

"Then how do you know she's dangerous?"

Agatha is suddenly in the middle of one of those awkward parenting moments. "It's just a feeling I get."

Jason looks at her the way he does the TV when he disagrees with a decision by the Red Sox coach. "Well, she probably has something unique to offer," he says. "You should find out."

* * *

Later that morning when they go to the grocery store, Jason spots the Interloper in the swatch of grass. "Mom, is that her? Is that the Interloper?"

Agatha looks. The Interloper is leaning against the "Cross Here" sign in the island, holding her can. "Yes, that's her."

"Mom, she looks sadder than anyone else in the whole wide world. Just like you."

As she drives, Agatha thinks about the Interloper and reflects on what a group of sad humans might be called. She starts with the collective nouns she's memorized for people and professions:

a tabernacle of bakers
a discretion of priests
a school of clerks
a feast of brewers
a diligence of messengers
an execution of officers
a goring of butchers
a giggle of girls

a melody of harpists
a body of pathologists
a flood (or a flush) of plumbers
a sprig of vegetarians
an amble of walkers

So many. And so appropriately named. But what of a group of sad humans? What should one call them?

a gloom
a bleak
a misery
a mood
a melancholy
a grief
a sorrow
a woe

Yes, perhaps the last. A woe of brokenhearted souls.

* * *

Agatha: I hate you Dax.

* * *

The goatscaping experts arrive in a pickup truck with "Hello Goat!" painted on its side.

"Step one is a feasibility review," Agatha was told when she'd called. The woman is wearing a dark blue sweatshirt with a large pale goat on the chest. She carries a clipboard. The man has a goatee. He is wearing overalls and strangely thick waders. "These protect me from poison ivy and brambles," he tells Agatha when he catches her eyeing his legs.

Tap tap tippity-tap.

Agatha and the woman stay on the perimeter of the overgrown yard but the man strides through the knee-high weeds. "Buckthorn," he hollers. "Common and glossy."

"Check." The woman checks the invasive species on the chart.

"Porcelain berry."

"Check."

"Lots of dandelion and clover. Our goats will love that. Like icing on a cake."

"Check."

The man dons a pair of gloves that go up to his shoulders, then leans over and moves a bush out of the way. "Poison ivy," he calls. "Lots of it."

"And that's okay?" Agatha whispers. It doesn't seem possible that anything could eat poison ivy and not be harmed.

"Oh, yes, goats love poison ivy."

"It doesn't hurt them?"

"No, ma'am. They have four stomachs. They can process almost anything. Except . . ."

"We'll have to fence off this azalea," the man hollers.

"Except azalea," she says. She makes a note in the margin.

"And these rhododendrons," the man calls.

"And rhododendrons. A few bites and . . ." The woman sticks out her tongue, bulges her eyeballs, and makes a horrid gaggy noise.

"Dead?" Agatha asks.

"Dead."

"They can eat poison ivy but a beautiful rhododendron will kill them?"

"Strange world we live in, isn't it?"

Agatha nods. "In so many ways."

"Fences are lifesavers," the woman says.

Agatha tries to imagine a fence between her and Dax. Another between her and the world. "Do what you need to do," says Agatha. "I do not want to be responsible for a goat's death."

"No, you don't," the woman says. "That would be an expensive misstep."

Tap tap tippity-tap.

"Oriental bittersweet," the man hollers.

The woman checks the box. "Good thing you called us and not a traditional land clearer. Bittersweet clogs chainsaws."

"Really?" Agatha says.

"Yes, indeed."

Agatha points to the goat on the woman's sweatshirt. "Is that a random goat or one of yours?"

The woman smiles, puts her hand on the goat, and rubs lightly. "Oh, this is my Thelma. Louise is on the back." She turns. Agatha sees a darker goat nibbling at a pile of brush. "If you're lucky, this pair will be part of your team. Two of our best."

Agatha wonders what the goats are best at. Being goats? Meh-ing? Eating poison ivy? She's about to ask, but, at the same moment, the man reaches the midpoint of the yard where the remains of the shed are half buried. "There's a lot of good equipment out here, ma'am," he calls. "Sure you don't want to clean it up before the goats come? They'll walk all over it and possibly break a few things. Our lovely beasts will do anything for a good vantage point."

The woman laughs and points to Thelma. "Especially this one."

Agatha thinks about climbing the tree across from GDOG's house to take photos of her husband and his lover. She understands doing anything for a good vantage point. "No, no plans to clean it up. If the goats break something, they break something. I'll take full responsibility for that."

"You'll have to sign a waiver," the man says.

"Not a problem."

The woman makes another note in the margin.

"What about the grass?" Agatha asks. "You know, under the weeds."

"Goats don't care for it much."

"Oh. Really?"

"Really."

The man steps onto the driveway and peels off his waders. "Looks good," he says as he drops them into a woven bag.

"How long do you think it will take?"

The woman surveys the yard. "Half an acre. Three goats. A week or two, depending on the weather."

"That's wonderful."

The woman hands a copy of the list of plants to Agatha. "We'll email a contract to you by tomorrow. Once you sign and return, we can let you know the date for the installation of the fence."

"The fence?"

"Yes, that's how we keep the goats in and predators out."

"Predators?"

"Coyotes. Fisher cats. Foxes."

"I hadn't thought of that."

"We have."

"Have you ever lost a goat to a predator?"

"Not yet, but we don't take chances."

"Makes sense." Agatha thinks about the neighborhood fisher cat. Then, as the goat people climb into their truck, she says, "Tell Thelma and Louise I look forward to meeting them."

Tap tap tippity-tap.

* * *

Agatha clicks onto Willow Bean's Instagram feed and stares at a photo of her boys tossing a beach ball with Willow at the beach. For fuck's sake, she hadn't even known they'd gone to the beach. Her own kids. "Mine, mine, mine!" her heart screams. "They are mine!"

She texts Dax. "Are the boys there? I need to talk to them."

"Right now?"

"Yes, right now. If they're with you, I need to talk to them."

"Okay, okay. It might be loud. We're at the Sox game."

He might as well have taken a bat to her head.

"The playoff game?"

Dax doesn't answer.

"You took the boys to a playoff game without me?"

He still doesn't answer.

"Dax, is GDOG there?"

There is a stupid long pause so she knows the answer even before Dax texts it. "Yes."

"Have them call me now. I don't care about noise."

"Sweet Caroline" sings from her phone. "Hi Mom," Dustin says.

"Hi honey."

"We're at the . . ." Dustin's voice drifts off. Clearly someone is at bat. Then there is a huge cheer. "Yah!" Dustin yells into the phone. "Mom, Mookie just hit another homer. Did you see it?"

She wants to say, "No, I'm not at the game with you. Your dad took his chippie instead," but the one thing she is good about is not badmouthing Dax to the boys. The other thing she's been good at so far is not driving that cleaver into Dax's head. "No," she says. "I haven't turned on the game yet. What's the score?"

Dustin is distracted but after a short silence says, "3–2, us."

"Okay, honey, enjoy the game. Let me talk to Jason for a minute."

Unlike Dustin, Jason is easy. "Mom!" he yells into the phone. "Oh, my god, Mom, did you see Mookie's home run? It was just the kind you love. It's a great game. A few minutes ago, I told Dad, 'Call Mom and make sure she's watching this,' but he said no. Then you called! You're like magic!"

Finally, Agatha smiles. Her Jason. She is still like magic to him. After all the changes of the past few months, she is still like magic.

"Are you having fun, sweetie?"

"I am, but it would be better if you were here. Willow won't let me get popcorn."

"Why not?"

"She says it's bad for my teeth."

"Oh, for god's sake," she says.

"You mean, for Big Papi's sake." He giggles.

She smiles. "You're so right. Hey, you go watch the game. Pass me to your father."

"Okay," he says. "I love you, Mom."

"I love you, too, sweetie."

Then Dax. "What?" he says.

"What the hell, Dax? Get the boy some popcorn. The Grande Dame of Grapefruits does not get to decide what my boys eat at baseball games."

"Fine, fine. I'll get him popcorn. Now can I go watch the game?"

Agatha hangs up, trying to remember how anyone knew anything before social media was a part of their lives. Her grandmother used to tell a story about her neighbor calling on the house phone, picking up the extension in the kitchen, and learning that the cops had stormed a house a few streets away but no one yet knew why. Her grandmother says she and the neighbor speculated a bit, leaning out of their mutually facing kitchen windows to try to get a glimpse of fire or flight, but didn't learn anything until a third neighbor buzzed in with news from her police scanner. This was in the glory years of call waiting when you never missed a call, back in the olden days when people actually wanted to talk to other people. They'd never thought of texting or sending an email or posting a GIF or ending an exchange with a poop emoji. No, they'd called each other and answered when the phone rang. Can you imagine?

Back then, the old-fashioned mom connection worked in its own slow, clunky way, with one mom calling another on a landline and that mom telling the "whatever" to the next mom when she put the first mom on hold to answer the other line, etc. But today, the mom connection via social media is lightning fast. Things happen and, seconds later, you know it. Everyone knows it.

Like the turkey incident. And the cupcake battle. And the arrival of the Interloper.

But is this immediacy a good thing? What does it do to hearts and minds and anxiety levels to know everything—bad and good—at every moment?

* * *

Agatha climbs the stairs slower this time. She eases the red door open and breathes. It had been much easier to enter this bastion of pain when she'd been pissed at Stella Bender. When she'd been trying to prove to a loony Mom that she's full of stuff and nonsense. Now not so easy. But she needs her dictionary. Her beloved, dog-eared, 400-pound, coverless dictionary. An online one won't do.

She walks to the desk and touches the corner. So beautiful. So her.

She drags the giant dictionary across the desk and thumbs to "H."

H-a-t-e.

The definition sucks: "intense or passionate dislike."

So mild. So impersonal. So non-hate-y.

She thumbs to "A."

Abhorrence is better, much better: "a feeling of repulsion; disgusted loathing."

Yes, disgusted loathing. That's what she feels for Dax.

But she doesn't. Abhor him. At least not all of her doesn't. Some of her abhors him, for sure. But some of her still loves him. She kneels next to the desk and presses her palm against the wee door carved into the side. The photo of her boys, the three of them, is still in there, a magical thing tucked tight.

She stands, turns, walks out, and pulls the door closed behind her.

Chapter Twenty-Nine

"You're not writing another 'The 12 Days of the Wallingford Moms,' are you?" Shrinky-Dink asks.

Agatha pulls the draft from her bag. "Of course I am. They'll be expecting it."

"Maybe ten years was enough."

Agatha sighs. "Nope, it's much too much fun, the highlight of my year."

"But it makes you miserable."

"It doesn't make me miserable. It makes me laugh. *They*, the Moms, make me miserable."

Shrinky-Dink grunts. "Read me what you have so far."

Agatha clears her throat. "Lalala la!"

"Get on with it."

"On the twelfth day of Christmas, the Moms gave to me, twelve penis cupcakes . . ."

"Stop there."

Agatha stares with her mouth agape. "What?"

"That's going to upset them."

"It's only one day."

"And it's too much."

"I'm keeping it."

"Forewarned is fair warned."

* * *

Kerry Sheridan knocks on Agatha's door.

"Hello, Kerry."

"Hello, Agatha."

"Can I help you?"

"Is it true?"

"Is what true?"

"Are you getting goats to eat the ground cover? To clear your yard?"

"How do you know that?"

"Word got out."

"How? I haven't told anyone."

"Okay, I was watching when they came by."

"Spying, you mean?"

"Watching."

Agatha sighs. "Yes, Kerry, I've hired goats to come for a week or two to eat all the brush."

"What about the poison ivy?"

"They love poison ivy."

"This is marvelous, Agatha!"

Kerry is smiling. She never smiles at Agatha. Agatha didn't know she had teeth.

"It is?"

"It is! I'm so happy. The boys will be delighted." She leans over and hugs Agatha. "I can't wait to see our boys playing ball again in their favorite field."

And then she's gone.

* * *

While downloading and organizing the day's photos, Agatha happens upon a folder containing a dozen or so pictures of the boys and Dax that she had taken a year before. One minute she is seething over photos of the Interloper, the next she is sobbing over Dax throwing Dustin into the ocean. Best vacation ever. The smile on Dustin's face is so big and so pure she is pretty sure she stops breathing. She clicks through the lot.

Jason holding a crab.

Dustin on Dax's back.

Jason holding a lobster.

Jason on a boat gripping a big tuna.

Dustin with the wind in his hair.

Dax with a kite so high in the air, the kite itself isn't even in the photo. The string disappears off the top edge.

Agatha wants to believe that string leads right to her heart . . . from Dax's loosely clenched hands to her heart, hovering somewhere above the photo, in the sky, above her two boys and her husband. That taut string with the distinctive pull, to something. To her.

The final photo in the series is just Dax. She remembers taking it. He is sitting on top of a picnic table with the sunset and ocean behind him. He is leaning forward, arms resting on his knees, hands clasped in front of him. His head is cocked to one side, just slightly, and he is grinning, like he knows something delicious and can't wait to tell her. Even though you can't see them in the photo, Agatha remembers that the boys are sitting in the sand at Dax's feet. It could have been a photo in which Dax was glancing down at them with love, but it was a photo about her. About them. There is no kite string in this one, but there is something even stronger tying them together.

The next photo is of the Interloper. That day, Agatha had taken ten photos of this woman, and in every single bloody one she is wearing the same lifeless expression. It is as if her body is standing at the intersection, shoving the can at cars as they pause at the stoplight, and nodding ever so slightly when they contribute, but her mind/heart isn't really there at all.

Agatha dates each photo and tucks them into the Interloper folder on her desktop. Then she clicks back to the photo of Dax. How could he be giving that same look to the dog walker today? How is that possible?

* * *

Agatha picks up her phone, types, and hits send. *I abhor you, Dax.*

That's more like it.

Tap-tap. Tippity-tap.

* * *

"Bite thy tongue, Agatha, bite thy tongue." Shrinky-Dink shakes her head.

* * *

Despite all her efforts to do otherwise, Agatha accepts Melody Whelan's invitation to her yoga class.

"I must be possessed," she tells Shrinky-Dink.

When Melody texts a reminder, Agatha texts back: "Where & when?"

Of course, she once again covers her ass in case of foul play by leaving a note on her kitchen table that says "I'm going to a yoga class with Melody Whelan at Bright Yoga Center. The class is at 9:00. If I'm not home by 11:00, please begin a search. She is likely singing 'Kumbaya' to me in her basement while feeding me crackers of kindness." It's the kind of note you post before setting off on a hike in the wilderness. If a mountain lion devours you, the search party needs to know where to look for your remains.

The fact that there is no one in Agatha's house to read the note doesn't stop her. Eventually, the boys will get worried and insist Dax call the police. Eventually, Officer Henry and his cohorts will break down her door.

She even tells the Tush where she's going. He shows no interest despite her carefully chosen low-cut leotard, but she shakes her stuff at him anyway. "Coulda had this," her butt hollers as she waggles her cantaloupes back and forth all the way down the driveway to her car.

When she arrives, Melody is stretching on her mat, which is positioned in the front row of the room. Agatha smirks, or maybe winces, sneaks in, and starts to unpack her brand-new mat in the very, very, very, very, very back corner behind the two women who clearly had chosen the very, very, very, very back spots in order to hide, but Melody catches sight of her, jumps up and down, waves, and calls, "Agatha! Agatha! Up here! I saved you a spot." Clearly the woman doesn't hold a grudge. It is as if the entire "nasty note to the Interloper" incident hadn't even occurred. Agatha is not used to forgiveness, especially offered up so quickly and easily.

The empty spot Melody saved is directly in front of the instructor, Paula O'Ryan, also a Wallingford Mom, one to whom Agatha has given a hard time for a variety of infractions. Paula, as lean and taut as a pole vaulter's pole, smiles when she sees Agatha.

Agatha's thigh muscles groan. Karma is tough.

She trudges to the spot Melody has saved. When she unrolls her mat, a poisonous stench rises up and threatens to suffocate everyone in the room. It reeks like a tire factory on fire.

Paula winces and inches toward her. "Agatha, where did you buy this mat?" She coughs and wipes her watering eyes.

"Dollar store."

"I suggest investing in a better mat before your next class," Paula says, but she smiles even through the stink. "You don't want to knock out your yoga mates, do you?"

Um.

She picks up Agatha's mat with two fingers and totes it to the door. "I'll put this out back," she says. "I have an extra you can use today."

The whole class is staring, and although Agatha is sure many want to snicker or make a snide comment, it is a yoga class so most are trying to smile warmly. Peace, love, blah, blah, blah.

Agatha turns to the class, brings her hands together in prayer, and bows. "Namaste," she says. As she tries to match IRL faces with tiny profile pics on Facebook, she begins humming "The 12 Days of the Wallingford Moms."

Melody says, "Agatha . . ."

Agatha smiles and is about to burst into song, but Paula starts the class with Sun Salutations. Within minutes, Agatha is too winded to sing, hum, or even think a snide word. Obviously this has been Melody's plan from the start. Shrewd, shrewd woman. Agatha's Sun Salutations start off fairly strong, but pretty quickly begin to look like she is doing a piss-poor job of miming "The Itsy Bitsy Spider." They move through Balancing Straddle, Standing Hand to the Big Toe, Firefly, and a few others. During Standing Hand to the Big Toe, Agatha tries her best to lift one straight leg into the air so it's up near her noggin, while holding tightly to her big toe. On her seventh attempt, she flies like a bowling pin hit by a strike and knocks Melody and another woman so hard they both fall over too.

Balancing Straddle goes no better. Agatha rolls out of this pose so many times she gets dizzy and nauseated. Motion sickness in yoga class. Who knew? Not once does she manage to hold it for more than a millisecond.

Still, no one yells at her. Paula smiles serenely, moves to her side, closes her eyes, and rests a hand on Agatha's hip to steady her. When she manages to hold the pose for five full seconds, Agatha feels like an Olympic gold medalist. Like Rocky running up those steps.

But the final pose before Corpse almost does her in. It's Firefly, the one where you put your hands flat on floor, stick your legs straight out in front of you off the ground, and lift your body (including feet). This takes some intense arm strength. Agatha tries a few times, but ends up settling for her version of the pose: Shaky Potato Bug. Basically, her curled in a ball on the not-smelly borrowed mat with all limbs shaking uncontrollably. She is damn good at this one.

As they move into Corpse pose, Paula says, "Drink water," as Agatha's shaking limbs begin to create earthquake-like tremors in the room. "Lots of water. And breathe."

Surprisingly, Melody is really, really good at yoga. Agatha knows she's not supposed to judge people's yogic ability—namaste and all—but damn, she is strong and graceful. She gets into and holds each and every pose Paula throws at them . . . without shaking. Agatha is shocked.

"Hey, Melody," she shout-whispers from Corpse pose, "how long have you been doing yoga?"

"Sshhh."

"Come on, how long?"

"Ten years. Now shush."

Agatha whistles. "It shows," she says.

Melody leans up on an elbow, looks at her, and smiles. "Thank you," she says in this super silky sincere tone that says, "I win, I win. You gave me a compliment."

"Oh, just be a corpse," Agatha says, closing her eyes and willing her limbs into stillness. She has no idea how long it is going to take to calm down her body. "By the way," she shout-whispers, "this was damn hard for a beginner's yoga class."

"Oh, this is not a beginner's class," Paula interjects, bending her body into some contortion Agatha can't even imagine. "This is an advanced class. My beginner class starts in an hour."

Agatha drags herself to all fours. It may be the hardest thing she's ever done. Then she dog-paddles through her pond of sweat toward Melody's mat and slaps her leg. "You said this was a beginner's class!"

Melody doesn't move or open her eyes. Such a good corpse. "Agatha Arch, I said no such thing," she whispers. "You simply assumed I was taking you to a beginner's class."

Agatha slaps her again and worm-crawls back to her now-cooling pond of sweat. "Damn you, Melody Whelan."

* * *

On the way home, Agatha stops at the birding store.

"May I help you?"

"I must get rid of a woodpecker," she tells the clerk. Three men in peculiar-looking outfits pivot on their heels and lock her into their gaze.

"Shhhh," the clerk says. "Those buzzards will eat you alive for even discussing a sin like that. Don't you know where you are?" He jabs a finger at the sign above the door: Bird Love.

Agatha leans forward and whispers, "I must get rid of a woodpecker. He's pecking holes in my house. He's pecking holes in my sanity."

The clerk nods. "You are not the first. Come back at 5:05, just after closing, to the back door."

"After closing? Are you serious?" Agatha says loudly.

"Sshhh! Of course I'm serious."

The man with the beak nose juts his head out like a turkey and makes a noise.

"What's he doing?"

"Practicing."

"Practicing what?"

"Gobbling."

Agatha laughs.

The clerk taps her arm. "Don't laugh. There is no laughing in a birding store. This is serious business."

As if on cue, the sun breaks from behind a cloud and a sharp ray cuts through the door, lighting up the display of expensive binoculars. A silver scope gleams in the sunlight, the price tag reads in the thousands. The thousands! Holy crap, this is serious business.

The warble deepens, then crescendos.

Agatha's eyes get wide.

"That's the mating call," the clerk says.

Agatha feels something deep in her stir. "It sure is," she says.

The stout birder wobbles to the other side of the store and cracks open a wilder call. Who knew a man of such girth could offer up such a sound.

"The mating response?" Agatha says.

"Indeed."

Agatha thinks about Abby Smith and the turkey that was squashed on the street near the hardware store. Abby should have come to Bird Love.

"Five o'clock?" Agatha says.

"*Five* after five," the clerk says. "No earlier. We have to be sure all is clear. Back door." He makes a chirpy noise.

Agatha raises her eyebrows.

"Nuthatch. My favorite."

The door opens. A singsong erupts. A sharp-beaked woman carrying three long-nosed scopes shuffles in. She lays them on the counter. "I need something stronger."

The clerk looks at Agatha. "Bring cash."

* * *

Tap tap tippity-tap.

* * *

Next step, electric fence. The goat experts are in the yard-cum-meadow even before Agatha has finished her first cup of coffee. They have a third goat person with them. "Intern," the goat lady explains when Agatha asks. "His name is Anthony. He'll be shadowing Fred."

"You can intern to be a goat person?" Agatha asks.

"Of course. This is a growing industry. We need young people to learn the trade so they can grow into the profession."

Agatha nods.

Putting up the fence takes longer than Agatha expects. Fred and Anthony drive posts into the ground every eight feet or so, then unspool an electric wire. They stretch three rows of wire between each set of posts.

"You don't realize how big a half acre is until you're putting up fence for goats," Fred says. Anthony listens attentively.

"I didn't realize this was going to be an electrified fence," Agatha says.

"Oh, yes, a solar battery will keep it charged."

"Will my sons get hurt if they touch it?" She can't imagine them keeping their hands off it.

"No, they'll get a little zap, but it's nothing more than they would get from an invisible fence for dogs."

Agatha nods again. Maybe she could have Kerry test the zap first. "But you've never lost a goat to a predator?" She's fretting about the fisher cat again.

The man straightens, puffs out his chest, and says, "No, ma'am. We've never lost a goat. Can't say the same about our competition though."

"You have competition?" Agatha asks. Goatscaping seems like a very noncompetitive profession.

"Oh, you'd be surprised. In Vermont, where they've been goatscaping for years and years, there's a decade-long feud between two family companies. While there's no proof, the story goes that the feud started after one family cut a hole in their competitor's electric fence. A bear wandered in, and the next morning, nary a goat left alive."

Agatha gasps. "Nary a goat?" She is excited for the opportunity to use the word *nary*.

"Nary a goat."

"Why would someone do that?"

"Like I said, it's a competitive business, ma'am."

Agatha nods. "I guess so. Well, no bears here, I can assure you of that. But we do have a couple of coyotes and a fisher cat. Fox, too."

The man nods and tightens the wire. "Foxes are too small to bother a goat, but the coyotes and fisher cats can bring one down pretty quickly. That's why our fence is the highest quality." A sharp end pokes out from the top. "Anthony, run to the truck and get my wire cutters, please. Can't let this end stick out like this. A deep scratch could be the beginning of the end of a goat."

"Wait," Agatha says. She reaches into a pocket and retrieves her Leatherman Super Tool 300 EOD. Then she pulls the wire-cutting tool into place. "Will this help?"

Fred looks at her with new respect. "Sure will." He snips the tip of the wire and finishes the fence. "Time to build the shelter."

"The shelter?"

"Yes, ma'am. It's a vital part of goatscaping," he says. "Goats don't mind a light shower, but they do not like heavy rain. The shelter gives them a place to go in inclement weather."

"Where are you going to put it?"

"As far from those rhododendrons as possible. Best to avoid temptation."

Agatha laughs. Temptation is the very thing that brought them to this place and time. "What's with the grain?" she says, gesturing to the bag of grain on the ground. "Aren't I paying for the goats to eat the plants and poison ivy? Won't grain fill them up?"

"If it rains, the goats will stay under the shelter. They'll need grain until the weather clears. Besides, *filled up* is not a term with which most goats are familiar. *Always hungry* is more like it."

Tap tap tippity-tap.

Fred looks up at the woodpecker, then back at Agatha. "That is one determined bird," he says.

"You have no idea," Agatha says.

* * *

At 5:05, Agatha is standing at the back door of the bird store. She's not sure if she's supposed to knock or not, so she leans close to the door and says, "Caw! Caw!" An embarrassing elementary crow call, but the only one she knows.

The door creaks open. An unusually hairy hand pokes out and waves her in. Agatha looks back at the parking lot. Stepping through the door seems like a brave choice as not a soul knows where she is. She didn't leave a note or post on the Moms group. This bird store guy could chop her up and feed her to the buzzards, but, if she wants to take down the woodpecker, this is her only known option. She takes a breath and steps through the door. In the dim light, the clerk hands her a dart gun.

"I don't want to kill the woodpecker," she says. "Well, not really. Not if there are more peaceful options."

"The ends of these darts are blunt. It's like getting hit by a ball of yarn," the clerk says. "No damage at all. This gun is your most peaceful option."

Agatha imagines such a strike. "And it will work?"

"Tried and true in the realm of secret birding techniques. Just don't let any birders see you, and do not ever let anyone know you got it here. We must protect the reputation of Bird Love at all costs. You must swear to secrecy."

"Is it illegal to hit a woodpecker with a soft dart?"

"Not technically, but I'll lose my store if this goes public. Birders are mean-ass people."

"How much is it?"

"Fifty dollars."

"Fifty dollars?" The gun looks like something she could get at the dollar store.

"Fifty dollars."

"How many of these do you sell a year?"

"Hundreds. This is New England, you know, heart home of the woodpecker."

Agatha takes a credit card from her wallet. The man shakes his head. "Cash only."

"This better work," Agatha says, pulling two twenties and a ten from the front pocket of her spy pants.

"Trust me."

Agatha takes the gun and starts out the door.

The man grunts and grabs her arm. "For God's sake, woman, hide it," he says.

She slips the gun under her coat as the clerk opens the door and shoves her through it.

* * *

That night, still aching from yoga, Agatha lies in bed and watches footage of a feathery fluff-ball plummeting down the side of a cliff. It bounces off rocks, flips upside down, and bounces again.

Holy crap. What kind of nature show is this?

A British accent breaks in: "The barnacle gosling must make the ultimate choice. Starve in its nest at the top of a cliff with no food source or plummet down the side of the cliff to the grass feeding ground at the bottom."

Turns out barnacle goose parents—enormous black and white feathery beasts with a mean-ass stare not unlike the one of the man in the birding store—don't feed their littles. They birth them at the top of the cliff where their nemesis, the Arctic fox, can't eat them, then move, without their baby, to the bottom of the cliff and call out, "Come on down, sweet one. We love you. The food is here!"

BUT SO IS THE ARCTIC FOX!

Good god! What kind of parenting is this?

Agatha rewinds the clip and watches the feathery fluff-ball peer over the side of the cliff, weighing its options.

"The gosling can anticipate a four-hundred-foot free fall," the Brit says.

Fothermucking hell.

Of course, the gosling hesitates. Even a days-old gosling knows that plummeting down the side of cliff is fucked up.

But the baby bird is imprinted, the Brit explains. Listen to Mumma's voice. Follow Mumma. Mumma! Mumma!

In the end, almost all goslings make the ultimate leap of faith. There are no statistics on how many survive.

Agatha saves the video in her Hard Truths file.

Chapter Thirty

When the mailman climbs out of his truck, calves firm and shorts short, a sure sign of a true New Englander, a little streak of fiery something races through Agatha's middle, and that fiery something reminds her of the ginger-infused vodka cocktail she drank at her agent's holiday soiree last year, the one that shot straight up and out of the top of her head and made her happy, bloody fothermucking happy. And although she knows damn well *mail carrier* is the current politically correct term, horny and heartbroken Agatha cares only about the *man* in *mailman*. "I'll be politically correct next week," she tells the tomato plant as she sashays past, setting Who Can I Bonk? Part II into motion.

She meets Mailman at the mailbox, rubs her bottom against the post, and coos, "How about coming inside for some iced tea?" Her voice is low and gravelly, and, once again, she is holding a sweaty glass of iced tea at breast height, dipping its icy freshness ever so slightly into her cleavage. Sweaty glasses of iced tea are becoming part of her modus operandi, a strange and unexpected development.

She loves the idea of screwing Mailman, whose name she knows but can never remember. Years before, she called him Rick, but Dax insisted that wasn't his name. Now she's spent days fantasizing about dragging Rick-not-Rick into the house by the official mail pin on his lapel, dumping his bag onto the couch, tugging his blue shorts down around his ankles, discovering a pair of jocks covered with stamped letters, then straddling him and bonking the shit out of him, all the while yelling, "Postage due! Postage due!" It's a ridiculous fantasy, but it's hers.

Tap tap tippity-tap.

When Rick-not-Rick leans in and says, "Excuse me?" she has a glimmer of hope that things might go her way. But when she repeats herself, this time more loudly, less coo and more caw, with even more swiggle in her bottom, his eyes jolt wide, he jammers, and his face turns a brilliant shade of magenta. Is it possible Rick-not-Rick has never been propositioned by a client on his route before?

To Agatha's credit, she doesn't take his wiffley-waffley response lightly. While he backs away as if she has Ebola, jabbing his mailbag at her like a sword, she continues to dip the sweaty iced tea glass into her cleavage, dropping it a little deeper each time. Hinting, hinting. When the glass gets stuck a little too deep, she yanks and tea splashes down her front. Little brown dribbles trail all the way to the crotch of her spy pants.

Desperate, she pitches it as a convenient trail for Rick-not-Rick to follow. "This way," the iced tea dribbles call. "This way! Follow me! Follow me to a slice of heaven!" But Rick-not-Rick is not following. He is not interested in heaven. He is running away so fast he is already too far to even see the dribbles. He leaps into his mail truck and guns the engine.

Defeated, Agatha looks down. Her spy pants are ruined. She'll have to pull another pair from the box. Thank god she bought so many extras.

Tap tap tippity-tap.

She turns. The Tush is on the east side of the house, paused on the ladder, paintbrush high, obviously entertained by the exchange. She bends over, wags her ass in his direction, and picks up her mail. "This, baby," she whispers. "You coulda had this." Then she tries to take a dramatic swig of iced tea, but the cubes give way and crash into her nose and mouth. She sputters and swears, then sashays into the house, horniness once again humiliated into check.

* * *

Melody covers Agatha with a mottled brown afghan and turns on *Beaches*.

Agatha snuggles in, but then sits up. "I can't stay," she says.

"Yes, you can, Agatha. Relax."

"I really can't. I'm still sweaty from yoga. I should . . ."

Melody pushes her down, covers her again, hands her a cup of chamomile tea, and curls at the opposite end of the couch. Agatha glances at her, still wary of this thing that feels like friendship, but also grateful. It's the first time she's felt comforted and cared for since the shed incident. And it's kind of lovely. She blubbers through the movie, hums "The Wind Beneath My Wings," and after the credits roll, stays under Melody's wretchedly ugly, insanely soft afghan and talks about death and love and loss and other friendship-affirming topics.

She's so relaxed that when Melody suggests going to meet the Interloper the next day, she has barely enough energy to resist. "You have nothing to be afraid of," Melody promises. "Lucy is young and kind and innocent."

"She's deceptive and deceitful and not trustworthy at all," Agatha says.

"How do you know? You've never spoken to her."

Agatha remembers Jason's comment about the Interloper looking sadder than anyone else in the whole wide world. His heart is so open, but hers just isn't. "Any human who comes to a town in which they've never lived," she says, "sets up a begging shop at the busiest intersection, and rakes in cash is deceptive, deceitful, and not trustworthy. If she's capable of these things, she's capable of anything."

"A begging shop?" Melody asks, eyebrows up.

"You know what I mean."

"Agatha, she's wounded and homeless and sad and hungry and lost, but she is not dangerous."

Agatha shakes her head. "There is no way that you can prove this girl is not dangerous."

"I can. By introducing you to her."

"Nope."

* * *

Agatha sets "The Wind Beneath My Wings" as Melody's ringtone. The first time it sings, Melody says, "Let's go meet Lucy. If you're free to answer your phone, you're free to go meet her."

Agatha runs to the dryer, presses her head and phone against it, and yells over the ruckus, "JUST STARTED ANOTHER LOAD OF LAUNDRY. NOT A GOOD TIME!" She hangs up.

* * *

The following day when Melody calls, Agatha bangs together a bunch of pots and pans. "I'm cooking. This meal won't be done for hours."

"You hate cooking," Melody says. "You don't cook."

"New life, new leaf," Agatha says, rubbing the colander against the phone.

"Fibber."

* * *

The third day Dustin answers when the sappy song plays. "Hi, Melody," he says, then hands the phone to his mom.

"Ha!" Melody says when she hears Agatha's voice. "Got you!"

Agatha stuffs a dish sponge into her mouth and mumbles, "Toofache! Ow. Ow."

"Yuck!" Dustin shouts.

Chapter Thirty-One

"The Interloper is broken," Agatha says.

Shrinky-Dink waits.

"She has folded, given in, surrendered."

"To?"

"To whatever broke her heart."

Shrinky-Dink nods.

"And?"

"If I'm not mean and tough and mouthy, if I don't fight like I do, I will fold, give in, surrender."

"You will become the Interloper?"

Repeat the words. Change the pronouns.

"I will become the Interloper."

Shrinky-Dink waits again. The chime goes off but she doesn't call a halt to the session. This is a first. "What other option do you see for yourself?" she finally says.

"I can make the ultimate leap of faith." Agatha says it in a British accent.

Shrinky-Dink pulls her "eyebrows-up, I have no idea what you're talking about" face.

"Watch this," Agatha says. She takes out her phone, opens her Hard Truths file, and scrolls to the clip of the nature show. Shrinky-Dink leans forward and together they watch the baby barnacle goose peer over the side of the cliff, then plummet down the mountain toward its parents and life-sustaining sustenance.

"That's quite a leap," Shrinky-Dink says. Agatha can tell she's impressed. This is a first, too.

When the camera pans to the lying-in-wait Arctic fox, Agatha harrumphs and Shrinky-Dink nods.

"You see? I am the gosling," Agatha says. She fingers the crease in her cheek.

Shrinky-Dink gets it now. Agatha can tell by the look on her face. "And what," Shrinky-Dink says, "is your Arctic fox?"

"Huh?"

"Instinctively the gosling is most afraid of the Arctic fox waiting at the bottom of the cliff. What is your Arctic fox? Of what are you most afraid?"

"This again?" Agatha asks.

"This again."

Agatha thinks about Susie. How do you leave something behind that has haunted you forever?

She returns to thinking about Dax. About expecting so much from him. Too much. Was that it? Does it even matter?

When Agatha finally leaves Shrinky-Dink's office, the woman in gray is not in the vestibule. This, too, is a first. For three years, they have overlapped in this quiet in-between space. For the five seconds it takes Agatha to close Shrinky-Dink's office door, cross the vestibule, pull her coat from the rack, put it on, and head out the exterior door, she and the lady in gray have overlapped.

Until today.

* * *

A few more days, a thousand more texts, dozens of calls, and Melody wears her down. "Fine," Agatha says. "Fine, fine, fine. I'll talk to her."

On the night before the rendezvous, she sleeps very little, and when she does, she dreams about being kidnapped, flown to a secret location, and eaten with fava beans. Hours before the "eaten with fava beans" part, the kidnappers text a ransom note to Dax, "$1,000,000 for the lady to be returned," but he, her husband, her estranged husband, her husband-who-screwed-the-dog-walker-in-the-shed-and-left-her misses the text and the opportunity to redeem himself even a little bit because he's canoodling with the Grande Dame of Grapefruits.

Good god.

Despite the dream, Agatha meets Melody in the parking lot of the grocery store at Apple54. It is early Saturday morning, a slow traffic hour, though, as the Interloper explains, the dads on their way to soccer games are often much more generous than the moms, handing over fives and tens instead of their change from Starbucks.

Up close for the second time, but seeing her awake for the first, Agatha has to admit the Interloper doesn't look quite as intimidating as she expected, shorter and thinner and much more fragile-like-glass than she looked in the Krug. "I can take her down if she tries any nonsense," Agatha whispers to Melody.

"Agatha," Melody says, ignoring the takedown comment, "this is my friend Lucy. Lucy, this is my friend Agatha."

Her friend?

Her friend?

Melody refers to this homeless ne'er-do-well as her friend?

To this, Agatha can barely sputter a response, so to make it easier on herself, thinking nothing of how hard this might be for the Interloper, she employs a tactic Dustin used when he was a toddler. Whenever she tried to get him to do something he didn't want to do (eat broccoli, brush teeth, say "up," put away blocks, go to bed, etc.), he refused to look directly at her. No caterwauling, no kicking, no tantrums, just complete avoidance.

Melody wastes no time, perhaps out of fear that Agatha will flee, perhaps out of respect for the Interloper's work hours, but either way she unpacks a picnic breakfast with cut fruit, cold juice, hot coffee, and steaming bacon and egg sandwiches.

"Agatha, Lucy is from out west," Melody says, handing Agatha a slice of watermelon, which she can't eat, won't eat, mostly because the longer this nonsense with Dax goes on, the harder it is to chew, swallow, consume, but also because the terror stirred by the Interloper makes her belly ache.

In every photo Agatha has taken, the Interloper has had a horribly dour, serious, flat-like look stuck to her face, a look that screams "Watch out, I'm going to get you," a look that made Agatha sleep with two lights on rather than the usual one, but when Melody says "out west," the little, glass-like ne'er-do-well smiles a little, not just around the mouth but also the eyes, the brown ones that suddenly shine with a bit of light, a wee smile that gives Agatha a different feeling, a feeling that maybe things aren't quite what she thought, though there's no way in hell she'll admit that to Melody.

"Out west?" Agatha says. "And you believe this?"

Melody nods. "Of course I believe it."

"Do you have a driver's license with a home address on it?" she asks the Interloper.

The Interloper shakes her head.

"Agatha," Melody says, "that's rude."

"It's not rude. It's a question. If the girl says she has a home somewhere out west, let's see something with an address on it."

"Why don't you show her your driver's license?" Melody says.

Agatha shoots her a look that could vaporize a demon. She does not want this young woman to know anything about her private life, especially details about her home or her children. Melody knows this.

"My life is private," she says to Melody, poisoned harpoons shooting from her mouth as she does.

"I hate to tell you," Melody says, "but no one's life is private. Isn't that what you tell the Moms on the Facebook page when they use that defense?"

Agatha grimaces.

"What brought you to Wallingford?" she asks the Interloper.

When Melody leans forward and opens her mouth to speak, Agatha holds up her hand just an inch from her nose. "Stop," she says. "Let *her* answer."

Finally the Interloper speaks. "Money," she says. Her voice is low but strong. "Money brought me here. I'm homeless but not dumb. I know enough to beg where the money is."

The Interloper turns and looks at the traffic building up at Apple54. The line of cars now stretches ten long from the light. Without looking at Agatha or Melody, she takes a final bite of watermelon and stands.

"Thank you for breakfast," she says.

Melody puts a hand on her arm. "Wait," she says. Then she wraps the three remaining sandwiches in foil, puts them and two bottles of water in a plastic grocery bag, and says, "Take these for lunch."

The Interloper takes the bag and trudges toward her post.

"Well, that sucked," Agatha says.

Melody shakes her head. "Only because you made it suck."

"*I* made it suck?"

"Yes, you. Couldn't you have been kind and generous, just for a few moments? Couldn't you have stepped out of your own crap and seen that others have crap way worse than you?"

Agatha is stunned. Melody never talks to anyone like this. She never even says the word *crap*. Agatha didn't know she was capable. "Are you kidding?"

Melody slaps a Tupperware lid on the picnic table and glares at her. "I am not kidding," she says. "Grow up. Put your ridiculous fears away for a bit. Listen to someone else. And, yes, you will see that lots of people have it worse than you, and everybody deserves some kindness."

Ridiculous fears?

Ridiculous fears?

"Melody Whelan," Agatha sputters, "do you know what I've been through these past few months? Do you have any idea how I've suffered?"

"Oh, shut up, Agatha Arch."

Melody Whelan says *shut up*. Shut up. To Agatha Arch.

"Listen, Agatha, yes, your husband cheated and broke your heart. Yes, it sucks. But you've still got your wits. And your home. And your boys. Can't you, you terrible selfish beast, can't you find it in your heart to show just the slightest bit of kindness and generosity? Who are you? How do you live with yourself?"

Then, without looking at Agatha again, Melody smacks the Tupperware containers into her picnic basket and marches to her car in the grocery parking lot.

Agatha sits there, taking in her words, trying for the first time to balance her fears with the possible truths Melody had just spoken. She watches the Interloper work the intersection without a single flash of expression on her face. If what Melody said was true, did the fact that the Interloper was suffering take away the possibility that she could commit heinous crimes in their community?

She has no idea.

Chapter Thirty-Two

The goats arrive. Finally.

As promised, Thelma and Louise are beautiful and sweet and funny. Thelma is the jumper and proves it when, less than five minutes after discovering the remains of the shed, she decides that atop the hidden ride-on mower is her best vantage point.

"She'll settle down and start eating soon enough," the goat lady tells Agatha.

"Are you sure?"

"Absolutely. She's a seasoned 'scaper. She knows her job and she does it well."

Just after the boys get home from school, the goat people deliver a third goat, a youngster named Timothy. "An intern?" Agatha asks when the goat lady leads Timothy from the truck on a leash.

The goat lady smiles. "Yes, an intern. You can take him to the pen." She hands the leash to Dustin.

This is Timothy's first job, and he has a lot to learn. While Thelma and Louise set to work, nibbling on brush near the property line with the Sheridans, Timothy runs and bucks and mehs, acting like he's at recess.

"Don't worry, he'll get the hang of it," Fred says. "Hunger will get the best of him. Never met a goat who didn't like to eat."

Agatha's phone pings. The Moms. She opens FB. The arrival of the goats is breathing new life into the Shed on Sutton Circle thread. "Check this out," Kerry Sheridan writes with a photo of Thelma and Louise being led on leashes into the fenced area in Agatha's yard. "The goats have arrived!"

Within an hour, the Moms are lined up on Sutton Circle in their cars. Charmed and curious, they start to park. Pretty soon, fifty Moms are crowded at the streetside fence.

"These goats are adorable!"

"*That* one is the cutest!" a Mom says, pointing at Timothy.

"Did you know you could do this?"

"Is there a waiting list for the goats? I'd love to book them for my yard."

"Can the goats clear wetlands?"

"Are these Nubian goats?"

"What is a Nubian goat?"

"Ooh, I'm going to bring carrots and celery scraps tomorrow. They'll love it!"

As the Moms talk, the goat lady walks up to their group, parts them, and hangs a sign on the fence: "Do not feed these goats. They are working. No treats."

"Oh, come on," one Mom says. "No treats at all?"

The goat lady faces her. She is quite stern. "No treats at all. If you're interested in feeding, the local farm has goats. These goats are working, and we can't have them filling up on snacks. Think of them like your children an hour before dinner."

Kerry Sheridan steps forward. "Don't worry. No one will be feeding these goats on my watch."

That afternoon, Agatha watches the goats from the porch. The daytime moon hangs in the sky above them.

* * *

Tap tap tippity-tap.

Agatha pulls the gun from her bag and loads a cushioned dart into the chamber. When she cocks it, the woodpecker stops. It's as if he knows. As if he's riddled many houses with holes and heard that click before. She lays the gun in her lap.

Tap tap tippity-tap.

She lifts it again. Takes aim. The woodpecker stops, turns, and looks. She drops the gun to her lap.

She can't do it.

* * *

Dax: Agatha, the boys saw you taking photos at our house last night and got upset.

Agatha: You guys were at our house last night?

Dax: Not OUR house, Agatha. Our house. My and Willow's house.

Agatha: Oh THAT "our house." I thought you meant OUR house. Yup, I was at the House of Sin last night. Needed a few shots for the portfolio.

Dax: The boys were upset.

Agatha: More upset than they are about the fact that you cheated on their mother, left her, and moved them into a new house with a new person half the time? More upset than that?

Dax: I'm sorry, Agatha. I am sorry.

This is Dax's first "I'm sorry" that feels authentic, heartfelt, real, and even though it's via text, a seemingly impersonal transmission, she knows him well enough, deeply enough, to recognize when something shifts.

As tears blur the letters on her phone, she almost, almost, texts back "I know," but she can't, not quite yet, it feels too much like "it's OK." And it will never be okay.

* * *

"I don't have an Arctic fox," Agatha tells the tomato plant.

"Liar!" the tomato plant says.

"Oh, shut up," Agatha says. She rips the still-green tomato from the vine. It is split like a lip on one side. "Rotten thing." She hurls it at the remains of the shed. It hits Thelma in the rump, not enough to hurt, but enough to make her jump off the ride-on mower. "Sorry, Thelma!" Agatha yells.

The last of the tomatoes is a rich red on all but one spot. Agatha turns it toward the sun.

* * *

During the second night with the goats, Agatha hears the scream of the fisher cat. It's late. Maybe one or two in the morning. She tears down the stairs and out the door. Susan Sontag is in the yard. As the fisher cat flashes past, Susan raises her tail, Agatha yells, "Noooooo!" but it's too late. She takes a direct hit.

The boys race out onto the porch, but stop when the stink hits them. "Mom!"

"Get my keys," she says.

They drive to the pharmacy, thankfully open all night, and the same young man is at the window. He tugs off his headphones when they pull up.

"You again?" he says.

"I could say the same about you," Agatha says.

"Same skunk?"

"Same skunk."

"I've still got the wash if you prefer, but I suspect you're going to stick with the wives."

"You got that right."

The young man holds his nose. "Your choice," he says. "But come around to the back door. I've got a couple of cases this time. It will be easier than passing all those cans."

Agatha nods. The boys are asleep in the back seat. The car is going to have to be fumigated.

* * *

"Lucy is not at Apple54," Melody texts Agatha. "Hurt? Sick? I'm worried."

Agatha rolls her eyes. She's quite sure the Interloper has simply taken advantage of the dark and stormy day to commit the crimes Agatha knows she's destined to commit: theft, kidnapping, murder. "Don't worry," she texts back. "I'm sure she's fine. Likely pulling off a heist at the bank. Check the news."

"The Wind Beneath My Wings" sings from Agatha's phone. She answers.

"Agatha Arch," Melody says, lecture-tone firmly in place, "I'm going to be the wind that busts your wings to pieces if you don't stop this nonsense. Lucy isn't capable of nefarious activities."

"You're so trusting, Melody. How do you know she isn't? I didn't think Dax was capable of cheating on me, breaking my heart, and shattering our family into pieces, and look at the reality of that. Every human—no matter how seemingly innocent—is capable of nefarious activities."

"Once again, Agatha, I am sorry your husband was so brutal. Once again, if I could make it any other way, I would. I hate that you're in pain. But once again, not everything in this world relates back to you. You have to let go and learn to trust the world again."

Agatha huffs. Melody has no idea Agatha never trusted the world to begin with. She had simply buffered her fear and mistrust of it with Dax. Wielded him like a shield between the world and herself. No Dax, no shield. Without him, without that protection, who can she be in the world?

"If that's how you feel, why are you telling *me* about the Interloper's absence?" Agatha says.

"I want you to check on her."

"What?"

"I want you to check on her. Make sure she's okay."

"Check on the Interloper?"

"Yes."

"Go up into the Krug *again* to check on the Interloper?"

"Yes."

"You're joking?"

"I am not joking. Go to Lucy's spot in the woods. Only you know where it is. Only you can find it."

Well, isn't this a pip? Talk about setting yourself up for something.

"You've got to be kidding me," Agatha says.

"I am not. You're the only one who can do this. Go, before something terrible happens to her."

"Or before she does something terrible to someone else."

"Agatha Arch."

"Melody Whelan."

"Agatha."

"Melody."

"Go."

"It's supposed to rain, you know."

"Only a fifty percent chance."

"A fifty percent chance of thunderstorms, a thing of which I am terrified."

"I need you to do this. Please."

Agatha finds it hard to believe she has arrived at a point in life in which she jumps when the Kumbaya Queen says jump. But there you go.

"Fine," Agatha says. "Fine, fine, fine. But if I die, it's on your head." She hangs up, dons her spy pants and a rain jacket, sets her GPS for the Interloper's spot in the woods, and drives to the grocery parking lot. When she sees Melody, hope rises in her chest. "You're coming along? Oh, thank god."

"No, I have an appointment. But take this food to Lucy." Melody hands her a bag of muffins, bread, and Twizzlers. "She likes Twizzlers."

"Seriously, Melody? I can't carry this up there in the rain. It's going to be hard enough."

"You can do it. I know you can. Text me as soon as you know something." Then she turns Agatha by the shoulders and gently shoves her through the trampled brush into the Krug. "Go now. Hurry."

And Agatha does. She slogs up as the rain sloshes down. Her spy pants get soaked and mud splashes to her hips. By the time she's halfway up, it is nearly night dark, and while her headlamp lights a good path, she can't see what is going on in the periphery. She once again thinks about the wild animals released by the now-dead cuckoodoodle in New Hampshire, the grizzly, the lion, the gorilla, the unknowns. Agatha knows the Krug would be a perfect spot for a wild animal to thrive. Good food sources. Dense cover. She pauses, sure she's heard a growl, a howl. "Please no, please no, please no," she chants. She pulls Bear from a pocket and presses him to her cheek. "Fear sharpens us . . . fear sharpens us . . . fear sharpens us."

That morning, a journey that usually takes forty-five minutes takes twice that, and Agatha cheers when she finally glimpses the Interloper's tree through the sheets of rain. The first crack of lightning hits as she realizes the Interloper is not slumped against her tree, and then *kaboom*! Thunder.

"Help!" she screams. "Help! Interloper lady, are you here?" As Agatha stumbles around in the clearing, her headlamp catches on a branch, flips to the ground, and clicks off. Without its artificial glow, it is dark. Night dark. Super night dark, as Dustin used to say when he was little. She kneels and feels around on the ground, trying to find the lamp.

"Interloper lady!" she screams. She curls into a ball, wraps her arms around her knees, and rocks like a baby. "I hate you, Bear Grylls! I hate you! I hate you, Melody Whelan! I hate you all!"

But then, during a quiet moment between thunder and lightning and the swoosh of rain, she hears a strange *ssshhh* from somewhere in the woods.

OMG. A ghost!

A stream of water gushes past her, and Agatha knows her headlamp is being washed downhill, gone forever.

Then a hand grips her arm. The hand of the ghost! Agatha starts to fight but she's wet and muddy and slippery and she can't shake the grip. She flails and strikes at whatever she can hit, which isn't much.

Then a voice. "Lady, stop fighting. It's me. Lucy. I'm trying to help."

Interloper lady? Interloper lady?

Agatha reaches out and feels what she hopes is the Interloper's head. "Interloper lady? Is it really you?"

"It's really me."

"Where were you?"

"Come on. I'll get you to a safe spot."

A safe spot? Out here? Normally Agatha would have debated the ins and outs of a safe spot with the Interloper in the Krug in a raging storm in the super night dark, but she doesn't have time. Another crack of lightning splits the sky. The Interloper pulls her to her feet and drags her through the trees. Agatha sees a tiny light in the darkness, then she's pushed through a door.

A door?

A door?

A door out here in the middle of nowhere?

Is she hallucinating?

As Agatha falls to the floor of this unexpected place, she expects Bilbo Baggins to offer her a cup of mead. "Gandalf? Gandalf? Are you here?" she cries.

"Woman, what are you jabbering on about?" the Interloper says.

Soaked and muddy. Exhausted. Heart pounding. Breath ragged. Agatha hears the door close behind her. Thunder booms, but she's out of the rain. When her body stills, she lifts her head and looks around. She is in a tiny hut. Her head is inches from one wall and her feet are touching the other. She twists and sees the Interloper leaning against the door, soaked and muddy, too. No Gandalf. No Bilbo Baggins. No mead. "You saved me," she says. Her voice is raspy and raw.

"Not really," the Interloper says. "You would have survived as long as lightning didn't hit you."

"But it would have. I know it. You saved me."

"Whatever."

Agatha sits up. The hut is not really a hut. More of a shack with four walls, a door, and a decent floor. "Did you build this place?"

"No."

"Who did?"

"Dunno. Mountain bikers probably. They're the only ones ever up here besides me and you."

"It doesn't leak?"

"Nope. Whoever built it did a good job."

There is a single camper's lamp on the floor in the corner. "Where did you get that?"

"That woman friend of yours."

"Melody?"

"I guess."

Agatha is a little shocked the Interloper doesn't know Melody's name, especially after all the advocating Melody has done for her.

"Has she been here?"

The Interloper shakes her head. "No."

"Has anyone been here?"

"Just you."

"Are you living in this hut?"

"Don't worry about it."

"Where's all your stuff?"

"You know where my stuff is. You've been through it enough times."

Caught. "The tree?" Agatha says.

The Interloper nods. "Probably soaked and ruined now."

Agatha thinks of the bag of goodies Melody had forced her to tote up the hill. It is long gone.

"Will you have anything to eat after this storm is over?"

"I'll be fine. I'm always fine."

Agatha sits for a few minutes, listening to the thunder. She doesn't expect a cathartic conversation, but the two of them sitting together, soaking wet, surviving a storm, has a *Beaches*-like quality Melody would adore.

"Why did you save me?"

"Do we have to talk? Isn't it enough that I got you out of the storm? I could have left you there, scared to death, screaming like a baby."

"I wasn't screaming like a baby."

The Interloper smirks.

"Aren't you frightened being up here at night by yourself all the time?" Agatha says.

"Nope."

"Wouldn't you rather be back home, wherever that is? Out west?"

"Nope."

"Aren't there people missing you?"

"Probably."

"Don't you want to go home to them?"

"Nope."

Right then the Interloper stands. Sure she is going to pull a machete from behind her back and hack her to bits, Agatha tucks her head into her arms. A pool of water has formed around her. Now it is going to be mixed with blood. "Don't kill me!"

Instead of murdering Agatha, the Interloper opens the door and steps out into the storm.

"Hey," Agatha yells over the pelting rain. "Where are you going?"

"Away," the Interloper says. "You're fine."

"You can't go out there. You might die."

But the Interloper is gone. And just like that Agatha is left alone in the tiny shack with lightning crackling all around her.

Seconds later, the big one hits not far from the hut. The smell of burning wood permeates the shack, and when she peeks out, Agatha watches a twirl of smoke rise into the sky. "Please don't let it be the Interloper. Please don't let it be the Interloper," she chants. Melody will kill her if anything happens to that young woman.

When the rain subsides, the lightning eases, the thunder moves away, and the sky lightens, Agatha steps out of the hut. She follows the smoke and sees that the Interloper's tree has been struck. All her things, few as they were, black and charred. Agatha sighs, relieved. Lucy's things, but not Lucy.

* * *

With the most dangerous elements receding, Agatha gets her wits about her. She pulls her cell phone from its waterproof pouch and takes a selfie with the smoking tree. It's a keeper. Hair plastered to her head. Twigs poking up out of her shirt. Mud everywhere. And, yikes, blood all over her face and neck.

The rain shrinks to a drizzle as she makes her way back down the hill, and by the time she bursts through the final copse of trees into the parking lot, the sun is shining and a rainbow is hanging over the grocery store. She couldn't have set the scene any better. Three cars slow to a stop as she gives herself the once-over. Besides the blood and twigs and mud, the left leg of her spy pants is shredded, revealing the lower part of her buttock. Thank goodness for the seven brand new pairs of spy pants still in the box.

The first two cars slide past her suspiciously, but the brave guy in the third car pulls to a stop and lowers his window. "Hey, lady, are you okay?" he says.

"Sure," she says, smiling "what could be wrong?"

He shakes his head and drives away.

Agatha sits on the curb, pulls out her phone, and pops onto the Moms FB page. "In the Krug once again—this time in that crazy lightning storm—protecting all of you from the Interloper. Everyone, say, 'Thanks, Agatha!'" She adds the selfie of her with the Interloper's smoking tree and hits *post*.

Seconds later, the page fills with responses.

Ava Newton:	"Agatha, what were you thinking? You could have been killed."
Blonde Brenda-What's-Her-Name:	"You aren't protecting us from anything, you nincompoop. That young woman isn't dangerous; you are!"
Jane Poston:	"I wish you'd been struck by lightning, Agatha Arch. It might have shocked some sense into you."

Yikes.

Priya Devi:	"I thought you were afraid of storms."
Agatha Arch:	"I am. I did this for you. For all of you."
Rachel Runk:	"No, no, you didn't, Agatha. Not one of us supports you in this craziness. Go back to spying on your husband and his lover."

Ouch.

Melody Whelan: "Ladies, Agatha actually went up the mountain at my request. Lucy was absent from her spot at Apple54, and I got worried. I asked Agatha to go. Despite what she says, she was making sure Lucy was all right."

Agatha types a series of sticking-out-your-tongue emojis and clicks off. When she looks up, Melody is standing in front of her, hands on her hips. "Really, Agatha? After everything you just went through, you're bad-mouthing Lucy on the Moms page? Have you seen yourself? You look like a crazed maniac."

Agatha throws up her hands. "Seriously, Melody? You're the one who demanded I go! What are you hollering about? Besides, you'll never believe what I found."

"I don't want to know."

"Yes, you do. The Interloper has a shack up there."

"Lucy. You mean Lucy."

"Blah, blah, blah. Yes, Lucy. Lucy has a shack up there."

"A shack?"

Agatha smirks. "I knew you'd want to know. Yes, a shack."

"You saw her?"

"Yeah, she actually pulled me to safety out of the storm."

"She's okay?"

"I'm assuming so. From what I saw up there, I'm pretty sure she's immortal. Anyway, I'd lost my headlamp. Lightning was popping all around me. She dragged me into her shack."

"Wait. Lucy saved your life, but all you can talk about is the suspicious stuff about her? Why didn't you tell the Moms she saved your life?"

"I'm quite sure her reasons were purely selfish."

Melody huffs and puffs. "What selfish reasons could this poor girl have for saving your pathetic life? Tell me, Agatha Arch, tell me. She doesn't know you from Adam. She's full of great sadness. She has absolutely zero reason to save your life on the top of a mountain other than, like you, she's a good person."

"You just don't understand, Melody."

"What don't I understand? That you're a suspicious, scared little girl who has to bully people who show their feelings? Is that what I don't understand?"

Bully?

Bully?

Agatha stands up. She is still unsteady on her feet and sure could use a cold beverage. "I am not a bully," she says. "I am a realist."

"You're a bully."

"That is not nice, Melody. I've never heard you say anything so not nice."

"You have pushed me to this place, Agatha Arch. No one has ever pushed me to this place. Ever! But I promise you, I will not be pushed to this place again. I'm done trying to help you through this. Done." Then she turns and walks away.

Crap. Agatha pops back onto the Moms page and types: "Just pushed Kumbaya Queen Melody Whelan to her limit. That's a first." But instead of pressing *post*, she presses *delete*. She isn't sure this is something she wants to brag about.

Chapter Thirty-Three

"Hi. It's me. Agatha Arch."

"Hello, Agatha. How are Thelma and Louise doing?"

"I think they're sick."

The goat lady's tone changes abruptly. "Sick? You didn't let them near the rhododendron, did you?"

"Of course not."

"Then what's wrong?"

"They're just lying around. Not eating anything. Only Timothy is active, and he's acting like an ass. Not eating either."

"Ah. I see," says the goat lady.

"See what?"

"This is typical goat behavior. I believe we mentioned that goats have four stomachs, so they need time to lie around and digest. If there are no other symptoms, that is likely what is happening."

"Seriously? I thought they were more earnest than that."

"They're animals, not people. We can't command them to do our bidding."

"Hm."

"Leave them to rest. I'm sure they'll be back at the job within a few hours."

"Hm."

* * *

"Hey, Hummingbird. Is that you?"

Agatha is crouched ninja-like behind a silver Mercedes across the street from the House of Sin, hovering her drone at Willow Bean's living room window. She's hoping to catch GDOG in the act of something, anything, but so far all she's got is Willow putting a banana peel in the trash instead of the compost. It's weak, but it's a start.

"Hummingbird?"

Crap, Agatha thinks. Crap, crap, crap. She pretends not to hear.

"Hummingbird?" Blue says again. The drone-driving, skateboard-riding, coffee-guzzling, tech-savvy, super-smart, emotionally balanced, how-the-hell-did-she-get-to-be-so-grown-up, fifteen-year-old Blue puts her hands on her knees and bends to Agatha's level.

Agatha grimaces, pivots on her haunches, tilts her head, and locks eyes with Blue. "Oh, hey, Blue." She hops up from her hiding spot and leans against a tree, doing her best not to look like a middle-aged woman crouched in spy pants commanding a drone.

Agatha summons the drone, makes it do a loop-de-loop around their heads, and lands it skillfully at their feet. A gold medal landing.

"Very nice," Blue says.

"Thanks, teacher."

The woman standing next to Blue holds out her hand. "Hi, Agatha," she says. "I'm Penny Miller. Blue's mother. I've heard some really wonderful things about you."

Agatha shakes Penny's hand and tries to imagine what wonderful things Blue could possibly have shared about the grown woman she was teaching to fly a drone. "It's nice to meet you, too. Your daughter taught me everything I know."

They exchange pleasantries, but all the while Agatha is painfully aware that she is on the street across from the House of Sin, holding her drone, wearing her spy pants, engaging in nefarious acts.

"Is this your house?" Blue asks.

"No," Agatha says.

Penny smiles. When she meets Agatha's eyes, Agatha imagines her face as an FB avatar and realizes she's a card-carrying member of the Moms group. No secrets here. "Blue," Penny says, "I suspect this house may belong to friends of Agatha's. It looks like they were kind enough to let her polish her skills here."

Could it get any worse?

In her head, Agatha falls to her knees with gratitude so she doesn't have to be any more embarrassed than she already is. Agatha nods. Then she gives Blue one of those giant "I'm full of shit" smiles that grownups love to give kids. "Yes, these are friends who let me practice my drone maneuvers at their house," she says. "It's more fun to practice where there are lots of people to observe."

Just then, Willow Bean's front door flies open and the boys tumble out. Agatha tries to duck behind the Mercedes before they see her, but she's too slow.

"Mom!" Jason screams, and he races toward her at the same exact second an Escalade careens down the street. The driver slams on the brakes, and the Escalade skids to a halt just a foot from Jason. He falls to the ground, eyes wide. Agatha screams. The driver screams. Blue screams.

Penny Miller does not scream. She calmly walks to Jason, stands him up, brushes him off, whispers in his ear, and escorts him to Agatha.

The woman in the Escalade leaps out. "Oh, my god! I'm sorry. I'm so sorry," she says. "He jumped out from nowhere. I wasn't going fast."

Agatha wants to wallop the woman, but there is a train clanging and collumping through her head. Jason is in her arms but she can also see him lying on the ground in front of the Escalade in a puddle of blood. A million what-ifs race through her brain. What if the woman hadn't been able to stop? What if Agatha hadn't been spying from across the street so Jason hadn't been compelled to run to her? What if Dax had never had an affair? What if he hadn't left her for a girl nearly half his age? What if Jason had been killed? What if, what if, what if? So many goddamn what-ifs in the world.

In the middle of all of this, Dustin gingerly crosses the street to join them. He tiptoes. He looks both ways twice. He cocks his head and listens for a car. He's the cautious one. The one who will always look both ways both literally and figuratively. When he finally reaches them, he wraps his arms around his brother and mom. Blue is shaken, but her mother is clearly experienced in helping people through tough moments. Life of a librarian.

"These must be your sons," Penny says after the Escalade gets the okay to drive away.

Agatha nods. "Jason, Dustin, this is my friend Blue and her mother, Mrs. Miller."

The boys look up and smile. Jason is almost over his panic. Then without warning, the Grande Dame of Grapefruits is there. The silk muumuu-maxi surprise. Her face drips with concern. "Oh, my goodness, Agatha, is Jason okay? I saw everything from the living room." She points to the window Agatha had been filming at just ten minutes before.

"He's fine. No thanks to you," Agatha says.

Blue is watching closely, trying to figure out what is going on. "This is your friend, Hummingbird?" she says.

Agatha grimaces. "Yes, this is my friend." She nearly chokes on the word.

Blue holds out her hand to Willow and they shake. "I'm Blue, a friend of Hummingbird's."

"I'm Willow. A friend, too."

"It's so cool you let Hummingbird practice her drone at your window, filming and everything," Blue continues. "Most people would hate that."

In that instant, Agatha, Penny, and Willow Bean are suddenly united in that weird grownup world in which you pretend something so absurd you're sure the kids must know the real scoop but are incredibly thankful they haven't quite figured it all out. Willow Bean could so easily pop this bubble. Agatha is surprised and grateful she doesn't.

"Thank you, Blue," Willow says. "Being on camera so often, especially when I least expect it, has taken some getting used to, but now I sometimes forget the drone is there, recording nearly every moment of my home life." She is alluding to the time a few days before when Agatha had maneuvered the drone to the upstairs bathroom window and caught her gliding naked out of the shower.

"It's like reality TV," Blue says. "For real though. Real reality."

Willow Bean nods and smiles. "Yes, just like that."

"Are you going to put it on the internet?"

Willow coughs and looks at Agatha. "Oh, I hope not," she says. She has had no privacy for weeks.

After a collective awkward grownup laugh, Agatha says, "Right now, this is just for home use. Privacy and all."

Penny Miller takes her daughter's hand. "Time to go, Blue. Nice to finally meet you, Agatha."

Agatha nods and smiles. "You, too, Penny. Thanks for helping out with Jason."

Penny nods back. Then Willow nods. It seems like the thing to do. And so, for one additional very long moment, they are a really weird group of awkwardly nodding grownups.

Chapter Thirty-Four

Agatha's hormones swell.

"Part 3 of Who Can I Bonk? is about to commence!" she texts to Melody. She's sure this will make Melody talk to her again.

Nothing.

"The winner is the UPS guy," Agatha texts. Bait.

Nothing.

One more try.

"As long as you don't look at his face, he's kind of hot in his brown shorts and knee socks."

Dead silence.

* * *

Looking back, Agatha will admit that going for yet another deliverer of packages is dumb as hell, but in the moment she is keenly focused on convenience. Bonking a man who stops by her house on a regular basis makes sense in her "urge to merge" brain. She makes her move on the day he accidentally delivers Dax's blood pressure meds to her house instead of the House of Sin.

He knocks on the door, and when she sees him peeking through the window, she hikes up her skirt and does a flirty twirl.

The UPS guy jumps back. Agatha assumes out of joy and excitement.

She shimmies to the door and opens it. "Hello there, UPS Guy," she says in her sultriest voice.

The man is wide-eyed. A good sign, Agatha thinks. "Yes, ma'am, hello," he says. "I have a package for Dax Arch."

"Yes, that's my husband. My estranged husband. And if he has his way, my soon-to-be ex-husband," she says, shimmying a bit more and leaning forward so her cleavage is highlighted by the shaft of late afternoon sun coming through the window.

"Very well, ma'am." The guy is tall and as skinny as a straw. Agatha has never slept with a straw-like guy, and the thought of it jacks up her hormones another notch.

"Would you like to come in for a bit?" she says. "Take a rest. Have a coffee," she pauses, "or maybe a glass of wine."

The UPS guy stands as far from her as possible without tipping backward over the porch railing. He stretches his long, rubber-bandy arm toward her, package in hand. "Thank you, ma'am, but I'm on duty right now. No time for coffee. Or wine. Or anything else." He shakes Dax's box of meds in front of her face. The pills rattle inside.

When she steps through the doorway and moves closer, his eyebrows shoot up to his hairline. "Perhaps," she says, "I'm not being clear. I'd love for you to come in and have a bit of fun this afternoon."

"I am getting the message, ma'am," the guy says. "You're being quite clear. And while I appreciate the offer, I'm in a hurry."

Undaunted, Agatha lifts her skirt a bit, strokes her thigh, and gives him a wink. "I won't tell anyone. Please come in."

"I have to go," he says. He tosses the box at her feet.

"Not yet," she says. "We have so much to explore."

The last glimpse she has is the guy leaping over her porch railing onto the driveway, his needlelike legs higher than his head.

"No luck with Ichabod Crane," she texts to Melody.

Silence.

* * *

"I have to move," Agatha tells Shrinky-Dink at her next appointment. "I am mortified."

"We all have embarrassing moments."

"Like hurling one's scantily clad self at the UPS guy? Like that?"

Shrinky-Dink laughs. "Not quite like that, but equally embarrassing, I'm sure."

Agatha drops her head into her hands. "I doubt it."

"You could connect with a high-end escort service. There are a few in Boston."

Agatha lifts her head. How in the world has she fallen to a place in which her shrink is suggesting she find a sex partner via an escort service? "You're not serious?"

"I am. Physical need is a real thing. It's very do-able."

"How do you know this?"

"Agatha, I've told you many times you are not the only person who has gone through these things. You are not as different as you'd like to believe."

Agatha tries to imagine the woman in gray hooking up with an escort for the evening. She can't.

"I need sex, but not with some stranger by appointment."

"But the UPS guy would be okay?"

Agatha groans. "Seems so."

* * *

Awash in misery, Agatha climbs the stairs to her bedroom, flops onto the bed, and looks around. Every single thing is a reminder of Dax. They'd picked out the furniture together. Strands of his wiry hair are still sticking out of his hairbrush. A ratty pair of slippers pokes out of his closet. The book he'd been reading when all of this went down, the biography of a king, is still on his side table.

Suddenly enough is enough. Horniness transforms into rage.

Agatha stomps to the basement, grabs a couple of empty boxes, and stomps back up to the bedroom. Then she pitches all of Dax's stuff into the boxes, including anything of hers that reminds her of him. The navy bedspread (his favorite); his king book, slippers, and brush; his clothes, pillow, and crap from his bedside table drawer; his stash of sleeping pills. "I don't need these anymore," he'd told her the week before. "Sleeping next to Willow makes me sleep like a baby," to which Agatha had roared.

When the room is empty except for the furniture and her clothes, she hauls the boxes to the curb, pops onto the Moms page, and writes, "Free stuff at my curb. More to come." She adds photos. The Moms love "crap on the curb" posts, and happy face emojis pop like candy. When she hears a car pull up, Agatha clicks to her favorite furniture store. "Queen beds," she types. Then she orders a beautiful new bedroom set. On her own personal credit card. Screw this king-size monstrosity with Dax's DNA all over it. She doesn't need it. All she needs is a nice comfy queen that fits her, her books, and her fothermucking broken heart.

An hour later, she summons the We Haul It All truck.

"Finally ready to get rid of that mess?" one of the men says, gesturing to the shed debris.

"Nope, that stays," she says. "You're here for the furniture in the bedroom. Take it all."

* * *

"Agatha? Agatha?"

Agatha sits up on the lounger on the porch.

Kerry Sheridan smiles and puts a foot on the first step. "I thought I saw your head up there. Aren't you cold?"

Agatha shakes the heated blanket at her. "I'm plugged in. Nice and toasty out here."

"Ah, very good."

"Can I help you with something?"

Kerry climbs the steps. "Yes, I think so. I hope so."

Agatha slides over on the lounger. "Have a seat."

As Kerry sits, Thelma hops on the riding mower and lets out a long *meeehhhhhh*. "Those goats are marvelous. Looks like they're nearly done."

"A few more days. They're definitely good at what they do. Even Timothy." Agatha looks at Kerry. "So? You said I can help you with something."

"Yes, I'm wondering, . . ."

"Spit it out, Kerry."

"I'm wondering if I can borrow a goat for a few hours."

"What for?"

"Just a small patch of poison ivy on the far side of the house. Pretty sure it originated here."

Agatha pauses. "Kerry, I hate to say no. Truly. But the goat people are quite clear about using the goats only on the area they've approved. They did a whole survey of the brush and everything, making sure there was nothing poisonous to the goats. I signed a waiver about not allowing the goats to go off property."

Kerry sighs. "Oh. Okay. I was just hoping with our newfound camaraderie that this might be something you could help me with."

"It's not about you, Kerry. It's about the goats."

"Yeah. Thanks anyway, Agatha." Kerry heads back down the stairs, shoulders slumped.

Agatha moans. "Hey, Kerry?"

"Yeah?"

"How about I walk Thelma over for a bit on a leash? If she happens to find some poison ivy on our stroll, well, so be it."

Kerry grins, giving Agatha another glimpse of those teeth Agatha never knew she had. "Thank you!"

* * *

Who in their right mind could ever have predicted that one day Agatha Arch would miss the Kumbaya Queen? On what planet, in what galaxy, in what lifetime, in whose reality is this even possible?

But it's true.

Agatha misses Melody. She misses the quiet drumbeat of her approaching presence. Her oddly conservative blouses buttoned to the throat. The string of pearls. She misses the single question mark Melody often posted after Agatha said something not so nice on the Moms page. She misses their yoga classes. And the way Melody calls her Agatha Arch whenever she infuriates or bewilders her. Not Agatha. Not Arch. But Agatha Arch.

"I am lonely," she whispers to the tomato plant.

The lone tomato, now plump and red, whispers back, "I know what you mean." Agatha pokes it with her finger.

A normal person might have taken Shrinky-Dink's advice to call Melody and offer an apology, but instead Agatha posts a couple of photos from her most recent journey into the Krug on the Moms page: the Interloper walking away in the storm and a post-storm selfie in which Agatha looks like she was on the losing end of a duel. "What are we going to do about this?" she writes. Provocation is an art form for Agatha.

High Priestess Poston: "I think we should pitch in and get you to Salon Brava."

A load of ha-ha-has and laugh emojis follow.

Undaunted, she drives to North Circle Street and parks four houses from Melody's. She hops out of Coop, sneaks through a series of backyards, and hunkers down behind the mammoth rhododendron next to Melody's back porch.

She gives her drone a big smooch, then sets it into action. It buzzes to the first floor windows: living room, dining room, kitchen, bedroom, bedroom, bathroom, study. But no Melody. Minutes pass. Agatha's heart quickens. Second floor. Library, ginormous closet, guest room. No luck. But finally she locates Melody in the master bedroom on the third floor. She's lying on the bed with a washcloth draped over her forehead, pearls so perfectly in place it looks as if the string is glued to her high-cut blouse. What modern woman lies on a bed with a washcloth on her head and pearls around her neck? The whole scene is so 1950 and so Melody, it makes Agatha's heart burst with love. But Melody is still, so still. She isn't drumming her fingers or twitching her foot. She isn't scrolling on her phone. She is as still as a stick.

Oh, my god, Agatha thinks, Melody is dead!

Her dear friend, her BFF, the very first member of her zephyr, is dead.

"Melody!" she hollers in her head. "Melody! Melody! Melody!"

Hoping to jar her into action, Agatha bumps the drone against the window. Thank god for Blue's tutelage.

Bump. Bump, bump.

Nothing.

Agatha pulls the drone back a good five feet and slams it into the window so hard she's sure the glass will shatter. Blue would be proud. Or appalled.

But still nothing. Not even a quiver.

Just then Agatha notices that one, just one, of Melody's low-heeled, green-as-an-Irish-pasture pumps is lying on the floor, and she knows this is a sure sign Melody has indeed perished right there on her bed.

"Screw this!" Agatha yells, out loud this time. She tucks her drone into a pocket of her pants, plows through the rhododendron, and takes off for the front door. "I'll save you, Melody!"

As she runs, she tries to remember the lifesaving steps for mouth-to-mouth resuscitation. Open the airway. Pinch the nostrils shut. Make a seal over the mouth with yours. There aren't many people in the world on whom she'd put her lips in order to save their life, but Melody is definitely one of them.

Agatha reaches the front door and turns the knob. Thank god Melody never locks her house (welcome, ne'er-do-wells!). She throws open the door and runs through the foyer hollering, "Melody! Melody! Don't die! I'm sorry! I'm sorry!" She tears up two flights of stairs and into the master bedroom. Just as she slams into the bed, Melody opens her eyes. When she sees Agatha, she smiles like a cat that has devoured 4,390,822 canaries.

"Agatha Arch!" she exclaims, sitting up and letting her other pump drop to the floor.

With that simple happy utterance, Agatha's heart soars. She falls at Melody's bare feet and hugs them both. "Oh my god, Melody! I was spying on you with my drone because I missed you and I saw you here with that ridiculous washcloth on your head and one shoe off and I thought you were dead."

"Dead? Because of a washcloth and a shoe?"

"Yes! I was going to give you mouth to mouth. I was going to save you."

"You were?"

"Yes!"

"What about all those germs?"

"Fuck germs, Melody! You're my BFF. I'm sorry, so sorry. Sorry for everything." Agatha rests her head on Melody's knee and starts to sob.

And sob and sob and sob.

And sob.

And sob

and sob

and sobsobsobsobsobsob

"It's okay, honey," Melody says, patting Agatha's head and dabbing her tears with the washcloth. "It's okay." Then she stops and sits back. "Wait a minute. You did all this because you missed me?"

Agatha nods.

"*You* missed *me*?"

Agatha nods again. "So much," she says. Melody is a little blurry through her tears, but her smile is so bright the astronauts on the space station could probably see it.

"Oh, my dear Agatha Arch, that is music to my ears because *I've* missed *you*."

Then, although Agatha is not sure if it is real or if she is just imagining it, Melody starts to hum "Kumbaya."

Agatha closes her eyes, hugs Melody's knees, and hums along with the tune. Melody Whelan, her friend, her real and true best friend, the principal member of her zephyr, missed her, too.

Chapter Thirty-Five

The Interloper gets taken in to the police station on a Tuesday morning. The police storm the intersection, stop traffic with flashing lights and blasting sirens, escort the Interloper into the back seat of a squad car, and whisk her off to the station. It is all very dramatic, filmed and posted on the Moms page for about thirty minutes before Marty Snow takes it down. "Case of mistaken identity," she posts. "They thought she might have been the thief who broke into three homes last week. She wasn't. Move on."

Agatha is not sure who filmed the scene, but they'd been close enough to capture the Interloper's expression when she whipped back her hair and glared at the camera. She was pissed, which terrifies Agatha. She would have expected a frightened, skittish, "what's going to happen now" look, but instead, the Interloper looked like she might murder someone right then and there.

Agatha takes a screen shot of that look before the post is removed and sends it to Melody with: "Why am I scared of her? Why am I scared of her? THIS IS WHY I'M SCARED OF HER."

Within five seconds Melody texts back: "Pretty sure I've seen this same murderous look on your face during conversations about Dax and Willow Bean. Pretty sure it's the look you have on your face right now because I just dared to call her Willow and not the dog walker."

Ooh.

Ouch.

Grrr.

From anyone else, that text would have incited an all-out war, but because it is from Melody, Agatha pauses for reflection. After breathing deeply and channeling Shrinky-Dink's advice, she admits to herself that, yes, seeing the word *Willow* on the screen pisses her off, but even so, she knows that no matter what the circumstance, she never looks like she would murder anyone. To prove it, she switches her camera to selfie mode, rereads Melody's text, and looks.

SHIIIIIIIIIIITTTTTTT!

Murder face! Murder face!

Her eyes? A murderer's eyes! Dark and sharp and menacing.

Her mouth? Some kind of god-awful murder-y contortion.

Her eyebrows? Most murder-y eyebrows ever seen.

If she were someone else looking at her, she'd be terrified. She'd call the police there and then. She'd shout, "I have no evidence, but I'm pretty damn sure this loonybird is going to slay an enemy. Stop her!"

Agatha looks away from her image, then back again.

SHIT! SHIT! SHIT! SHIT! SHIT! SHIT! SHIIIIIIIIIIITTTTTTT!

She really and truly looks like a murderer.

Does she look like this often? Does she look like this whenever Willow's name is spoken? Dax's? Does she look like this in the grocery store? At Shrinky-Dink's office? Walking down the street? Do her boys see her look like this?

She takes one more shot of herself, flips the camera back into "photograph normal people" mode, and falls onto the bed.

Melody texts, "Agatha? Agatha? Are you there? If you don't text back, I'm going to call you." There it is again. The ultimate threat of the new millennium. A phone call.

"Fuuuccccckkkk!" Agatha texts back. "Do I look like this often?"

"You looked at you?"

"Yup."

"You shouldn't have looked."

"Just answer me. Do I look like this often?"

This time there is a good thirty-second silence.

"Yes, yes, you do."

"Don't call me," Agatha texts.

She stuffs her phone under her pillow and flops onto her back.

Her phone rings. "The Wind Beneath My Wings." She ignores it. The song stops, then starts again. She grabs her phone. "What?"

"You don't look terrifying all the time."

"No?"

"Absolutely not."

"How much of the time?"

"Just when something or someone reminds you of what Dax did."

"You mean what Dax *is* doing. Present tense."

"Yes, is doing. Present tense."

"Things remind me of what Dax is doing all the time. Every second." She sits up in bed and glances at her image in the mirror.

Fuuuucccccckkkkk. She looks even more murder-y than before. How is that possible?

"Melody, no wonder the Tush didn't want to do me."

"That's absurd."

"No, it's not. Here I am running around citing all the things in the world I am afraid of and the biggest thing that other people must be afraid of is me. Crazy fucking me. Right?"

"No, Agatha, no. People understand. Really they do."

"They might understand I'm in pain, but I don't think anyone can understand the murder-y look on my face."

"Are you still looking in the mirror?"

Agatha nods but doesn't speak.

"Agatha?"

"Yes, I'm still looking."

"Do me a favor?"

Agatha is pretty sure she is going to ask her to cover her head with a sheet, but that is already her plan.

Instead, Melody says, "Smile."

"What?"

"Keep looking at yourself in the mirror and smile."

Oh, for fuck's sake.

"Agatha, I'm serious. Look in the mirror and smile."

"I can't."

"Yes, you can. I want to show you something. Think of something spectacular. Then smile."

Agatha thinks about her crumbling marriage, her failed attempts at sex, her stalled writing career, her roller skates, the Tush, the mailman, the UPS guy, the Interloper, and a few other juicy bits and pieces of her miserable existence of a life. She has nothing. "I've got nothing, Melody. Not a damn thing."

"The boys," Melody says. "Jason and Dustin."

Immediately, Agatha is shot through with joy and love. She smiles without even trying to smile. She feels it before she sees it, but as soon as she does, she looks up at herself. Murder-y her is gone and in her place is shiny Agatha. Shiny, shiny Agatha who doesn't look scary at all. Shiny shiny Agatha who wouldn't make you cross the street to avoid her. Super shiny Agatha who might even make you want to hug her. Happy shiny Agatha.

"Well?"

Agatha laughs, actually laughs. And an even happier reflection appears in the mirror. She sighs. "Yes, it worked. I no longer look murder-y."

"Now, can you relax a little about Lucy and that image of her you saw today? It was one moment in which she was sad and afraid and angry and lost. It is not who she is, I swear."

Agatha takes a breath. "Okay," she says, "I'll cut her a little slack."

"Good. Now go look at yourself smiling for a while. You're beautiful. I'll see you later." And she is gone.

* * *

Agatha takes a selfie while saying GDOG's name out loud. It's hideous. Frightening.

She takes another selfie while thinking about the boys. It's beautiful. As beautiful as she gets.

She posts a mash-up on her Infidelity page. A side-by-side comparison. She's scared to present something so raw, but she has to own the truth.

#realme #nofilter

* * *

"Do you think this is permanent?" Agatha rubs the crease on her cheek. It is as indelible as it was the morning after the shed incident. A narrow sword-like crease that ends in a sharp point.

The esthetician shines her headlamp at the spot. "Hm. That's an unusual marking."

"It's not a marking. It's a crease. From lying too long cheek-down on my porch."

The lady lifts her spectacle and eyes Agatha. She looks again at the mark. "You've had it your whole life, yes?"

"No."

"No?"

"No. I just got it a few weeks ago."

"Really?"

"Really."

"It's not a normal crease." She's leans so close her nose brushes Agatha's cheek.

"Meaning?"

"Meaning it has special qualities."

"What?"

"It doesn't respond like the rest of your skin." She presses a finger to Agatha's cheek and quickly lifts it. "You see? The rest of your facial skin is responsive, like a trampoline, but this crease of skin is resistant to such buoyancy."

Agatha wonders if all estheticians talk this way. "Meaning?"

"Meaning, you're marked."

"Marked?"

"Yes, marked."

"For how long?"

"For life."

"For life?"

"Yes."

"Like Harry Potter?"

"Like Harry Potter."

* * *

"Why didn't you tell me about murderer face?"

"Excuse me?" Shrinky-Dink looks confused.

"Murderer face. This." Agatha thinks about GDOG and Dax in the shed and feels her face contort and twist into a mask of hideousness. She feels like Bruce Banner transforming into the Hulk. Buttons popping. Shirt splitting down the middle. Skin turning green. "This," she says when she knows she's in full murderer face, jabbing at her cheeks and chin with both index fingers. "This."

Shrinky-Dink sighs. "Oh, that."

"You knew about it, right? You've seen it a lot in here."

"Of course I've seen it. You've looked like this often since Dax's indiscretion. But I wouldn't call it murderer face."

"And I wouldn't call what Dax did an indiscretion."

"Agree."

"What would you call it? This look of mine."

"I'd call it, Agatha-is-in-pain face."

Of course she would.

Agatha folds at the waist and drops her head to her knees. She falls sideways and curls on the couch. "This is the look that scares me on the Interloper, but I often look the same way? What am I supposed to do with that?"

Chapter Thirty-Six

From the porch, Agatha spots GDOG creeping along the fence in the backyard, creeping along like only a sexy person can, hunched at the back, grapefruit arse in the air, sleek legs stretching out in daddy long-legs steps. Her heart squeezes and flops. WTF? What is this woman doing in her yard? "Hey!" she yells. "Hey!"

Willow stands, straightens into her willowy self, into her full "I am beautiful" height, and gives a small wave. "Hi, Agatha," she says.

Hi, Agatha?

Hi, Agatha?

This woman tosses out this friendly greeting as if slinking along the fence in this particular backyard is an acceptable activity?

WTF?

Agatha walks toward her. "Willow, what exactly are you doing in my yard?" The last time Willow had been in this yard she'd been slipping off that silky muumuu-maxi, screwing Agatha's husband in the shed, then running naked from Agatha and the hatchet.

"I'm sorry," Willow says. "I'm not trying to intrude, but Balderdash was spotted near here."

"Balderdash? Here? In my yard?"

Thelma, Louise, and Timothy let out a vigorous *meh*, as if the thought of a dog in their midst is too much to consider.

"Yes, two Moms spotted him around here late last night. Didn't you see it in the Moms group?"

"No, I've been trying not to look at that as often." Agatha turns in a circle and surveys the yard. "I don't see him anywhere."

The two women walk through the yard, a good five feet between them, a safe distance, Agatha thinks, a safe-ish distance. They skirt the fenced area around the shed remains.

"If Balderdash was here last night, he's gone now," Agatha says. "It looks like he's eluded capture once again."

Right then a low mournful moan spreads across the yard.

"What was that?" GDOG says.

"My soul," Agatha says. She means it.

The moan comes again, louder. Willow's eyes pop wide. "The goats?"

"That's not the goats," Agatha says.

"Agatha, it sounds like Balderdash." GDOG starts to run.

"So you know this dog's moan as well as you know his poop?"

GDOG ignores the question. She looks behind the row of lilac bushes and the Rose of Sharon, then under the porch. "Balderdash?" she calls. "Balderdash?"

The moan comes again.

"Where is that coming from?" GDOG says. "Balderdash?"

Agatha runs to the gate in the electric fence. On the other side, not far from Thelma, she sees Balderdash lying on his side, his furless body pink and bright, a shade reminiscent of the hideous hot-pink shirt Dax had worn to the house the morning she threw the coffee cup, the shirt with the ridiculous patchwork pocket on the breast. Bastard. "Here, Willow, here. He's inside the fence."

Willow lopes to the gate, her grapefruit hips chugga-chugging like a drumroll. "Oh, my goodness! Balderdash! How did he get in there?"

"No idea. He must have jumped the fence."

"Jumped the fence? There's no way this dog jumped the fence. Look at him."

"He didn't walk in, Willow. I know that. The gate is always closed and latched."

Agatha opens the gate and Willow runs to Balderdash. She kneels and runs her hands over the dog in the same way Agatha imagines she runs her hands over Dax. Balderdash lifts his head and licks Willow's cheek.

"He's okay," GDOG says. "Just scared."

"I heard the coyotes last night," Agatha says. "Maybe they chased him and he leaped over the fence. It's the only explanation that makes sense."

"I can't imagine this dog leaping over a blade of grass, let alone a fence."

"Fear does funny things to you," Agatha says. This is a big truth she's just starting to reckon with.

"Why wouldn't the coyotes follow him?"

"I don't know."

From the road, a car beeps and a Mom jumps out. Agatha recognizes her from her avatar, but can't come up with her name. Carol? Cathy? Catrina? She's sure it starts with a *c*.

"Hey!" the woman yells. "You found him? You found Balderdash? He's still here?"

"Yes, thank you," Willow yells. "Are you the one who posted last night?"

"Yes!" The woman jogs to the fence and snaps a few photos with her phone, then jumps back into the car and drives away. Seconds later, Agatha's phone beeps. The Moms.

"Don't look," Willow says.

"I shouldn't," Agatha says. But she does. She can't help it. She pulls her phone from her pocket.

"Balderdash found!" the post says. In the photo, Agatha, the goats, Willow, and Balderdash are all staring at the camera. The remains of the shed clutter the yard.

Agatha turns and looks at the shed, what's left of it. Willow's eyes follow. She lets out a breath. "Agatha, I'm sorry about so much."

Agatha swallows hard. "Sorry, Willow? You're sorry?" She yells it so loudly, Balderdash twitches and Timothy jumps up on the ride-on mower. "You screwed my husband in the shed on our property with our sons inside our house, with me, the wife, inside our house, *our* home, and you're sorry? That's all you've got?"

"I know," Willow says. "None of this happened the way I wanted it to."

"Willow, I need to say this once. I don't ever want my boys to hear it from my mouth, but I have to say it to you, once. I hate you. I hate you more than I've ever hated anything in my life." She takes a deep breath and lowers her voice to a whisper. "I hate everything you've done, everything you've changed, everything you've taken."

Willow drops her head onto Balderdash's body. "I get that, Agatha," she says. "I deserve that. But please know that I didn't plan to fall in love with Dax. I didn't plan for us to do what we did in the shed. I didn't plan any of this. And I'm so sorry."

Agatha is pretty sure these same lines have been spoken in hundreds of sappy movies to jilted wives. She also knows the hatchet is somewhere nearby, under a bucket or buried in the stack of sticks, likely within easy reach. "Here's the thing, Willow," she says. "Hating you for the past few months hasn't helped anything. It hasn't helped make life peaceful for my boys. It hasn't helped make life peaceful for me. It turns out I'm not good at hate and hate is not good for me."

Willow rubs Balderdash's ears. "So what do we do?"

"Well, I can't speak to the future, but right now I don't want that hideous shot of us to be the talk of the day," Agatha says. "Stand back."

Moments later, just as she snaps a photo, Timothy leaps over Balderdash, creating the best goat photo bomb ever. GDOG texts the pic to Gem Lily, and Agatha uploads it to FB.

"BALDERDASH!" the Moms cheer, and the photo garners more likes than any photo in the history of the Moms.

"I don't have a leash," Willow says. "I ran out of the house so fast, I left it behind."

"Use this." Agatha hands her Thelma's leash. "Just bring it back when you're done. I have to walk Thelma to Kerry's yard later for a poison ivy snack."

As GDOG leads Balderdash back through the gate and to the street, Agatha considers how some things—Balderdash, Melody, Kerry, Shrinky-Dink—come closer, while others—Susie, Dax, the Interloper—move farther and farther away.

* * *

When Dax calls a few hours later to thank her for helping Willow, Agatha doesn't yell or curse or seethe. She stands in the living room with her face pressed to the pane of glass looking out over the yard and the remains of the shed.

"Agatha," Dax says, "this thing, this thing with Willow, it had nothing to do with you, with anything being wrong with how you are in the world. You're perfect in this world. Your fears didn't drive me away. I just walked away. All on my own. And I'm sorry I hurt you."

And suddenly, just like that, there he is again, her Dax, her beautiful Dax, without the armor, the defensiveness, the bravado, just Dax. "It's not okay," Agatha says. "It will never be okay. But it's okay."

* * *

Thirty minutes into the delivery of Agatha's new bedroom furniture, the stubby man with cute dimples, says, "Ma'am, I apologize, but there's been a mistake. We only have one bedside table on the truck for you."

"No mistake," she says. "I only ordered one."

"One? Just one? Are you sure? I don't think I've ever delivered a set without two stands." He squints at the packaging slip. "Everybody wants two."

"Even single people?"

"Yes, ma'am, even single people. Symmetry."

"Well, you've probably never delivered to a pissed-off wife whose husband left her for a dog walker and who wants just enough furniture for herself and no one else. You only need two bedside stands if you have two people sleeping in a bed. If there's only you, and your husband is sleeping in the dog walker's bed not more than a mile away, well, there's really no need for the bastard to have a bedside table, is there?"

Agatha is quite sure a spiky thornbush springs from her tongue as she speaks.

The guy's eyes widen.

"As for symmetry," she continues. "It's overrated. It's for people who can't take a little imbalance in their lives. Weak ones. You know what I mean?"

The man eyes her, then steps back and says, "Yes, ma'am, I do indeed." The other two delivery men stop, turn, and stare. She's taken them all off guard.

"Okay, ma'am," Stubby says, giving a nod to his pals. "Whatever you say. I'm sorry to hear your news, but I'm glad you'll have a new bed to rest in."

"Do you have my new pillow?" she asks.

He pointed to a single box on the floor. "I do."

"I only ordered one of those, too."

"Yes, ma'am."

From then on, the men keep at least three feet between her and them. Perhaps it's a rule they were taught at headquarters that applies to both aggressive dogs and crazed, brokenhearted women: "Keep a piece of furniture and at least three feet between you at all times."

* * *

She has the men set up the bed in a new spot in the room. She wants a different view when she wakes. While they are still there, she lies down to check out the perspective. Instead of the door, she now faces the wall with two windows. Lots of blue sky to ogle. "Yes, this works," she says.

All three men nod slowly. Symmetry.

Once the furniture is in place, the pillow is unpacked, and she's signed the "yep, I got it all" paper, the men rush out the door to their truck as if they are being chased by a raptor.

* * *

Alone, she puts her new lamp on her new bedside table and sets Tracy K. Smith's *Life on Mars* next to it. She puts a few things in the drawer, journal, pen, lip balm, vibrator, then places a box of tissues next to the lamp, for crying. She shakes out the new set of cornflower blue, 700-thread-count sheets that she's already washed three times for softness, pulls the fitted sheet into place, stretches the flat sheet over, and finally lays out her new sunflowered comforter on top. Pillow in place, she strips down, crawls in, and closes her eyes. It is 4:30 PM.

The next morning at 11:00, she wakes, sun piercing the window. "These are the softest sheets I've ever slept under in my life," she says to herself. "Like fog."

* * *

"Where are you?" Melody texts. "Yoga starts in 5."

"Not today. Lounging in new bed. Watching Bear's latest season of *Running Wild*."

“👍🐻🖤” Melody texts. “Take notes.”

Agatha scans Bear’s Twitter feeds for gems as she watches. The @NBCRunningWild feed is fine, but the good stuff, the juicy stuff, is from @BearGrylls. She heeds Melody’s advice.

Tweet: Something about actress Courteney Cox eating a rotting sheep carcass with Bear Grylls?
Note: G-R-O-S-S

* * *

Tweet: An invite to explore a jungle filled with heart-stopping danger with Bear?
Note: Um, no, thank you. I’ll enjoy him from my new comfy bed.

* * *

Tweet: Bear says he never gets tired of the mud.
Note: I could have used this during that last climb in the Krug.

* * *

Tweet: Bear says that birch bark contains so many oils that it will take a spark, even when wet.
Note: Get birch bark.

* * *

Tweet: Advice about not setting up your tent in a river bed in the desert because of flash floods.
Note: Duh!

* * *

Tweet: For Big Papi's sake, he found a frozen bird and has to thaw it out.
Note: OMG, he stuck it down his pants!

* * *

Tweet: Some nonsense about having to dig deep in order to reap the rewards of the wild.
Note: yeah, yeah, yeah

* * *

Tweet: Bear swears that storms make us stronger.
Note: Bite me.

* * *

Tweet: Bear says you can eat a gecko but you have to squeeze out the excrement first.
Note: Show this one to the boys.

* * *

Tweet: "Fortune favors the brave."
Note: More rubbish about fortune favoring the brave.

After a few more tweets about tenacity and strength, Agatha starts sliding down the "Bear rocks; I suck" road, but midway down that very slippery slope, she recognizes that in some ways she and Bear aren't too far off. Granted, their goals are different, but each goes at them with gusto. Bear thaws a bird by sticking it down his pants; Agatha tries to score by donning a pair of roller skates. By the time the show is over, she is jumping up and down on her new bed and hollering "Yeah!"

Then she tweets:

"@BearGrylls, just binge-watched last season of
'Running Wild.' Inspired!
Needed to be! Life sucking right now. Grateful!"

Then:

"@BearGrylls, consumed by fear over here.
Any advice for a petrified woman
trying to piece her life back together?"

A few minutes later, she looks at her phone. Bear Grylls has tweeted her back.

From the man himself:

"@AArch, fear sharpens us"

Then this:

"@AArch, I believe"

Bear Grylls believes . . . in her.

Chapter Thirty-Seven

"You were right, Agatha." Shrinky-Dink looks more excited than Agatha has ever seen.

"About what?"

"About what? Haven't you seen it on Twitter?"

"What? What?"

Shrinky-Dink hands her iPad to Agatha. A first.

It's open to an article about a lion tranquilized in a town not twenty miles away.

Agatha's mouth falls open. "Oh my god. This is a lion. *The* lion. From that guy in New Hampshire."

"It sure is."

Agatha pulls the iPad closer and reads. "Holy shit, they found it alive. Eating local pets."

"Yes, they thought they were looking for a mountain lion, but got a tried-and-true African lion."

"There could be more."

"There could be more. Anything else today?"

"It's permanent," Agatha says.

"What's permanent?"

"This." Agatha points to the crease on her cheek.

"Your dagger?"

"Yup."

"Who says?"

"The esthetician."

"Really?"

"Yup, she says I'm like Harry Potter."

"That's kind of cool."

"I'm trying to think of it that way."

Shrinky-Dink waits.

"I'm not sure I want a permanent reminder of the day of the shed incident. I'm not sure I want to be reminded every time I look in the mirror."

"It sounds like you don't have a choice."

Agatha smirks. "Neither did Harry. But at least he got to go to Hogwarts."

"Consider life your Hogwarts."

The chime dings. Agatha stands, gathers her things, and heads for the door.

"See you, Harry."

* * *

Agatha is putzing around in the canned soup aisle on a boys-with-Dax Friday night, trying to decide between *Star Wars* chicken noodle and *Frozen* chicken noodle when the guy beside her sneezes so big that he tips over the giant R2D2 display of noodle soups and hundreds of cans clang and bang to the floor. When a *Star Wars* can rolls to a stop at Agatha's feet, she laughs, picks it up, and says, "Guess it's me and Darth tonight."

"This isn't for you, is it?" he says through a hot-red stuffy nose.

She nods, trying not to look like the most pathetic person in the store. "Yup, I've got a thing for R2D2."

The guy chuckles.

"And you?" she asks, eyeballing the can featuring Elsa and Anna in his cart.

"Sick," he says. "Terrible cold, away from home."

"It must be hard to be away from your wife when you're sick," she says. Shrinky-Dink will smile when Agatha shares this fishing line.

When he meets her eyes, holds them, and says, "No wife," a hot bubble of passion throbs between Agatha's legs. She imagines throwing the guy and his snotty, swollen, crusty nose onto the floor of the grocery right then and there, whipping down his britches, and straddling him as Olaf croons "In summmmmmerrrrr . . ."

"This may sound a little crazy," she says, "but would you like to share a can of soup with me tonight?" She catches him in the middle of blowing his nose. He gives it a final wipe.

"You want to share a can of soup with a guy whose temperature is over a hundred and who is losing half his body weight in snot?" he says.

She appreciates his humor and honesty. She needs both. "Better than having a can of soup by myself."

The man pulls a tube of hand sanitizer from his pocket, squeezes a bit onto his hands, rubs it in, then offers a hand to her. "Edward," he says. "Edward Weltz. Usually a healthy specimen of engineer who lives in Madison, Wisconsin, but today, on a business trip, I'm a snoggy mess in . . ." He looks around for a sign of where he is in the world.

"Wallingford, Massachusetts."

"Yes, Wallingford, Massachusetts."

His hand is perfect, Agatha notes. Not too sausage-y, not weirdly bony and skinny. Just a nice, well-sanitized hand. It is promising.

"Come on," she says. "I live nearby. You can follow me."

As she settles on two cans of soup, one *Star Wars* and one *Frozen*, Edward pulls his license from his wallet. "Just to show you I am who I say I am," saying without saying that he totally gets that she is taking a strange man to her house and he wants to make it clear he is not a serial killer who stalks his victims in soup aisles at grocery stores.

Agatha snaps a photo of it, and they head for the parking lot.

After climbing into her car, Agatha texts Melody. She is horny, not stupid. "Melody Whelan, project Who Can I Bonk? is about to get real! Taking an engineer from Madison, Wisconsin, back to my house. Met him in the soup aisle at grocery store. Name = Edward Weltz. Has an awful cold. Rental car is a . . ."—she pokes her head out the window into the rain and squints—"dark blue Honda Pilot. If you don't hear from me again, send the cops after him. If he decides to kill me, hopefully he'll screw me first." She attaches the photo of Edward's license.

By the time she pulls into her driveway, with Edward close behind, she has a text from Melody. She expects a reprimand for her impulsive, libido-driven behavior, but instead she gets, "What? Seriously? This is wonderful! Don't forget to yell olé!"

"What?" Agatha texts.

"Olé! Yell it whenever you feel like yourself."

Agatha laughs.

Then from Melody. "Check in so I know you're alive. And DO NOT talk about he-who-should-not-be-named. xo"

* * *

The early moments of the evening are uneventful. Two grownups sharing a can of too salty soup, stale oyster crackers, and a bottle of pinot noir. Agatha almost says, "Just broth for me," but for the first time in weeks, she's actually hungry. They talk about their kids, hometowns, and work. By the time they start on a third glass of wine, they move to the couch and are sitting side by side, watching rain hit the window. Edward's cold medicine has kicked in so his nose goop is more of a trickle than a roaring stream. He is cute. And like Agatha, lonely.

"She left me for a colleague at work," he tells her about his ex-wife. "It was such a cliché, it took me an entire year to even believe she was really gone."

Agatha starts to share details of Edward's indiscretions, but then stops. "My shrink made me promise not to roll around in a swamp of pain and heartache during my first post-marriage fling," she says.

"Mine, too," says Edward. "He actually says, 'Sidestep the swamp, Eddie. Reach for the stars.' I have no idea why he calls me Eddie. No one calls me Eddie."

"Is this a fling then?" Agatha says.

"Oh, I hope so," Edward says. "I sure hope so." Minutes later, when he "accidentally on purpose" brushes his hand on Agatha's thigh, her loins burst into flames, and she yelps so loudly he jumps a foot off the couch.

"What? What?" he says. "Are you hurt?"

"No, no!" she yells super loud. "Just hungry!" She doesn't know why she is yelling. Yes, rain is slamming against the windows but not so hard she has to holler to be heard.

"Hungry?" he says, sweetly concerned. "Do you want more soup?"

"Soup?" she yells. "Oh, god, no, I don't want soup. I've had more than enough Darth Vaders and Obi-Wans. No, no, I want you. I'm hungry for you." Her voice is screechy and rough. And still super loud.

When Edward sets his hand on her knee in response and squeezes, desire roars through her like a wildfire. She can't take the lack of touch one moment longer. It has been so long. Weeks. Months.

She whips around on the couch so she and Edward are face to face. She grabs his shoulders while the rain smashes against the window. Then she bolts in for their first kiss. This god of noodle soup and Sudafed is as ready as she is, and his lips, all lubed up with Vaseline and Vicks VapoRub, are soft and smooshy and minty and, at least for the night, hers, all hers. His mouth is a blend of noodle soup and wine and berry-flavored cough drops. His tongue? Salty and chicken-y and sultry. She groans and moans and bubbles. She squirms closer and closer, suddenly remembering how delicious mouths are . . . how many things hands can do on a body. Hands on arms. Hands on shoulders. Hands on hips and stomach. Oh, hands on stomach. And then SWEET JESUS!

HANDS ON BOOBS!

"Hands on boobs!" Agatha yells. "Hands on boobs!" And Edward laughs so hard he can barely keep his hands on her boobs, proving he is the exact right person for her to hook up with on this day at this time in her life.

He squeezes and rubs, pushing her boobs this way and that, all the while throat-whispering, "Beautiful. So soft. Oh, my god, so soft," which fans that crazy wildfire in her loins into house-high flames. She doesn't know if his voice is normally this gravelly or if the cold is causing it, but it is sexy as hell.

"Talk to me!" she yells. She can't stop yelling. It is all so glorious.

"Gorgeous," he whispers. "Lovely. Sweet."

The more he whispers, the more she yells. And when he starts to unzip her hideous blue grocery-store-on-a-Friday-night sweatshirt, the zipping sound rips through her like a lightning bolt. "Faster!" she yells.

When her sweatshirt is finally hanging from one hand, Edward shoves her bra aside and presses his mouth to her nipples. She dies right then. D-I-E-S. But just for a few seconds, because then his tongue, hot and fast like a serpent's tongue (yes! a serpent's tongue!), whips her back to life, and she yells, "Oh my god, NIPPLES! Hands on nipples! Mouth on nipples! More, more, more!" She falls backward onto the couch and thanks the gods for her decision to trudge to the grocery store to answer her craving for canned noodle soup. Then she thanks them for Edward's business trip and his god-awful cold.

Just as she is about to thank the gods for Elsa and Anna and Darth and Obi-Wan Kenobi, Edward shushes her and folds her up in his arms. With that invitation, she leaps onto his lap like a flying squirrel, legs splayed. Who knew she could even perform such feats of gymnastic prowess? Once in place, grinding ever so lightly—then not so lightly—on his lovely mound of manliness (yes! lovely mound of manliness!), she grips him between her legs and squeezes. She grunts, and he grunts back. She tugs his shirt over his head and discovers wee tufts of hair scattered across his chest. Gah! "Hair on chest!" she hollers.

Then Edward stands and scoops her up. "Which way to your bedroom?" he asks, pausing on their way to press her to the door and suck on her neck and ears, during which time she caterwauls herself silly.

Of course, she's totally forgotten she is wearing her spy pants, fully stocked with all the supplies she carries on a regular basis. Midway up the stairs, her headlamp falls out of a pocket and clunks down the steps. Edward pauses and glances at the bottom of the stairs where the headlamp has settled. "What's that?"

She jumps out of his arms, grabs the lamp, and pulls it onto her head. "Ah, my handy-dandy headlamp," she says, scrambling to make it seem normal. When she clicks it on, the beam of light shines on Edward's swollen nose. He squints. "The better to guide our path," she yelps. She grabs his hand and leads the way.

Once on the bed, her Leatherman pokes into his thigh. "Ow! Ow! Ow! What is that?"

"My Leatherman Super Tool 300 EOD," she yells. She may be the first human ever to yell *Leatherman* during foreplay.

He grins, wiping his nose. "Should I ask?"

"Nope," she says, and she frantically unpacks the rest of her supplies. The reel of fishing line comes undone and gets wrapped around both of them, and as they try to get her pants off, it nearly cuts off the circulation to her big toe. She pulls a pair of scissors from another pocket and cuts herself free. Once she is, Edward flops her onto the bed and peels away all remaining pieces of clothing. Then they

kiss
kiss
kiss
and
kiss

Then it is her turn. With great glee, she unsnaps his britches and begins the interminably long unzip. When his pants are loose, she tugs them down to his ankles and pulls them off. With her headlamp on, she can see tiny haystacks on his shorts. So darn cute. She reaches in, finds a strong stiff sword (yes, strong stiff sword!), and yells, "Penis in hand! Penis in hand! Oh my god! Penis in hand!"

It's been so long since she held one, she can hardly control her excitement. She rubs it. Shines it. Polishes it. Turns it this way and that. She honors the hell out of it.

Once all parts and pieces are free, she throws her headlamp to the floor, and she and Edward roll into action.

"Olé!" Agatha yells. "Olé!"

* * *

Hours later, as they lay there, sweaty and sticky and happy, Edward coughs, then whispers, "I reached for the stars, my dear Agatha Arch. I really did. I reached for the stars." And saying without saying (as they are both determined not to stick even a toe into their respective swamps of agony), he thanks his gods for her, for her decision to search out a can of noodle soup, for Sudafed, for her patience with his drippy nose, and for her crazy caterwauling wildfire self.

"Oh, Eddie, it was beautiful," she says, feeling all starry and shiny and twinkly from the tips of her toes to the top of her head. They nuzzle into each other and pull her new sheets and blankets into a warm nest.

As Bear Grylls often says, "Time spent preparing a good camp is never wasted."

* * *

Later, when Edward is snoring, Agatha rolls over, grabs her phone from her single bedside table, and texts Melody. "Glorious night. Alive and kicking."

Just before falling off to sleep, her phone flashes. Text from Melody. "Just drove past your house to snap a photo of Edward the Man's license plate. Just in case. A happy glow is pulsing from your bedroom window. See you tomorrow!"

Agatha snuggles into Edward and falls asleep.

* * *

The morning after their most glorious oh-my-god-hands-on-boobs night, Agatha gets a text from Edward. It features a math problem: soup can + a red heart = us.

For the rest of the day, she prances instead of walks and sings "La la la la la la la la la!"

She also starts sniffling and getting that no-no-no-no-no scratchy throat that tells you you've caught your lover's cold and you're going to feel like shit pretty damn quick. But does she care?

Hell no!

Cold be damned.

Olé!

She jumps into her car and, for the first time in forever, speeds down the street. Truly speeds. The lights on the police car flip on almost immediately.

Officer Henry pulls her over and steps up. "You!" he says.

"You!" she says.

"What's going on? You don't speed."

Agatha laughs. "I was practicing."

"For what? The Indy 500?"

"Life."

He nods. "Hey, I finished the book."

Agatha grins. "You read the whole thing?"

"The whole thing. And I loved it."

"I'm surprised," she says, "and impressed."

"Hang on a second," he says. He walks back to the squad car, and when he returns, she expects a ticket. Instead he hands her a copy of her latest book. "Will you sign this for me? It's next on my reading list."

"You have a reading list?"

"I do now. Will you sign it?"

"Of course."

"Are you writing again?"

"Not yet, but soon. But I'm almost ready to start."

"What's your next project?"

"A thriller."

* * *

"Thriller in process!" Agatha texts to her agent. "It's a'coming!"

Chapter Thirty-Eight

On the morning after Susan Sontag makes her final appearance of the year, heading into her winter den to succumb to a delicious state of torpor, something Agatha won't mind at all, the High Priestess posts a photo of the intersection at Apple54.

Jane Poston: "Hey, ladies, I haven't seen the Interloper in a couple of days. Apple54 feels strangely empty. Anyone else spot her?"

Agatha sits up, studies HP's fuzzy-ass photo of the intersection, so blurry Agatha isn't even sure it is the Apple54 intersection, and waits, first, for the Moms to weigh in and, second, for the text from Melody with a panicked "What? Lucy isn't there? What are we going to do?" In the minutes between those things, she clicks on Ava Newton's call for prayers, offers a bagful of Jason's discarded stuffed animals to Anne Pape, who is collecting for a charity, recommends Shrinky-Dink to a Mom who desperately needs a good listener, and offers a Bed Bath and Beyond coupon to Lila Due who needs a new rice cooker before ten cousins descend on her house for an anniversary dinner.

Before the text from Melody, a handful of Moms confirm that they have not seen the Interloper either.

phyliss-with-one-l-and-two-esses:	"so strange that you mention it, jane, as i was just saying to my wife, 'the woman at apple54 hasn't been around the last few days.'"
Rachel Runk:	"I haven't seen her either."
Meredith Wilson:	"I noticed her can wasn't in the grass yesterday afternoon but I didn't think much of it."
Kelly Prescott:	"Agatha, have you checked your basement? Maybe she's hiding there waiting to pounce."
Agatha Arch:	"Ha ha, KP."

A moment after Kelly Prescott's well-timed jab, Melody's text comes through. "Agatha, Lucy is missing! Have you seen her?"

Agatha is honest. "No, not in 2 days. Meet me in the parking lot in 15."

Melody shoots her a thumbs up.

Agatha puts on her spy pants, glances in the mirror, then changes into a pair of yoga pants that she fits into for the first time in years. As she hops down the stairs to the yard, she glances under the porch where Susan Sontag is likely sleeping, curled up next to Jerry Garcia for a long winter's nap.

"Research says that only female skunks bunk together in winter dens," Agatha tells Shrinky-Dink in her next session, "but I'm pretty damn sure Jerry Garcia is in there with her."

* * *

The air is crisp, the kind of crisp that will no longer succumb to warmth, no longer turn over to a few days of second summer. Agatha and Melody stand in the swatch of grass in which the Interloper has stood for the past few months, but as Jane Poston said, there is no sign of her. Her can. The coat she used to hang on the light post. The hand-scrawled sign about being unemployed and going through hard times. Even her essence. All gone.

"She's gone for good, isn't she?" Melody says.

"Looks like it," Agatha says. "Feels like it."

"I'm going to miss her."

Agatha rolls her eyes. "Not me," she says, "I'm going to sleep a little better now."

"Stop it, Agatha. That young woman was a good egg and you know it."

Agatha shakes her head because even after everything they've been through, no one, not her or Melody, not Willow Bean or Dax, not Jane Poston or David Watkins or any other Mom or Dad in the group knows for sure if the Interloper is a good egg or a bad egg. And now, no one ever will.

Agatha half expects Melody to ask her to hike into the Krug one more time to check, just in case, but instead Melody turns to the Krug and waves. "Goodbye, Lucy," she says. "Good luck."

Agatha does the same. "Goodbye, Interloper."

* * *

The waving goodbye on this first frosty day leaves Agatha unexpectedly teary, unexpectedly lonely, and even though it is ten o'clock, an hour in which all children, including Dustin and Jason, are in classrooms, learning things, disputing things, examining and exploring things, she drives to GDOG's house, the place where her boys most recently slept, most recently peed and pooped and ate breakfast. The place where just hours before, they'd fallen down, wrestled, snuck in a video game, and built two LEGO dinosaurs. The place where Jason had cried big tears, brushed mud from his sneakers, and stuffed a Captain Underpants book into his backpack.

Agatha thinks about home. Her home and their new part-time home at GDOG's house. Homes, plural. This place, these places, where the boys pull the heads off the neighbor's Barbie dolls and eat potato chips until their fingers are slippery with grease and stomp around like monsters and scare the shit out of each other by hiding behind doors and jumping out and yelling "Boo!" and not folding the laundry put on their beds and farting and burping and saying "I love you" in their funny, sheepish way and calling Agatha when they miss her and/or calling Dax when they miss him and letting their hair get too long and brushing their teeth superfast so they can get back to *Star Wars* as quickly as possible and sitting close together without meaning to but meaning to and fighting over the faded yellow Batman T-shirt and fighting over the last chocolate chip cookie and fighting over the TV clicker and fighting over who is going to go down the stairs first and defending each other when the neighbor kids threaten to steal their bikes and laughing like hyenas when SpongeBob loses his pants and throwing a baseball in the living room no matter how many times they are told not to and shattering a lamp with the baseball then hiding the glass bits in a box in the garage until someone says, "Where's the lamp?" and complaining about having to eat beets and complaining about having to drink milk that isn't chocolate and complaining about not having any candy in the house and so much more.

It used to be just one home in which these vital things happen. Now there are two.

Agatha parks under the pine tree and drops her head onto the steering wheel. Moments later when she hears footsteps approaching the car, she expects Officer Henry but instead sees Willow Bean. Unbelievably beautiful Willow Bean and her thumpa-thumping grapefruit hips.

"Hi," Agatha whispers when Willow reaches the car, not even trying to wipe the tears that are streaming down her cheeks. "I'm just sitting here, trying to be close to my boys."

"I know. I saw. I brought you these." GDOG hands Agatha the often-fought-over yellow Batman T-shirt and the much-loved Green Hornet T-shirt. "They wore them yesterday. I picked them up off the floor."

Even without bringing the shirts to her nose, Agatha can smell the boys. More tears roll down her face.

Respectfully, Willow Bean turns away and starts walking back to the house.

"Thank you," Agatha calls, her voice rough. Willow doesn't turn, just waves. Agatha buries her face in the shirts and sobs.

* * *

On this day of waving goodbye and crying in Coop outside Willow Bean's house, no one knows that in a year's time, catastrophic typhoons in Japan will hit so hard even the cherry trees will get confused and bloom in the fall. An autumnal bloom just months after the usual spring bloom. It is beautiful, of course. Pale pink. Fragrant. Intoxicating. It is always beautiful. But an off-season bloom means something. Everything means something.

* * *

"Come on," Melody says, tugging on Agatha's arm. "Get your yoga clothes on."

"Why? I'm tired. I want to sleep and dream about sex with Edward."

"Get dressed," Melody says. "You can dream about sex later. I have a surprise."

Agatha sits up. "Fine. Wait here. I'll be down in ten."

* * *

An hour later they pull into a driveway leading to a beautiful gray barn.

"What's this?"

"You'll see. Grab your mat."

"We're doing yoga in a barn?"

"Why not?"

The quintessential New England vibe warms Agatha's heart. The brown hills behind the barn. The scent of rotting apples from an orchard. The scent of cider donuts.

"Donuts?" Agatha says. "Now you're talking."

Melody opens the barn door and pushes Agatha in first. It's cozy and bright with sunshine streaming through skylights. They settle on their mats and a teacher comes in, then the goats, *trip-trop, trip-trop*.

"Goat yoga?" Agatha says, grabbing Melody's arm. "Goat yoga?"

"Not just any goat yoga. Look."

Just as Agatha turns, Thelma trots through the door. Then Louise.

"Louise!"

It's hard to know if the goats recognize her or if they are simply gluttons for attention, but they trot right over and snuggle as she feeds them grub from a nearby "Feed Them This" bucket. "I'll bet Hans Christian Andersen never considered this as the future of goats," she says.

"You might get peed on," the teacher says. "Or pooped on. It's all part of the joy of goat yoga. Call out if you need a clean-up." She gestures toward a young man with a spray bottle and rag.

The next hour is the best yoga ever. During Warrior pose, the baby Nigerian dwarf goats skitter under Agatha's legs. In Upward Dog, a sweet one nuzzles her neck. In a perfect Plank, two leap onto her back. "Hold it, hold it," the instructor encourages.

"Who's that tripping over my bridge?" Agatha says.

Tabletop is a favorite among the goats.

In Downward Dog, Louise has a snack under Melody. Then she nibbles on Melody's shirt and piddles. The young man wipes the floor, then breaks up a head-butting tussle in the corner.

Even Timothy makes an appearance.

During the more vulnerable poses when chests are exposed, the young man lures the goats to the corner with sliced carrots from a hip pouch. "We don't want any injuries," the assistant says.

"Let go of control," the teacher says as Thelma steps on Agatha's finger.

They move into Child pose, not the easiest to do with a goat on your back, but a good challenge.

As they leave, Agatha hugs Melody. "Thank you, thank you, thank you."

"Anything to help you avoid Murderer Face."

* * *

A day later, Edward texts Agatha: "Coffee before I head back to Wisconsin?"

"Soup?" she texts, not-so-secret code for "let's have sex again." But the whole time she's thinking how weird it is that sadness and happiness can consume a human at the same time. That those two gigantic feelings can reside in the same heart. That a human born in this world is expected to manage so much of both.

Edward sends back a long line of smile emojis, not-so-secret-code for "Yes, yes, yes! Sex again!"

They meet at a café that offers both soup *and* coffee.

"You are so cute, even without your cold!" Agatha says.

"What's in the bag?" she asks, pointing to the large tote on the chair next to Edward.

"Your books!" he says, and shows her a copy of each book, even the middle-grade series. "I can't wait to read all of these!"

Three Moms of preschool kids—protégés of High Priestess Poston—are having coffee and gossiping about the other preschool Moms who are not as great as they are, and they openly stare when they see Agatha give Edward a big smooch right on the kisser.

A waitress delivers a bowl of noodle soup and a steaming mug of black coffee to each. "Nutrition and octane," Edward says. With a red, swollen, crusty nose, he'd been super cute, but now that his cold has passed, he is downright handsome. And still so funny and kind.

"What now?" he says, getting down to noodles and business.

Agatha grins. Everything about him and their encounter is good. Delicious. Warm. Steamy. Happy. She doesn't want anything to screw it up. She doesn't want to get embroiled in something that may eventually make her think a single dark thought about this guy. She wants him and their encounter to be pure. She doesn't want to talk about Dax, and she doesn't want to talk about the departure of the Interloper.

"What now?" Agatha whispers, thinking how complicated it would be to try to have a relationship between Wisconsin and Massachusetts.

"We're grownups," he says. "We know the reality of our situation."

Agatha nods. She's feeling more like a grownup than she's felt in a long time. Maybe ever. It sucks. And it doesn't suck.

"Even if we decided this was the relationship of all relationships, neither of us would ever leave our kids," he says.

She nods again. "What do we do?" she says.

"I propose we have one more afternoon together, then I go home. We flirt via text for a few weeks, then we go back to living and working on our own separate lives, leaving us a delicious salty, soupy, soggy memory."

Agatha stands, picks up their bowls of soup, and carries them to the counter. "Can we get these to go?" she asks the girl.

* * *

Fifteen minutes later they are back in her just-perfect queen-size bed, and hours later, when Edward is readying to leave, Agatha says, "We can't sext, can we?" Thinking of how often her boys mess around on her phone and figuring his daughters do the same.

"No," he says, "but we can come close."

Later that night, he texts a photo of a can of *Frozen* soup.

She sends a photo of her Leatherman, then the reel of fishing line.

He sends one of his knee.

And sometime in the middle of night, his nose.

* * *

Dustin and Jason see Edward's text of a photo of his ear.

"Whose ear is this?" Jason says.

Agatha grabs her phone.

"No one's."

"No one's?" Dustin says. "It's somebody's ear. Why would someone send you a photo of their ear?"

"It's just a friend's ear, that's all. He's having a lobe issue."

"A lobe issue?"

"Yes, it's embarrassing for him. Please don't talk about it."

"Really, Mom?"

"Really."

Thank god they'd agreed not to sext.

"Who sends a photo of their ear?" Jason says an hour later. "That's gross. There was a bunch of hair inside it."

"Don't worry about it," Agatha says. "It's a grownup thing."

They head outside, and Agatha sends Edward a photo of her ankle.

* * *

"You survived your Arctic fox," Shrinky-Dink says.

Agatha smirks. "Yeah, I guess I did."

"And you had sex."

Agatha smiles. "Yup. Without hiring an escort."

"What now?"

"The thriller," Agatha says. "I know exactly where to begin."

* * *

When she gets home, she sees Kerry traipsing through the yard. The poison ivy is gone. The grass is trim. There's just a big pile of tools and wood stacked up like a sculpture.

"What are you going to do with all this?" Kerry says when Agatha reaches her.

"Why?"

"Well, Agatha, it is an eyesore."

Agatha turns and walks away. "Oh, Kerry."

* * *

The next morning, a thick frost covers the grass. Agatha calls We Haul It All, and the truck arrives within an hour. The same three men disembark. Agatha nods at the good guy as he hands her a blueberry muffin.

"*Gracias,*" she says.

"Ready?" he says.

"Ready," she says. "Take it away." She turns her back and starts walking to the house, but from the porch, she calls, "Wait!" Then she runs back to the shed debris. She lifts the tarp that just a few months before had covered naked Willow after she'd run from Agatha. She digs through the bucket of screwdrivers and hammers. She dumps a drawer from the red toolbox.

"Ma'am, what are you looking for?" the man says. "Can I help?"

She doesn't answer.

When she moves the rakes, she sees it. The hatchet. The hatchet she used to destroy the shed. She grabs it, then turns to look at the crew. They eye her, a little nervously.

She marches to the truck and hurls it into the bed.

"Now I'm ready," she says. "Take it. All of it."

* * *

Later in the day, Melody shows up, puts her arm around Agatha, and says, "Let's go sashay past the Tush. He's painting a house on my street this week. We'll remind him of the glory he missed out on."

Chapter Thirty-Nine

When Agatha decides to redecorate her office, she starts with the desk that Dax built, the monstrous beautiful beast with so many memories stuffed into its cubbies and drawers it should be writing its own book by now, and despite the tears that well every single bloody time she thinks about the men from the donation house hauling it off in their bright yellow truck, she calls and schedules a pickup time for it and the bookshelves and the purple stuffed chair by the window and the rocking horse on which the boys rocked while she wrote and even the lamp with scarlet fringe. She calls and says, "It's a roomful, for sure, and you must send a gaggle of men to move the desk," then hangs up and for the last time opens the door of the wee chamber on the side and removes the photo of her three boys. In its place she puts a silver coin with "fear sharpens us" stamped on one side, "fear propels us" on the other, Etsy again, with hopes another writer will find it at the precise moment she needs a boost to continue creating and writing and believing.

By the time the bright yellow truck pulls up two days later with four Zeussian men, Agatha is well past nostalgia and on to "Get it all out of here" so that only a few tears drip as the truck pulls away. With the absence of the oak blocking the window, the office is bright and sunny and new.

Agatha redecorates the boys' rooms as well, replacing every piece of furniture that she and Dax had bought or acquired in their eleven years together.

Dustin is flabbergasted. "Mom, even your desk is gone?"

"It's okay," she says. "It's only stuff. Objects. Wood and cloth and fiber."

"Only stuff?" he says. "All my life you've lectured me on the importance of symbolism in the things with which we surround ourselves." His tone mimics hers.

She clears her throat. "Well, things change. People change. I've changed."

"Because of Dad and Willow? Because of what Dad did to you?" Jason says.

This is the first time either of the boys has initiated a conversation about what their dad has done. Agatha is caught off guard. "Yes, because of what your father did," she says.

"Well, just so you know," Dustin says, "we think he's a butthead for all of it. We still love him and all, and Willow's nice. But we know butthead when we see it. We're not little kids anymore."

Agatha looks at her boys. Though she hadn't been able to see it earlier in this mess, trying as she had not to cry in front of the boys, not to say a bad thing about their dad in their presence, not to drive the cleaver through their dad's head, to use Willow's real name instead of GDOG, to at least look like she was holding it all together, it is now clear that they've been hurting too. That they've grown and changed. Both boys are looking at her with more seriousness in their eyes than she's ever seen. In some ways, she is sad about this. Every mom wants their kids to stay innocent and naïve, not be hurt by the realities of life. But really, it is impossible to be a human and not be a little bit broken.

"No, you're not little kids anymore, are you?" she says, then apologizes for doing some of the things that scared them, like the painted HEART on Willow's tree and the window-shattering hammers in the car. "Your dad kind of broke my heart," she says, "and I couldn't control my emotions for a while. I'm so sorry. I'm doing much better now."

Both boys curl in for a long hug.

"Now," she says, "go check out your brand new rooms." The sound of their feet stomping on the stairs and their fists pounding on the walls makes her grin. It feels good.

* * *

Edward texts a photo of a red and white swirly pillow. "New pillow!"

Agatha texts a photo of the gnarly bump on her elbow. "Bruised elbow. Altercation with nightstand."

"Favorite fork!" Edward. It is an awesome fork with only three tines.

"Enormous clock banished to basement." Agatha.

As predicted, things with Edward, quite naturally, begin to cool. It is hard. These two humans are too touchy-feely for long distance, and their relationship has served its purpose.

"Should we talk?" he texts one evening.

"Definitely," Agatha says.

When her phone rings, her heart bumps around in her chest like a teenage girl's. She loves this guy. Loves him for a million reasons. Loves him for cracking her open.

"Hi," he says.

"Hi."

For long minutes, they small-talk about colds and furniture and soup and their kids and how things are going in their everyday lives. Then they go silent.

"It's time, isn't it?" he says. "Time for us to say goodbye."

Little baby tears leak out of Agatha's eyes. Oh, she loves this man. His nose. His snot. His mucus. His hands. His willingness to hold a woman he just met in the soup aisle in the grocery store, a woman whose pockets are inexplicably stuffed with fishing line, a Leatherman Super Tool 300 EOD, duct tape, waterproof matches, and so much more.

She nods.

"Are you nodding?" he says.

She nods.

"Hang up. I'll FaceTime you."

She does. He does.

"Too hard?"

She nods.

"Too far away?"

She nods.

"I know."

They pause there for a long time, looking at each other, silently considering the possibility of moving to the same place and starting a life together, but then once again realizing how tied they are to their separate places and how neither could ever uproot and change that. At least not for fifteen years or so when their kids have grown and gone. Neither is up for long distance. They are lovey animals. They need lovey animals every day. Not once every three weeks after a plane ride and promises of "I'll see you soon."

"You can call me whenever you need help or if anyone hurts you or if the world gets too big or if you need a picture of my ear."

"And you can call me if you ever need advice on which can of soup to buy. *Star Wars* or *Frozen*."

Edward laughs.

"You saved me," she says.

"You saved me," he says.

"You saved me," she says.

"We saved each other," he says.

They both know they will never talk again.

"All right, my sweet Agatha, with fishing line around her toe," he says. "You hang up first."

She nods and closes her eyes.

"Wait," he says. He stares at her. "I'm memorizing."

She cries big gallumpy tears.

"Okay, I'm ready," he says.

She nods again.

"Wait! Wait!" he says. "Do you still have your spy pants?"

"Yes," she says, "but I'm going to burn them."

"Good," he says. "They're sexy, but you don't need them."

Agatha thinks about the way he'd tried to slide them off her, with finesse and seduction, but then all the stuff had started tumbling out of the pockets and the Leatherman Super Tool 300 EOD had poked him in the hip. "No," she says. "I really don't."

After a final pause, Edward whispers, "Okay, Agatha Arch, I'm ready now. You first."

Agatha takes a deep breath, blows him a kiss, and presses "End."

* * *

Twitter

Later on Twitter, Agatha tweets her idol. "Bear, I've enhanced your mantra. Fear sharpens us. Fear propels us." She's shocked when, a few minutes later, he responds, "Excellent addition. Stealing it!"

Chapter Forty

Agatha decides that the Transitive Property of Equality (if A = B and B = C, then A = C) actually does work with humans as well as math. It goes like this:

If Human A is kind to Human B.
If Human B is kind to Human C.
Then Human A is (most likely) kind to Human C.

"It's the Transitive Property of Love," she tells Shrinky-Dink. "It really does work."

* * *

With Christmas and Hanukah barreling toward them, Agatha and Melody send an evite to the Moms for the first-ever sing-along of "The 12 Days of the Wallingford Moms." The tune promises to be as biting and mocking as ever, but instead of rancor and resentment, they receive smile emojis and lots of yesses.

For refreshments, they order twelve dozen Minion cupcakes from Penis-Maker-Baker, and they coproduce two gifts for each attending Mom (or dad or grandparent or stepmother or so on):

1. A recipe book: *Pulled Pork Recipes for You and Yours*, which includes every pulled pork recipe ever posted to the Moms page, even the strangely simple "Pour a can of Coke in the slow cooker. Add pork. Walk away for six hours. Best pulled pork ever."
2. A T-shirt. On the front, "Fear sharpens us." On the back, "Fear propels us."

* * *

"Stop being creepy," Shrinky-Dink says at their second-to-last session. It's very direct and un-shrink-like.

"What do you mean?" Agatha says.

"I mean stop being creepy."

"I'm not being creepy."

Shrinky-Dink rolls her eyes, an even more un-shrink-like move.

"Are we ending therapy?" Agatha asks. "Is this shorthand for 'we're over'?"

"You know we're ending therapy. We've discussed it numerous times. I'll see you today and then next week and then we're done."

"I didn't think you were serious."

Shrinky-Dink laughs. "You knew very well I was serious."

Agatha smirks.

"Agatha Arch," Shrinky-Dink says, "you're done. You're good. You don't need me anymore. You've got this."

"What about all my fears?"

"What fears?"

"Well, they're mostly gone but, without Dax, how am I going to handle the ones that linger?"

"You're going to handle them the way you're handling everything right now. Beautifully."

"And if I need help?"

"Call me. I'm here."

"And the boys?"

"I've emailed a list of therapists to you. I'm sure there's at least one on there who will work well with the boys. I respect each of them."

"Thank you. I'll share it with Dax, too."

Shrinky-Dink smiles.

"But wait? What did you mean about the creepy thing?"

"Just stop."

* * *

Stop being creepy. Agatha hangs a blue sticky note in her kitchen with these very words written in black ink, and each time she looks at it, she disposes of one more maybe-creepy maybe-not-creepy object or behavior. She sells the long-nose camera lens on Craig's List for a fraction of what she paid for it. She burns her spy pants in the fire pit, gifts the million-dollar drone to Blue, who will use it to save the world, replaces the sentence "I hate Dax" throbbing in her brain with "I love Dustin and Jason," and practices calling GDOG by her given name.

This last one she practices as often as possible, while driving, pouring coffee, folding clothes, etc. Willow. Willow. Willow. Willow. GDOG. Willow. Willow. Willow. Willow. Willow. Willow. Willow. Willow. Willow. Willow. Willow. Willow. GDOG. Willow. The Goddamn Fothermucking Grande Dame of Grapefruits. No, no, no. Willow. Willow. Willow.

Though she's tempted to drop the Dax and Willow reflection dolls in the Krug near the mouth of the cave where she's sure one of the escaped animals from the New Hampshire dude's pseudo zoo is likely hiding, Agatha connects with her inner yogi and places them gently, but not too gently, in a small box with a tea towel. At first they are touching, Dax hip to Willow hip, but she shimmies them apart and fluffs the tea towel between them so that they can see each other but aren't touching. A little angst might be good for them. Then she donates the dolls to a local shelter with a bunch of the boys' retired robots and train sets. She'll let fate take it from here.

The GoPro goes to Jason and Dustin, who now take skateboarding and life lessons from Blue.

The dart gun goes back to Bird Love.

"How's the woodpecker?" the clerk whispers, slipping the gun into a drawer.

"Still pecking," Agatha whispers back.

His eyes pop. "What? This method has never failed before."

"Oh, I didn't use it. I figured that for whatever reason, that poor little bird must need to peck the hell out of something. Just like Susan Sontag needs to spray."

"Susan Sontag?"

"A skunk that lives under my porch. It's the nature of things. Who am I to steal their glory? Their instincts? Their animalism? Their essence?"

The clerk smiles and nods to the flock of birders trying on new hats down the aisle. "You might just fit in around here after all."

* * *

Agatha even apologizes to Rick-not-Rick, claiming temporary insanity, and promises to stick to mailperson/mail-receiver etiquette from now to the end of the world. He's wary but starts putting her mail into the mailbox again instead of dropping it on the ground as he flies by in his truck.

* * *

"Sing it to me," Shrinky-Dink says when Agatha describes the first-ever Moms sing-along, hosted by Kerry Sheridan and touted as *the* social event of the holiday season, during which hundreds of Moms squish-squashed into Kerry's house wearing their "Fear sharpens us; Fear propels us" T-shirts, stuffing their maws with bright yellow Minion cupcakes made by Penis-Maker-Baker, and belting out the latest edition of "The 12 Days of the Wallingford Moms."

"Oh, come on, do I have to?" Agatha says.

Shrinky-Dink nods.

"Fine." Agatha takes a deep breath. "On the first of Christmas, the Moms gave to me, an Interloper in the Krug . . ."

Shrinky-Dink holds up her hand. "How about starting on the twelfth day?"

"I knew you were going to say that. You steal all my fun. Here goes . . ."

On the twelfth day of Christmas, the Moms gave to me
twelve contraceptives
eleven pairs of spy pants
ten mensural cups
nine cats named Tuxedo
eight pulled pork recipes
seven coupon codes
six rabid foxes (or is that a coyote?)
five Bear Grylls bobbleheads
four Balderdash sightings
three penis cupcakes
two stink bugs
and an Interloper in the Krug

Agatha holds out "Kruuuuuuuggggg" for a good thirty seconds and Shrinky-Dink gives a slow clap.

* * *

While the Interloper has disappeared from sight, she hasn't disappeared from mind. Like many who pass through, she will be thought about, conversed about, dreamed about, for months, even years, to come, as is the case a few evenings later, when Agatha and Melody run into Dax and Willow at Westfall's. With a gulp of martini, an extraordinarily deep breath, and a sharp jab in the back by Melody's pointer finger, Agatha smiles and wishes the duo well, all while struggling to control the torrent of images of the past few months now streaming through her head like a movie in fast forward:

the shed
the cock
the hatchet
the muumuu-maxi
the spy pants
the Interloper
the pine cone
the mad mad mother
Dax
the Interloper again
Balderdash
Officer Henry
GDOG
the woodpecker
Bird Love
Eddie, oh Eddie
Janie Mae Crawford
Their Eyes Were Watching God

It's funny how time works, how so much can happen over what feels like forever, but then be condensed into mere seconds. By the end of the reel, Agatha is sweaty and Melody's gentle "Was kindness like that so hard?" feels like a dagger being stabbed into her eyeball.

"What now?" Agatha says.

They escape out a side door to a swatch of grass in the park near the statue of Wallingford's founder, not far from the spot where Blue taught Agatha to command her drone.

"Perhaps we should practice being in the moment," Melody says, and she moves into Tree pose like an aspen.

"What? Right here?" Agatha says. She looks around. The grass is crispy with frost and dozens of Friday evening dinner-goers are parking and walking and passing and looking.

"What's wrong with here?"

Agatha gestures at all the people.

"Oh, come on. Forget about what they think," Melody says. "Be in the moment. Be a tree." She closes her eyes.

"Perhaps your tree shall fall," Agatha says, nudging Melody's arm with her elbow.

But even nudged, Melody doesn't fall. Melody Whelan never falls, literally or figuratively. She holds that pose like she has roots all the way to Antarctica.

"Oh, fine," Agatha says. She pulls Bear from her purse and stands him up next to Melody. "Watch this," she says to him, then she lifts her right foot up into her crotch and raises her arms overhead. Immediately she topples onto the grass.

Melody smiles, eyes still closed. "Try again."

Agatha tries, falls.

"Try again."

She tries, falls.

"Again."

"Melody," Agatha says, trying again, "who stays in life?"

"What do you mean?"

"Susie died. My parents died. Dax left. The Interloper left."

"Oh, that kind of stay."

Agatha nods, falls.

"Nothing is a guarantee," Melody says. "Nothing is permanent, but very often, it's your friends who stick around. Now, try again."

The squad car pulls up as Agatha tries and falls once more. She expects Officer Henry to laugh or give her a warning about yoga in a public place, but instead he smiles, waves, and gives her a thumbs-up. She waves back from her spot on the ground.

"Agatha Arch, is Officer Henry flirting with you?" Melody asks.

"Maybe," Agatha says, smiling. "I don't think I'd mind."

Minutes later, as Agatha tries and fails to hold Tree pose for the tenth, maybe eleventh, time, Kerry Sheridan and Jane Poston pass on their way to Westfall's. They stop, pile their coats at the founder's feet, then join Melody and Agatha in their quest. Foot in crotch, arms overhead. Kerry sucks at it, but, not surprisingly, Jane is one hell of a tree.

Then Rachel Runk and phyliss-with-one-l-and-two-esses come along. Neither is a master, but both try really hard.

When the streetlight flickers on, twelve women are gathered on the green, all standing or trying to stand in Tree pose, and even not-there-but-there Interloper is there-not-there, a ghost or a ring of light or a crest of frost.

Melody smiles and nudges Agatha with her elbow. "See?"

A charm of goldfinches flutters in Agatha's mind. Then a dazzle of zebras.

"See what?"

"Friends."

But what to call friends, Agatha thinks, if I have them?

Maybe a flicker.

A flash.

A quiver.

A clementine.

A zephyr.

Whatever I call them, she thinks, they are here.

Knees and bum wet with frost, palms scuffed, Agatha pulls into Tree pose and holds it, finally, finally, holds it. "Like this?" she whispers to Melody.

"Just like this."

Acknowledgments

To publish a novel in any year means a lot, but to publish a novel in 2020, the year of the COVID-19 global pandemic and the Black Lives Matter movement, means even more. As many of our kids shift to remote learning, it feels important to acknowledge the teachers who helped me along the way. Sending out big thanks to: Mrs. Mangus, my 2nd grade teacher who introduced me to Indigenous Australians, the life cycle, and the importance of experiential education; Marcia (Klimo) Rosen, my 6th grade English teacher whose trip to Aruba inspired me to look at maps and dream about faraway places; Gloria Feather, my 7th grade English teacher, who talked to us kids like people and taught me that the past participle of *lie* is *lain* (right?); my 9th grade English teacher Mrs. Van Gorder, who taught *connotation*; Mr. Rubright, for teaching me to type and pay attention to patterns; my chem teacher Mr. Pollack, for seeing me and prompting me to quietly celebrate Linus Pauling's birthday every February 28; that high school creative writing teacher who took us to the cemetery to write our own epitaphs and demanded *something happen* in each story we wrote (I didn't get it then; I get it now); my 12th grade English teacher Mr. Mochnick, who dressed up like a lion and literally shivered with excitement about words and literature at the very moment I needed to know that was an okay thing; Mr. George Taliaferro, my social work professor at Indiana University, who got me thinking deeply about race and white privilege and making a difference; Kitsey Ellman, my creative writing TA at Indiana University for somehow convincing my shy self to read one of my first stories out loud—out loud!—to a group of visiting professors; Lynda Hull, for metaphor and fragility; Randy Albers, for seeing and listening and being; and so many more.

Acknowledgments

Writing *Agatha Arch* has made me think deeply about friends and family, love and loyalty, vulnerability. Cheers to all those in my zephyr, past and present, visible and invisible, including but not limited to Sandy Huffman, Julie Samra, Marissa Hsu, Christi Sperry, Katrin Schneck, Becky Stelmack, Mishi Saran, the three best sisters in the world who've cheered me on from my earliest days as a writer (Traci Gere, Nancy Bair, and Amy Berg), and my folks, Peg and Jim Bair, two of my fiercest supporters.

Thanks to Zora Neale Hurston, Bear Grylls, and Steve Irwin, for showing me what bravery and passion look like in writing and life; my agent, Barbara Poelle, and my team at Alcove Press for believing in Agatha; that special soul at the intersection near Market Basket who I hope finds her way from lost to found; all the moms (and dads and guardians) in Facebook mom groups . . . I love you; my darling kiddos, Tully and Yao, who remind me daily why I'm a pantser, not a plotter; and my dear husband, Andrew, who has gotten me through lockdown during a global pandemic with love, laughter, margaritas, and way too many tubs of Oreo ice cream.

Throughout the book, I reference several sources, as follows:

Chapter Six—Peterson, Christine. "Ten Strange, Endearing and Alarming Animal Courtship Rituals." *Cool Green Science: Smarter By Nature*, February 9, 2016. Accessed August 19, 2020. Web, https://blog.nature.org/science/2016/02/09/ten-strange-endearing-and-alarming-mating-habits-of-the-animal-world/.

Chapter Fifteen—Coelho, Paul. *The Alchemist*. New York: HarperOne, 1993. Print.

Chapter Twenty-Six—Walker, Alice. *In Search of Our Mothers' Gardens: Womanist Prose*. New York: Harcourt, 1983. Print.

Chapter Twenty-Nine—"Barnacle Goose Freefall." BBC FOUR, Life Story, October 20, 2014. Accessed August 19, 2020. Web, https://www.bbc.co.uk/programmes/p028w8yc.